CW00589681

TJ GREEN

STORM MOON
SHIFTERS (BOOK 1)

STORM MOON
RISING

Storm Moon Rising

Mountolive Publishing

Copyright © 2023 TJ Green

ISBN eBook: 978-1-99-004758-9

ISBN Paperback: 978-1-99-004759-6

Cover design by Fiona Jayde Media

Editing by Missed Period Editing

Contents

One

Maverick Hale, owner of Storm Moon and alpha of the Storm Moon Pack, made his way through the crowd in front of the stage to the bar at the far end of the room.

It was Thursday evening in the middle of November, and his club was busy. A local rock band was playing, and the heavy thump of the bass guitar thudded up through his feet. The atmosphere was heady, the excitement palpable. They were popular, with a good-looking frontman, and many of the crowd were scantily-clad women—despite the freezing weather outside. The scent of sweat, perfume, and spilled beer was strong, although he was probably more aware of it than most, courtesy of his superior wolf senses.

He familiarised himself with his customers' moods as he passed through the crowd, detecting paranormal creatures among the humans, who were for the most part unaware of the company they kept. There were shifters, predominantly wolves like he and his pack, but there were also bird shifters and therians—who could shapeshift to any animal—as well as witches. They chatted about work, holiday plans, relationship problems, and flirted. Nothing to give him any concern. There was never much trouble at his club; his security staff ensured that. They were discreet, polite, and vigilant, easily disarming conflicts, but also swift to eject anyone who caused trouble. Apart from a couple of humans, his security team were all wolf-shifters, tall and packed with muscle, and that helped, too. Other than the occasional rowdy drunk, they hadn't had real trouble for a long time.

As he reached the bar area, festooned with Christmas lights already, he spotted his friend, Kane, propped against the bar, having a drink and watching the dance floor. Another shifter, and the deputy manager of the club.

"Expecting trouble?" Maverick asked as he joined him.

Kane grinned. "No. Just thought I'd take a moment to enjoy the band. They're good. Going places, I reckon. They might be too expensive for us to book in a couple of years."

"The club who helped them in their early years? I hope not!" Maverick caught the eye of one of the bar staff and signalled for a drink. In seconds, she passed him a rum and Coke, his usual.

"Hey Maverick, I know it's a bit short notice, but I was hoping to get a couple of days' leave next week. There's a couple of things I need to do."

Kane asked this casually enough, but he kept his eye on the crowd, and an uneasy feeling that he couldn't explain settled over Maverick. "I'm sure we can juggle the shifts. Someone always wants extra money at this time of year. Is there a problem? No family issues, I hope?" Maverick knew Kane's family was up north, and hoped no one was ill.

Kane shook his head, finally looking at him. "No, nothing like that. I might head up there to see them anyway, seeing as I won't go up at Christmas. Nothing serious. I thought I could tag the days on to my days off. Monday and Tuesday would work well." Kane was obviously unwilling to elaborate, eyes on the band again.

"No problem. Have you talked to Arlo about it?" Arlo was the pack's second in command, and the club's manager.

"No, actually. It's a very recent decision."

"Are you sure nothing is wrong?"

Kane flashed him a grin before staring at the stage again. "Mate, you're paranoid. I'm fine. Just need to wrap a few things up."

"Fair enough. I'll head up to the office now and get it sorted out. Do you fancy a game of poker after the club closes?"

"Sorry, I can't hang around tonight."

It was unlike Kane to turn down a game. It was a regular event that took place in Maverick's flat, but it was obvious Kane wasn't going to share any further information. Taking his drink with him, and trying to dismiss his worry, Maverick headed to the office. The club was in Wimbledon, London. It was an upmarket establishment in a rich area, but the club appealed to everyone. The rich, the poor, and those in between. That was mainly because he pitched his prices right, and booked bands, mainly rock, to play regularly. The club was in the basement, and a bar was on the ground floor. He lived on the first floor above it.

A tug at his elbow made him look down. "Tamara! I haven't seen you for a while."

"I've been skiing." Tamara was blonde and tanned, with whiter than white teeth, a dirty laugh, and an even dirtier mind. They were not a couple in any sense of the word, but they certainly had hooked up on occasions. It was an arrangement that suited him—most of the time. She stepped closer, pressing her body to his, her perfume wafting around him. "I missed you. Can I come up later?"

A night with Tamara was probably better than a night spent playing poker. "Sure. I have a few things to organise, but I'll come find you when I'm done."

She reached up and kissed him, a promise of things to come. "Don't keep me waiting."

Thinking his night was looking up, he turned down a corridor that ran between small rooms, all with plush couches, low tables, and atmospheric lighting that allowed for more intimate conversation, finally reaching the stairs at the end that led upward to a mezzanine office. Brody, one of the younger pack members, stood sentinel on the door, and Maverick nodded in greeting before passing inside. Immediately the raucous noise and pounding beats vanished, thanks to the soundproofing that insulated the room.

It was a mix of office space and lounge area, with a small kitchen and personal bar, plus a couple of security monitors with feeds from cameras around the club. A huge window overlooked the stage and bar, and a desk topped with a computer and the usual office paraphernalia was at the far end. It was Domino's desk, but seated behind it was Arlo. His office was upstairs, but he liked to use Domino's at night.

He was the only person in the room, and he looked up as Maverick entered. "I hate staffing rosters. They stink, beyond anything else that I have to do. Even the accounts."

"You don't do the accounts. Our accountant does."

"You know what I mean!" He leaned back in his chair, huffing with annoyance.

Arlo was in his thirties, like Maverick, and one of his most trusted friends. He'd been a pack member for years, and had supported Maverick when he had challenged for the alpha position years before. He wasn't interested in the role for himself. He just wanted a secure and functioning pack. The low light cast his strong features into relief, making snakes of his dreadlocks that fell to his shoulders. He was mixed race; his dad Jamaican, his mother English.

Maverick took the chair opposite him. "Is this your usual pre-Christmas grump?"

"I like Christmas! I like mince pies and rum cocktails, and all of the ridiculous shenanigans that go with them. I'm not grumpy. Well, maybe I am over Christmas lights. There are hundreds of them!" He gestured to the room in general. "Jet and Domino have gone mad. It's not even December!"

Maverick couldn't disagree with that. At least they hadn't put up the Christmas tree yet. "Which is exactly why I haven't let them decorate my flat, despite their pleas. But I actually have other things on my mind." He leaned forward, placing his drink on the table. "Kane wants some leave next week. It's a last-minute request."

Arlo groaned. "See? Rosters! I'll bring up next week. Bloody Kane..."

"Something's wrong with him, I know it."

Arlo was already flicking through files on the computer. "Because he wants leave?"

"He wouldn't look at me while he asked. It was odd."

Arlo stared at him. "I know you have your alpha super-sensory perception thing going on, but I really think you're being paranoid."

"I'm serious. Have you been watching the floor tonight? Has he met anyone?"

"No, I've been stuck behind the desk. Domino and Grey were watching earlier, but they're watching the band now." He studied him a moment more. "It's probably family business, and Kane tends to keep that stuff to himself. Don't worry about it. And I can give him the time—a couple of guys want more hours. It's all good."

Maverick tried to brush his concerns off. Maybe he was just tired and overwrought. He had been working some very long hours lately, as well as monitoring the activities of the North London Pack, the other big shifter pack in London. He walked over to the window, looking down to the bar where Kane had been standing, but he'd gone. He searched the crowded floor, but there was no sign of him. Potentially he was in one of the side rooms, or even upstairs in the bar.

Arlo was right. Kane just needed leave for personal business, and he should let it be.

Kane watched Maverick walk away, feeling terrible that he'd lied to his friend.

It couldn't be helped. In fact, it was safer this way.

For the briefest moment, he had considered taking him into his confidence. Kane knew he could trust him, and certainly knew Maverick could handle himself, but there were some things not meant to be shared.

He smiled as the crowd parted in front of Maverick, as if they knew he was the alpha.

It was the way he carried himself. His tall stature, good looks, and his tightly controlled air of authority. A blonde reached out to tug his elbow, and leaned in. *Tamara.* That guaranteed there would be no poker game tonight, and it made him feel slightly better about lying.

Kane checked his watch. Another few hours yet before his meeting. Perhaps he should call his father, just in case.

Maverick was entertained for hours with Tamara's naked body and wicked smile.

It was probably a stretch to say that he'd missed her, but he certainly appreciated having her back in his bed. He knew she felt the same.

It's why their relationship—or lack thereof—worked. She had her life, and he had his. Their between the sheets activity was a fun side-line. He was also pretty sure that he wasn't her only romantic interest, and that was fine, too. He had several willing females who shared his bed, and he was happy to keep it that way. He was not about to settle down any time soon. *The perks of running a club.*

As the weak winter light cracked through his blinds, Tamara stretched against him, all smooth skin and heat, and his hand lowered to cup her bottom and pull her onto him. She nuzzled his neck and straddled him. "I can't stay long. I have to work."

"So do I. We better make it count."

Unfortunately, before he could start making *anything* count, his phone rang, the buzz carrying it across his bedside table. He ignored it. Whoever it was could wait. Lost in Tamara's heat, he was vaguely aware of the call ending.

And then it rang again.

Bollocks.

He answered it gruffly, seeing Domino's name on the caller ID. She was the head of his security team, and another shifter. "This better be good."

She didn't waste time on preamble. "You need to get down to the club. Now."

Tamara nuzzled his neck.

"I'm busy."

"I'm not fucking kidding, Maverick. Get down here. Now. It's..." She hesitated, a catch in her voice. "It's Kane. Just come. I'm out back."

She ended the call, and his worries for his friend eclipsed all other thoughts. "Sorry, Tamara. Rain check."

"Now?"

"Right now." He rolled her off him, deciding a shower could wait. "Help yourself to breakfast, and I'll see you soon." He pulled his jeans and t-shirt on, not even bothering with underwear.

She sprawled naked on his sheets, pouting. "Can you come back? I'll wait."

Unfortunately, fear was chasing all other thoughts from his mind. "It sounded urgent. Sorry, Tam."

Heart in his mouth, he raced down the stairs to his private entrance that was situated at the side-rear of the club, rounded the corner, and descended the steps that led to the open-air loading bay. There were two entrances to the club's lower level there. Double doors, which led directly to the rear of the stage where the green room and storage areas were, and a single door that provided an emergency exit. It led to a corridor that ran alongside the stage onto the dance floor. The area wasn't ideal. The steps from the ground floor carpark meant bands had to carry their gear up and down, but that was just the way it was.

Domino waited by the open emergency exit. She was a tall, athletic woman, with long, chestnut hair that glinted with red in a certain light. Her lips were pressed so tightly together, the skin around them was white. She had earned her place as his head of security because of her astute nature, brilliant combat skills, and diplomacy. All qualities he valued highly. And she was also a good friend.

"I have very bad news." She led him inside, not waiting for questions.

The smell of blood struck him before he was even in the room. It was in darkness except for one spotlight onstage, which lit up Kane's dead body. As if dreaming, Maverick walked up the steps, silent as he studied the torn throat and bloody mess that now constituted one of his best friends.

His silence masked a building anger and utter shock, quickly followed by a desperate urge to find and kill whoever had done this. He couldn't trust himself to speak. He crouched down to close Kane's sightless eyes, taking a moment to compose himself. He wanted to shift right now and head out to the London streets to chase the murderer down, but in broad daylight, that was impossible. He could, however, search the club from top to bottom.

Domino spoke as if she'd read his mind. "I've already checked the immediate area while I waited for you, and I found one strange scent on Kane's body, but that's all."

He shifted from grief and anger to practicalities, standing to face her. "Wolf-shifter?"

"Hard to tell. There are so many other scents around—the band from last night, their crew, the customers, and the shifters who were customers. To be honest," she hesitated, "I think shock impeded my senses. He was one of my best friends." Domino's eyes filled with tears for the briefest of moments before she brushed them away.

Maverick suddenly felt horribly selfish for not even considering her feelings. His own had been so overwhelming. "Sorry, Dom. I'm shocked, too. Are you okay?"

"No. I am very far from okay. I want to kill whoever has done this."

"That makes two of us." His tongue stuck to the roof of his mouth, and he moistened his lips, aware he hadn't even had a drink yet that morning. "Who the hell would kill Kane? I can't get my head around this at all. But I want answers, and I want them now."

"I know—so do I. The thing is, there's no sign of a break-in. Kane either let the killer in because he knew who it was, or they were here all night."

"But your team searched the place before locking up, right?"

"Of course. But maybe it was a therian-shifter who was a tiny animal. Maybe it came through the vents." She raked her hands through her long, thick hair. "I don't know anything right now, but I will find out."

He squeezed her shoulder. "I know you will. We all will. When did you find him?"

"Minutes before I called you. I let myself in upstairs, as usual, made my way down here."

"Everything okay upstairs?"

"It all looks as it should. But down here, the spotlight was already on."

"The killer lit him up, like a bloody stage act." Maverick took a deep breath and rolled his shoulders that were so tight they were bunched up around his ears. "I just don't understand why he was here so early. He never normally arrives until mid-afternoon."

"Maybe we have to consider the fact that he was meeting someone."

Maverick stared at Kane's dead body once more, considering the conversation they'd had the night before, and then surveyed his club. They didn't open until the evening. The bar opened at five, and the club opened at eight. That meant security could sweep the building, and the shifters could do it in their wolf form. *What was he thinking? There was no way the club would open that night.*

"Dom, I want the team to search every nook and cranny, but they need to especially take notice of the roof spaces, cupboards, storage, anywhere where someone could have hidden." He took a deep breath, grief threatening to overwhelm him. Just because he was part wolf didn't mean he didn't feel human emotions. They had a reputation as fighters, but like any wolf, they cared about their pack, and their family. He focussed on his anger. That was the only thing that would sustain him now.

"What about Maggie Milne?" Domino asked. "We have to tell her. I know you want to handle this yourself, but we must involve her."

"Bollocks. Not bloody Maggie!" Maggie was the Detective Inspector of the Paranormal Policing Team in London. She was razor-sharp and relentless. "Holy shit. She will drive me insane."

"I know, but…"

"Yes, of course. We have to. If she finds out any other way, it will be worse."

Domino nodded. "I've called Arlo, straight after you. He should be here soon."

"He'll be devastated."

"Everyone will be. Kane was popular. I also have four shifters on the way. We can search this place in an hour, and call in Maggie then. Sound good?"

"Perfect. I'll help search, too. What about Grey?" Grey was Domino's deputy. He was human, and ex-forces, and like a bulldog when it came to investigating anything.

"On his way, too. I haven't told them anything over the phone. Just said it was urgent."

The snick of the club's entrance door opening had them both whirling around, but it was just Arlo. He lived in Wimbledon, only minutes away. He froze when he saw the body on the stage, and then he finally stared at Maverick and Domino. "Kane?"

Maverick nodded. "I'm afraid so."

With a visible effort, he gathered himself together and reached their side. "Bastards. Who would do this?"

"Excellent question, and one we've just been discussing. Thanks for coming so quickly."

Arlo shook his head in disbelief. "When you said there was an emergency, Dom, I didn't really envisage this."

"Sorry. I didn't want to say over the phone."

"It's fine. There's really no easy way to break this news, is there?"

Domino lowered her voice, searching the dark shadows of the poorly lit room as if someone might lurk there. "Who would *dare* to do this? Everyone who knows the shifter world knows they'd be starting a war they could not win. What's their end game? Is this an individual vendetta? Did Kane piss someone off, or is there more to this?"

Maverick stared down at Kane's body as he considered her questions. Blood had spread around him, congealing in thick, dark pools. His throat was ripped out, and huge claw marks shredded his abdomen. Kane was tall and powerfully built, like most shifters. "He's not in his wolf, but his injuries suggest a wolf did this—or another wild beast. Why didn't he change? That's the most obvious thing to do when we're threatened. We're more powerful as a wolf!"

"Perhaps he did," Arlo suggested, "and shifted back before death."

A horrible thought stuck Maverick. One that made his anger flare again. "If this was one of our own pack..."

"We don't know that," Domino said, cutting him off. "We don't know *anything*. Let's not jump to conclusions."

Arlo nodded. "I agree. Second-guessing the loyalty of our pack will not do us any favours. Could this have anything to do with that leave he wanted, Maverick? You said he seemed off."

"What leave?" Domino asked.

Maverick quickly summarised their conversation from the previous night. "Arlo convinced me I was overreacting, but now I'm sure something was troubling him. He seemed guarded. Like he was keeping secrets."

Domino shook her head. "He was never forthcoming about his family. Some people are like that."

Arlo drew their attention back. "The pack. When are we going to tell them? It has to be soon."

"This afternoon. Once Maggie's been here." Maverick could barely wrap his head around this, never mind think about telling the pack. "Can you arrange it, Arlo?"

"Of course." He raised his dark eyes to Maverick's, his concern apparent. "This will cause absolute disruptions."

Domino folded her arms across her chest, drumming her fingers on her arms. "Perhaps this is what the killer wanted to do. Split the pack from within by creating distrust." She was almost as tall as Maverick, and she held his gaze, something that not many people could do. "If someone is seeking to challenge your leadership, they would do so by creating discontent and making the pack feel unsafe. You have to be stronger now than ever before. Our pack, and your position, depend upon it."

Maverick knew the shifters would be angry and nervous. Always a bad combination. "I am fully aware of that. But I need to check this place out for myself, first." He stripped his clothes off and handed them to Domino, aware he shouldn't leave them close to the crime scene.

When shifters changed, they did so naked, or their clothes would rip. They had learned to abandon any modesty within the pack, because often they shifted and ran together at night, under the stars. Or in the day, if they could find a sufficiently isolated spot. While Wimbledon Common and Richmond Park beyond it offered miles of green space, they were also popular places, which made them too dangerous to shift there in the daylight.

Maverick shifted in seconds, the fluid movement of changing from human to wolf as natural as breathing. There was a misconception that it was painful, like they used to show in the old werewolf films, and that certainly might be true for werewolves. They were human, and it wasn't their natural state to change; the moon's cycles made it impossible for them not to. However, for him and his kind, it was a second skin.

Being a human in a wolf's body meant he kept his human intellect, thoughts, and reasoning, but benefitted from a wolf's superior senses. It also meant that as a human he was much stronger and faster than a normal person, because he had inherent wolf abilities.

Maverick raised his nose, the many disparate scents assaulting him. He detected individual pack members, and the scent of humans—particularly the band who had been on the stage and their crew from the night before. However, Kane's scent overwhelmed all others, especially the sharp tang of his blood pooling around him. Thanks to the slope of the stage and the angle of Kane's body, there was no blood on one side, and he could sniff his body easily. Domino was right. There was an odd, unknown scent on him.

Maverick moved on, investigating the wider stage, and then progressed to the dressing room, essentially one long room with a sink and fridge, and finally the bathroom and storage rooms. He spent a while investigating the double doors that led to the loading bay. The killer could have entered that way, but again, Domino was right. There was no sign of a break-in. Failing to detect the strange scent anywhere, he explored the main floor. Unfortunately, he found nothing obvious. The killer had been too clever for that.

Maverick needed space to think. He headed to the bar, situated at the opposite end of the dance floor from the stage, and shifted back to human. His reflection in the mirror behind the rows of spirits did not paint a pretty sight. Framed by his shoulder-length dark blond hair, grief made his face look older than his years, and his eyes smouldered with orange light that displayed his anger. A faint scar marked his clavicle and stretched down his sculpted chest to his abdomen, the result of an old fight, but a few others were invisible in the low light. Shifters were born fighters. It was rare to find one without scars. Potentially, by the time this was over, he may have a few more.

Sighing, he stared at the scene on the stage, feeling the chill of the cold room on his bare skin, but unwilling to move. He held on to the moment's peace and quiet. Once Maggie arrived, and the pack and the staff were told, there would be no peace for days, maybe even weeks. There were things he had to do. Calls to make.

Killers he had to hunt.

"They're good. Have you ever been?"

"No! Have you?"

Stan was tall, lanky, and quiet, and looked like he'd never listened to rock in his life. "Yes, actually. I used to be a drummer for a band in my youth. I like rock."

For once, Maggie was actually lost for words. "You're kidding me. You?"

Stan looked offended. "Yes! I was pretty good. And then the band fell apart due to creative differences." He shrugged. "I couldn't be bothered after that."

She tried not to roll her eyes. "Rock's loss, my gain!"

"I know." He said it without the least hint of sarcasm. "You want Irving to join us?"

Irving Conrad was the other Detective Sergeant on her team. "No. Let him finish up with Burton and Knight." Burton and Knight was an auction house in Chelsea that traded primarily arcane and occult objects, and that morning they had called in a theft. "Has he reported what's been stolen yet?"

"No. I think he was going to make some enquiries with Sam at The Alley Cat after that." He shrugged at Maggie's doubtful expression. "It's worth a shot."

"Sam won't say a word, even if he knows."

The Alley Cat, a wine bar close to the Embankment, was also a front for some shady auctions that sold occult objects obtained on the black market, or magical objects made by private individuals who didn't want to advertise their skills too widely.

"He might if he thinks we'll be looking over his shoulder."

"Perhaps," Maggie said, not wanting to shoot Stan's suggestion down, but thinking it was highly unlikely. "While we're on the way, call Forensics and get them to meet us at the club. I have a bad feeling about this. Killing a shifter in a prominent pack is bad news. Maverick will hit back, hard. We need to find out who did this before he does."

She didn't need to explain why. Stan had been around long enough to know the implications. If they weren't careful, they'd have a shifter war on their hands, and no one wanted that.

Arlo stood next to Maverick and faced the assembled pack who were gathered in the bar while the Scene of Crime Officers finished downstairs, dreading the next few minutes.

It was two o'clock on Friday afternoon, and they were about to break the news about Kane's death, although from the pale, strained faces in front of them, he was pretty sure some already knew. It didn't help that the SOCOs van was parked outside, and Maggie was here with her sergeant. After they told the pack, they needed to tell the staff. While a few of them knew about shifters, most of them had no idea of the paranormal world in which they worked. They intended to keep it that way.

He glanced at Maggie and DS Walker. Despite Maverick's insistence that this was pack business, she had pulled rank and insisted she stay, as part of her investigation. The memory of it almost made Arlo smile. *Almost.* Kane's death overshadowed everything.

Maverick cleared his throat, quelling the whispers, and then told the group about Kane. While he talked, Arlo watched them closely, looking for any signs of guilt. Domino and her team were spread among them, listening for murmurings of insider knowledge, although Arlo doubted that anyone would give themselves away. The killer would be too clever for that. Most of the shifters just looked horrified and upset, turning to each other for reassurance, but a good number were also furious, and tension started to build.

Renwick, one of their older and more outspoken members, a grizzled veteran of pack fighting, muscled his way through the crowd to the front, and glared at Maverick. "This place is supposed to be safe. It's our headquarters. My kids work here! What the hell is happening, Maverick?"

Maverick's voice was low and even, but anger radiated through every word. "Like I told you, Renwick, I don't know, *yet*, but I will find out."

Brody, one of the newer members, stepped forward, too. He was of average height, stocky with muscle, rather than lean. He had a sneer on his face, and a challenge in his eyes. "If you can't keep us safe, Maverick, who can?"

Fuck. That was quicker than expected. He and Domino knew there might be dissent about Maverick's leadership, but they didn't expect it this soon. That alone made Arlo suspicious. Brody was either very brave, had some backing, or was a complete idiot.

Maverick acted quickly, eyes already smouldering to a molten orange as he crossed the space between them with lightning speed. He was tall with long limbs and powerful shoulders, and he radiated the magnetic power of the alpha. He picked up Brody by his jacket collar and lifted him clean off his feet. "If you question my leadership, that means you have to fight. Are you prepared for that, Brody? Because if so, we can settle this tonight. But you won't walk away alive. What's it going to be?"

The pack, as one, stepped back. The security team waited, as did Arlo. Maverick dealt with this alone. It was the alpha's responsibility to handle any threat to his leadership.

Brody stuttered out his words, face almost purple. "I wasn't doubting you."

"Really?" Maverick growled. "Because it sounded like it to me. Think you have the balls to be pack alpha? To keep this pack functional? Because you're barely out of school, and I seriously doubt you'd have much support."

"No! It was just a question. Kane was a good fighter. If he couldn't survive, what chance have we got?"

Maverick stared at him for several long seconds. If he chose, Maverick could insist on a fight just to prove a point, but instead he lowered Brody to the floor. "Questions are fine, Brody, but challenges are not. I do not appreciate your tone. You talk to me like that again, and we fight over it, understood?"

Brody dropped his eyes to the floor. "Yes. Sorry, Maverick."

Maverick pushed him aside and addressed the wide-eyed, mute pack. Even Renwick had backed off. "I know that this is distressing for everyone. Kane was a good friend to many of us, but infighting and bickering will not solve this. I'm your alpha for a reason." He paused as he scanned the crowd. "You need to let me and my team find his killer and bring him or her to justice. Are there any other questions or comments? Anything you've seen that might shed light on this?"

Jensen, loyal to Maverick and an old pack member, said, "I don't know anything about this, but I trust you, Maverick. No one wants a shifter war, and I know that you won't let that happen." He stared at the others, particularly Brody. "I've been in this pack long enough to know good leadership and stability when I see it. If you need any help at all, Maverick, just ask."

Maverick nodded. "Thanks. Anyone else?"

"Who will tell his family?" Frieda asked, a middle-aged shifter who had three children in the pack. They stood next to her, two boys taller than she was, and a daughter. None of them worked in the club. "They're up north, I think."

"I'll arrange it with the alpha," Maverick answered.

She nodded, her fingers clasping those of one of her sons.

The tension ebbed, but the shock remained, and when it was obvious there were no more questions, Maverick turned to Maggie. "Do you need to speak to them?"

"Yes, please." She stepped forward, hands on her hips. Maggie was of average build and height, with light brown, shoulder-length hair. She wore little makeup, but her clear features didn't need it. However, her pleasant looks were offset by her steely demeanour and her lack of patience for anything and anyone. "I'm Detective Inspector Maggie Milne of the Paranormal Policing Team. Behind me is Detective Sergeant Stan Walker. I appreciate that you see this as pack business, but I don't agree. I take murder very seriously. This is not one of your inhouse alpha spats. Kane was murdered. I want to know what he's been up to over the past days—and weeks, if necessary. Everything! Meetings, girlfriends, boyfriends, club activity... You name it, I want to know. I'm sticking around for the next hour, and I'll start with close friends." She turned to Maverick. "I will also need to speak to his family. Maybe through an officer in their hometown."

"Not a problem." He addressed the group again. "You heard her. Stick around, get seats, have a drink. Domino and Grey will also be talking to you, so please share anything."

A swell of chatter arose as Maverick walked to Arlo's side, face grim. His eyes still smouldered, but grief was mixed with anger. It exaggerated the fine lines around his eyes, more apparent now because his hair was tied back. Maverick was confident, cocky even sometimes, especially when he needed to be, but Arlo knew him well enough to see through that. He was stretched tight, like a guitar string, and that didn't bode well.

"Do you need to get out of here?" Arlo asked, voice low.

"No. I need to be seen. I could kill that little shit Brody."

"You handled it well. Best nip it in the bud now."

"If I don't get answers, I may get more of that."

"And you'll knock them all back. Most of the pack, though, like the stability we have right now, and the freedom you give them. They won't trade that easily."

"He asked a good question, though. Kane *was* a good fighter, and clever. It wouldn't have been easy to take him unawares. And he's not just injured, he's dead! How can I keep the pack safe? He was attacked here, in this club, on the damn stage!"

"It's not just your responsibility. It's mine too, and Domino's. You want me to approach Castor?" Castor Kershaw was the North London Pack's alpha. They did not have good relationships with their rivals. They tolerated each other. "Just to make enquiries, obviously. Any unknown shifters in the area, odd behaviour observed? They have their fingers in all sorts of sticky pies."

Maverick shook his head. "Not yet. Let's make our own enquires first. The whole place is closed tonight, anyway. I presume you've cancelled the band?"

"It's done. It means we can search the whole place again later, which is a good thing."

"We'll re-open tomorrow, though. If we're being watched, I want whoever did this to know we are not afraid. We carry on."

"Okay." Arlo checked his watch. "The staff are due in at three-thirty. Want me to handle that?"

"Yes, please. I'll call the alpha in Cumbria."

Hunter Lawrence, member of the Cumbrian Pack, sipped his pint of Grasmoor Dark Ale as he watched Ollie, the pack's alpha, and Tommy, a good friend and shifter, finish their game of pool.

He sat at a corner table in the bar of The Slaughtered Lamb, dimly lit and busy on a Friday afternoon. A Christmas tree filled one corner, and fairy lights twinkled overhead, reflecting in the mirrors behind the bar. A few years back, this room would have been filled with cigarette smoke, stained yellow with nicotine, and inhabited by grumpy old men who viewed all newcomers with suspicion. Now it was updated, modern, and featured a gin bar. Well, the lounge area had a gin bar. The main bar retained a more local feel.

The impending Christmas depressed Hunter. Only a few weeks earlier, his girlfriend, Briar, a witch in White Haven, had dumped him, and even though he knew she was right about the distance between them, it still stung. She lived in Cornwall, close to her coven, and he was miles and miles away. He finished his pint, pondering whether to have another. He may as well. Work was slow. He part-owned a family business with his brother and two sisters that offered tours of the Cumbrian wilds. They were very busy in the summer, but winter and the wild weather that accompanied it always slowed the business.

Wishing he could shake his mood, he stared through the window, noting it wouldn't be long until it was dark. He could shift then. Head to the hills, run off his pent-up energy, and attempt to cheer himself up. He definitely had time for another pint.

He called over to Ollie and Tommy. "Another round?"

"Yes, please. And some pork scratchings," Tommy added, eyes on his shot.

Ollie rolled his eyes. "Disgusting stuff." His mobile phone rang out, rattling across the table. "Get that, will yer, Hunter? Tell Jen I won't be long."

Hunter looked at the caller ID. "It's unknown. Not Jen."

"Get it anyway. If they're selling something, tell them to piss off."

While Ollie watched Tommy take his shot and lined up his own, Hunter answered. "Ollie's phone. Can I help?"

"My name is Maverick Hale. I need to speak to Oliver Noble. It's urgent."

That name rang a bell, and he spoke in a London accent. Ollie loathed Londoners. "Maverick Hale? Does he know you?"

"No." He hesitated. "Who is this?"

"Hunter. One of his best mates. He's busy right now. Can I give him a message?"

"Tell him I run Storm Moon in Wimbledon."

It suddenly clicked. The Storm Moon Pack was in south London. "Hold on."

Hunter carried the phone to Ollie. "Pack business."

Ollie finished his shot and straightened up. "Who is it?"

"Maverick Hale." Ollie knew who all the pack alphas in England were, and Maverick was more well-known than most.

Ollie nodded. "I'll take it outside."

Tommy leaned against the wall, hands gripping the cue as he watched him leave. He was a big man, all muscle and hair. His shaggy brown hair fell over his eyes, but he'd recently trimmed his beard after one of the pack kids told him he looked like a young Santa Claus. "That can't be good."

"Might be just Christmas greetings."

"Yeah, and an invitation to his posh club, I'm sure."

Hunter smirked. "Would you go?"

"No, I bloody wouldn't. Would you?"

"I might. I could do with a change of scenery."

"You need to get over Briar, and the best way to do that is with another woman."

"That's your way, not mine."

"Oh, get over yourself."

Refusing to get into another discussion about his post-split recovery, he watched Ollie through the window instead. He paced outside, face twisted into a grimace. "This is bad news. I just know it."

In another minute, Ollie ended the call and entered the pub, drawing them both to the table where they could talk without being overheard. He was very different to Tommy; lean in muscle, clean-shaven and short-haired, and unlike Tommy who loved to fight, he was self-contained and quiet. But that exterior hid an icy interior. He had achieved pack alpha by killing Cooper Dacre the previous year at Samhain. It was a bloody coup, and a couple of White Haven witches had helped them overthrow him by neutralising the witches who supported him. It was how he'd met Briar. Hunter had fought Cooper before the coup, and near death, after a brutal, uneven fight, his family had rescued him and fled Keswick for the opposite end of the country. They'd ended up in White Haven.

Right now, Ollie's eyes were hard, his jaw clenched. "We need to find Harry Elliot, now. Any idea where he'd be?"

"At his workshop, probably," Hunter guessed. Harry owned a carpentry and joinery business on the edge of Keswick. "I know he's busy. What's happened?"

"His son, Kane, is dead. Murdered." Ollie finished his pint, eyes distant. "He'll be devastated."

"Back up!" Tommy instructed. "What do you mean, murdered?"

"I'll tell you in the car. There's no time for another pint. I can do this alone, but I'd rather have company."

Hunter was already rising to his feet. "I knew Kane, and his dad is a good bloke. I'll come."

"Me, too." Tommy was already puffing up. "I'll help find the bastard, too."

While Ollie drove the short distance to Harry's workshop, he filled them in on the scant news that he had. Hunter was dreading the coming conversation. However, when they exited the car, there was silence. None of the usual sounds of jigsaws, hammering, and all the other usual noise associated with his workshop.

Hunter lifted his head and inhaled. "Blood."

"I smell it," Ollie said. "Stay close."

Harry's workshop was in an old, converted stable. It had huge double doors that were wide open in the summer, and closed tight in the winter. Now, however, despite the cold weather, the door was ajar. They crossed the yard quickly, Hunter already fearing what he would see inside.

As they pushed the door open, they could see Harry's dead body spreadeagled on the floor. Just like his son, his throat had been ripped out, and his body gouged with claw marks.

Tommy howled and punched the door frame, an unearthly, eerie sound that was wracked with rage, but Ollie stood stock-still, fury building as he thrust his keys at Hunter. "Go and check on his wife—now!"

Three

Domino Franklin moved from one staff member to another, offering comfort where she could, all the while veering between wanting to go out and hunt Kane's killer and cry in a corner.

Arlo had just broken the news to them, leaving out the gruesome details of Kane's death. As predicted, the staff had been shocked, upset, and scared. They were a mixture of pack members and humans, almost thirty in total, of which about half were human. They had a range of roles—security, bar staff for both floors, club attendants, the DJ, and a kitchen crew. Storm Moon wasn't a full restaurant, but they did offer bar snacks and light meals. The pack members, of course, already knew, but had been told to pretend they knew nothing for the benefit of those who had no idea about shifters. Kane's body had already been removed hours earlier.

Now, as Domino spoke to everyone, she couldn't help but suspect them. *Did someone know something? Was someone being a good actor?* She finally ended her rounds, leaving the staff to comfort each other, and headed to the bar. She sat on a stool and leaned on the long, polished copper counter, and having finally sat down, realised how exhausted she was.

Arlo was behind the bar, watching everyone from his vantage point. After breaking the news, he'd opted to offer comfort by way of free drinks, and he poured her a glass of white wine. "You look like you need this."

"I need answers, but this will help." She sipped the cold drink, savouring the crisp notes of Sauvignon Blanc. "Any news from Maverick?"

He nodded to the floor above. "He's still in his flat. I thought I'd give him space."

"You handled this well. Telling them, I mean."

"Thanks, but it sucked. I hope I don't ever have to do it again." He poured himself a pint of beer, and then gave a sad smile to another staff member who joined them. "How are you, Jet?"

Jet, a petite and stunningly pretty young woman with impressively tattooed arms, was employed as a waitress and spy. Because of her looks, the customers loved to talk to her—male and female. She always looked dramatic, favouring black clothing, skilfully applied makeup, and lots of jewellery. She was human, but knew all about shifters, and was considered one of the inner team. She befriended everyone, knowing all the regulars and what they did—on or off the premises. Currently, she was less self-assured than normal, which wasn't surprising.

Her dark, lustrous hair fell around her pale, heart-shaped face, and she wiped tears from her eyes and blew her nose. "I've been better. Rum and Coke for me, please."

"I'm sorry we had to tell you with the rest of the staff," Arlo said as he fixed her drink. "It seemed better that way."

She brushed it off. "It's fine. I completely understand. I just can't believe it. It seems...impossible." She turned to Domino. "Has your team found anything?"

"Not so far. I picked up one strange scent on Kane's body earlier, but it could have been from something innocuous. The others noticed it too, but we haven't found it anywhere else in the club."

"Which is surely unusual," Jet reasoned. "There are hundreds of people in this place every night."

Arlo leaned closer as he put her drink in front of her. "Exactly. We need to work out who that scent is from."

"I can't stop wondering why he was here before me," Domino mused. "It's my job to come in and open up. And we know Kane! He was not an early riser. There was no sign of a break-in. And no sign so far that a therian-shifter hid in here overnight. Which suggests he was meeting someone here and let them in himself."

Jet groaned at Domino's implication. "You think it was someone he knew." She glanced behind her, at their friends, and the pack that should support each other no matter what. "Oh, shit."

"You know what I'm going to ask," Domino said.

"You want me to spy on everyone."

"Just be aware of anything unusual." She glanced at Arlo. "We'll all be extra careful over the coming days. I'll get my staff to review everyone's background—again. Just in case we missed something. Anything strike you now?"

Jet shook her head. "No. But I'll do as you ask, of course."

"Where's Grey?" Arlo asked Domino.

"Downstairs with John. They're in the office, watching the SO-COs." John was a Scottish shifter who was part of her security team. In his forties, with red hair and a clipped beard, he had blue eyes that seemed to see right through you. "Maggie was not happy at them being there, but seeing as the office was locked, and there was nothing in there to suggest it was part of the murder scene, she let them stay. I'll head down to see him soon." She considered the office her bastion of power. The door had a multitude of locks and featured a steel core.

Arlo's phone rang and he stepped aside to take the call, but it lasted seconds only. "Maverick wants to see us. You too, Jet. Everything just got a whole lot worse."

Hunter tried to calm Tommy down, while the local police secured the dead bodies of Harry's wife, Donna, and their youngest child, Maria.

As soon as Ollie had asked them to leave, they had driven to Harry's house, but again they were met with the scent of blood. After confirming they were both dead, they had left the house.

"Stop scowling at the police, Tommy. It's not their fault."

"I know! But I'm fucking angry!"

"So am I, but let's do something productive. There seems to be a vendetta against Kane's family," Hunter reasoned. "But why kill Donna and Maria? They surely never harmed anyone."

"Because there are some sick wankers out there." Tommy was wild-eyed, and it was obvious to Hunter that he was spoiling for a fight. "I will rip them limb from limb."

Hunter ignored him as another horrible thought crossed his mind. "Harry had another son—Riggs. He's in Birmingham, right? I haven't seen him in years."

"What is it with Harry's kids and their need to move? What's wrong with our pack?" Tommy grumbled. "This is a good one, right?"

"Some people like to travel, that's all. Harry used to before he settled here. There's nothing sinister in that." Hunter bristled with impatience. "Focus! We need to warn him! What if he's next?"

"I never knew him that well. He was older than me, left when I was in my teens. Maybe some of the other members kept in touch. Ollie must know. Or Jimmy." Jimmy, a shifter in his forties, was the pack's well-respected second in command.

"I reckon Ollie has got enough on his plate right now. Besides, he asked us to get the pack together. Let's start calling. Tell them to meet us at my place. One hour."

Maggie prowled around Maverick's flat while he made a few calls, half-listening as he spoke to various alphas.

Arlo and Domino had been summoned from the bar, along with a girl called Jet she hadn't heard of before. *Interesting that Maverick was allowing her to be here*. She must have importance to his team. *Good*. They needed all the help they could get, because this was going to be big. She could feel it in her blood. Another shifter dead in Cumbria, and his human wife and daughter, with another shifter son in Birmingham who the police were trying to track down. By the sound of it, so were the shifters. From what she could gather, there were three packs in Birmingham, but she wasn't sure where Riggs was. She trusted that they did.

However, it wasn't just their deaths to be concerned about. There were others, news she wouldn't share just yet, news she was pretty sure even Maverick didn't know.

While Maggie waited for Maverick to finish his calls and the others to arrive, she examined Maverick's richly appointed flat for any signs of a violent struggle, although she seriously doubted that he had killed Kane himself. Fury radiated from him, and she didn't think he was that good an actor. Besides, the place was immaculate. His club must turn over a lot of money, because it had a lot of top-quality goods in it. It was furnished in a loft style. There were bare brick walls, huge windows with black metal frames, rich furnishings of leather and velvet in dark materials, tons of artwork, a high-end sound system, and state of the art kitchen. Under one of the windows was an original Eames chair in cream leather with a matching foot stool. A fancy wood burner was suspended from the ceiling, its bulbous burner hanging clear of the floor. A fire was burning in it, warming the huge floor area, and Maggie was grateful for it. It was a cold day, and would be a colder night. Snow threatened.

Through half open doors, she could see a couple of bedrooms, and a very well-equipped gym with a punching bag. She wondered if this place had been designed by a professional. The style reflected the bar décor, but there were a lot of personal touches. Maverick had rock star swagger, and elegant tastes. However, she also knew from her own run-ins with him, and from the current tone of his voice, that he was not a man to be trifled with.

He ended his calls the same time as the others arrived. Domino and Arlo stood shoulder to shoulder with him, their stance wary, violence reined in on a tight leash. A reminder that beneath their very human appearance, wolves lurked. Deadly, fast, and powerful. A flare of fear threatened, and she quickly squashed it down. It would never do to show them fear. In fact, Maggie never liked to show *anyone* fear. She studied the far shorter woman who stood next to them. She was petite, dark-haired, and must be Jet. They all stared at Maggie with a mixture of hostility and wariness.

"For fuck's sake," she said, rounding on them. "I'm not the fucking enemy. I'm here to help! I know all this blah blah pack shit, *I'm the alpha, we do it my way* bluster, but this is too big! And," she stepped forward to meet Maverick as he advanced across the living room, eyes already smouldering with liquid fire, "don't try that eye shit on me."

Maverick snarled. "I am very angry right now."

"Me, too. I don't like dead people on my patch, and I especially don't like what looks to be the start of a shifter war." She glared at the other three. "I presume you don't, either. Of course," she took a breath and stepped back, "I can't discount any of you doing this. There's no sign of a break-in downstairs."

Maverick didn't break eye contact with her. "You can take every single one of my clothes and search this flat from top to bottom. There is nothing here to link me with Kane's death—I even have an alibi. I'll provide her number if you like. And I would stake my life on the fact that Domino, Arlo, and Jet weren't involved, either. Or Grey."

"Ah, the Jason Statham lookalike downstairs. Your security second, I gather?" Domino nodded. Maggie had been all too aware of her own attraction to Grey when she met him earlier, so she was glad to hear that Maverick trusted him. Not that she could take his word for it, obviously. "Regardless, I need to know where you all were last night. And yes, Maverick, I'll have the name of your alibi. I presume Brody is on your hot list. That stupid little upstart who challenged you. I'll look into him."

"It's already taken care of," Maverick said, a growl in his throat.

"Not to my satisfaction it isn't. Now," she gestured to the comfortable velvet sofas in dark grey that she wanted to sleep on for a week, and said, "can we be civilised and sit and chat for a moment? I'm fucking knackered."

Maverick extended his arm toward it dramatically. "Be my guest."

Arlo smiled, tension easing. "Tea or coffee?"

"Coffee, please. Strong, no sugar. Black."

"Done." Arlo headed to the kitchen, looking comfortable with its setup. Domino and Jet each took a seat, but Maverick warmed himself in front of the fire.

"Is it true?" Domino asked, crossing her legs and leaning forward. "Kane's dad is dead, too?"

"I'm afraid it is. I presume their pack alpha told you, Maverick?" He nodded. "And his wife and daughter are dead, too, neither of whom were shifters. Now the race is on to find Riggs, his other son." Maggie had more news to share, but that could wait. First, she pulled her notepad out. "Where were all of you last night? Domino?"

Domino's eyes widened with surprise. "Oh, of course. At home, in my flat. I arrived home at about three in the morning after everything was locked up here, but there's no one to corroborate it."

"And you left this place secure?"

"Of course."

"I find it odd that the head of security locks up herself. Don't you have minions who do that?"

Domino's jaw clenched. "My staff are not minions. Some nights they do, or Grey oversees it. Last night, it was me. Sometimes it's Arlo."

Arlo agreed as he brought over a tray loaded with a coffeepot and mugs, and placed it on a low table. He passed her a mug of steaming coffee as the others helped themselves. "Yes, I take my turn locking up. I left at about two last night. Went home to my flat. I share it with another shifter. Jax."

"He was awake?" Maggie sipped her drink, glad of the shot of caffeine.

"No. Night off. He was asleep." Arlo looked honest enough, but like all three shifters he was wary, tightly controlling his fury and grief. "You'll have his details from earlier."

She made a note to follow up with him, and then turned to Jet, who was watching and listening intently. She may not be a shifter, but she certainly had an edge to her. However, purely from her size alone, it was unlikely she had killed Kane—unless she had an accomplice. "What about you?"

"I was here until closing, and then I went home, too. I live with three other girls. They were all asleep." She huffed, clearly incredulous as she reached for a mug of coffee. "But look at the size of me. You think I could have killed Kane?"

"Unlikely, I agree, but I'm not ruling out your potential involvement." She studied them, hoping they weren't involved, because having someone in the shifter community that she could trust would help a lot. Paranormal communities were closed in general to outsiders, especially police, although Maggie had been in her job a long time, and knew that many of them trusted her to do the right thing. She played on that now. "I can see you're all devasted. Your staff, too. Unfortunately, people are very good at lying. However, it's also pretty clear there must be more than one person involved. To get from here to Cumbria would take hours, and on first impressions, the deaths were only hours apart. It's possible, but unlikely."

Domino frowned. "Kane's family was killed this morning?"

"Early, yes. Just after eight, we estimate. Kane was around three."

"That hadn't escaped my attention," Maverick said, finally sitting next to them. His knuckles were white as his hand gripped the mug. "A coordinated strike."

"Exactly. Are you aware of anyone who had a problem with him, or his family?"

"No!" Domino was emphatic. "He was a good mate. Funny, loyal, and a good pack member. He mentored the younger shifters."

"The family in general, then?" Maggie's own anger boiled over. "They're all bloody dead! Even the humans! Was there a possibility that they were involved in something underhand that had gone wrong?"

Arlo answered this time. "No. I've known him for years, and although, of course, you never know everything about anyone, I seriously doubt it."

"Unless," Jet suggested, casting an uneasy look to her friends, "he was being punished for something Riggs has done. Maybe it's all a warning to him."

"Interesting," Maggie conceded. "But I have more bad news, I'm afraid. There have been other shifter deaths across the country, and as far as I'm aware, they aren't related to Kane's family."

Maverick's mug shattered from the strength of his grip, and ceramic shards and the remains of his coffee splattered across the sofa, rug, and table. Jet took a sharp intake of breath, but Arlo and Domino both froze in shock before quickly recovering. All looked at Maverick for guidance.

Maggie was pleased she had been the one to break the news, because every single one of them looked utterly blindsided. She'd put money on the fact they weren't involved. Their response made her breathe a little easier.

Ignoring the hot coffee that was splashed across his skin and furnishings, Maverick leaned forward, eyes boring into Maggie's. "How many?"

"Half a dozen, so far. I found out only within the last hour."

"Where?"

"Packs all across the country. The Peak District, North Yorkshire, Lincolnshire, Scottish border, Wales. I don't have details yet."

Domino's eyes narrowed. "How have you collated all that together so quickly?"

They didn't know about the government's Paranormal Division that kept tabs on all sorts of paranormal activity, and she wasn't about to tell them about it, either. One of the team had informed her. Instead, she lied. "We paranormal policing units have connections. We're more specialised than other divisions. We'd be stupid not to be."

Maverick was already reaching for his phone. "I'll start making calls. We need to respond. And call a security team meeting. We need a strategy."

Arlo stood, ready to leave, but Maggie waved him to sit again. "The North London Pack. Where do they fit in here?"

"I have no idea. I haven't called them yet."

"You guys don't get on." It wasn't a question. She knew they didn't. "Isn't it better, considering the circumstances, that you stick together?"

Maverick interrupted. "No. Not until we know more."

"You distrust them that much?"

"Yes."

"You think they would kill other shifters? Why?"

"Knowing them? Just for the sheer hell of it."

Maggie studied all of them. "I don't buy it, and deep down, neither do you. I know they run black market activities. Drugs, gambling, stolen occult objects that they fence. They wouldn't bring attention to themselves this way, and you're all fucking idiots if you think they're behind this."

"Has anyone died in *their* pack?" Domino asked, a challenge in her stare.

"No. Not yet. But the way this thing is heading, who knows what's going to happen next."

Darkness had fallen while they talked, and the only light in the apartment came from the fire. The flames reflected in Maverick's glittering eyes. "Will you be throwing the full weight of the police behind this investigation, Maggie? Or will it be the usual lowkey to non-existent response when it comes to paranormal matters?"

"If you're suggesting that I don't care, then you're a bloody idiot. Why else have I spent hours here, rather than leaving this to you? I know you're spoiling for a fight. Don't pick one with me. Besides, there are human deaths too, unless those are irrelevant to you. My investigations are lowkey because you and your kind, like me and my team, don't want the general public to be aware of this shitshow that exists below their day to day lives, or there'd be an uproar. Don't mistake my discretion for not giving a shit." She stood, ready to leave. She was over shifter egos and politics, and this investigation had barely begun. "We've had dealings before, so you know I'm better than that. I'll leave you to your plans, but don't any of you do anything stupid, because I'll be watching. And I'll be back."

Four

Maverick didn't bother turning on any lights after Maggie left, preferring to remain in the shadowy darkness of his apartment. Besides, his eyesight was superior to that of most humans as a result of the wolf that resided within him. The wolf that badly needed to run.

His companions remained with him. Arlo and Domino were still sitting on the sofa, talking quietly about possible motives. Maverick stood once again by the fireplace, enjoying the warmth, and letting his thoughts drift. He debated sending shifters to the affected packs. He wanted to have people on the ground there, rather than relying on second-hand information.

Jet, standing at the window watching the road and the carpark, interrupted his thoughts. "I know it's not what you want to hear, Ric, but Maggie is right. You should talk to the North London Pack. They might know something."

He crossed to her side. On the carpark, the forensic team was packing up their van, ready to leave, although yellow police tape still cordoned off the carpark and doors. His bar, normally a hive of activity by now, was dark and deserted.

She continued, staring up at him. "I know you don't like them, for good reason, but you can't let that get in the way of investigating Kane's death. They could help us."

"What about you? You're my spy. Have you heard any rumours of a possible attack, or..." He floundered for words. "Anything unusual at all?"

"Of course not. If I had, I'd have told you already."

"Did you know he wanted some days off next week? He was cagey about what they were for."

"No, he didn't mention it to me."

Maverick watched the forensic team leave, desperate to do something to avenge Kane's death. Now, more than ever, he suspected that Kane had business he needed to deal with on his leave, business that might well be behind his murder. Right now, his churning emotions were overriding his objectivity. He needed to get it back. He turned and leaned against the cold window. "What do we know about Kane?"

Arlo and Domino broke off their conversation, and Arlo said, "He's a traveller, or was for many years. I gather it's a family thing. It's why he's here and his family is spread across the country. It's what Domino and I were just talking about. We think he may have cousins in other packs, too."

"Could they have been the ones targeted?" Jet asked, alarmed.

"Perhaps, but without names it's impossible to say. And I expect Maggie would have mentioned that, which makes me think they are unrelated."

"Kane never said why he was a wanderer," Maverick mused. "I presumed it was just what he liked to do. After all, some shifters never settle."

Domino nodded, the firelight highlighting the copper in her hair. "True, but normally they have a problem with authority. They clash with alphas, or rub the pack the wrong way. Sometimes the alphas want them gone because they stir up unease and dissent. Kane did none of those things."

"Exactly." Maverick paced across the wooden floor and thick rugs, aiming for his drinks cabinet. He picked up a bottle of rum and poured a shot. He knocked it back, and the shock of its tanginess fired up his brain. "Rum, anyone?" They all nodded their assent, and as he poured, he said, "I never really questioned why he would travel, and when I asked him once about it, years ago, he replied with a question. '*Why not?*'" Maverick laughed at the memory, and handed out the glasses. "It was a night much like this. Cold, dark, snow on the way. We'd just finished a game of poker after the club had closed for the night. I didn't think twice about his answer. But now…now I'm questioning everything. Maybe I didn't know him as well as I thought. Maybe he was running from something."

Arlo sounded sceptical. "Like what?"

Maverick huffed. "That's the question, isn't it?"

Jet gave a dry laugh, just as sceptical as Arlo. "Kane never looked like he was running from anything. He was self-assured, relaxed, and was never afraid of being seen. Wouldn't someone on the run just keep running? Or maintain a low profile? He worked in the club most nights!"

"I agree," Domino said. "He never once kept to the backrooms."

"But Wimbledon features a wealthy clientele, and London, in general, has a lot of overseas visitors," Maverick pointed out. "Maybe he thought the city offered anonymity."

"The other thing London offers," Arlo added, "is low pack numbers. Not many shifters live here. Not considering the population."

"Because of the lack of greenspaces? It's something I've always wondered about," Jet asked.

"Pretty much." Arlo shrugged. "I mean, there are lots of parks in London, big ones, but they tend to be cultivated with roads running through them. That's why more packs live on the edge of national parks."

"Okay," Domino waved an arm airily. "I'll humour you. This is a good place, despite first appearances, to hide. So, what from? What did he know that has just got him killed? And his family, too? And what links him to the other deaths? There must be *something*."

"Whatever it is will be from his past. We'll start there. Maybe Ollie will know more in Cumbria. After all, more of the family was based there." Maverick tapped his glass as he considered his options. "Domino, will you call him? See what you can find out. Then, tomorrow morning, I want you to go up there."

"To compare for scents?"

"Exactly. And to ask around about Kane's family. I think in person will be better than just phone calls. Tell Ollie you're on the way. You okay with that?"

"Absolutely. Grey can manage things here."

"In the meantime, Arlo, we'll start ringing around the affected packs. We may even need to set up a meet. And then, when everything is quiet later, we'll search the streets, wolf-style. See if we can find that damn scent. I think we do need to visit our neighbouring pack, but not just yet. Let's see what else we can find out first."

"What about me?" Jet asked.

"Your turn will come tomorrow," Maverick told her. "With luck, we can reopen the bar, and I'll push for the club, too. Then you can do what you do best. Act as my eyes and ears."

Maggie saw Irving hunched over his desk as she entered their office. Her own room was at the end of the main one, but she didn't bother crossing to it. Instead, she sat down at Stan's desk, which was closer.

Irving was in his fifties, of average height, and with an impressive beer gut that showed dedication to his regular pastime. His greying hair was thinning, but his eyes gleamed with intelligence and cunning. He was an excellent DS, and if he hadn't been so insulting to his superiors in so many ways, he might have achieved a much better rank than he had now.

He had moved from one department to another for years, every senior officer sick of him, until he arrived in the paranormal unit five years earlier. He had liked it—a lot. Probably because it was a small unit that most departments either ignored or knew nothing about. Maggie, like him, had little room for pleasantries and small talk, although she at least knew how to be civil with her superiors. She had found working with him a breath of fresh air. She also liked his dogged pursuit of clues, his unwillingness to be brushed off, and his breezy acceptance of the paranormal. Fortunately, he got on with Stan, too. They were an unusual team, but they worked well together.

He stopped scribbling on a notepad and looked at her. "Hi, Guv. No Stan?"

"No. It's been a big day, so I sent him home."

"The shifter death get messy?"

"Very, and getting bigger by the second. There are more. At least eight now." She summarised her day and the reported deaths. "I could do with going home, too, because there's bugger all else I can do today, but then you phoned. It better be good."

He leaned back, tapping his pen on the pad, a broad grin spreading across his face. "Well, Burton and Knight was interesting. They have an upcoming auction on occult items relating to mythology, specifically shapeshifting." He cocked an eyebrow at her, but Maggie waited. He pulled a crumpled, glossy pamphlet from his pocket, and straightening it out, he read in his most pompous posh accent, "'This magnificent collection comprises of paintings, sculptures, ancient books of mythology, inlaid boxes that are rumoured to have spells attached to them, jewellery, and many more fascinating objects themed around shapeshifters from all over the world, but particularly mythology based on the British Isles.' It goes on, but you get the drift. It's a work in progress, because items are still arriving. The auction is planned for early in the new year. It's one of their biggest, apparently. Young Arbuthnot, that snotty little oik with a stick up his arse, is very excited. He is also outraged because the theft is from this collection."

He waited, again. He always loved a dramatic pause. Maggie leaned forward, heart beating faster. "What was it, you shitbag?"

"A rather impressive bone and antlered crown, set within a double circle of gold and other metals. Bloody huge, from the photos. Must weigh a ton. The tines were tipped with precious metals, and studded with gems. There were also bones in it. A bloody skull. They think it's a wolf." He slid the glossy brochure over.

Maggie gasped. "Wow."

"Tricky to date, but they think Bronze Age. The thief also stole a small acacia box, richly carved, containing animal parts. A withered hare's paw, sealskin, a portion of a stag's antler, a bird skull, and fish scales. All creatures that are associated with shapeshifting."

"You're kidding me!"

"Would I do that to you?" He spread his hands wide. "But there's more. The wood was remarkably well preserved. Apparently, acacia wood has water resistant properties and is highly resistant to warping, but magically it's used in spells of protection, psychic power, and it symbolises the afterlife. An inscription on the box, written in ancient Celtic Welsh, said, 'Here lies the truth of shifters.'"

"Which means what? It's a bit vague."

"No one knows—yet. You see, some of this collection came from a dead man's estate. It's the usual story of eccentric collectors and rambling houses filled with crap. Their family doesn't see the point of keeping it. Most of his belongings were disbursed elsewhere."

Maggie had visions of dusty old boxes, cobwebbed attics, and shadowy libraries where everything creaked. "There are other things in the auction from the estate?"

"A couple of shifter sculptures in bronze. Weird things." He shuddered dramatically. "I wouldn't like them on my mantel piece. And some dusty old books. Leatherbound, arcane."

"But the thief only took the box and the crown?"

"Yep."

"Any idea how the thief broke in?"

"None. No sign of a break-in anywhere. But the cameras were sabotaged. Nothing captured at all. They were out for an hour between midnight and one o'clock in the morning. Of course, they flatly deny an inside job, and with good reason, really. They have the key swipe IDs. Logs people in and out, and no one entered."

"Well, this can't be a coincidence, can it? Dead shifters, and a mysterious box of shifter shit stolen from Burton and Knight. No, I don't like this at all. Did you get the team in?" She meant the forensic team.

"Just the general one to dust for prints in the area. Nothing unusual there, either."

"So, no damaged locks or windows, or anything?"

"Nope."

"You haven't approached Sam yet?"

"No, or any of the other occult shops, either. I thought I'd find out a bit more first. Sound okay?"

"Perfect. I don't want you to approach anyone. I don't want the thief to be alarmed, or to think that we're watching. But potentially we could rope someone else in to watch for us."

Irving grinned. "Your favourite Orphic Guild collector, Harlan Beckett?"

"He is not my favourite. He's a pain in the arse. Especially when he associates with those bloody Nephilim and Shadow. But yes, him. Everyone knows him in that world." Maggie nodded to herself, pleased with the decision, and she rose to her feet. "I'll phone him in the morning. That will be a nice start to his weekend."

As his wolf, Arlo investigated the carpark behind Storm Moon, safe in the knowledge that no one would be there that night.

The club was on a main road that led into the centre of Wimbledon Village, and had a large amount of foot traffic passing it constantly. Fortunately, the cold November night deterred loiterers, but additionally, not only had the police cordoned off the area, the pack had stationed their own security staff around the club grounds, too.

Arlo sniffed the many scents in the loading area behind the stage, but could not find the strange scent they had all detected earlier. He looked up at the roof. *Could someone have been up there? Surely not. There would be no way to enter the club from there. Maybe air ventilation bricks on the ground?*

He moved to the front of the club, knowing that if anyone saw him, they would assume he was a big dog. He took his time, identifying the scents one after another—both human and shifter. Most of the wolf-shifter scents were recognisable to him, as they were from his own pack. A few were unknown, but again, that wasn't unusual. Shifters, like anyone, visited London and frequented their club. It was a place where they felt safe to meet and conduct their business, or just kick back and have fun. Shifters liked to deal with each other, just because they had common interests, and didn't have to hide who they were.

Again, there were no scents there that gave him any alarm. But Kane had been killed by a shifter, of that there was no doubt. The tearing of his throat was a very shifter way to kill—well, wolf-shifter, anyway. Which brought him back to therian-shifters again. They were humans who could change into any animal at will. *What if they had entered the club as a rat, and changed into a wolf?* He considered Kane's body, laid out on the stage under a spotlight. He knew the security team had investigated the ventilation spaces, but what about the area above the stage?

He headed to the rear of the building again, changed to human form, and whistled. The pounding of four paws announced Maverick's arrival. He was a big wolf, with huge paws and powerful haunches, his fur dappled with grey and black. He shifted as well. "Have you found something?"

"I have an idea. Follow me." Arlo grabbed his bundle of clothes, pulling on his jeans as he entered the club. It was eerily quiet. Although Kane's body had been removed, most of the blood was still there. Arlo ignored it, and pointed above them. "The stage area. There's a crawlspace up there, right?"

"Sure. For maintenance on the lights. But the team went up there."

"Are you sure? It's separate to the other roof space, after that water leak we had a few years ago. I had it sealed off."

A look of resigned impatience crossed Maverick's face. "I presumed they had…"

"And you might be right. Domino is thorough, but she may have presumed, too. I want to check now. No harm, right?"

The access to the area above the stage was through a small storage room where they kept various supplies for the kitchen and toilets. A ladder ran up the wall to a hatch in the ceiling. Pushing it open, Arlo pulled himself through the opening. It was hot in the narrow, confined space. He shifted, and proceeded carefully across the beams. Wiring ran across the area in thick bundles leading to various spotlights, and he edged forward carefully.

Within seconds the strange scent became apparent, growing stronger as he reached the area above where Kane had been found. This is where the murderer had waited for him, potentially dropping down on him from above.

The only thing remaining was a small, black feather. But feathers were useful. They carried the shifter's scent, and were part of its body. Witches could cast spells with such things.

Hunter raced across the moors, muscles flexing and stretching, the rough grass feeling coarse beneath his paws.

It was close to midnight, and a shaft of moonlight cast a band of silvery light over the landscape, but he didn't stop to admire its beauty. He knew it so well already. The hills that surrounded Keswick were wild and untamed, and they sang to his shifter blood, especially when he was a wolf.

The rich, earthy scents mingled with grass, heather, distant water, the promise of snow, and the scents of the other shifters that were up ahead. The pack was meeting in a hollow, tucked into the hillside, one they kept for their meetings when they wanted to be out in the wild. It housed a small hut with a fireplace and spare clothes, but that was it. Most of the time, they conversed as wolves up there.

Their old meeting place in Castlerigg Stone Circle had been abandoned once they parted ways with the Devizes, the family of witches. Their new meeting place was far from their prying eyes.

Howls erupted into the air, signalling that Ollie had broken the news of the deaths to those who didn't already know. The sound was plaintive, heart-breaking. Hunter stopped running and joined in the lament, lifting his head to the heavy, cloud-filled skies that swallowed the shafts of moonlight. When he'd finished, he loped up to the rim of the hollow and looked down on the pack gathered below. His home. His siblings, Holly, Piper, and Josh, were down there, too.

Suddenly, Hunter couldn't bear to join them. He lay flat on the ground, head on paws, the chill wind ruffling his thick fur. He was used to violence. Shifters were often violent and territorial, especially in the wild, as he considered these moors to be. Other packs sometimes encroached on their territory out here. They had to be forcefully reminded not to. Recently, their closest neighbour had been doing just that, and Hunter, one of their strongest fighters, had been happy to repel them. Now, he pondered that. *Why had they been more aggressive lately? Was it something to do with Harry and his family's deaths?*

Surely not. What had territory disputes have to do with their deaths? And who the hell could have issue with Harry? He was harmless and hardworking. He didn't threaten pack stability, and had no interest in being alpha.

The other deaths, however, added confusion to all that. Word had reached them only a couple of hours ago. He had volunteered to spend time with Domino when she arrived tomorrow. He wanted answers, and was prepared to do anything to get them. He had a reckless disregard for his own safety after splitting with Briar, and would relish having something else to do.

A prickle ran down his spine as another scent reached him. Something was close. Something that hadn't seen him because he lay so quietly. Ignoring the pack below, Hunter focussed.

Was this the start of an attack?

No. He detected only one strange scent.

Remaining motionless, he scanned his immediate surroundings, and was rewarded moments later when a kestrel perched on a rock close by to watch the gathering below. But it was no ordinary bird. It was a shifter, but he was reasonably certain it wasn't a therian. He could tell by the scent and indefinable aura of magic that comprised power and Otherworldliness, a difference that no ordinary human would ever detect. Potentially, the closeness of his pack was enough to disguise his own presence.

Why was it here? Was this who had slain their pack members, or was this someone else who had come to watch and gloat? Or was it just a random shifter who had stumbled across the meeting?

Hunter had spent hours on these moors, and had often come across other types of shifters, but most kept to themselves. The fact that this one was watching the pack made him uneasy. Hunter weighed his chances. He wanted to catch it, clench it tight within his jaws to take it captive, but he'd never reach it before it flew away. He was to its right, well within its eyeline if he moved. Besides, it could shift at any point to something larger than him, shattering his jaws and injuring him. Death was the only option.

Once he'd studied it, absorbing its size and shape and its unique scent, he sprang to his feet and launched himself at it.

The kestrel rose with an outraged squawk, and Hunter swiped it with his huge paw, bringing down a cascade of feathers. But that was all he had. The kestrel rose quickly, winging away on the night. It hung above them for seconds only, before wheeling out of sight.

Five

Harlan Beckett, the American collector who worked for The Orphic Guild, an organisation that was paid to find occult and arcane objects for their usually rich clients, studied Maggie across his latte and breakfast burrito.

"*You* want *my* help? Wow. This is unusual. Should I break out the champagne?"

"Sarcasm is not your friend, you American jackass."

"Ah! Stooping to American insults now. How lovely."

They were sitting in a modern café not far from Harlan's apartment, after Maggie's early morning phone call when she had more or less demanded a meeting with him. His concession had been to meet here after his gym session. He had worked up an appetite, hence the burrito. Maggie was tucking into a bacon and egg sandwich.

After swallowing a mouthful, she said, "I've got a dead shifter on my patch, and several more across the country. What do you fucking expect?"

Harlan laughed. "I've missed you and your foul mouth."

"I haven't missed you. I seem to run into you all the time lately, especially as you've taken up with those psychopathic Nephilim, and the crazy fey madam." She leaned forward. "Didn't I hear that you were involved in that very lucrative find recently?"

"The Templar gold. Yes, that was an interesting job."

"You're rich now?"

"I'll be a bit better off." That was an understatement. He was already wealthy, courtesy of commissions on the objects he found. That particular commission had been enormous.

"You're not giving up the day job, though?"

"And miss all the fun of the chase? No chance."

"Good. Because this could get messy." She used a napkin to wipe a smear of tomato sauce from the corner of her lip. "Actually, it's already messy. The killer—or killers—is not fooling around. You could wind up in the crossfire."

"It's a risky business."

"I think this will be worse than most." She held his gaze, her expression serious. "These deaths were violent. The shifter who was killed was one of Maverick's best friends."

Harlan pushed his empty plate away and cradled his coffee cup. He'd seen the death at Storm Moon splashed across the news, but obviously the report did not specify that it was a shifter death. They would have no idea. "How is Maverick? I only met him once, but I liked him."

"He's furious. I am very worried that this will start a shifter war. So is he."

"Any idea who did it?"

"None at all. Yet. But we have a potential clue, which is why I'm here. It involves mythological objects. Before I go on, I trust I have your absolute silence on this?"

"Of course. But despite my latest hefty commission, I do need to get paid for this, or Mason will ask questions." Mason was The Orphic Guild's director, and he would need to justify his hours spent on a new job.

Maggie shook her head. "It stays off the books. On your own time. And before you even bloody start, I have bailed you out of some shit before, so you owe me!"

Harlan considered complaining and refusing, but he was already intrigued. Plus, after his one and only meeting with Maverick Hale and his team, he had always wanted to know more about them. The more connections you had in his business, the better. "Fair enough. On my time, and my lips are sealed. But I presume you'll leap to my rescue if things go 'tits up' as you Brits say?"

"I will try my best."

Harlan grimaced, but nodded anyway. "Go on."

She outlined the theft from Burton and Knight. "So, no sign of a break-in, and no evidence of an inside job. But bollocks to all that. That's my concern. I want you to find out about that box and the crown! What about them is so important? Is someone trying to fence them on the black market? Or was it stolen to order? We can't go charging in asking questions without setting off significant alarm bells, but you..." She batted her eyelids and Harlan nearly choked on his coffee.

"Seriously Maggie, that's freaky. Don't ever do that again."

"I won't if you say yes."

"Yes, then! I admit, I am intrigued. What did you say the inscription on the box was again?"

She checked her notebook. "Here lies the truth of shifters."

He made a note on his phone. "And a bone crown. Intriguing. And there were other objects from the man's estate?"

"Yes. They weren't touched. Do you know much about shifter mythology?"

"Not really, other than what they are, and that there are different types, including the trickster therians. Shadow swears they all have fey blood—that it's a fey gene passed down through generations."

Maggie nodded. "I get it. It would all have begun when the borders between worlds were thin, and humans and fey passed back and forth. And bred together, obviously."

"Yeah, and that makes sense, right? She says that there are shifters in the Otherworld. Birds, deer, bears, and others."

"So potentially this box could reference that, or she could be wrong and their origins are very different here."

"Or it's some weird mix of the two," Harlan suggested. He considered his options. Delving into shifter mythology would be fascinating. "Why would those two things be worth killing over? Presuming the deaths and the theft are related."

"It's too much of a coincidence for them not to be." She sighed, her finger idly making a pile of spilled sugar. "As to their importance, I have no idea, but there are *a lot* of deaths in the span of twenty-four hours."

"Are there links between the deaths? I mean, are the victims related, or do they have common elements connecting them?"

"It's what we're looking into now. I presume if there's a link somewhere between them all, it could connect to the box of tricks and the crown."

"That's what I'm thinking, too." Harlan finished his coffee and grimaced at the cold dregs. "Okay. I'll approach Burton and Knight and see if I can preview the rest of that collection, and go from there. I'll make up some client who's interested. Any objections if I approach Maverick? I'd like his take on their origins."

"Knock yourself out. In fact," she checked her watch, "I haven't even told him about the theft yet. I don't know if he even knows of their existence." Her eyes kindled with mischief. "I'd better do that now, and I'll let you know how it goes."

It was an almost six-hour drive from London to Keswick, in Cumbria, and it was mid-afternoon by the time Domino arrived outside Ollie's house at the outskirts of the town. She was grumpy and cramped.

Admittedly, the view for the last hour or so had alleviated some of her annoyance. The Lake District was beautiful, and once she was off the motorway, the road led her past Lake Windermere, Thirimere, and then on to Derwent Water. The small town of Keswick was situated at the northern point of the lake. She had stopped the car a couple of times to stretch her legs and take in the view, but the biting cold had quickly driven her back to the warm confines of the car. It was far colder there than in London. She'd already checked into her hotel, and her mood lifted even more. It was cosy, with a restaurant and fire, and would suit her stay perfectly.

On the drive she had mulled over Kane's death and the investigation. He had been a good friend, even more at one point, but that had been short lived and a long time ago. His death had blindsided her. She berated herself for being head of security, and yet failing to save Kane. But that was a stupid sentiment. His death was not her fault, and he had been killed when the club was closed. Leaving the city and the grief-stricken pack would allow her time to think, and be rational, away from the drama.

Focussing on the present, she studied Ollie's house and its surroundings. It was more of a large cottage really, built of stone, and with a sagging roof and numerous chimneys, all of which belched smoke.

It was situated in a small garden full of shrubs that suffered from the cold, and all was set against a backdrop of magnificent hills, bruised by dark clouds that pressed on the landscape. Perhaps here she would find answers.

She marched up the path and knocked on the door, and within seconds, a tall, slim man, wiry with muscle, opened the door, his face etched with grief and anger. Emotions she was seeing all too frequently recently. His gaze raked over her, and she recognised the dominant superiority that all alphas carried. The eyes that said, *Don't screw with me.*

"I'm Domino, from Storm Moon. I think you're expecting me."

He gave her a weary smile, and extended his hand. "Oliver Noble, but call me Ollie. Everyone else does. Come in."

After taking her coat and making polite enquires about her journey, he led the way to a chaotic living space, filled with mismatched, squashy sofas and armchairs, and a huge window that looked out onto the wild landscape behind the house. It could not have been more different to Maverick's flat—or her own, for that matter.

Four other shifters were there, including one woman, and they all rose to their feet as he made the introductions. "Jimmy is my second, and knew Harry well. Holly was a good friend of his daughter. Tommy—" he cast an amused glance at Domino, "who really is as feral as he looks, sort of invited himself here. And this is Hunter, who'll be helping you while you're here. He's Holly's brother."

"I am not fucking *feral*, yer cheeky shite! I'm your muscle!" Tommy complained. His lips pursed as he looked at Domino. "Head of Security? Interesting."

Domino was used to sexist men questioning her qualifications. "You don't think a woman is up to the job? I thought I'd travelled a few hundred miles, not back in time."

Holly snorted. "Ignore him, Domino. He's not as backward as he looks. He's just got a weird sense of humour. I'd blame it on the death of our friends, but he's always a moron." She smiled, but it looked more like a scowl. "I'm sorry you're here under such awful circumstances."

"Me, too. I'm sure together we'll find who did this." She was itching to take control and get to the heart of the matter, but Ollie was the alpha, and she didn't want to upset him. First impressions suggested he was reasonable, but they could also be misleading. Plus, northerners and southerners sometimes clashed, and she didn't want to seem arrogant. Instead, she asked deferentially, "How shall we play this, Ollie?"

"I think we need to share as much information as possible." He gestured for everyone to sit again. "I'll make coffee, and then we can start. Back in a tic."

For a few minutes they made small talk, about the journey and the weather, and Domino took the time to study them. Jimmy, the pack's second in command, was in his forties, weather-beaten and burly, but with a look of calm authority. He listened well, and was studying her as much as she was them, weighing her up. No doubt a good support for a young alpha. Tommy was a shaggy-haired and bearded monster of a man, with broad shoulders, thick forearms, and thighs solid with muscle. He was rough and judgemental, but clearly loyal and a valued pack member. Holly also appeared calm and level-headed, but she bristled with watchfulness and energy. She looked like she wouldn't back down from anything. Then there was Hunter, her main contact while she was here. He was tall, and lean with muscle, with thick dark hair and a cocky manner that was apparent even though he wasn't saying much. It was the way he looked. Confident, assured, with a deadly glint in his eye. He oozed sex appeal. He wouldn't back down from anything, either.

Out of courtesy they waited for Ollie before discussing the murders, and as soon as he returned and they were settled with drinks and plates of biscuits, they began. Domino started, describing Kane's death and how they had found him, and Ollie picked up what had happened after Maverick's call.

He shook his head, clearly perplexed. "I don't understand why they would kill Harry's wife and daughter. They weren't shifters. And Harry was never mixed up in anything bad. He just ran his business."

"Unless there was something in his past," Domino suggested. "Something his wife would have known. Something Kane would have known, too."

Jimmy sighed. "I've been thinking on that all night. I've known them all since they moved here, nearly twenty years ago. The kids were young then, of course. He was pretty closed about his past. He moved around when the kids were younger, but said it was important to be settled for them. I often got the impression he liked it here because it's remote."

"As if he was hiding from something?" Ollie asked.

"Maybe? But he wasn't jumpy. He just got on with life, set his business up. He was a good carpenter. Busy."

"I must admit, there was nothing about him that worried me," Ollie said. "He just kept his head down. I made it my business as soon as I became alpha to get to know the whole pack, and while he was always polite, he never shared much, either. I had to respect that."

"Keeping your head down is a good way to avoid people noticing you, though, isn't it?" Domino said. She turned to Holly. "You knew the daughter well?"

"I did. I really liked her. She wasn't a shifter, but she was a similar age to me, and knew all about shifter politics. She was great to chat to when I wanted to offload. Get some perspective."

She cocked an eyebrow at Domino, and didn't need to say any more. Domino knew what she meant. Dealing with big egos and being one of only a few women shifters in the pack was hard, and sometimes exhausting. Always having to defend yourself or assert yourself. It was both good to know that she wasn't alone in this, and disappointing that this issue affected packs across the country.

Holly continued, "But she never reciprocated with any major concerns of her own. Because she wasn't a shifter, she got on with her own life. She was young when she came here, like Jimmy said. I think they spent time in Scotland at one point, but that's as much as I know."

"Has anyone had any luck in finding Riggs?" Domino asked. Hopefully, if he was alive, he would shed light on *something*.

"Aye. Well, I know what pack he *was* in," Jimmy said. "He was in one in North Birmingham, in Sutton Coldfield, actually. Small market town, edged with a lot of green area and a park in the middle. Thing is, the alpha can't find him, and the one phone number we found in Harry's belongings he doesn't answer. We asked around the pack last night, but no one could offer any more information."

A silence fell, broken only by the crackle of the fire, until Hunter leaned forward. "We have got some news, though. Our meet last night, up on the fells, was watched by a shifter bird. Or was, until I nearly caught it." He pulled some feathers out of his pocket and placed them on the table. "These belong to it. A kestrel."

Domino caught a faint familiar scent, and took a sharp intake of breath. She eyed the feathers warily. Despite what the scent suggested, she asked, "You're sure it was a shifter?"

"I wasn't born yesterday." Hunter looked amused.

Domino picked the feathers up and sniffed them again. "It's the same scent I found on Kane's body. We found a feather, too. Black, though. It was above the stage." She felt sick with rage. "At least we know it was the same killer."

Hunter nodded, eyes hooded. "It would have travelled quickly as a bird. Effective. Unlikely its responsible for all the deaths, though. There were too many."

"Agreed," Ollie said. "From my intel, it seems at least three of them died in the same timeframe. Too much even for flight to achieve."

"Have you any idea where the shifter went last night?" Domino asked as she placed the feathers on the table again.

"Wheeled away to the west." Hunter's eyes lit up. "I tracked it for a short way, but it dipped out of sight. Thought I'd search again tonight. Do you want to come?"

"Of course." The prospect of hunting across the wild moorland exhilarated Domino. "But can I see where they died first? It would satisfy my curiosity."

"After dark," Jimmy said. "The police have cordoned the house and workshop off."

Domino grinned. "Perfect."

Six

Arlo had argued for a long time with Maverick about his next course of action, and very unwillingly, Maverick had finally agreed. Now he looked at the gloomy gothic mansion ahead of him, and wondered if he was doing the right thing.

Moonfell belonged to three witches.

In the gloom of the chill autumn twilight, it was wrapped in mist, and the trees that clustered around it reached their clawed branches toward the house in a spiky embrace. Arlo was not a superstitious man, or easily scared, but Moonfell was uncanny, and the witches who lived there even more so. There was also the added complication that he'd had a brief, unforgettable relationship, with one of the witches.

His footsteps echoed on the hard stone as he trudged up the path, and the door swung open before he'd even knocked on it. He grimaced. He did not appreciate Hammer House of Horror parlour tricks.

"Is that you, Birdie?"

A slender woman materialised out of the deep shadows beneath the curving staircase. "No, it's me." A shaft of light from the lamp in the corner illuminated Odette's smooth ivory skin and thick curls that fell to her shoulders. "It's been a while, Arlo."

Arlo's heart sank. Odette was the last person he wished to see. "Birdie told me that you were out."

"She's just a tease, isn't she?"

"Liar and troublemaker, more like."

"Missed me?"

"No." He stood in the doorway, not sure whether to advance or go home. The hall stretched ahead into the gloomy interior, with doors partially open on either side. Rooms he knew to be filled with heavy oak furniture, thick rugs, oil paintings, and all manner of strange ephemera. The sound of 1920s jazz came from somewhere in the house. *The kitchen, perhaps. Morgana's domain.* However, he needed information, and he had already waited all day. Time that could have been spent chasing down Kane's killer. "Is Birdie here?"

"Upstairs, in her rooms." She stepped fully in the light, revealing her high cheekbones and full lips that he remembered kissing so well. Her eyes narrowed and she moved closer. "You carry grief like a cloak. What's happened?"

"Kane is dead."

"I'm sorry. You seek justice."

"I will deliver justice. I just need to find his killer." He shut the door behind him. He was here now. He may as well see this through. "Birdie said she would help. Will you take me to her?"

"A drink first?"

"No. It's important, Odette."

Wordlessly, she turned and led him up the stairs, her hips swaying to her own music, and lifting his head, he stared instead at the landing above. The scent of incense curled around him, cloying and thick, and like the hall below, darkness lay thick on the first floor, the only glimmer of light showing from under one of the doors.

Odette knocked on it, then ushered Arlo in, following on his heels. The room was stiflingly hot, but despite the heat, Birdie sat only feet away from the blazing fire in a huge, wing-backed chair with a rug over her knees. The rest of the room was lost to darkness, but his keen eyes picked out the huge four poster bed at the back of the room, draped in heavy curtains, and the chest of drawers and wardrobe that comprised her bedroom. He'd expected to be shown into her spell room, not here. She turned at his approach, and he almost gasped in shock.

Birdie had aged considerably since he saw her last. Her flesh clung to her bones, and her small hands were withered where they rested on the arms of the chairs. She had shrunk into the nickname that she'd been given as a child. Her milky eyes swept over him. "Arlo. I may not be able to see you properly anymore, but I'd know you anywhere. Your aura is dark today. Your friend is dead."

"Yes, he is. But I have something that may help me find the killer. If you'll help me."

She patted the chair next to her. "Sit. Odette, bring me my scrying bowl. The silver one. And a sherry." She cocked her head at him. "One for you?"

"Why not?"

"Good." She smiled, revealing her gap-toothed mouth. She'd lost a few more teeth, too, since he last saw her. "Let's be civil before we conduct business. How are you?"

"In general, I'm fine—aside from this ugly business. But how are you?"

"As well as can be expected for an old woman. My eyes are failing, my body is weak, but my magic is strong. Not strong enough to keep me young, unfortunately." She cackled with glee. "But youth is overrated."

"I'm sorry. Your eyes? Cataracts?"

"Yes. Magic keeps them from worsening, but only a little. It would take magic I'm not prepared to do to heal them completely." She pulled her woollen wrap around her shoulders, as Arlo took his jacket off. Sweat was already beading on his brow.

Odette planted a feather-light kiss on Birdie's head before giving her a glass of sherry, and then passed one to Arlo. Arlo felt like a fool. No wonder Odette had answered the door. He doubted Birdie could use the stairs now. He cast her a look of apology that she silently acknowledged.

"Odette. My bowl!" Birdie commanded.

"It's coming." She moved to a long sideboard against the wall, the pouring of water and clink of metal filling the silence.

Birdie leaned toward him. "You said you have an item of this person. The bringer of death."

"A feather. That's all." He placed it in her outstretched hand, and she clasped it and closed her eyes. "This creature is agitated. Scared, too."

"Scared? Why?"

"I don't know." Her eyes flitted beneath her closed eyelids. "But fear and panic are the overriding emotions I sense."

"Scared of Kane? That doesn't make sense. He wasn't a violent man."

"As far as you know." Her eyes opened again, pinning him beneath her milky gaze. "Scrying might tell me more."

Odette had positioned an inlaid wooden table in front of Birdie, and she now placed the silver bowl on it, filled with water, and a small bowl of dried herbs and petals next to it. Birdie extended one hand and ran it clockwise over the bowl, murmuring words Arlo didn't understand. She sprinkled the herb mix into it, and continued her incantation. The water swirled lazily, carrying the herbs and uncurling petals with it. A sweet fragrance filled the air, and the water turned opalescent. She dropped the feather onto the surface of the water where it bobbed for a few moments before disappearing into the depths, and Birdie leaned over it, her face inches above the surface.

Arlo glanced at Odette, but she was focussed on the old woman, and Arlo, almost holding his breath, watched her, too. The water bubbled and a faint steam rose, tendrils wafting around Birdie's bent head. Her breathing quickened, and her hands gripped the bowl. For endless moments she was locked in place, and then she jerked backward, the bowl upended, and water sloshed everywhere.

Birdie clutched her throat, her ragged intakes of breath shredding the silence, before she fell forward, insensible, on the floor.

Burton and Knight Auction House was a bustle of activity as prospective buyers hurried into the warm reception area, Harlan amongst them.

He wasn't interested, however, in the auction that night—a collection of Greek and Roman objects that included *katádesmoi*, curse tablets designed to impede your enemies, amongst other things. Instead, he was looking for Rose, his friend and reliable contact, who he'd arranged to meet after a phone call that afternoon.

He picked up a glass of champagne from a table in the entryway, and threaded through the crowd and into the auction room. A few familiar faces were already seated, and the low murmur of conversation filled the air. He nodded to his acquaintances, but didn't loiter, anxious not to get caught up in tedious conversations. Spotting Rose talking to the auctioneer at the far end of the room, he headed to her side.

She finished her conversation, and he drew her aside. "Thanks for agreeing to see me. Popular auction."

She smiled at him, her pale face stark against her red hair. "Classical objects always are. They never lose their appeal." She noted his glass of champagne. "I didn't think you were bidding."

"Surely I'm a regular customer, and therefore deserve a glass of your finest?"

She rolled her eyes. "I suppose so. Look, I can't spare you too much time with the collection, okay?"

"I don't need much time. I just want to see what's in it. My client is very interested, but lives abroad and wants to know if it's worth travelling for."

"It's still weeks away. Couldn't this wait?"

"No." He didn't elaborate. Lying was best when it was kept simple.

She stared at him for a few moments longer, her nostrils flaring as she frowned at him. "I smell a rat, so it's a good job I like you."

"And know me to be reliable, trustworthy, and honest."

Looking sceptical, she led him out of the main auction rooms, through a door marked *Staff Only* that required a key card to swipe through, along a warren of corridors, and then finally downstairs.

Harlan took it all in. "I didn't know you had a basement."

"We don't always use it to store the lots in, but we do now..." she trailed off.

"You think there'll be another robbery?"

She stopped and stared at him. "I didn't mention a theft. Harlan?" Her hands rested on her hips and she tapped her expensively-shod foot.

Herne's horns. "Ah. Just something I heard."

"Liar. It's been kept from the press."

"I have contacts..."

"Of course you do. What's this really about, you lying bastard?"

He considered fabricating some more nonsense and then thought better of it. "A death. You saw the news about a member of staff being killed at Storm Moon, that club in Wimbledon?"

Annoyance made way for fear. "Yes. Are you saying the theft here is linked to that?"

"It's very possible. I need to see the other objects. They might help shed light on the issue."

"The police didn't mention anything."

"The connection came to light later." The narrow passage seemed to press in on them. "Look, can I just see it? I swear I'm not going to advertise what happened." He leaned in conspiratorially. "I'm helping the police. You need to keep quiet, too. A pact?" He extended his hand.

Rose, however, crossed her arms across her chest. "Are we in danger? Because if we are, you should tell us. The police should tell us!"

"No. If you were, I promise they would have said so." He continued to hold his hand out. "If I find out anything that looks like you might be at risk, I'll tell you. Deal?"

She finally shook on it, and spinning on her heel, she opened a door a short way down the corridor. "They're in here. Don't touch anything!"

The room had a long table in the centre, and various locked cupboards against the walls. She unlocked the largest one, and started to place a collection of artefacts on the table. "These came from the same collection."

"The one the crown belonged to? The man's estate. Ivan Baldwin."

"Yes. You are well informed."

"It's part of my job. I'm good at it."

"I'll reserve my judgement on that." She pointed out the objects, naming them one by one. "Books on mythology—a couple are Medieval in origin, beautifully illustrated, one in block ink, and the others illuminated. This one—" she tapped a small, pocket-sized book, "is estimated to be earlier still, written in Latin. And this very lovely short story, which is modern, but again, beautifully illustrated."

Harlan was desperate to open them, but his attention drifted to the bronze sculptures that stood a couple of feet high. One was of a man changing into a wolf, the other half-man, half-bear, again mid-change. They were beautiful in a muscular, energetic way, as if the figures were about to come to life. Then there were the masks. "I didn't hear about those. Birds and animals."

"Yes. Unusual, aren't they? They remind me of Venetian carnival masks, but they're much less sophisticated—all acacia wood. Eagle, raven, owl, wolf, stag." She pointed them out in turn. "Arbuthnot is managing this collection and knows far more about it than me, but he isn't working tonight."

"Good. He's annoying." Arbuthnot was a fussy little man with odd mannerisms. He could cope with those, but his clipped, arrogant tone drove Harlan crazy, and he tried to have as little to do with him as possible. "I bet he was apoplectic about the theft."

Rose huffed. "Don't get me started. Of course, it was awful—and worrying. God knows how they got in. We know how they got out. Waltzed through the back door."

"Can I open the books?"

"I'll set the older ones up on a stand, but you can look at the short story—carefully!"

While Rose arranged the books, Harlan looked over the rest of the collection that was still in the cupboard. "Are those animal skins?"

She glanced over her shoulder. "Yes. Shamans used them to assume the creature whose power they were calling on. Again, wolf, bear, stag...popular animals because of their strength and other attributes. They are not antique, but will illustrate other themes of shifting mythology. Part of the display to accompany the auction. Arbuthnot wants it to be an immersive experience. There are a couple of scrolls with spells on them that will also be up for auction."

"Spells to change shape?"

"Yes. Therianthropy. You know, witches changing into black cats or owls. It's lucky, really. Another deceased estate approached us at a similar time, and it enabled us to put this collection together. It's not just about shifters, however. There are other mythological creatures. Some painting of fairies, Golems, phoenixes. Here you go."

Harlan tried not to react at the word *therianthropy*. Therian-shifters were not well liked in the shifter community. They were considered tricksters, untrustworthy, and potentially it was one who had engineered this theft. She stepped aside and Harlan took her place, turning the pages of the illuminated manuscript carefully. They were filled with mythological shapeshifting creatures.

"You know, the Gods could shapeshift, too," Rose said. "Well, a few of them. Zeus probably being the most famous. He shifted mostly just to have sex with young women. Wanker."

Harlan sniggered. "Not sure he'd appreciate being called that."

"I don't care. Misogynist prick. The Greek Gods also transformed lots of people into animals as a punishment. It's a huge subject, and shifters have been a part of many cultures for hundreds, if not thousands, of years."

"Perhaps that's why shifters in general—mythologically—are distrusted. After all, if you can't see who they really are, it's unnerving."

"Which is why wearing masks at carnivals carries so much power. You're hiding your true self."

"But if it's your nature," Harlan said, thinking of the Storm Moon Pack and the young kid, Blaze, the therian-shifter who'd been killed earlier that year, "then you are being yourself."

"I thought we were being hypothetical."

"I am. I'm putting myself in a shifter's place—*hypothetically*."

"Interesting thought. You know, vampires are shifters, too. They have the ability to become bats. Dracula and his children of the night. And his affinity with wolves."

"I hadn't considered that. But, about the box that was stolen. I understand there were bits of dead animals in it?"

Rose nodded and shuddered, listing them for him. "Shrivelled things. Ugh."

"There was no paperwork, right?"

"Correct. Arbuthnot had examined the box, looking for hidden compartments. It was lined with threadbare linen, and that was it. There was only the inscription on the cover. *Here lies the truth of shifters.* He took photos, so I can forward them on."

"Please do. The two estates that contributed to this collection. Where are they?"

"One's in Yorkshire, the other the middle of Wales. I guess there's no harm in me giving you the addresses, but obviously the men who curated the collections are now dead—and we didn't take all of it."

"I know. I'm just trying to get the context. What about the crown? Sounds big."

Rose's eyebrows shot up. "Huge!" She fished a brochure from a pile. "There's a photo of it on here. Now that it's been stolen, we've had to pull them. God knows how anyone would wear it. It must be just decorative."

Harlan shuddered. "It's macabre!"

"I know. Old, too. Very old. Should fetch quite a price if it's ever found." She sighed, as if resigned to the fact it was gone for good. She was probably right. "I'll get those addresses."

"Thanks, Rose."

While she hunted for them, Harlan studied the books. "This short story is intriguing. Very fantastical. Modern, you say?"

"Yes. Early twentieth century. *The Wolf King and The Witch Queen*. Rather a tragic end. It won't fetch a lot, but the illustrations are rather lovely."

Harlan found that the more he looked at it, the more he liked it. "Can I borrow it?"

"No!"

"Please? I'll sign for it, and if I damage it, I'll pay. I'm just really intrigued by it."

Rose tutted and finally agreed, and he had a feeling she was agreeing just to get him out of there. That was fine by him. *Whatever worked*.

Seven

Maverick was glad the club was open on Saturday evening. It was a welcome distraction from his constant mulling over Kane's death.

Despite, or maybe because of the death, the club was even busier than usual. The morbid curiosity of the masses had swelled their regular crowd, and in anticipation, Grey had drafted in a few extra shifters. He was now patrolling the floor, leaving Maverick alone in the office, thinking about Maggie's news of the stolen objects.

She'd visited a few hours earlier, and he had lied when he said he'd never heard of such things. He wasn't sure she believed him. She had looked at him with barely concealed impatience. Of course he'd heard of the box—or rather, the collection of objects that could reveal the mystical beginnings of their race that was lost to history. However, he hadn't heard of the crown, and that was curious.

In his position, Maverick made sure to know such things, although it wasn't anything as fantastical as information being passed down through the alphas, like a wise elder bestowing ancient knowledge. The change of hands from one leader to another could be a calm and rational affair, but all too often, it wasn't. It was rare for the new alpha to actually kill the old one; often there was a bloody fight and then the old alpha moved aside, usually leaving the pack, but not always. Occasionally, it was a fight to the death. However, old alphas knew the wisdom of moving aside for youth, although this potentially would lead to a fight between shifters as to who would assume the leadership position. That was exactly what had happened in his pack. Their old leader stepped aside, inviting those interested in the job to fight for it. Maverick had won, after several bloody battles. So, no, there was no mystical handing over of lore and myth to the next in command. His knowledge came from his own curiosity. A need to know his roots.

His first assumption years ago was that the objects were a child's tale, like many other stories from the oral traditions. However, the news that they existed and now had been stolen made him wonder if there was something to them after all. *Was the man who had owned them a shifter?* Maggie hadn't known, but was looking into his background, and although she told him the name, he hadn't recognised it. She had also been cagey about what else had been in the man's ownership. Another mystery to add to the feather and its odd scent.

He was glad when Arlo arrived. Maverick had been going around in circles, and needed a distraction. Rising to his feet from behind the desk where he'd been sitting, feet up on the surface, he crossed to the bar. "How did you get on?"

"Well, I have answers, but you won't like them." Arlo threw his jacket over the back of a chair. "I need a whiskey. A big one."

Maverick fixed their drinks, and Arlo threw back the first one immediately. "Like that, is it?" Maverick said, worried for his friend. "I'll get you another."

"According to Birdie, the feather belongs to a shifter, but not a human one—if we are to believe her, and I do."

Maverick's first instinct was to deride Birdie and her witchcraft. He didn't like her and didn't trust her, but curiosity overcame him. "What do you mean, not a human one?"

"She says it's an ancient fey creature. A Pûca."

"A Pûca?" Maverick's own drink was forgotten. "I've heard of those. Thought they were just myths. And how does she even know that?"

"Because the scrying glass shows her such things—and her eyesight is going. It's sharpened her other senses. She sees less with her eyes than her mind." He sipped his second drink. "I thought the vision had killed her. It didn't, fortunately, or Odette would have killed *me*. She just passed out." He sat heavily in one of the chairs in the seating area, weighted down with worry. "She's frail now. I never thought I'd see that. She was always such a force of nature."

"We all have to grow old, Arlo." Maverick sat opposite him, wishing to talk more about Pûcas than Birdie, but it was obvious that Arlo was shaken up. "Was she okay when you left?"

"Yeah. She was a bit woozy initially, but a large sherry helped sort that out—some things don't change—and then some weird, herbal tea that Odette gave her."

"How was she?"

"The same. Beautiful, aloof, infuriating." Arlo stared at him, lips twisted ruefully. "You told me not to get involved."

"But you made it out alive. Maybe a little scarred."

"That's one way of putting it."

Arlo had been in a relationship with Odette for only a short time a couple of years earlier. A matter of months, perhaps. But it had been intense despite its brevity, although of course Arlo had never elaborated. Maverick had just seen the aftereffects. The brooding silences, the sharp responses, the anger, and the hurt. Maverick had experienced his share of intense passion, but had never felt a fallout as bad as Arlo's. "I'm sorry it ended so badly. You shouldn't have gone there today."

"We needed answers. I got them."

"So, this Pûca, did she tell you more about it?"

"In typical Birdie style. She said she saw a twisted, writhing creature, full of evil intent. It shook her up, there's no doubt about that." He shot Maverick a worried look. "Not much does, so that on its own worries me. She said it wasn't working alone, either."

"How many?"

"She wasn't sure, or where to find it. The feather enabled her to see what it was, and allowed her to get a general feel for its emotions, which were not good. It's angry and intent on doing harm—or rather, *they* are. But she also said it was scared. Seems contradictory, but I guess it isn't, really."

Maverick leaned back, swirling the remaining whiskey in his glass as he tried to take it all in. "Pûcas... How do we find it—or them?"

"I have no idea. Birdie said its magic was effectively blocking any way to cast a spell to find it. They're old, powerful creatures, not often seen by men." He tapped his nose. "We have to rely on this to hunt them down. Someone must know something about them."

Maverick nodded. "Thank you. I know it was hard."

"It was worth it. Odette said to call on them if we need help."

Over his dead body. He said more politely, "I doubt that would be wise."

"I know."

"Okay. I have some news for you, too." He updated Arlo on Maggie's visit. "The theft and the deaths have to be connected."

Arlo snorted. "Do you really believe in the mythological shifter relics? That's nuts. That's like..." he wafted his hands around his head. "Airy fairy rubbish."

"I think we have to. They were stolen. Shifters are dead! And some bollocking fey creature is involved. *Shit.* Domino." Immediately, fear for Domino's safety shot through him, and he called her. "She's not answering."

"Which means she's already hunting," Arlo said, reassuring him. "She's got pack support. I'm sure she'll be fine."

"But they don't know what they're up against. And it's not our pack."

Hunter loped up the steep hills that cradled Derwent Water and Keswick, exhilarated by the race. A few pack members were accompanying him and Domino, their intention to spread out and pick up the shifter's scent again. An exploration of Harry's house and workshop had been fruitless as far as detecting any clue of their attackers.

Tommy and Domino were a short distance away. Tommy was a huge wolf, just as he was a huge man. Domino was sleeker, long-legged, and quick. She pulled ahead of Tommy, but still couldn't catch up to Hunter. Further out were Ollie, his sisters, Holly and Piper, his brother Josh, Jimmy, and Evan, Holly's mate.

The area was blessed with numerous peaks. Skiddaw, Blencathra, and further west were Grisedale Pike and Grasmoor, the landscape riddled with hiking trails, forests, streams, and lakes. They finally stopped on the crest of the hollow, situated between Underskiddaw and Skiddaw, where the pack had gathered the night before, and Hunter led them to the place where he had seen the bird. The scent was fainter now, and even though Hunter had pondered on it all day, he still could not place it.

Hunter looked to the west, the direction where the bird had flown. That was where they would try next. Northwest was Bassenthwaite Lake, but just below was Thornthwaite, and Whinlatter Forest beyond it—a thickly wooded area. Expecting to find anything there was madness, but they had to try.

When the shifters had exhausted their search, they made their way back to their cars. Although wolves could cover long distances, time was against them; it would be quicker to drive to their next destination and shift again.

Tommy shook himself like a dog as he changed back to human form, quickly pulling on his jeans and jumper. "What kind of smell was that? It was feral. Dirty and...old."

Hunter laughed. "We're sort of feral."

"Not like *that* we're not."

"It makes me uneasy," Holly said, shivering in the cold. "Who could have a problem with Harry and his family?"

"I hate to say it," Jimmy admitted, "but they must have something in their past that makes them a target. Them and the other victims. Where shall we meet, Hunter?"

"Whinlatter Visitor Centre. It will be deserted at this hour."

Hunter drove Tommy and Domino there in his old Volvo, the lanes quiet on the cold winter's night. Domino laughed at the scenery. "Wow. This could not be more different to London."

"Better, obviously," Tommy growled.

"Different." Domino was undaunted by his gruffness. "But I will admit that it's wilder. You have a lot of room to roam up here. How big is your territory?"

"Up to Carlisle," Hunter told her. "Another pack has the territory around there—and all around the Solway. Another pack is in the North Pennines."

"Really?" Domino looked surprised. "I hadn't realised there were so many shifters up here."

"There's a lot of land. It makes sense. Why live in the city when you have all this?"

Tommy grumbled again. "Stupid southerners."

Hunter snapped. "Shut up! My girlfriend was a southerner! And there's nowt wrong with Domino, you dick."

Tommy cast Domino a sly glance. "Just my opinion."

She grinned. "It's okay. I always thought northerners would be brutish idiots. I wasn't completely wrong, it seems."

Their banter and insults continued all the way to Whinlatter, and by the time they parked, it appeared that Domino and Tommy had become unlikely friends. Tommy, always reluctant to give female shifters their due, was now looking at Domino in a wholly different light.

The other cars arrived within minutes of each other, and they all gathered in a dark corner far from the centre. The trees were already thick around them, nudging the road and carpark, pale ribbons of lighter areas marking paths between the trees. It would be impossible to hunt there in the day. It was a popular place for hikers, and even in the winter many visitors used this as their base.

"Let's split up," Ollie suggested. "We'll cover more ground that way. Me and Piper will head north, Evan and Holly east, Josh and Jimmy south, and you three can go west," he said, nodding at Hunter. "Happy?" They murmured their agreement. "Be careful, and howl if you find anything. And Piper—" he glared at Hunter's headstrong younger sister, who they'd pretty much had to bring or she would have charged out on her own, "you stick close."

"Yes, sir!" She gave him a sarcastic salute that he ignored.

"Let's meet back here, three hours tops. Sound good?"

They nodded and stripped, ready to change, Tommy's gaze lingering a little too long on Domino. Hunter glared at him and he turned away, mouthing, *piss off* to Hunter.

Hunter brought them west, leading them off the main paths to weave beneath the trees. Domino and Tommy vanished from view, and the night sounds filled the silence. Owls hooted and mammals scurried. Hundreds of different scents filled the forest, but Hunter was only interested in one, and that was a longshot.

The further they moved from the Visitor Centre, the wilder the terrain became. Off the main paths the trees clustered together, and the land undulated. Every now and again he called softly, a low yip rather than a full sound, and an answering call indicated that Domino and Tommy were still close.

And then a bloodcurdling howl halted their progress—a summons. *North*. Hunter changed direction, hurtling through the trees. A flash of fur to either side showed the others alongside him. More howls filled the air, and Hunter finally burst into a clearing on a rise, the ground silvered by frost—and blood.

He barely had time to take in the strange snarling and snapping creature that morphed in the centre, Ollie and Piper wrestling with it. A few other pack members had arrived, but the creature was moving with such speed and strength that they could barely keep pace.

Hunter bounded across the distance, jaws wide, snapped at a flailing leg, and was immediately thrown into a tree. Domino didn't fare much better. Tommy gripped the creature by the scruff of the neck. And then it became clear what the issue was. There wasn't just one strange creature, there were two, twisting and shifting between creatures at incredible speed. Bear, wolf, stag, snake in a constant whirl.

Hunter bounded to his feet and raced in again. The creatures' scent was odd, earthy and wild, and so strong that it added to the confusion—almost like a drug. By now, the rest of the pack had joined them. Hunter could barely see where one wolf ended and another began.

Just when Hunter thought they had one creature trapped, it shifted again into an enormous bear, swiping the wolves away like they were mice. For a moment, there was a lull. Everyone was bleeding—the creatures and the wolves—and the tumult of the snarls, growls, and howls faded. In the space gained for the two of them, the creatures changed into birds and flew out of reach. But it was clear that one was wounded badly. It flew raggedly, dipping in and out of the trees, until it finally vanished from view.

The wolves were injured, too. Nevertheless, Hunter gathered himself for pursuit until Ollie intervened. He howled another summons. A different one this time. One that commanded obedience. Two creatures had fought viciously against nine of them, inflicting a lot of injuries, and survived.

It was time to retreat.

Eight

It wasn't until Domino was back at Ollie's house that she finally checked her phone and picked up Maverick's message.

They were a ragged, angry group, all with a range of injuries. Domino had deep gashes along her forearms that were fortunately already starting to heal. If she slept in her wolf they would heal even quicker, and as soon as she reached her hotel, she aimed to do just that. Right now, however, they needed to regroup. Strategise.

Tommy paced in front of the open fire, a black eye already swelling. Jen, Ollie's girlfriend, a human who knew the pack well, had offered him an icepack, but he refused. "I'm not a bloody sissy."

"Honestly, Jen," Ollie reassured her, arm hanging limply by his side. "We'll be fine. You know that."

"I haven't seen you this badly injured in a long time. Have you dislocated it?"

"I did. It's back in now, though. Just a bit sore."

Her eyes raked over the rest of them, jaw tight. She was a petite woman, with pale red hair cut into a blunt bob, but her anger made her seem bigger. "You all look awful. What the hell were you fighting?"

"Harry's killer," Jimmy explained. "Something I've never seen before."

Domino, her attention momentarily diverted by Maverick's message, said, "It was a Pûca. Another type of shapeshifter." She wiggled her phone. "Maverick told me." He'd also told her about the theft from Burton and Knight, but she wasn't sure whether to share that news yet.

"What's one of those?" Hunter asked. He was sitting next to Piper, who had managed to pick up an impressive number of scratches and a bite on her leg. Hunter was just bruised.

"An ancient, shapeshifting creature. That's as much as he knows right now." She'd texted Maverick so he knew she was okay, but held back on the details. He would just worry, and she could do without that right now. "I guess now we have to scramble for info on them."

"I think first-hand knowledge counts for a lot!" Piper said, jaw jutting out. "It was like a shifter on speed. How can it change that quickly?"

"Or be so strong?" Jimmy added. "Two of them fought off *nine* of us. One of us on our own wouldn't stand a chance."

"At least I know how Kane died," Domino said. At the thought of his death, her energy flagged, and she leaned back in her chair. As her adrenalin ebbed, her injuries started to throb, and all she could think about was a long, hot bath. "We wondered how someone could have killed him. He was so strong. One of our strongest. I still don't get why he was at the club on his own. Did he know them and arrange to meet them there? Did they offer him something?"

"What?" Hunter asked. "Money? A deal?"

"Kane wouldn't be interested in anything like that." Domino sighed, perplexed. "Unless, of course, he was mixed up in something no one knew about."

Jimmy shook his head. "That suggests Harry was, too. I don't believe it. Perhaps we're thinking about this all wrong, and they have something the Pûca would want?"

"But that raises even more questions," Evan argued. He had been quiet up until now, checking Holly's injuries as he listened to the conversation, but now he settled cross-legged in front of the fire. "What could a Pûca want from us? Or rather, them. We have never interacted with each other before. I've never even heard of them! We're familiar with other shifters. They're part of our community, but these... They don't even smell right."

Piper scrolled on her phone while they talked, her finger winding around a strand of her purple-dyed hair, and she now sat up straighter. "They're full fey creatures, according to the internet."

"Yer can't believe everything that's on the net," Tommy scoffed.

"That's because you're an old man and you don't trust technology," she shot back.

"I'm barely ten years older than you, you cheeky shit!"

Ollie cut in. "Fully fey creatures how?"

"I don't know." She shrugged and pouted. "Like gnomes and pixies, I suppose. The fairy folk."

"Like bloody flower fairies?" Tommy guffawed.

"They didn't look like flower fairies tonight, did they? They kicked your arse. And unless you've addled your brains with beer, you should remember the fey warriors in White Haven at Samhain last year. There was nothing remotely *flower fairy* about them!"

Tommy's eyes widened. "I'm not likely to forget that in a hurry. That was a night and a half."

"Then you should know not to underestimate the fey."

"Hold on!" Domino held her hand up. "What are you talking about?"

Hunter grinned. "We helped some friends out last year when the Wild Hunt rode into town. Herne himself crossed over, with an army of fey warriors. We sent them back, but they left a fey behind. Shadow." He gave Tommy a sly grin. "She'd make mincemeat of you, my friend."

"Don't have to look so pleased about it."

Domino recollected the name. It was unusual. "I met a woman called Shadow before. She was at the club months ago with a guy called Gabe, and Harlan from The Orphic Guild. They were searching for a therian-shifter named Blaze."

"That's her!" Hunter was grinning broadly now, eyebrow cocked. "Fights like a demon, that one. Evan and Ollie were with us. Dined out on that story for months."

Ollie and Evan nodded in agreement, with Ollie adding, "One of the best fights of my life."

Domino thought back to their meeting, about the way there was something different about Shadow that she couldn't place. Her height, slenderness, and inner strength. Her ability to detect shifters. "She's fey?"

"Yep. Uses glamour to hide her Otherness." Hunter gestured to his sister. "Piper is right. These Pûcas can't be underestimated. The fey are wild, dangerous. They have their own laws. Their own reasons for doing stuff."

Domino could not shift her focus from Shadow. "Are there other fey warriors here? In this world, I mean."

Hunter shook his head. "Not that we know of, just little fey forest folk, and they keep to themselves. They don't care to interact with humans, so it must be big for them to do so now."

Domino mulled over the rest of Maverick's text while the conversation batted back and forth, reasons and explanations being offered and rejected. Maverick's news about the theft of the crown and shifter body parts—like weird relics of the saints—might have relevance that someone could understand. For some reason, she felt it was information she should protect, but that made no sense. They needed answers, not secrets. She broke into the conversation and updated them, but was met only with confusion.

"Mystical bloody objects? Sounds like bollocks," Tommy protested.

"Everything outside of the pub and brawling sounds like bollocks to you," Piper pointed out. "Moron."

Ollie looked at Jimmy. "What do you think? I've never heard of anything like that."

"Me neither, I'm afraid, but maybe some of the older shifters might know. I can approach a few."

"Good." Ollie fell into a thoughtful silence for a moment. "What we need to decide is if we should search the woods again tomorrow night, with a full pack. If the creatures are there, we need to find them. Perhaps they live there all the time?"

"We should look," Jimmy agreed, "but they'll have probably fled. We won't find them again—unless they come after us for revenge, which I think is unlikely."

Ollie rubbed his face, his weariness apparent. "I can't work out why they would attack Harry's family. The answer must lie in their past, or why were they so cagey about it? We need to sleep now. Go home, everyone. Rest, heal. I'll contact the other packs with dead members again tomorrow. Today they were all just as confused as us, but now we need to meet and compare notes. Especially after tonight. We're under attack, and we need to know why. And we also need a response. A big one."

Nine

Maverick spent hours on Sunday morning either making phone calls or receiving them. Alphas were worried, and packs were unsettled. They agreed to meet in Birmingham, a place that was central for all of them.

Riggs's pack, in Sutton Coldfield, had agreed to host, especially seeing as Riggs was still missing. After arranging to meet Domino there, he had another hour before he needed to leave, so Maverick wasn't happy when Maggie Milne pounded on his private entrance at the rear of the club.

"Maggie! You don't need to knock it down."

She smirked as she sidled past him and up the stairs to his flat. "I wasn't sure if you'd hear me."

"I have excellent hearing. I could hear your car chugging up the road from the roundabout. Your oil needs changing, and it could use a service."

"You're a mechanic now?"

He took a deep, calming breath as he headed to the coffee machine in his kitchen. "I haven't got time for this. Why are you here?"

"I have news. And yes please, I'd love a coffee." She looked perky this morning. Satisfied. Her hair was brushed, and she'd even worn make-up. He must have been staring too much, because she said, "What?"

"You just look a little more groomed than normal."

She self-consciously ran her hand through her hair as she sat on a barstool by his counter. "I showered. Get over it."

"Always so prickly."

"Always so insulting."

"*Touché.*" He passed her a tiny cup of espresso, presuming such a small cup rather than a mug would infuriate her. He was right. She stared at it in distaste. "It's strong. You don't need a bucket. Shall we stop this delightful banter and move on?"

"The victims all have one thing in common. They're from Wales."

"Wales?" He stared at her, but there was no hint of amusement on her face. Instead, she watched him over the rim of the tiny cup. "I didn't know Kane was Welsh!" He floundered, which he hated doing. It was very un-alpha like. "Are you sure?"

"I happen to be very good at my job, as are my staff. Yes. Wales. What does that mean to you?"

"Leeks, mountains, sheep, and rain."

"Nothing to link it to your weird shifter lore?"

"We do not have *weird shifter lore*—the box of odd relics aside. No."

"Well, at this moment in time, Wales is the only thing that links them. So, it has to be something in Kane's murky past that he didn't want to share."

Maverick sagged against the counter behind him, his cup hot in his hand. He sipped the strong drink, avoiding eye contact with Maggie. He honestly had no idea about Wales and what it could possibly mean regarding the deaths. But he did know about Pûcas.

She prompted him. "Maverick. What do you know?"

He brazened it out. "Nothing. There's a pack meeting in Birmingham I have to get to. I may find out more then. I can share this news, so thank you. It may help."

Maggie looked as if she would say something more, her face creasing into a frown. "You're a shitty liar, Maverick. What are you hiding?"

"*Nothing*. I need to make this meeting, and if I find out anything more, I'll let you know."

"It's like that, is it?" She rose to her feet, eyes not leaving his. "We'll work together until you find out something you don't want me to know?"

Maggie's ability to read him was unnerving, almost like she had some paranormal senses, too. He regarded her coolly, his alpha strength radiating out of him. "You're imagining things."

"Like I said, you're a shitty liar. It's lucky I have ways of finding things out, too." Grinning maliciously, she turned her back and left, leaving Maverick wondering what other means she had at her disposal.

Maggie was in a foul mood by the time she tracked down Harlan Beckett at The Orphic Guild in Eaton Place. She scowled at the opulent décor as he escorted her up the stairs, thick carpet underfoot as they passed exquisite paintings and sculptures.

"Must be nice to work in such elegant surroundings. Does it feel good to rip people off?"

"Wow! You are cranky. We don't rip people off. We work hard for our money. And I risk my life regularly, in case you've forgotten." He pushed open a sturdy wooden door on the second floor. "I'm in here, and have been for hours, working on your damn case!"

"And will you share, or will you be just as cagey as that bastard Maverick?"

"Oh!" His eyes widened. "I should have known. Keeping secrets, is he?"

"I suspect so." As her anger abated, she took in her surroundings.

They were in a library, shelves filling every wall space, all lined with books, old and new, as well as manuscripts and folders. A couple of round tables with chairs filled the central space, but Harlan had set up under the window, his table strewn with books and an open laptop.

"Nice place."

"Not too ostentatious for you?" he drawled.

"I like libraries, although I have little time for reading. Especially this kind of thing." She studied the titles. Books on the occult, art history, world histories, lost civilisations, conquering armies, the renaissance, Medieval history, mythology, fairy tales, and lots of maps—both ancient and modern. She lost track of it all. "Have you read all of these?"

Harlan snorted. "No! I read what I need to. Right now I'm looking at shifter mythology, and there are reams of it. Until I was talking to Rose last night—my contact at the auction—I didn't realise how many types of shifters there were."

He sat at the table, the cold November light highlighting the creases at the corner of his eyes that indicated his age. He was in his forties; she knew because she had run background checks on him years ago. He was good-looking, kept himself fit, and generally favoured a studied scruffiness rather than suits. He had no police record, but knew he skated close to breaking the law sometimes. It was the nature of working in the occult; she knew that more than anyone. While parts of it were legitimate—as evidenced by Burton and Knight who were known for their auctions of occult, magic, and witchcraft-based lots, many goods passed along the black market, or through agents such as Harlan. Objects that were found in strange places that were not advertised—like tombs, lost libraries, and estates whose owners had amassed private collections.

She sat opposite him. "It was a successful trip, then?"

"You could say that." He tapped the keyboard and turned his laptop to face her. "I took a few photos of Ivan's collection last night. Irving was right—the sculptures were uncanny. However, the books, although interesting, aren't particularly valuable, except for the illustrated one." His eyes clouded with the memory. "Stunning imagery. The others, though, were similar to the ones I have here, but early editions. Apart from a rather interesting short story, which was modern. Rose told me about shifter stuff I'd never considered before, like the Greek Gods who changed either themselves or others, as punishment or for safety." He tapped the book under his fingers. "Shifter mythology is worldwide."

"What has it got to do with the *truth of shifters* and the box of tricks?"

"I have no idea! Give me a chance here."

"Could it be to do with Wales? The country, not the big fish."

"It's a mammal, not a fish."

"Whatever."

"Why Wales?"

"It's where all the dead shifters lived, at one point."

"Really?" Harlan looked out of the window, across the busy street below, and over the rooftops of London. He rubbed his chin and turned back to her. "Wales is rich with mythology—King Arthur, *The Mabinogion*—"

"The *what*?"

"A collection of tales set in early Wales. The earliest prose collection from the 12th and 13th centuries, written in Middle Welsh. They link to *The Matter of Britain*."

She nodded. "Another place that argues the connection to King Arthur."

"Not surprising. There are places that are named after him, and a few books put forward strong arguments."

"But what about shifters?"

"There's a very famous shifter in those tales—Taliesin."

Maggie was not a romantic soul, but she'd heard of that name, and it made her smile. It conjured a land of forests, castles, swords, and kings. "The bard. He comes with mystical baggage, doesn't he?"

"He accidently drank from Ceridwen's cauldron and gained the gift of foresight. Ceridwen was not happy. He changed into a multitude of creatures to escape her wrath, and after a convoluted chase, he ultimately survived." He smiled, eyebrows raised. "Odd, the tales that survive and take root in our subconscious."

"Is this related to him? An old story?"

"I don't know. His is probably the most famous character from the many Welsh tales—well, Arthur aside. All the tales would have been oral, originally." He shuffled and leaned on his elbows. "I've got to be honest, having skim-read *The Mabinogion* years ago, I found them to be convoluted and long-winded— I'm not sure they'll tell us anything. What about Ivan, the owner of said box? Has he got an interesting tale?"

"Not that I've found out so far. He was a teacher, and collected as a hobby. There doesn't seem to be anything sinister about him."

"I wonder where he found the box and the crown, or whether they were even together. They had no provenance, Rose told me. It was one of the things they were trying to establish before the auction. It adds value."

"The thief must have known they were there from the few promotional brochures they had printed. Well, the crown, at least. That was on the front page." Maggie sighed and pinched the bridge of her nose. "Maybe the crown was the target, and the box was secondary. That wasn't advertised. More mysteries. It's all intriguing."

"Can we check out Ivan's place?"

"It's been cleared out and sold. What's the point?"

"Context."

"No. It would be of more value to find out if he'd travelled, or who he bought things from. Shops he frequented. Irving is looking into it."

Harlan ran his hands across his stubbled jaw, face wrinkling in thought. "He probably just stumbled upon them. To be fair, from the photos I've seen, the crown looks amazing. Rose forwarded me a couple of images of the box, too. It's bigger than I anticipated. I'll put some feelers out, see if I hear rumours, but somehow I doubt it."

"I do, too," Maggie agreed. "Someone is killing specific shifters, as if to wipe something out or cover their tracks, so I think the thief will hide the objects, not sell them." Another thought struck her, something she had meant to do earlier. "I need to look at a map of Wales."

Harlan leapt to his feet and headed straight to a section of shelves. Extracting a map, he spread it out on an empty table. "What are you looking for?"

She joined him, extracting her notebook from her bag. Finding the right page, she placed it on the table so Harlan could see it, too. "I want to check these old addresses."

Working together, they quickly identified the places, all clustered around Gwydir Forest Park in North Wales. A shiver ran up her arms. "Well, that's interesting."

"It's close to Snowdon. Lots of trees, trails, and hills. Is there a pack there? Or *was* there?"

"I don't know, but you can be sure I'll find out."

Ten

"I hate these big meetings," Hunter confessed to Domino. "All posturing and ego. Drives me mad. I'd rather be on the moors."

"Why did you come then?"

"Because revenge drives me. Like it does you." He studied her profile. She was watching the gathered alphas and the shifters who'd accompanied them. She took her time, methodically moving from one to the next, as if she were committing them to memory. "Do you know any of them?"

"A few, but not well. You?"

"Just Caleb from the Pennines, and Eddie from Carlisle. Wanker." He pointed them out.

"Eddie?"

"Of course. Always trying to hunt on our land, as if he hasn't got enough." Eddie returned Hunter's stare, smirked, and then turned away. Amused, Hunter studied the rest of the room.

They were at the alpha's meet in Sutton Coldfield, Birmingham, gathered in a boxing club owned by one of the pack members. It was a large, no-frills area, with punch bags, weights, cardio equipment, and a couple of rings. The stale scent of sweat and testosterone hung around them, and Hunter hoped the rings wouldn't end up being used. The shifter who owned it was muscled and hulking, with a broken nose and shaved head, and he sat behind the Sutton Coldfield alpha, watching the room dispassionately. It was also where Riggs had worked.

Ollie and Maverick were mingling with the gathered group, having informal chats before the meeting began. There were more there than they had all expected. Alphas were attending not just from the affected packs, but all over the country. Fortunately, Hunter and Domino weren't staying. As agreed by their alphas they were going to search Riggs's place to look for clues as to where he might have gone. Or why.

As the Sutton alpha summoned the meeting to start, Hunter nudged Domino. "Come on. Let's go."

No one paid them any attention as they strolled to Domino's car, Hunter's own parked next to it. They had driven separately, knowing it was likely they would be heading in different directions after the meeting. "You have the address?"

"Yep. You're going south, edge of Sutton Park."

After fifteen minutes of weaving along non-descript roads, they pulled up in front of a semi-detached house. "Very suburban," Hunter noted, feeling his insides shrink. "I couldn't live here. My soul would wither and die."

Domino laughed. "Very poetic."

"Could you?"

"It's a bit of a no-man's land, isn't it? No. I couldn't. It's London or die for me," she said as she exited the car.

It was late afternoon and the November twilight had fallen, dark clouds amassing overhead and promising rain, and they sheltered beneath the porch as they knocked. As expected, no one answered.

"I would have thought they'd have someone guarding his place," Hunter said as he watched the road, protecting Domino's actions from view. It turned out that as head of security, knowing how to break into places was one of her skills. "We would."

"Perhaps they have been. Or they're out patrolling." She fiddled with the skeleton keys and he heard the lock slide open. "Done."

The house was warm, the heating still on, although it had the feel of having been empty for days. Hunter lifted his head and sniffed, following the scent of rubbish to the kitchen bin, while Domino investigated the lounge. Everything was tidy, nothing out of place except for an unwashed mug on the counter. He opened a few cupboards, but found nothing beyond what he expected.

He found Domino on her hands and knees in the living room, lifting rugs and sofa cushions. A huge TV was mounted on the wall, a games console beneath it, with games stacked around it. "Might be worth checking the games boxes. I'll head upstairs."

She nodded but didn't answer, and he left her to it. Their search was broad, because they weren't sure what they were looking for. *Maybe an address where he might be. Any old letters—not that people really sent those anymore. A computer, perhaps. Maps...* The more he thought about it, the more ridiculous the idea became. *What were they doing?*

There were two bedrooms, one tiny box room, and a bathroom upstairs. One bedroom had gym equipment in it and not much else, the other was Riggs's bedroom, with all the usual furniture. The wardrobe, however, looked half empty, as did some of the drawers, and there was no overnight bag or suitcase around, either. Everything suggested that he had planned to leave.

The box room, lined with shelves and filled with boxes and files was the most promising place, and within minutes Hunter had stacked boxes on the floor in the home gym. It was in the fourth box that he found a pile of old family photos, and when Domino found him, he was surrounded by them. She moved some aside and sat cross-legged next to him.

"Oh, my God! A young Kane." Her voice caught and her eyes welled with tears. "It still seems unbelievable that he's dead."

Hunter looked over her shoulder. "That's Riggs next to him. Same height and build, but Riggs is fairer." He shared a photo he'd found of Harry, his wife, and the kids in a forest, dappled by sunlight. "This is the whole family. They look happy." He flipped it over, and there was a date on the back. "1998. I wonder where it was."

"I went out with him for a while," Domino said, sounding wistful. "I thought we might actually go the distance at one point, but…"

Hunter wasn't sure whether to ask more or not, but seeing as she had brought it up, he may as well. She was flicking through the photos, one after another, lost in her thoughts. "Why did it end, then?"

"It was my fault." She stared at Hunter. "I ended it, because he wouldn't share things with me. I felt like he was holding part of himself back, all the time. He'd shrug things off. Wouldn't really talk about his family, certainly never about his childhood. But look at these photos! What's so secret about these?"

"Certainly looks normal enough." She didn't answer, her lips twisted, jaw tense. "You're angry."

"I'm bloody furious! Was it me? Was there something about me that made him not want to share?"

"I doubt it." He took in the clean lines of her face, her long hair and fresh scent, and her very good figure that had curves in all the right places. The room was almost dark, a faint light only coming from the windows, and he was acutely aware of her heat. Maybe Tommy was right. Perhaps the feel of another woman would make getting over Briar easier. "Ask me. I'll share anything."

She laughed. "Funny."

"I'm not joking."

She met his eyes, understanding dawning, and Hunter felt un-mistakable attraction between them, until she pulled away. "Maybe another time. I think we should focus on this for now."

Hunter grinned. "It wasn't a no, so I'll take that for a win." He opened another pack of even older photos and flipped through them. "These look like the eighties. Bloody hell. Harry looks young. What the hell is he wearing? Is this a commune?"

He held out the photo showing a collection of wooden houses like chalets spread across a clearing in the middle of trees. A few men were standing next to Harry, and a few wolves, too.

"An old pack he must have belonged to." She took the photo and flipped it over. "Llanrhychwyn, '89." She laughed, stumbling over the word. "Where's that?" Hunter looked it up on his phone while she flicked through the other photos. "There are lots of photos of this place. It looks big. Organised. And remote. I wonder why they left?" She was talking to herself more than him, and she answered herself, too. "Maybe it was *too* remote."

"Or maybe tourism made it too busy. It's in North Wales, not far from Betws-y-Coed. It's a popular place. Lots of hiking trails, surrounded by miles of forests, fields, and mountains."

"I've heard of it. I don't think there's a pack there, though."

"I'm pretty sure there's one in Snowdonia, and further south. Maybe it was a secret one."

"A secret one?" She sniggered, her gaze drifting from his eyes to his lips and back again. "Like a cult? Or an inner circle? Hunter Lawrence! What a fervid imagination you have."

"You'd be surprised what I can imagine."

Disappointingly, she returned to the subject at hand. "Perhaps something happened there. Some huge fight that the family didn't

want to talk about. Or maybe, it was something as mundane as needing a job."

While she continued to flip photos, Hunter leaned against the
weights bench, feeling the cold metal press into his back, his gaze
absently roaming the room. He thought how nondescript the house
was, not just the area. Anything personal was in these boxes. It was like
a safe house. Somewhere to hole up and keep your head down. Weird
though, because Harry didn't live like that. He was surrounded by
life's detritus. And then he considered what Domino had said about
Kane not sharing. "Was Kane's place like this? Sort of soulless?"

She glanced up, thoughtful. "It was, actually. I didn't really think
about it too much. Just thought it was a man thing, but looking
back…"

"You know, that's quite insulting to men. My place isn't soulless. I
have lots of soul."

"It wasn't meant to be an insult. To be fair, women can have soulless
houses, too."

"That's okay, then. Would hate you to be sexist."

She grinned. "That's rich, coming from a male shifter."

"I'm progressive."

"I'll reserve my judgement on that."

Thinking that sounded promising, he mulled on the house. "He
has boxes packed full of stuff, so why hasn't he taken it all? This
place feels ready to be abandoned quickly. He must have thought his
trip to wherever he's gone to was short-term, and that he'd be back.
Interesting…"

Domino continued to flip photos, and found names on the back of
one. "Oh, shit. These sound familiar. Aren't these the names of dead
shifters?" She read them out and the room become even darker.

"Herne's horns. Yes, they are."

"I hate to say this," Grey said to Arlo, "but we have a mole."

Arlo had been studying the computer screen in the security office, hands a blur over the keyboard, but now he jerked his head up, eyes narrowing. "We *what*? Are you serious?"

"Of course, I'm serious, you half-witted wolf! I've had him watched for a while now, and I'm sure of it."

Arlo leapt to his feet, seat crashing back against the wall, his dark brown eyes already smouldering with a yellow light. "Who?"

"Who do you think? Young, cocky, a bit too brash. Maybe a bit secure in his place?"

"Brody."

"Yeah." Grey gestured Arlo to sit. "Calm down. It's in hand."

"I hate people telling me to calm down."

"I know." Grey knew Arlo well. They were good friends, were part of Maverick's regular poker group, and he knew all the buttons to push—while knowing he could get away with it. He headed to the fridge and grabbed a couple of beers. "Want one?"

"Why aren't we doing something?"

"We are. We're talking."

Arlo strode across the room, took the offered can, and popped the top. "Go on."

"I've had my suspicions for a while, and because he's a superior, cocky young shifter, he ignores me—a mere human." He gave Arlo a feral grin. "Little does he know that it's my lethal weapon."

"You're such a tit."

"I know. I have mates outside of this place, ex-Services like me, mates who need a bit of cash in hand sometimes. They can look after themselves, and they know all about shifters, so they know the risks."

"How do they know about shifters?"

"Because I told them. I'm not about to send old mates in blind, am I?"

"Why didn't you use our staff?"

"Because I didn't know how far it went. Do you trust me?"

"With my life."

"Good." Grey took a long sip of his beer, suddenly realising how thirsty he was. It was Sunday evening, and he'd been so busy that he'd barely eaten all day. "Something about him unsettled me, can't say why, just did. I've got good gut instincts, though. I had my mates start watching him a few weeks ago, just to see where he went, who he chatted to. I was about to take them off surveillance because he seemed fine, until he started turning up in some of Kane's haunts. Then he went sniffing around the North London Pack territory. He met with a couple of their guys, and then this guy I've never seen before—my team took photos, obviously. They met in a very seedy pub. Money was exchanged."

"For what?"

"Information, I suspect. Probably on Kane, considering he's now dead, but that's a leap." It was frustrating, because Grey was sure his team were unobserved, yet Brody had remained very careful. He'd used half a dozen men, so it would be hard to pin any one of them down.

"Did he kill Kane?" Arlo was angry again, the can crumpling within his clenched hand.

Grey rolled his eyes, frustrated that Arlo's normal composure seemed to have left him, but the death of a close friend would do that. "No, or I would have said, *obviously*. We were watching him. It definitely wasn't him. But I increased surveillance, and he's preparing to leave town. He's been filling his car with bags all day. He's sure of himself, though, because he's here tonight." He jerked his head upstairs toward the bar. "Having a drink with Jet and a few others."

Arlo threw the can into the sink, beer still in it, and sank onto the closest chair. He stared at Grey, hands steepled in front of his lips. "Is there anyone else involved from this pack?"

"No, unless they have been very clever, but I think not."

"But you think he had something to do with Kane's death?"

Grey folded his muscled arms in front of his broad chest, and leaned against the sink. "Yes. I think he's been watching him, and passing on information. He cultivated a friendship with Kane, too. Maybe was the one who facilitated the meeting between him and his killer." He shrugged. "I'm speculating now. We haven't heard a thing, but it all adds up. Especially his little outburst when he questioned Maverick's ability to lead the other day."

"He backed down quickly."

"Of course he did. But he planted the idea, didn't he? And I've noticed he's asked a lot of questions about what we're going to do now to avenge Kane's death."

Arlo, always the diplomat, countered, "So have a lot of people."

"Not like him. He's stirring, even as he asks. Plus, I think it's a genuine question. If I was on the inside, I'd want to know as much as possible of the planned response before I scarpered."

"I want him in this room, now."

"All right. Although, you'll have a club full of punters in another hour." It might be Sunday, but Storm Moon was always open. Tonight, there was no band in the club, just music, and it was lower key. A mix of lounge, dub, jazz, and other varieties that he hated.

"Which is why I need to see him now. Plus, it's soundproofed."

"I want a plan, Arlo. What are we going to ask? We have one chance before you either kill him, or he escapes."

"We want to know who he's working for, obviously, and why Kane was a target. And who the bloke was that he met with. Then, I'll tear him limb from limb."

"I'm not sure that's wise. We have the police crawling around this place. Another death is not a good look."

"Well, we can't just let him go!"

"Unless we follow him out of town and stop him then." But even as he was saying it, Grey knew that wouldn't happen, and Arlo huffed with derision. "All right! I'm following orders, too. Domino told me to make sure no one went off half-cocked. Now look what's happening."

"Does she know?"

"No. Only me and my men. I'd have sat on it longer, just to be sure—it's not like Brody is learning anything important—but now that it looks like he's going, I can't."

"Domino won't like you keeping secrets from her."

"I'll grovel later. Besides, she'll understand."

"Not if she thinks you didn't trust her, either."

"Arlo. Shut up. I'll deal with it. What about Brody?"

"This ends tonight. Get one of your men to fetch him, and say I need to talk staff rosters with him."

Grey nodded and headed to the door. Things were going to get very ugly, very quickly.

Eleven

averick flicked through the photos, frustration building as he passed them to Ollie. "So, the dead shifters were all in this pack at one point. I don't know any of them except for Kane. Ollie?"

Ollie shook his head, a crease settling on his forehead. "Harry's family, obviously, and maybe this guy." He tapped a photo of a middle-aged man, "but I don't know *how* I know him. Maybe he was a friend of my dad's. I certainly don't know the place."

Maverick sipped his pint, finding it hard to focus. They had found a pub after the meeting had ended. The meet was tense, and the mood had become ugly. Accusations had been levelled against a few people. Old rivalries brought up. However, news of the strange fey shifters had put an end to that, and instead started a whole new level of speculation.

Through it all, Maverick kept quiet about the crown and box of shifter relics—that was the best word he had to describe them. Until he was sure of their significance, he wanted only a few people to know about them. But now these photos had added more confusion, rather than clarity. Hunter and Domino were silent, both seated at the corner table with him and Ollie, after explaining what they had found.

Maverick sighed and shook his head. "You did well to find these, but I don't know where to go from here."

"To Wales. We must," Hunter said immediately. "We have to chase down every clue. It could be where Riggs is."

"I'd rather that we don't race there. I know we have the name of a village, but we have no idea where exactly *this* place is, or why they vacated it. It does look off-grid, which suggests it's remote. Besides, some of them could still be there."

Ollie nodded. "Agreed. More importantly, we don't know why a bunch of shifters associated with the place are all dead now."

"But we're wasting time," Hunter argued, leaning forward to state his case. "If we wait, we lose any advantage we have."

"Or you walk into a trap." Maverick stared at the photos again. "What if Pûcas chased them away from the place? It could be infested with them."

Domino's fingers drummed the table, and she shot Hunter a look of apology. "It's frustrating, but they're right. We need more information first. We certainly need to narrow down where it is. The name of the closest town isn't enough."

"Say it is off-grid," Ollie suggested, "up in the hills in a forest. Why? Are they guarding something? And what do your relics have to do with it?"

Maverick laughed. "They're not *my* relics, but it's interesting that we've started calling them that. Maybe that's exactly what they are. Remnants of early shifters that led us to who we are now."

"'Relics' makes them sound like saints! Like a religion." Hunter's eyes widened with surprise. "Yer having me on. Most shifters don't do religion. Not in the Christian sense of the word, anyway."

"No, not in that sense." Maverick mulled over how to say what he was thinking without sounding like a nutjob. "There are world mythologies about shifters, but I'll be honest, even though I am one, I have never heard a definitive beginning of our race, have you?" His companions shook their heads. "We just *are*! I mean, we know that males are more common than females. That female shifters always give birth to shifters, while other women do not. We're territorial, like our wolf. The pack *is* family. We fight. We hunt. We're supernaturally strong and have powerful senses, just like our wolf. And we have always existed. Our origins go back millennia..."

"Or so we assume," Ollie interjected.

"Fair point," Maverick conceded. "But *how* are we as we are?"

Hunter huffed. "That's a big question to ask over a pint."

"I've always assumed it's just genetics," Domino said. "A quirk that allowed us and other types of shifters to exist. Like witches who tap into elemental magic."

Ollie smiled. "Now you're talking. Magic is a much more interesting explanation than boring old genetics. That's how we get the little fey creatures, the Gods and Goddesses, ghosts, and the whole range of oddness in between." He snorted with disdain. "*Genetics*."

"Magic or genetics," Maverick spread his hands wide, "with the discovery of this box and the crown, it's a question we have to ask. The crown is made of antlers and has bones on it. That *must* be significant."

A contemplative silence fell, the noise of the pub suddenly loud. Maverick let it wash over him, fascinated by their current dilemma, despite the deaths and the theft. A few days ago, he would never have contemplated that he would be here, in this position, with Kane dead. Instead, he'd been focussing on his club and the run up to Christmas. Staffing, bookings, drinks, and food would be his primary concerns.

And that day's meeting. It was a horrible reminder of how some packs could be. Overbearing alphas, and enforcer seconds. He took a moment to study Ollie, gazing into his pint, a finger stroking his chin. Another young alpha, like him. Someone who broke the mould.

Arrogant and self-assured, yes, physically strong, and strong willed, of course, but a breath of fresh air considering some of the older alphas who were stuck in their ways. Sexist, posturing, controlling. Maverick hoped he wouldn't turn into that. And then there was the just plain rotten, like Castor, alpha of the North London Pack who had turned up late to the meeting, watchful and brooding. Perhaps that was why Maverick liked Ollie. He sensed a leader with similar ambitions to his own. Something fresher.

Ollie broke the silence. "Let's presume the whole camp is empty. Perhaps they split up to make it harder to track them all down, which suggests that more are out there, somewhere. I refuse to believe that the entire old pack are dead. Maybe that's why," he stared at Hunter and Domino, "Riggs's place was plain."

"And why Kane was so cagey about his past," Domino chimed in. She looked tired, her grief weighing on her, and she rubbed her forearms. The ugly red welts from her fight with the Pûcas were still healing. "But we're presuming a lot. A pack could still be there, even though some of them left."

Maverick felt another wave of guilt wash over him. Since Kane's death, she hadn't stopped. She'd driven hours to Cumbria, had a huge fight, and then driven here. If she was attacked now, she wouldn't be at her strongest, and he couldn't lose her. She was one of his best friends and most trusted staff.

"I'm sorry," he said to her, changing the conversation. "You must be shattered."

"It's fine. I want to do this—I *need* to do it."

"You need to rest."

"Mav..."

"No. You do."

"I'll have a good sleep tonight, and that will do me for now. Ollie is right." She stared speculatively at him. "Despite the recent deaths, some of the people in that photo must still be alive, and Riggs is on the run."

"Or out for revenge," Hunter pointed out. "I would be."

"He might have returned to Wales," Maverick suggested. "It's possible."

"Or the pack regrouped elsewhere," Ollie suggested. "Just because some shifters joined other packs doesn't mean they all did."

Maverick's head ached, and tension knotted between his shoulder blades. "We know fuck-all so far. That's why you shouldn't go to Wales yet, Hunter."

Hunter grimaced and held up his fingers, one after another. "We know Pûcas are deadly little bastards who fight like demons and kill shifters like we're regular humans. We know that someone, maybe one of *them*, stole the relics. We know a mysterious pack was living off the grid for some weird reason, several of them are dead, and one is missing." He pulled the photos toward him. "There are names on this. More than those that are dead. There has to be a way of tracking them down."

"Maggie?" Domino raised an eyebrow, looking hopefully at Maverick.

"Absolutely not." The thought of Maggie poking into everything made his headache worsen.

"Then we split the photos between us," Ollie said. "We have a few older members in our pack. Jimmy was going to speak to them today, but showing photos might help trigger their memory. I know it's a longshot, but if they knew Harry better than we did..."

Maverick nodded in agreement. "We'll ask around, discreetly. We also have a couple of old wolves who might know something. Generations tend to stick together." He picked his pint up and finished the last few mouthfuls. "We'll go home, investigate, but keep in touch. Sound good?"

"It does to me," Ollie said, quelling any arguments from Hunter with a stare. "But whatever we find, we share, and we act together. I also suggest we watch our backs, because this isn't over. Not even close."

Arlo burned with fury as he watched Brody through the one-way glass from the office. He crossed the empty dance floor below, an easy swing to his stride, looking unconcerned at his summons. He cast one glance at the stage, but from this angle it was impossible to see his expression.

Arlo swallowed, trying to keep his temper in check. *After all*, he reminded himself, *Brody could have a perfectly reasonable explanation for his behaviour.* Brody lifted a hand to greet the bar staff who were restocking before opening. There was an exchange that Arlo couldn't hear, but it looked relaxed. The only other people downstairs were three shifters on the security team. Cecile, a blonde from France with a dry wit, and Monroe, black and musclebound who towered over most people, were doing their usual routine patrol before opening. Vlad, a blond, blue eyed shifter from Denmark, was accompanying Brody. They disappeared from view as they entered the corridor leading to the office.

Grey watched one of the monitors. "He looks relaxed enough."

"I doubt he'll stay that way, but let's see what he has to say for himself."

There was a quick rap at the door, and when Brody came in, Vlad entered too, standing just inside the door.

If Brody suspected anything, he didn't show it. "Hey, Arlo. Staffing issues again?"

"Sort of. Take a seat." He gestured to the informal seating area in the corner of the room, and sat opposite him before nodding at Grey. "I'll let him start."

A puzzled look crossed Brody's face, and Grey didn't waste time. He threw a couple of photos on the table, but remained standing. "You were seen meeting with some of the North London Pack, and then this dodgy-looking bloke who was giving you money. We want to know why."

"You were spying on me?" Brody stood up, scowling. "You cheeky shit." Dismissive, he looked at Arlo. "You should control the humans in your employment."

"Answer the fucking question," Arlo growled. "And sit down."

"Where's Maverick?"

"Busy, and I said *sit down*." Brody glowered at him, but Arlo was Maverick's second, a role that carried considerable authority, and he was powerful, with a stare to match. He fixed it on Brody, his pupils widening, as control rolled from him. It was almost impossible to break a stare from the alpha. It was part of the power they wielded to control the pack. The second in command had that power, too. "Don't make me say it a third time."

Brody swallowed and blinked, unable to look away, although he tried to. Unwillingly, with stiff limbs, he finally sat down. "Yes. I met with some of Castor's crew. They were friends from way back. What of it?"

"You should have disclosed it. We don't get on with them. You know that. Our business is not their business."

Brody shrugged it off, still locked within Arlo's stare. Sweat beaded on his brow. "It was nothing."

"I decide that, not you. And the money?"

"I did a cash in hand job, that's all. A shift at a pub."

"No, you didn't," Grey said, and Arlo released his hold so Grey could question him. Grey stood over him, forcing Brody to look up. "Because I've been watching you for weeks, and you haven't done a shift anywhere." He lowered his face so it was inches from Brody's. "What was the money for?"

"Nothing. A favour."

Grey eased out of his face and paced away, changing tack. Brody's face relaxed, his shoulders dropping. A good tactic, keeping him unbalanced. "And your meetings with Kane? The way you met up with him. Got into his space."

"What the fuck? We were friends. So what?" He looked at Arlo. "What's his problem?"

Arlo didn't answer, and Grey continued. "No, you weren't Kane's friend. You watched him. Watched his flat a few times. Stalked him. Who were you watching him for, Brody?" He threw another couple of photos on the table. "That's you, outside his flat."

Brody's eyes darted around the room before settling on Arlo. If he was expecting sympathy from Vlad, he wasn't getting any. The big Dane glared at him, anger barely controlled. He'd been a good friend of Kane's, too.

Brody licked his lips. "It looks weird, but I was worried about him. My mates in the North London Pack said people were asking questions about him. I thought I'd keep an eye on him."

Arlo wanted to rip his throat out, but he reined it in. "And yet, despite all this worry and concern, you didn't tell us. Sounds like bullshit. Because, unless you've forgotten, Kane is dead, and I think you had something to do with it."

"No! Absolutely not."

Arlo had been seated, but he bounded across the space between them, pinning Brody in the corner of the couch. "Who was the man you took money from?"

"Just a guy."

"I want a name."

Brody's pupils dilated. "I don't know it. He needed to know Kane's shifts. When he worked, where he lived. That's all! He could have found that out just by coming into the club!"

Arlo paused, thinking. That was true. Kane didn't hide. He worked in the club, coming and going just like everyone else. *Was he losing his mind? Was Grey imagining things?*

Grey's voice broke his doubts, but Arlo and Brody remained fixed on each other, Brody unable to look away. "No. No one would have told him those details, and Kane kept pretty much to the office upstairs. You know that, you lying little turd. Who was it?"

Arlo's fury built, and he knew his eyes were glowing molten yellow. It changed the way he saw the room. A wolf's vision, not just human. He could hear the beating of Brody's heart, and smell the blood running through his veins. But what was surprising was the steadiness of Brody's heart. The pulse that was slowing, not speeding up.

A cocky smirk twisted Brody's lips. "You have no idea what's happening here. There are secrets, and then there are secrets that people die for."

His eyes flashed yellow as he propelled himself past Arlo. He rose to his feet in one powerful movement, lifting both of them as he tried to break free. He swung his fist at Arlo, but he was too close to him, and the punch was useless. Grey snapped out a beefy arm and caught

Brody's forearm in a powerful hold. But he wasn't strong enough, and neither was Vlad quick enough.

Brody had seized his chance well. He wrestled Arlo to the window, and then sprang at it, and rather than let go, Arlo went with him, smashing through the glass and onto the empty dance floor below.

Shards of glass fell with them as they crashed to the floor. Arlo twisted in mid-air, shifting to his wolf, and managing to keep Brody beneath him, but despite Brody cushioning the fall, it was a crushing landing.

The crunching thump threw Arlo off Brody, and he rolled across the floor. Brody had also shifted, and he ran for the outer door at the side of the stage, trailing shredded clothing. He'd have to shift to open it, but Grey wasn't in sight, nor Vlad.

However, Brody's gait was awkward, and his speed slowed. Blood poured from him, and as Arlo gained on him, he collapsed on the floor, tongue lolling. A huge piece of glass was wedged in his throat. He was choking on blood, unable to breathe, his life draining away, and before Arlo could even think to do anything, Brody was dead.

Then Arlo realised that he was bleeding, too.

Twelve

G rey pressed the thick compress to the bloody wound in Arlo's abdomen, and then addressed Vlad. "Keep pressing, before he bleeds out." He glared at Arlo's sweating, ashen face. "Jumping through a bloody window! Are you mad?"

"I was trying to stop him." Despite his injuries, Arlo still radiated fury. "At least I survived."

"Only just."

The club was in chaos. Brody was dead, body spreadeagled on the floor surrounded by a pool of blood that was already congealing. The scent of blood was overwhelming, even to a human. Arlo was propped against the stage in a seated position, covered in minor cuts, but the biggest was the one that pierced the side of his abdomen, caused by a shard of glass.

And there was so much glass. The security office window was huge, and now razor-sharp slivers of it, as well as huge chunks, were spread all over the floor.

While Vlad helped Arlo, Cecile and Monroe waited for instructions. The two bar staff, both humans, were watching from behind the far counter, mute with shock. And Maggie Milne was on the way.

Grey stood over Brody's dead body, watching him dispassionately. He wasn't pleased that he was now dead. Far from it. He'd wanted answers, and had instead heard only riddles. He also knew he'd been right. Brody had betrayed Kane. He'd betrayed them all.

He turned back to Arlo. "Why don't you change into your wolf? You'll heal quicker that way."

"No. I'll do it later. Have you called Maggie?"

"Of course I have. And Domino and Maverick." He checked his watch. "They'll be here soon. I've also cancelled the DJ, and told the staff the club is shut again tonight." He addressed Monroe. "Go get some water for Arlo, before he passes out. And a blanket." He crouched next to Arlo, feeling his pulse. "We need a healer. Why don't I call Odette?"

"No! I'll be fine."

"You've lost a lot of blood, and you're going into shock."

Arlo grimaced, his eyes still holding traces of yellow around his pupils. "Odette is not a healer."

"An ambulance, then?" Arlo's light brown skin was looking greyer by the second, and his rapid breathing did not fill him with confidence. "I'm worried about you, my friend. I need to call someone, just to stabilise you."

"Definitely not an ambulance! There are more witches than Odette in London."

"But ones that we trust?"

Arlo looked away. "I don't trust her."

"Liar. You saw her last night."

"I saw Birdie."

"Bullshit. I'm calling her."

"Fine." He glared at him resentfully, adding, "But Morgana is the healer."

Of course. Grey had forgotten that.

He stood and moved away to make room for Monroe, who had returned with water and a blanket, Vlad still pressing hard on the compress on his wound. He briefly considered if he was doing the right thing calling the Moonfell witches, and then ignored his misgivings. Odette used to frequent the club regularly, Morgana too, but neither had since the split. They had always helped them before if they had needed a witch, and he was sure they'd help now. After all, they had the previous night.

Odette answered the call within a few rings. It was strange to hear her voice, and once again, he wondered what had happened between her and Arlo. He quickly explained the problem, and she didn't hesitate. "We'll be there as soon as we can."

"Come to the stage door. We'll be waiting. And there'll be police. Just so you know."

As he ended the call, right on cue, there was a pounding on the back door, and Cecile, who leaned against the wall in readiness, opened it.

Maggie shouldered past her, her DS behind her, walked to the edge of the stage and then stopped, her attention immediately drawn to Brody's dead body. Then her eyes swept the rest of the scene, before landing on Grey. "I presume you're in charge. What the fuck happened?"

Arlo was technically still in charge, but seeing as he was halfway to unconsciousness on the floor, he didn't say that. "Brody here, the dead guy, betrayed us. He was responsible for Kane's death—somehow." He gestured to the shattered window up above. "We were questioning him upstairs in our office when he decided to make a bid for freedom. Arlo, stupid bugger, went with him. I took the stairs. It was an accident."

Her eyes never left his face. "You sure you didn't push him out of it?"

"Very sure. I would have made his death a lot tidier than this."

"Good to know." She studied Brody's body again, now back in its human form. "I can't believe he's not a mangled mess, considering the height of the drop."

"He was a wolf when he landed. They survive falls like that better than humans. He changed again when he died."

For the first time Maggie studied Arlo, and she hurried to his side. "Ambulance on the way?"

"No. A witch."

Arlo croaked out. "No ambulances!"

"For fuck's sake." Maggie rounded on Grey. "You listened to him? He's nearly dead!"

"Yes. Odette will be here soon." He hated being questioned on his actions, especially as he knew Maggie was right. He should have ignored Arlo's request. It made him snap. "Arlo, change, and rest. You'll be better for it." Arlo didn't even argue, and in seconds he had shifted into a huge wolf with a thick black and tan coat, and he sprawled across the floor.

Maggie turned to Stan, who had remained silently by the stage until now. "Start interviewing this lot. Grey," she rounded on him, eyes sharp, "is going to take me upstairs, to see what happened up there."

"Fine. Vlad, stay with Arlo. Cecile and Monroe, remain on the door. Let Odette and Morgana in when they arrive—but do not let them wander off alone. All of you," he eyed all the staff, including the bar staff, who looked terrified, "please accommodate the nice policeman."

Without waiting he led the way upstairs, aware of Maggie's eyes burning a hole in his back. When they arrived in the office, he said, "See! Nothing dramatic here except a shattered window. No torturing devices. Just a chat."

She shut the door behind her and leaned against it, arms crossed over her chest. "Why didn't you call me when you suspected him?"

"We wanted to talk to him first. I might have been wrong. I wasn't, obviously." He crossed to the bar and poured a shot of whiskey. "Want one?"

He expected her to say no, trotting out the usual line of being on duty, so he was very surprised when she said, "Hell yes."

He smirked. "Like that, is it?"

"What do you think?"

"I presume that's a rhetorical question."

He poured her a generous measure, and sipping it, she walked around the room, inspecting it carefully before ending up at the window. Parts of the glass still clung to the frame, and shards were on the floor, but she stepped over them to watch the proceedings below.

"It's a big drop."

"I must admit, I couldn't quite believe it was happening." He wasn't lying, either. He could still feel his fear deep in the pit of his stomach when he saw what was about to happen. "I couldn't stop them. I got a hand on Arlo's ankle, but..." he grasped the air, opening his palm. "They were gone. I nearly broke my neck running down the stairs." He gave her a sheepish grin. "That would have added to your woes, wouldn't it?"

She didn't answer his question, instead asking a new one. "I've been here a couple of times in the past, not too many, fortunately. Maverick keeps a clean house. I don't remember seeing you before."

"I try and blend in. Grey, like my name."

Her eyes raked over his broad chest and up into his eyes. "I hate to break this to you, but you don't really 'blend in.'"

"You'd be surprised. It's the shifters who draw the attention around here. Even though most of the punters don't know why they're drawn to their animal magnetism." He sniggered. "Maverick hates it when I say that."

Maggie smiled broadly. "Good to know. I'll save it for when he pisses me off. Again." She turned to face the room. "Walk me through what happened, and tell me why you suspected him. I'm serious. I'm bloody furious that I wasn't kept informed. I try to keep an even hand with paranormals. It falls below the radar of normal policing, and I know you lot—I know you're human, but I'm lumping you in with them—like to exact your own vengeance. But even so, there are rules."

"To be fair, although I'd had my suspicions for a while, I only told Arlo tonight, and I only told him because Brody was preparing to leave. It actually all happened very quickly." He ran through his team's observations again, and their line of questioning that night. "His final words were, 'There are secrets, and then there are secrets that you die for.' Turns out, he was right." Grey sat behind the desk, all of his energy draining from him.

Maggie sank into a chair well away from the mess. "What do you think this is all about?"

"I have no idea, and I'm not lying. In all the years I've worked here, I've never seen anything like this."

"How long have you worked here for?"

"Close to five years, give or take. I like it here. It's interesting, and Maverick is a good boss."

"Did you know the old alpha?"

"Sure. Barratt is still here. He could have left, but Maverick per-suaded him to stay. The change was before my time. To be honest, though, he keeps to himself now. He didn't even attend today's meet-ing."

"Is that unusual?"

"Not for him."

She nodded. "I'll need Brody's address. We'll search it."

"I want to come."

"Not a chance. But I'll share what I find." She turned to the security monitors against the wall. "Have you got footage of the fight?"

"No. There are no cameras in here, but..." He headed to the computer where the feeds were stored, and Maggie followed him. "We'll have footage from the club. Might not be a good angle, though." He was familiar with how the system worked, and quickly accessed the recordings. There were a couple of angles available, and he pulled them up. "Here you go."

The best shot was from across the floor, from the camera high up near the ceiling that offered a broad view of the dance floor. It caught a good portion of the almost invisible window with its blackened effect so that it blended in with the wall. However, as the glass broke, light poured from it, showing the action inside. Even though he knew what happened, he still winced to see Arlo and Brody crashing through the window and onto the floor, and him desperately reaching for Arlo as he slipped through his fingers. He hadn't realised in all the confusion that Vlad had also grabbed for Brody, but hadn't been able to keep hold of him. He'd have to thank him for trying.

Maggie took a sharp intake of breath. "Holy shit. That's bone-crunching." She looked up at the ceiling as if seeking inspiration, and then back to Grey. "Okay. I haven't called in SOCO, because I wanted to see what had happened, and based on this, and that for some strange reason I actually believe you, I'll just call them in to pick up the body."

"Thank you. I thought you would have to dust the whole place. Again."

"I'm in charge, and I make the call. The perks of the paranormal team. Nothing works like the real world."

Some of the weight lifted off Grey's shoulders at that admission. *One less thing to worry about.*

"But, I still need statements, and I want those photos." She gestured to the ones spread on the table. The pictures of Brody's contacts.

"What's your phone number, or email? I'll send you them electronically."

"Sure." She dipped her hand in her pocket and extracted a card. "My details are on that. Just promise me that you won't head into some mad act of retribution for Kane."

"No, ma'am." He winked and saluted. He wouldn't, but he couldn't predict what Maverick might do.

Maggie looked as if she was about to argue about his cheeky salute, but a commotion below had them both on their feet and looking downstairs. Maverick and Domino had arrived at the same time as Odette and Morgana.

Grey heaved a sigh out, the next few minutes rolling out like a film in his mind. The shouting, the pacing, the build-up of magic and power, and the instinct to act, *now*. "Maverick will not like what I have to tell him, but we better get down there and get it over with."

Thirteen

"That settles it," Domino said decisively, before Maverick could even get a word in. "We speak to Castor *now*."

Maverick's eyes were already kindling with a fierce yellow fire, power and anger radiating off him in waves. "Sure you're not too tired, Dom? This could get messy."

"I'm more than ready for this." Watching Odette and Morgana tending to Arlo, seeing him so badly injured, although accidental, had filled her with rage. "I can't sleep until we've spoken to him."

Maverick nodded as he paced. "We take a small team. I don't want to fight, but we must be prepared if they attack."

Maggie's acid tone broke into their conversation. She had listened while Grey had explained the circumstances, assessing them with her cool, speculative gaze, but now she snorted. "Don't want a fight, my arse. You're spoiling for one!"

He rounded on her. "Is one of your best friends lying on the floor, half dead? No. Did one of your best friends die two days ago? No. You bet I'm spoiling for a fight, but neither am I stupid. We have enough going on without starting a war. However, I need answers. Plus, for all we know, Castor has no idea about this, either. We might do him a favour."

Domino highly doubted that. Castor and Maverick had kept a wary but polite distance from each other at that afternoon's meeting. He'd hardly see Maverick strolling into his base to expose his shifters as a favour.

"No. He'll hate you for it. If he doesn't know, he'll look like he isn't in control, and if he does know, then he's behind all of this. This is a no-win scenario. And if Brody was one of his all along and he's now dead..."

Grey shrugged, lips twisting with doubt. "I doubt it. We never saw Brody talk to him, but he's clever. He'd keep his face out of all this. Either way, it's a shitshow. Who are you taking?"

Maverick nodded at the gathered shifters. Jax, Arlo's wiry-framed flatmate, had been upstairs in the bar, but after hearing about Arlo, he'd come to help. "Vlad, Jax, Domino, and Cecile. That's enough. You stay here with the rest and monitor this place. And if Arlo deteriorates..."

Odette looked up at him while Morgana continued her ministrations, her ivory-skinned beauty radiant, even squatting on the floor of the club. "He won't. We've got this. But I want him somewhere more comfortable. And quieter." That accusation was levelled at all of them. Their discussion had been spirited.

"Fine. Grey will help you. Don't let me down, Odette." He turned and strode toward the door. "Let's go."

Maggie knew she should go home. A two-man team were on the way to pick up Brody's dead body and take him to the morgue, and Stan could wrap it all up, but she was very curious about Odette and Morgana.

Leaving Stan in the main hall with Monroe, a man who looked like he could crush bricks with his bare hands, she followed Grey up the stairs, Arlo cradled in his arms, with Odette and Morgana behind him. Maggie knew she was prickly with a big mouth, and in fact, she cultivated it. But she also knew she could blend in when she wanted to, so when they arrived in the office, and Arlo was laid on the couch, she retreated to the chair behind the desk to watch.

She'd heard of the weird, gothic mansion called Moonfell on the edge of Richmond Park, and the three witches who lived there, but she knew few details. Although it was her job to police the paranormal world, there were too many paranormals to know them all, especially if they kept out of trouble, and as far as Maggie knew, the three women did. And yet, still there were whispers about them and their powers. Their abilities to bring you your heart's desires that always came at a cost. The potions they brewed, love spells they sold, and secrets that they kept.

Right now, they seemed pretty normal—magical powers aside, of course. Odette was probably in her early thirties, slender and willowy, with creamy skin and thick chestnut hair with rampant curls that Maggie was a tiny bit jealous of. Who was she kidding? Very jealous of. Morgana looked to be a little older, with a streak of grey in her long, dark hair. She'd curled it up on her head in a messy bun, and half of it tumbled down her back as she bent over Arlo. She had a carpet bag with her, now open on the floor, a jumble of pots and jars inside. A strong smell of herbs and incense wafted from it. Both wore black. Odette was in slim fitting jeans that clung to her lithe form, while Morgana was draped in a voluminous dress, so that it was hard to know what kind of figure lurked beneath. From the shape of her wrists and forearms, and the sharp point to her chin, she was probably of a similar build to Maggie. The two witches didn't look alike in the slightest, and she wondered about the nature of their relationship.

Arlo was still in his wolf, and unconscious. He seemed to have deteriorated rapidly in a short time, and although Morgana tried to rouse him to change form, he wasn't responding. With a huff of frustration, she chanted something commanding and arcane, words of power that seemed to take root in the air. Arlo groaned, a shudder racking through him as he turned from wolf to man again. He was naked, his clothes having shredded when he turned mid-leap.

"About time," Morgana muttered.

Grey dropped a blanket over his lower half, and glared at Morgana. Anger burned in his eyes, but fear was there, too. "What did you do?"

"I banished his wolf."

Banished his Wolf? Maggie didn't even know that was possible.

From the shocked look on Grey's face, neither did he. He recovered quickly. "He heals quicker as a wolf! He was probably unconscious for a reason. It's what they do."

"You called me to treat him, and it's much easier when he's human. It means I can see his wounds properly."

Maggie couldn't fault her logic. Arlo's wounds looked terrible under the full light of the office. Long cuts marked his arms, and his torso was scored with them, but the wound in the side of his abdomen was the worst. Morgana eased off the first dressing she had pressed into the ragged abdominal wound, and dropped it into a plastic bag next to her. The wound stayed dry, and she sniffed it.

"At least it's clean, and I've staunched the bleeding. Deep, though." She poked into it with forceps. "Damn it. There's still glass in it; I'm going to have to dig deep to pull it out. Grey, hold down his arms. This will hurt him. Odette, his legs." She called over her shoulder.

"And you. Come hold him down, too. You may as well do something useful."

Ignoring her peremptory tone, Maggie knelt and leaned across Arlo's legs with Odette as Morgana poked in the wound. Arlo writhed and groaned, and it took all their strength to restrain him, but Morgana finally extracted a long shard of razor-sharp glass, and threw it on the pile with the others. She placed a thick herbal paste directly into the wound, coated more of it onto a cotton pad, and strapped it over the injury with a bandage that wrapped around his toned and muscular abdomen.

She sat back on her heels, evaluating the rest of his wounds. "Good. It doesn't matter how often he changes, the bandage will keep everything reasonably secure. I'll put my herbal paste on the rest of his cuts, turn him back into his wolf, and with his own healing, that will suffice."

"Are you sure?" Grey asked, loosening his grip on Arlo's arms.

"I'm sure." She looked up at him, a sympathetic smile on her face that softened her stern features. "I've stopped the bleeding and removed the glass. That was the most important part, and I've got more spells to do. After that, sleep will help."

The tenseness dropped from Grey's broad shoulders. "Thank you, Morgana. Once you're done, I'll take him up to Maverick's flat. He's got a spare bed he can sleep in, and I can keep an eye on him while I clean up this mess. In fact," he looked around with a grimace, "I'll start now, before anyone else gets injured. I must admit, while I knew confronting Brody would have consequences, I didn't expect *this*."

Morgana snorted with derision. "Then you're a moron. Shifters all cause havoc. All that damn testosterone. And you backed him into a corner. What else would he do?"

"I *wanted* him backed into a corner! I wanted him to talk."

Morgana just tutted, head down, applying paste to the other cuts, and Maggie stood, knowing she wasn't needed anymore. She walked to the table to pick up her bag. She should leave. It was late, she was tired, and she had nothing more to gain by being here. In fact, for all that she liked eavesdropping, she felt like she was intruding. There was a strange intimacy to this scene, and she sensed that these people all knew each other well.

However, before she could say her goodbyes, Odette stood too, appealing to Grey. "I can stay with him tonight."

"Not in Maverick's flat you can't."

She bristled. "I'm not a thief."

"I didn't say you were, but you know how Maverick feels about witches."

"His dislike is illogical."

"It's perfectly logical. A witch killed his parents."

Maggie froze. She didn't know that.

"A rogue witch," Odette shot back. "Nothing to do with me. And that was years ago. Witches do not kill people. It's not what we do."

Grey rolled his eyes. "It's what some witches do. Those who betray their own code—your witchy creed. *Harm none.* There are always those who break the rules for their own ends. Witches are still people at the end of the day, and people are driven by their desires, their hate, their egos. You're no different. Besides," his voice softened, "I don't think Arlo would like it either, and you know that."

Odette looked as if she might argue, her chin lifting, but after a pause, she just nodded. "No, he wouldn't. But I'm worried."

"I'm not, not anymore, thanks to you and Morgana. He'll be fine."

Morgana's commanding voice cut into their conversation. "Yes, he will be. Be satisfied that Grey called us. At least he has sense."

Grey laughed. "A compliment from Morgana. Wonders will never cease."

Maggie saw her chance and stepped forward. "I must go. I just wanted to see that Arlo would be all right." The two witches looked at her, eyes narrowed, Morgana's lips twisting with amusement, as if she knew exactly why she'd stayed. Maggie met her gaze defiantly. "Good to meet you two. Grey, I'll be in touch." And without another word, she left them to their strange dynamics, wondering about Maverick's parents, and the three witches of Moonfell.

Fourteen

averick led his team to the door of the Apollo Pool Hall, and stopped in front of the shifter guarding the entrance. He was a hulking brute, solid muscle with a sneer that suggested he knew exactly who Maverick was. His gaze swept over him and his team, a lascivious smile spreading as he checked out Domino, and then landed on his face.

"You're not welcome here, Mr 'Ale."

"Believe me, I have no wish to enter your dreary little establishment that stinks of beer and B.O., but I need to see Castor as a matter of urgency."

He spoke slowly, with a mock-affected accent. "I will call him to see if 'e will grant you an audience."

Maverick wanted to smack the sneer off his face. He settled for sarcasm. "Grant me an audience. What is this? Ancient Rome? The king's court? It's a fucking pool hall."

"I have my instructions." With exaggerated patience, he pulled his phone from his pocket and made the call, eyeballing Maverick the entire time. "Mr Maverick 'Ale, leader of the Nancy-boys in Wimbledon would like to see Castor. Shall I let them in?"

Maverick clenched his fists, but waited, knowing that the idiot in front of him was spoiling for a fight he wasn't going to get. *Yet.* He could feel his team's anger, but didn't turn to look at them. They would exercise some patience, too.

The bouncer nodded, eyes gleaming with malice. "I shall inform him." He addressed Maverick again. "The nature of your business? Mr Pollux has had a long day."

"Tell whoever you're talking to that I don't communicate with an inbred lackey. Just know that it's important, or I wouldn't waste my time here. I'd rather be wading through shit, in fact, than be here."

Speaking into the phone again, he said, "Seems I am not important enough to be granted the reason for Mr 'Ale's business. Shall I turn him away?"

Maverick itched to charge inside anyway, but he schooled himself to patience. He'd take care of him on the way out. *Cocky shit.* And then, as he knew would happen all along after this pointless display of power and insult, the shifter stepped back.

"Mr Pollux will see you now. The office is at the back, on the right."

Maverick didn't reply, instead shouldering past him into the gloomy interior, his team right behind him. A dozen pool tables were spread out across the large room, circles of yellow light illuminating the baize surfaces, and most of them were occupied. A bar was on the left, and huge TV screens were placed around the room, along with barstools and benches around the sides, mostly lost in the shadows. Murmurs of conversation and laughter mixed with the noise of the TVs showing a football match.

The clientele was a mix of shifters, wolf and therian, as well as humans, witches, and a few hunters, too. Hunters of ghosts, poltergeists, and other paranormal creatures that caused havoc in the population. He recognised a couple and nodded to them. A few customers stared as they passed, shifters mostly, hands braced on pool cues. Maverick kept going until he reached the back of the room. Another smirking shifter silently opened the door, showing a dimly lit office beyond.

Maverick turned to his team. "Domino, with me. The rest of you, wait here."

They nodded and settled in, and Maverick hoped they would keep calm. They should do. Vlad, Cecile, and Jax were old hands, not easily riled.

As soon as they entered the office, the bouncer shut the door behind them, and Castor's unmistakable North London drawl greeted them. "To what do I owe the pleasure?"

Maverick studied the room before he answered. Castor was seated behind a desk, feet up on the surface, face in shadow; behind him, a shifter moved in front of the door as if to block their exit, while a couple more sat in the corner on worn leather armchairs. Hostility bristled from all of them.

"I wish I could say it was a pleasure, Castor, but we both know it isn't. As you know after today's meeting, my friend, Kane, was killed the other night, as well as several other shifters. I have been searching for Kane's killer."

"And found it, I thought. A Pûca. Nasty little things when provoked. Gave poor Domino," his voice purred with malice, "a bit of a beating."

Maverick ignored his tone, glad that Domino hadn't reacted. "We haven't actually found it. It's still on the loose, and there's more than one if you had paid any attention to what was happening today. But I want to know why they attacked. We didn't provoke them, and we don't know why Kane was targeted. So, we have been doing some digging, and my team found something very interesting. One of my pack has met with a couple of your members."

Castor shrugged. "It happens. What of it?"

"It doesn't *happen*. Our packs keep apart. We don't like each other. And I'm not talking about a casual meeting on the street. It was clandestine, in a pub in Clapham, and everything about it was suspicious. I just wondered, seeing as you're the alpha and must know everything, what the meeting was about."

Castor leaned forward into the light, his black hair swept back into a ponytail, which revealed his sharp, high cheekbones and dark eyes. The pupils were huge in the light, and they bored into Maverick. "I don't keep tabs on my pack, Maverick, despite what you think. I'm not a Neanderthal."

"So, the fact that some of your members were meeting with mine doesn't bother you? The fact they might have been trading secrets?"

"Or your member was trading your secrets."

"I doubt that. I haven't got any." *That was far from true, but Brody knew none of them.* "But he may have been trading Kane's. He'd been poking into his business. If your shifters had anything to do with Kane's death, I will deal with them."

Castor stiffened. "You will not *deal* with my pack. Besides, I doubt your information. They know repercussions would be severe."

"How can there be repercussions? You don't know anything. In which case, I'll approach these individuals on my own."

Castor didn't budge. "Who are they? I presume you have proof. And who did they meet?"

Maverick had taken copies of Grey's photos. He'd scanned the room for the shifters when he'd entered the club, but hadn't seen them in the dark, crowded interior. "Brody, one of my newest members. He was a stray for a few years, I took him in, but now I wonder why he came to me, if he knew some of your men."

"Perhaps I rejected him. I have specific requirements."

"Really? You shock me. I thought a pulse would be enough." He placed the prints on the desk. "I want their names."

Castor examined the images, jaw tightening. "I'll deal with them."

"Not good enough. I need to know what they talked about." He leaned on the desk, lowering his head to stare at Castor. "This is trouble. You know it is. Shifters are dead, and there might be more. We have no idea what the Pûcas want. If they know something that will help us stop this…"

"I said, I'll deal with it. And your guy. You'll talk to him. I have no objection to collaborating on this, although I'm sure it will turn out to be nothing." From the tightness to his jaw and the fury building in Castor's eyes, it was obvious he didn't believe that, but Maverick decided to drive his doubt home.

"Arlo questioned Brody tonight. Looked like he was getting ready to run. The interview didn't go well. He jumped through a glass window onto my club floor, and now he's dead, and Arlo is injured. Why did he run, if it was nothing?" He leaned in even closer, smelling Castor's aftershave, mixed with the sweat on his black t-shirt, and the scent of beer on his breath. "Something is very wrong. We both need answers."

Castor considered Maverick for a long moment. "Because I know you won't let this drop, and because Kane was your friend, I'll call them in here, right now, and put this to bed. It will be nothing." He eased back in his chair, and then without breaking eye contact, he said, "Danny, fetch Charlie and Harry."

Maverick took a breath and stepped back, gaze flicking to Domino. *This was progress. Good progress.* Castor would not want Maverick chasing around his turf, so this was the safest way to do it. And actually, although Castor had an excellent poker face, Maverick was pretty sure he had no idea what was going on.

But then the sound of raised voices from outside had Castor's team on their feet, and the shifter outside the door stuck his head in. "Boss. Trouble."

In seconds, they were all in the main room, and Maverick realised his words were a huge understatement. A fight had broken out around the far pool table that was closest to the bar and the door. Fists were flying, and pool cues were swinging around in a cracking arc. At the centre of it was Danny, Harry, and Charlie. More people poured in to back Danny up, but as they intervened, others on the periphery got caught up in it, too. In seconds, it had escalated into a full brawl. Danny was smacked on the head with a cue, and the blow carried him onto the pool table where he lay dazed under the swinging yellow light.

Every shifter in the place piled in, Castor included. He shouldered his way across the room, a brooding mass of power that deterred no one. By now the fight was spreading across the whole place. It was late, some were drunk, and the atmosphere when they had entered the hall had seemed poised on a knife's edge anyway.

"What the hell is happening?" Jax asked, bewildered. "What did you ask?"

"Castor was bringing the shifters in for questioning. I guess they resisted." His team remained fixed around him, and Maverick was torn between leaving Castor to it—this was his business and his pack, after all—or getting involved and helping secure the two for questioning.

Domino echoed his thoughts. "Surely this will be over quickly; it's two of them against the whole pack."

But her words were lost amidst howls, shouts, and breaking furniture as the two under suspicion fought furiously. Those who didn't want to get involved were now trying to get around the spreading fight and out onto the street. Charlie and Harry were getting closer to the door, and they had friends who were helping them. It became clear that Maverick didn't have a choice. In fact, he didn't want a choice. He was itching to let off some steam, and so was his team.

He barked out his orders as he charged in, grabbing a pool cue en route. "Stop them from getting out! *Now*!"

Fifteen

The fight was a blur of brutality, but that was nothing new to Domino. When shifters fought, it escalated, until it seemed that partway through you couldn't even remember what you were fighting about.

Trading blows, rolling, ducking, counter-punching, and smashing furniture to use as weapons fuelled her adrenaline and the bloodlust that was at the root of every wolf's most basic desires. She still ached from the fight from the night before, but that was a very different fight to this, and very soon she forgot them and became a weapon. She trained hard, and fighting was something she was good at.

The team focussed on one thing, however, and that was blocking Charlie and Harry's escape route. Thoughts of Kane drove her onward. But while one was blocked from the door, the other had made it through. His panic and desperate sense of survival turned him into a fighting machine, and he was aided by his human friends who were trying to stop the pursuit. While Jax and Cecile tackled a couple of them, Domino spun on her heel and kicked a man in the throat, knocking him off his feet. She dragged him by the ankle away from the door and charged through it, stepped over the groaning bouncer on the ground, and found Castor next to her.

The shifter was fleeing down the street, and she started to race after him, but Castor grabbed her arm. "Take the next street to the right, and then left—you'll intersect him. Charlie is heading to the park. I'll make sure he gets there."

Hoping Castor wasn't sending her on a wild goose chase just to lose her, she did as he asked. Out of the corner of her eye, she saw Cecile leave the club too, taking off after Castor, and Domino hoped that if she failed, Cecile would succeed. The next few minutes were a blur of pounding pavement. She ached to change to her wolf, but it wasn't safe right now. There were still too many people on the roads, and she could hear sirens in the distance. She hoped it wasn't the police heading to the bar.

The clean scent of trees and grass wafted out to her, and as she reached the corner, she saw a park ahead. A huge, grey wolf raced over the road and leapt over the iron fencing into the park, pursued by Castor and Cecile, already tearing their clothes off and ready to shift. Shifting in clothes was horrible. Belts and shoes constricted their wolf, so unless it was unavoidable, they always stripped first. But Castor was right. She was closer. She pulled her jeans and t-shirt off, changed into her wolf, and leapt into the park.

Immediately the city sounds vanished, and earthy scents surrounded her. She could smell Charlie up ahead, but he was fast. Cecile and Castor were to her left, fanning out as they chased the wolf down. Castor pulled ahead. *Not surprising.* He was an alpha; fast and strong. His power rolled out from him and she could feel it, even at a distance. But Charlie was not slowing down, and was already some distance ahead.

Head down, Domino kept going. *They couldn't let him escape.*

Maverick was returning to a more reasonable mental state after the bloodlust had threatened to overwhelm him, and he knew his team was, too. After a bloody fight, the one shifter who hadn't escaped, Harry, was now face-down on the floor in a pool of blood and beer, arms twisted behind him, and a bloody gash on his head.

Harry had fought furiously, but despite the brawl perpetuated by his human friends that had vastly complicated things, the pack had prevailed.

Even though Maverick's team were now supposedly on the same side as the North London Pack, that hadn't stopped old resentments from rising, or the settling of old scores on both sides. Every time Maverick was within reach of the fleeing shifter, a pack member deliberately intervened, and with Castor now outside, no one had called them to order. In fact, Castor's second, a lean, scar-faced man called Hammer—Maverick internally rolled his eyes at the utter stupidity of the name—seemed keen to encourage the fight, and engaged Maverick personally.

It was only when Jax and the door thug finally managed to wrestle Harry to the ground that the fight stopped, and Maverick took stock of his surroundings and his injuries. He thought the bloodlust had turned his vision into a red mist, until he realised blood was actually dripping into his eye from a deep cut above his right eyebrow. His arms were bruised after being struck with the pool cue, his ribs ached from repeated punches, and his knuckles were bloodied from the punches he had delivered.

In fact, looking at the mix of shifters and humans in the bar—it was now empty except for about twenty of them—they all looked battered with cuts, bruises, broken noses, and black eyes.

But at least they had restrained Harry, and it was good to note that only his human friends had supported him. Hammer promptly threw them out of the club. "Consider yourselves banned. I know all your faces, and all your names, so don't come back here again if you want to keep your balls. Understand?"

One short but stocky man, swaggering with belligerence despite his injuries, gestured to Harry. "We'll take Harry with us."

"Don't be stupid. He stays. Now fuck off."

"But..."

"Out. *Now*. Or I'll keep you for questioning, too." When the half a dozen humans had left, he sent a shifter outside to guard the door. "No one comes in except Castor and the Nancy-boys—or should I say Nancy-girls?" He grinned at Maverick, blood streaming down his face from a broken nose. "At least you fight well, Nancy."

"I know. My fist looked good on your face." He pointed to Harry. "Where can we question him?"

Hammer scanned the room. "We'll strap him to a chair by the bar." He raised his voice, "Barney!"

A man with grey hair emerged from the room behind the bar, a glass and a cloth in his hands, his grizzled face looking bored. "What?"

"We want ice. Lots of it. And the first aid kit, before I bleed all over the bloody pool tables. And a bottle of whiskey." As Barney turned away, he shouted, "And thanks for your help, you miserable cock. You lot," he instructed the pack, "start clearing this shit up, or Castor will do his nut."

Maverick looked at Vlad, amused, as the clean-up began. "Well, this is fun."

Vlad laughed as he used his torn t-shirt to stem the flow of blood from a cut on his cheek. "Not my normal Sunday night. Feels good to let loose, though. I think a few old feuds were aired again." He nodded at Harry, who was now being hauled to a chair. "I doubt he'll tell us much."

"No. But we have to try." He dabbed ineffectually at his own cut, which was already starting to clot. "I hope Domino and Cecile are okay."

"They'll be fine." Vlad lowered his voice. "Do you trust Castor?"

Maverick snorted. "No. But I believe he's as surprised as us."

"I agree. I think they all are, or else this was a well-staged fight." He rubbed his jaw as he scanned the room that was already returning to a semblance of order.

Vlad was a square-jawed, blond giant, with close-cropped hair and piercing blue eyes, and as far as Maverick knew, had no relation to Vlad the Impaler. His name wasn't actually Vlad, but Valdemar Rasmussen, a Dane who had moved to London with his brother, Mads, in his early twenties. Both were in the pack, but Mads wasn't working that night.

The slam of a whiskey bottle and glasses on the bar drew everyone's attention, and with a deftness that belied his grizzled appearance, Barney free poured a row of shots without spilling a drop. He then threw a large first aid kit and a wad of bandages onto the closest pool table, and casting a disparaging glance at Hammer, disappeared back behind the bar.

Vlad's lips twitched with amusement. "No love lost there."

"Right." Hammer drew them all to order. "Let us begin."

Domino's fist was plunged in a bucket of ice back at Storm Moon, reflecting on the outcome of the night. One missing shifter, and another nearly dead from some crazy bar fight, and all they had was the name of a supposed go-between. *Jake.* Plus, a whole lot of injuries.

With her free hand she sipped her gin, willing herself to remain alert for at least another hour before she could crawl into bed, and said, "We won't find him with only a first name to go on. It's probably not even his real name."

"But from his description," Jax pointed out, "we know he's the guy that met with Brody, and thanks to Grey's crew, also the pub he met him in."

Maverick was brooding. "We need more. What the hell is going on? The more we seem to find out, the less I realise we know."

It was close to one in the morning, Storm Moon had closed, and Vlad, Jax, Cecile, Grey, Domino, Jet, Monroe, and Maverick were gathered in a large corner booth. The only lights on were behind the bar, and the one above their table.

"Are you sure Arlo is okay?" Jet asked Grey.

"I'm sure. I wouldn't have left him otherwise. He's curled up as a wolf on Maverick's spare bed. Morgana did a good job." He winked at her. "He'll be right as rain tomorrow."

Cecile examined her swollen knuckles. "Better than us, probably. Charlie was fast, but I really thought we'd catch him."

"He got too much of a head start," Domino said. They had chased him for a while, until he left the park and vanished into the streets the other side of it. It was far too difficult to track him as a wolf because of the number of humans around, and they didn't have any spare clothes to chase him as a human, so they'd had to return to the pool hall, defeated. Castor had been stony faced throughout, and only interrogating Harry had lifted his scowl.

"So, what now?" Grey asked. "Are we working with Castor?"

Maverick shook his head. "I wouldn't go that far. We have agreed to keep each other informed on our line of questioning. We'll chase down the mysterious Jake, and Castor will look into Charlie and Harry's connections."

"Their human friends?" Jet asked.

"Amongst others," Domino answered, knowing how she'd proceed. "The fact that they helped them escape won't go down well, and while they let them go tonight, they'll surely round them up tomorrow. Unless they've had the sense to disappear."

"Would they have known they were shifters?" Jax asked. "They might not have, and they may not have any idea what they have blundered into."

"Neither do we, for that matter," Grey pointed out.

Monroe grunted. "If we're involving witches, it has to be bad."

Maverick stared at Grey. "Did you *have* to call Odette?"

"Yes. He was bleeding—*a lot*. He had a deep wound. I know you don't like witches, but it was the right call. Maggie stuck around. Curious about them, I think."

"Maggie is curious about many things, but I suppose she did us a favour tonight. And I guess so did Odette and Morgana, little though I like it." Maverick drained his drink. "Right. I need sleep and time to think. We all do." He stared at each of them in turn around the table. "I don't know where this is going to go. I don't know what the relevance of those relics is, and I don't know how big this will get. If you want nothing more to do with this, and you just want to carry on with normal pack business, say so now. I won't hold it against anyone. Equally, I don't want you talking about this openly, either. Not the details, at least."

"Count me in," Monroe said, glaring at the rest of them. "I'm a bit pissed I didn't get more involved tonight."

Vlad laughed. "Your time will come, my friend. I'm in. Mads will want in, too."

There was a general chorus of nods around the table, and Jet said, "I can't do much, but I'll do what I can."

"As usual, you're our eyes and ears," Grey said. "But what are you telling the rest of the pack, Mav?"

"Very little. We're honest about the fact that Brody died. We keep quiet about the details. But, we will ask a couple of the older members about that place in Wales, discreetly, in the office. Rumours will circulate, but we'll keep shutting them down until we know more. Agreed?" They nodded again, and he stood. "Great. Go home, rest, and be here at ten tomorrow."

Sixteen

On Monday morning, Harlan checked his schedule. His current jobs weren't urgent, and most were near completion, so he could carve some time into his day for the shifter issue.

His curiosity was growing by the second, and even though Maggie had told him Irving was looking into Ivan, Harlan knew he had to investigate him, too. But he'd also said he would put feelers out into the community, so maybe he should start there.

There were several occult dealers and shops in London, and a few across the rest of the country. He knew the main contacts for all of them, but phoning wouldn't do him any favours. Cold calling, and being able to see their reactions, would tell him more. He considered contacting Jackson Strange at the Paranormal Division, but he knew he was side-tracked by the more pressing issue of Black Cronos, so perhaps that was a bad idea.

Harlan drank his espresso and shuffled through the books on his desk, the ones he'd brought down from the library on the floor above. His head was full of myths and legends after his immersive reading yesterday, but he had no idea what was relevant or not. Or even if any of it was. That was the trouble with this business. Filtering through the crap was not easy. But he kept circling back to *The Mabinogion* and Welsh myths. If the root of all this was in Wales, then it would make the most sense to focus there.

Unable to stomach doing any more reading, he finished his coffee, grabbed his leather messenger bag, and headed to the closest tube. *Time to clear his head.*

However, four hours later, and with his feet aching and nothing achieved except a bag full of books and oddities he felt compelled to buy for the so-called client he'd made up for cover, he was ready to abandon his search. He'd dropped by Seekers by Stealth, Keepers of Magical Artefacts, Silver Hawker, and The House of Hecate, as well as Atlantis Bookshop, and while all of them had been very kind and helpful, none of them could shed light on his hunt for unusual early shifter mythology. He didn't name Ivan, but asked if they had a regular client who was interested specifically in shifter ephemera and who might be interested in selling a collection. He'd hoped it might jog a recollection of old sales, but unfortunately, they couldn't confirm that, either.

Lunch was calling. Harlan had circled London and was close to the office again, but he had one last stop to make first. Fighting through the crowded tube station, he emerged in Lambeth and made his way to a small establishment called Seekers of the Lost, owned by a middle-aged couple who'd been running the business for years. It was a narrow building, the door painted bright red, with a small window to the side that did very little to illuminate the interior of the shop. The shop name was written in suitably gothic font above the door, and a bell announced his presence as he pushed inside. The smell of incense and moth balls struck him first, and then the welcome scent of toast and coffee.

He weaved through the crowded interior that was filled with curiosities. Stuffed animals that made Harlan shudder—he hated taxidermy—ornate jewellery, books, tarot cards, wands, heavy oil paintings with occult content, statues of Gods and Goddesses, and all sorts of other occult-related items. Some things looked new, others were clearly very old, and some objects looked like utter junk.

A small, round man with thinning grey hair pushed through some beaded curtains at the rear, coffee in hand. "Harlan Beckett! What trouble has brought you to my door?"

"Trouble? I don't know what you mean." Harlan grinned as he reached the counter and shook Albert's hand. "I'm just making a few inquiries."

Albert settled on a stool, pursing his lips. "Rubbish. I know you. What are you searching for today? Something for yourself, or a customer?"

Harlan rolled out his prepared story, and smiled encouragingly.

Albert frowned. "The origins of shifters? That's an interesting angle."

Harlan laughed. "I know, right? My clients are always interesting. He's prepared to pay good money, too." He glanced at the crowded shelves and displays. "You have a decent selection of books here, and those weird stuffed animals. Anything in that line?"

"They're stuffed birds, Harlan, not stuffed shifters." He raised an eyebrow, amused.

"You know what I mean. The weirder, the better."

"Rumours have reached me that Burton and Knight are running an auction on just that subject in a month or so. They would be a good bet. But..." he slid off the stool and waddled over to the books. "I do have a few mythology books. Nothing specific, though." He pulled a few books out and placed them on the counter for Harlan to look at, attention drawn to the bags in his hand. "Looks like you've been visiting my competitors."

"No stone unturned, Albert." Placing the bags on the floor, he opened the first book with a tooled leather cover, and found it had full-page colour illustrations in it. "Nice. How old is this?"

"1953, small print run only, nothing too valuable, but you won't find many of these around. The usual standard fare of shifter stories in there. A few Gods, and tales of shape-changers all over the world. Elaborate illustrations. If I wasn't so averse to destroying books, they'd look good mounted in a frame."

"They would, but I couldn't do it, either. And I'm certain my client won't."

Even though Harlan had no previous interest in the subject, he found himself drawn to the book, especially after everything he'd looked at earlier that day. He had his own small reference library at home where everything that he'd bought would be placed, and this book would join it.

Albert retreated behind the counter, picking up his coffee again. He rummaged beneath the counter, and extracting a half-eaten pack of chocolate biscuits, took one and pushed them toward Harlan. "Help yourself. Unusual subject, shifters."

"Is it?" Harlan crunched on a biscuit. "What makes you say that?"

"Well, people are obsessed with vampires, witches and faery folk, demons, angels, and the Gods, but shifters always seem to take a back seat. Maybe not werewolves, but you know what I mean."

"I guess I do. Although, they're not unpopular." He thought about all the films he'd seen and books that seemed obsessed with shifters.

"Yeah, but in our line of work, it's all magic and witchcraft, isn't it? Summoning demons and alchemical weirdness. This is less...esoteric, shall we say."

Harlan saw an opportunity. "Any regular clients of yours interested in this stuff?"

"Not really. I had a guy who used to come in regularly a few years ago, but I heard from his son a few weeks back that he's dead now. Asked me if I wanted to buy back his stuff. I passed. He wanted more money than I wanted to give, and it wouldn't sell quickly, anyway. I recommended Burton and Knight."

Harlan felt his excitement mounting. "Was his name Ivan Baldwin, by any chance?"

"Nah. Bloke named Thompson. Who's Ivan?"

Harlan shrugged, disappointed. "It doesn't matter. I'll give Burton and Knight a call. That's a good suggestion. I'll buy this book anyway."

Harlan pulled his credit card out as Albert placed the book in a bag, preoccupied. "Maybe I should have taken that stuff back. I've had a couple of people asking about shifter things in the last couple of weeks. They're not exactly banging my door down, but I might have made money on it after all."

Harlan half wondered if Albert was messing with him. He seemed to be dripping him information slowly, but maybe he was just getting paranoid. "Anyone I'd know?"

"An older woman saying she was looking for presents for her granddaughter, and some tall guy loaded with muscle and a scowl. Didn't look the collecting type at all. A bit brusque, actually. Not the slightest bit interested in those books. Was asking about an old wooden box and a crown. I hadn't got a clue what he was talking about. Nor was I about to find out for him, either."

"Did he leave a name, by any chance?"

"Brody something. Left me his number should anything come in, but I told him same as I told you. Check out the auction house."

"Bloody hell," Cormac said as he studied the photos on Hunter's phone. "I haven't seen some of those faces in years."

"You know them?"

"A few, a long time ago. But I didn't live there. I knew Leo," his thick finger jabbed at the phone, "from the pack I used to belong to in Scotland. Beyond Edinburgh. Good group. Friendly. Loads of space to roam and hunt. This place reminds me of there, but warmer."

Hunter laughed. "It's really not that warm here."

"Compared to bloody Scotland it is! One of the reasons I moved." Cormac had a thick Scottish accent that hadn't softened with distance or time.

It was late on Monday morning, and Hunter and Ollie were the only ones talking to Cormac in Ollie's living room. They had agreed to keep their enquiries as quiet as possible, especially from Tommy, who tended to become excitable. They had also opted not to tell Cormac all the news at once, wanting to gauge his reactions.

Ollie intervened. "Is Leo still there?"

"No. Had a heart attack a few years back..." He flicked through another couple of photos, and then looked at Hunter and Ollie, puzzled. "Why are you asking about these?"

"Because Harry is in them. We're trying to work out why he was killed."

"And you think one of these people did it? You're mad."

"Of course not," Ollie said hurriedly. "But we are trying to work out why they left the pack, and if it still exists. Did Leo give any reason?"

A vacant expression crossed Cormac's eyes. "Not really. It wasn't a subject we talked about. It's in the past."

Hunter exchanged a disappointed glance with Ollie. "You said you knew a few of them. How? Any names?"

"They were all spread through packs across Scotland. At most, a couple to a pack. Weird really, like you say—why split up? I never asked, though. Not my business." He grinned suddenly, his face dissolving into wrinkles. "The packs were all friendly enough, we got together regularly, and that's why I know them. Hogmanay was a right old knees up. Howled the night away up in the Highlands. Those guys knew how to party. As for names, maybe there was a Jim? Emyr? I remember that because it was odd. Not sure about the rest. Like I said, I didn't really know them."

"The other thing that troubles me," Ollie confessed, "was that Harry wasn't Welsh. Were the others?"

"Just Emyr. Big, thick accent. Good Celtic blood. Don't know what took them to Wales, but we move around, right? Look at me."

That was true, Hunter reflected, *but even so, something was unusual about all this. It might not have looked odd at the time, but retrospectively, it was very weird.*

"The other issue is that all of the shifters killed on Friday," Ollie said, studying Cormac, "were in this pack."

"*All* of them?" Cormac's hand shook. "Seriously?"

"Unfortunately, yes."

Cormac slumped in his chair. "That's...uncanny. Which ones?"

Hunter pulled the list of names from his pocket and read them out loud.

"Jimmy. Oh my God," Cormac said, horrified. "He was James Hatfield, I'm sure of it. And Warren, I remember him. Bloody hell." He stared at Ollie and Hunter. "They're dead? Murdered?"

Ollie nodded. "I'm sorry, but yes. These two at least must have moved from Scotland. Potentially the others, too."

Cormac shook his head. "Maybe, but I don't know some of those names you mentioned."

"Which means some shifters in this photo could still be alive."

"Of course they could be! We're not decrepit!" He looked resentful. "Let me have another look through the photos."

"Not saying you are," Ollie said, watching him scroll through the images again. "They could still be in Scotland, for all we know."

Hunter leapt to his feet as if he was going to tear out the door. "Herne's bollocks! Those bloody Pûcas could be hunting them right now!"

"Wait! Sit down." Ollie instructed. "We need to think this through. We need information on this pack, Cormac, and you knew some of them. Can you suggest who I should try?"

Cormac was now looking grey, his eyes haunted. "Emyr. He was the Welsh pack's alpha at one point, from what I remember. Certainly, they all seemed to defer to him when they met up. Try him. He was a long way up though, and as far as I know is still there. Ballater, in the Cairngorms."

Ollie nodded. "Cheers, but do me a favour. Don't mention this to anyone. I don't want to alarm anyone, or set off wild rumours."

Cormac mimed zipping his mouth. "Not a word, Ollie. But, you should know there are already questions. Everyone has heard about the other deaths."

"Just say that we know very little right now, and leave it at that. Do *not* talk about Wales. I don't want anyone else to die."

Ollie escorted Cormac out of his house, and Hunter paced to the window while he waited for him to return, mulling over the conversation, and not really paying attention to the dark clouds that gathered above the mountains around the lake. He felt unsettled, like his life had been turned upside down. Hunter didn't indulge in introspection, especially about his origins. Life was for living *now*. It had been his creed for years. What his race was or where it had come from didn't really interest him. But now? Well, now it seemed fascinating, and also darkly disturbing. His friend, Shadow, the fey warrior who lived in White Haven, had once said he was part fey—a remnant of the fey-shifters that had once crossed back and forth between worlds hundreds of years before. In the light of this new information about a box of relics, and Pûcas, perhaps it merited more attention.

Movement behind him heralded Ollie's return. His face was grim. "I don't like this at all, Hunter. What the hell is going on?"

"I have no idea! What's so bad about our origins that people would die to hide it?" He told him about Shadow's theory.

Ollie prodded the fire, and turned his back to it, warming his legs as he talked. "It makes sense that we would be part fey. I mean, let's face it—we are magical, but the fact that we live and work as humans most of the time means I don't even think about it. We just *are*! And who cares, anyway? What does it matter?"

"We don't really mix with other shifters," Hunter mused, "but I wonder what their take on their origins are—especially therians. Might be worth asking."

"I'm reluctant to ask anyone anything right now. I don't want to exacerbate anything."

"Hopefully, Emyr can enlighten us. When are we going to Scotland?"

Ollie considered his question for so long that Hunter wondered if he'd heard him, but finally he nodded. "We need answers, and can't delay this. We should leave today."

"And the survivors of that Welsh pack? They could potentially be in danger."

"The names of the dead will spread, and anyone who knows anything will have fled already. Look at Riggs." He reached for his phone. "I better tell Maverick our plans."

Seventeen

By the time Arlo awoke, it was late morning. He could tell by the light, and also from the rich scent of bacon drifting in from the room next door. He could also tell who was cooking, from the man's citrus aftershave and unique scent. *Grey*.

The strong scent of Maverick also told him where he was, before he'd even registered the room that he was in. For a moment, he just stretched, mentally searching his body for wounds. He could feel scores of them, like tiny burns across his body. But he lay on a soft, warm bed, a thick duvet beneath him, and he'd slept deeply.

He shifted to his human form and examined his injuries. He winced to see the amount of cuts that scarred his arms, even though they were almost healed. In the heat of the moment, as he wrestled with Brody, all he'd thought about was stopping him, and when he plunged through the window, Arlo didn't consider releasing him. He definitely didn't feel the glass shard plunge into his side. Fortunately, his deep wound had clotted well, leaving only a dull ache in its place. He stood carefully, wincing as it pulled, and then spotted the pile of clean clothes on the bed. He needed a shower first. He was covered in dried blood and stank of sweat. He padded to the ensuite bathroom and turned on the shower to heat the water.

"Ah! Sleeping beauty awakes," Grey called sarcastically from the next room. "Get dressed, you lazy bugger."

"Only if you make me coffee," Arlo called back. "And food. I'm starving."

By the time he was showered and dressed, a steaming cup of coffee was on the kitchen counter, and the smell of bacon, eggs, and sausage was strong.

"Well, you look better," Grey said, eyes sweeping over him. "How's your injury?"

Arlo pulled up his t-shirt to show him. "Almost healed." He sat at the long breakfast counter on a barstool and sipped his drink. "I have a hazy memory after the fall. Did Odette and Morgana come?"

"Of course." Grey placed a pile of thick-cut bread with butter on the counter, and started to plate up the food. He shot him an amused look. "Odette was suitably concerned about your well-being. Morgana was a bit cranky. Good, though. She filled your wound with her potions and pastes. And," he shot him a concerned glance, "did something I didn't expect."

"What?" Arlo asked, reaching for the bread.

"Commanded you to shift. And you did."

Arlo froze. "Oh, that's what I remember." A vague memory of strong words had ripped him from a deep sleep, and he remembered the sharp cold of losing his fur. "I thought it was a dream. I felt cold."

"No dream." Grey came around the counter and sat at the next barstool, placing the plates in front of them. He studied him, a deep crease between his eyes. "I didn't know that was possible."

"Neither did I. That makes me feel a bit sick, actually."

"You don't want your breakfast, then?" He reached for the plate, as if to pull it away.

"Of course I do! I'm starving." He tried a mouthful of crispy bacon dipped in egg yolk and sighed dramatically. "This is so good!"

"That's because I'm a great cook."

"Have you been watching me all night like a creepy stalker?"

"I call it being a concerned friend, actually. But no, I haven't. Not once Maverick got back."

Yesterday's events flooded back. "He got back from Birmingham? Everything okay?"

"Kind of. After your fight, he raced off to see Castor."

"Shit!" Arlo froze. "And?"

"It got ugly." He related the whole evening, including the news of the off-grid Welsh pack, Maggie's arrival, and the removal of Brody's body.

Arlo stopped eating, fork on the counter. "I forgot he was dead. How could I forget that?"

"Shock." Grey shook his head. "You were in bad shape. I know you didn't want me calling Odette, but it was the right thing to do." He nodded at Arlo's half empty plate. "If you don't want that, I'll have it."

"I want it! I'm just thinking! You're like a bloody vulture." He pulled the plate close and edged away from Grey. "Where's Maverick now?"

The door clicked open behind them. "Right here."

Arlo turned to see his best friend stride into the room, his lips set in a thin line, and a black eye decorating his face. "Nice shiner."

"Bloody Hammer. Wanker."

"Well named, though."

"I had my own back." He crossed the room and entered the kitchen area, his long, even gait showing no sign that he'd been in a huge fight the night before. After pouring himself a coffee, he studied Arlo. "You're looking a bit messed up, too."

Arlo shrugged. "I'll live. So, any information from our old alpha?"

"Diddly fucking squat. But Ollie phoned, and he has *very* interesting news. A shifter called Emyr was the alpha of the mysterious pack at one point. Apparently, he's in Scotland, so they've gone to find him." He outlined their plan and what they'd found out.

Arlo couldn't help feeling that he'd missed out on a lot, especially with the news of the mysterious pack in the wilderness. He pushed his empty plate away, eager to be involved now. "What are we doing?"

"*You* are recovering."

He rolled his eyes. "Don't do this to me. I'll be fine."

"Tomorrow, maybe." His tone did not allow for argument, and Arlo knew better than to try. Maverick was usually upbeat, positive in his mindset. He kept the pack energised. Now, however, his jaw was clenched, and it was clear he had little time for humour. "Now, we wait to see if Domino has any success in finding the mysterious Jake. We have a name and a pub, and that's all."

"And if they can't?" Grey asked.

"Then we'll see if we can find Riggs. Hell, maybe we should be doing that anyway."

"But isn't the Birmingham pack doing that?" Arlo was frustrated. "We're chasing our tails here! Maybe we should search for Pûcas. They killed Kane."

Maverick's voice rose. "They fled to bloody Cumbria! Has your injury addled your brain?"

Arlo took a breath before he answered, seeing the fury building in Maverick's eyes. He was as frustrated as Arlo was. As they all were. But, as the alpha, the pack were looking to him for results, and he had very little to give them. "I just thought that maybe we should check out the wild places here. The common, and Richmond Park. It's unlikely they flew straight to Cumbria. Maybe we'll find a base here. A cave! A hole in the ground!"

"A Hobbit hole?" Grey suggested, amused despite the circumstances. "A womble den beneath the common?"

He resisted flipping him off. "They are wild fey-shifters, but they have to have a base." He appealed to Maverick. "Have we even checked the common? We searched around here, but what if they *are* there, waiting for their chance to strike again?"

Maverick's hips leaned against the counter, hands cradling his mug. "We are constantly in the common and the park, and we have never scented them before. But, you make a good point. I don't think it will achieve a damn thing, but fine, if possible, we'll search tonight. Or some of us will. You're injured."

Arlo said nothing. He would go hunting, whether Maverick wanted him to or not.

The pub at the end of the street was small and grubby, and clearly catered to the locals rather than any tourists. The sign, The Bell, hung crookedly over the door, and Domino could smell the malt and hops from her seat in the car, as well as the stench of cigarette smoke from those gathered around the main door.

She grunted with frustration. "We'll get stared at in there."

Vlad, seated next to her, shrugged. "Who cares?"

"I care. Strangers mean trouble in places like that. We could scare Jake off."

"That's assuming he's a regular. He might have come from out of town." He accelerated past the pub and down the next street. "There's a limit to how many times we can keep circling around here."

"We've only circled three times! Stop exaggerating."

"It feels longer. I'm bored."

"Reconnaissance is important."

"And boring."

Domino groaned, feeling cramped, and stretched her legs into the footwell. "I can't disagree. Besides, there's no sign of Jake anywhere."

It was after six on Monday evening, dark, and very cold. They had explored the area around the pub for hours, making sure they knew the lay of the streets, alleys, exits, other shops, houses, and anything else that might help them track him—if they were lucky enough to find him. They had also purposefully waited for dark before they went in the pub. If they had to chase him in their wolf, it was easier at night. That was, of course, presuming he was a shifter, too.

"Pull into the nearest parking spot," she instructed Vlad. "Let's get this done. I'll call the others and make sure they're ready."

Mads and Jax were in one car, and Cecile and Monroe were in Cecile's van. They were trying to prepare for all eventualities, as they weren't sure if Jake was a human or shifter. If he was therian, that would cause even more problems. Despite her misgivings, Monroe had brought a tranquilliser gun with him, but she desperately hoped they wouldn't have to use it. The others would position themselves around the pub, while Domino and Vlad went in. She didn't want to lose him like they lost Charlie the night before.

After confirming their plans with the others, she swung her long legs out of the car and headed for the pub, Vlad at her side. Passing the smokers at the entrance, they pushed through the heavy wooden door and entered the bar.

It was bigger than it looked from the outside, the room stretching back a long way. The front of the bar had a dartboard mounted on the wall, and a pool table in the middle of the floor, and tables were at the rear of the room. As expected, heads swivelled as they entered, the conversation pausing, but fortunately, there were only half a dozen customers inside, and after buying a couple of pints of local beer, they found a table at the rear.

Both positioned themselves with their backs to the wall. Domino spotted a door to the side, and feigning a trip to the toilet, investigated the short corridor beyond. As she suspected, it ended at the rear exit door, and had several doors leading off it, two of them male and female toilets.

With a nod of satisfaction, she returned to Vlad. "All good down there. One exit route. Now, we just wait."

By eight o'clock on Monday evening, Harlan's head felt ready to explode. After his trek around London's occult stores, he'd headed back to the office, completed a few other jobs, and then went home to read his newly acquired books.

After turning on his expensive gas fire with real effect flames, he'd settled on the sofa, his purchases strewn at his sides. Notebook in hand, he'd made a few notes as he read. Now, however, lifting his head and finally focussing on the room around him, he realised that apart from the lamp at his side, and the orange glow from the fire, the rest of the room was in darkness.

His stomach rumbled, and he reached for the bowl of tortilla chips beside him, but unfortunately only crumbs remained, his only sustenance for hours. He groaned and rubbed his eyes, stretching out the kinks in his neck, reflecting on what he'd learned. Many stories he'd read that evening were repeats of ones he'd seen the day before, albeit told in a slightly different way. The book he bought from Albert, though, was captivating. The illustrations were rich and detailed, and he felt like a child again as he read through them. But what was more intriguing was the fact it was the only book that had the story in it that he'd borrowed from Burton and Knight, although it was shorter and altogether less elaborate than the single, highly illustrated edition.

The tale called *The Wolf King and The Witch Queen.*

It was about a great wolf-shifter who lay dead beneath a mountain next to a lake, the place bewitched by a powerful witch who loved him beyond anything. But he was no ordinary wolf; he was a Wolf King, a mighty leader of his people, until he was grievously injured in battle. The story suggested he was still there, waiting to be brought back to life, to lead the wolves once more.

It made Harlan smile, because it reminded him of the King Arthur tale, the powerful King of Britain who was seriously injured in battle, and was taken to Avalon by the priestesses to rest there until he was ready to rise again. Shadow had told him about a human boy who had travelled to the Otherworld and woken him up, insisting that Arthur was alive and well and living life to the fullest there. She'd said it with a completely straight face, and Harlan had looked at her sceptically, but she'd just shrugged and said, "It's true! You have no idea what goes on in the Otherworld."

It made him reconsider the shifter story. King Arthur was probably England's greatest myth, and generations of people had investigated if, at its root, it could be true. It had gripped everyone's imagination for centuries. The British royal family still carried the tradition of naming royal heirs 'Arthur' somewhere in their big list of names. And England wasn't alone. There were many cultures with founding myths. Why shouldn't the wolves or other shifters have one, too?

Harlan wasn't prone to flights of fancy, but he had worked in the occult business for too long to dismiss things. He searched for cursed or bewitched items, alchemical documents, grimoires, and plain old treasure. He worked with Shadow, a fey warrior, and Gabe, the Nephilim, and his six brothers. Only a few months ago they'd discovered the Igigi, the ancient slaves to the Sumerian Gods who had disappeared from history, living beneath the desert in Turkey—not that he could ever tell anyone that, though. And of course, there was Black Cronos, the monsters of transformation. All of that meant that he couldn't dismiss this story either, especially when coupled with the box of relics and a huge crown.

His need for answers overcame his desire to sit in front of the fire. In half an hour, he could be walking into Storm Moon in Wimbledon, questioning the shifters himself. With that thought, he hauled himself to his feet, and prepared to leave.

Eighteen

Domino glanced up from the phone on which she and Vlad were playing a word game, checking who had walked into the bar bringing a blast of cold air with them. It wasn't Jake. "Bollocks. This is a waste of time."

"There are still hours left before closing." Vlad stretched his long legs under the table, and returned to the puzzle. "I'm just grateful that I can drink three pints of beer and still be sober enough to drive. Being a shifter totally rules."

"You don't say that when it costs you a fortune to get drunk, you moron."

"Moron! Five letter word that fits! Brilliant." He winked at her. "Nice one."

"You're a *double* moron."

"That doesn't fit. It's not even a thing."

She sighed, aware of the curious glances they were receiving. "Even if this is his local, it doesn't mean he'll be here tonight. We might end up staking this place out all week."

Vlad finished the game, and shuffled to look at her better. "There's no way we can come here every night for a week. We're not regulars. Someone will ask questions."

"We could be new regulars."

He lowered his voice. "Look at us. We do not fit this pub. We both look too well off and healthy, for a start, and I'm presuming we both have double the IQ of most people here. This is not a pub we'd be a regular in, and everyone watching us knows that, too."

As annoying as that statement was, Domino had to concede that he was right. "So, if he's not here in another hour, we ask the barman if he knows him."

"That's pointless, too. He's been staring daggers at me on and off all night. He'll lie, regardless. In fact, the longer we stay here, the more uncomfortable I'm becoming."

Domino casually glanced around the bar that was considerably busier than it had been a few hours earlier. Despite the level of noise from both conversations and the football match playing on the TV by the pool table, there was an air of unrest. Of waiting. For what, she wasn't sure. "I can't sense therians or shifters of any type, can you?"

"No, but that doesn't make me feel any better. As much as I enjoy a fight, I really don't want to get into one here. Fighting with shifters is a whole different thing. These are humans." He reached for his almost empty pint, and nodded to hers. "I think we should drink up and go. Oh, no." His eyes cut to the entrance and back to her. "Therians. And still no Jake."

Their unmistakable energy signature reached her before she even casually looked around. There were four of them, all young, three males and one female, and they all stared at Vlad and Domino as they crossed to the bar.

Domino shrugged. "That's okay. We have therians in our club. We don't hate each other."

"You say that, but one of them is heading our way, and he doesn't look impressed." Vlad downed his pint and stood up, and Domino did the same.

The young man had cold, calculating eyes, and his jeans hung low on his hips, as he confidently crossed to their table. "You two don't belong here."

Domino answered, knowing a woman was more likely to diffuse the situation than a man. "We were just having a drink, but—" she wiggled her empty glass, "we're leaving now."

She made to brush past him, but he stood his ground. "Why are you here?"

She spoke slowly as if he were stupid, Vlad watchful next to her. "Just a drink. It's a pub. That's what people do."

He was itching for a fight, his entire being resonated with it. "My mate has had trouble with you lot before."

She desperately wanted to ask if that was Jake, but realised it would be like putting a match to a stick of dynamite. "Well, that wasn't me or my friend." She glanced around at the customers who were openly staring now. "Can you move? We're trying to leave."

He looked as if he might say more, but with them on their feet, they weren't giving him much room for argument. Then again, some people didn't need anything to start a fight. However, he looked at Vlad's height and threatening demeanour and seemed to reconsider.

"Fine." He moved aside, allowing them to walk past, but not before saying, "Don't come here again."

Domino didn't answer, and willed Vlad not to, either. The entire pub would most likely join in a fight, and they still needed to find Jake. It felt like a long walk to the door, and Domino didn't breathe easy again until they were a short distance down the road. Although, when she glanced back, two of the therians stood on the threshold, watching them until they rounded the corner and were out of view.

"Thanks for not making things worse," she said to Vlad.

"It was tempting, but we have a job," he shrugged, "best all 'round."

Her phone pinged, indicating a message, and she checked it, adrenalin rising. "Jax has spotted Jake around the corner, walking this way." Her intention had been to corner him in the pub where she hoped they could talk without making a scene, but that was out of the question now. She phoned him. "What road, which direction?"

"He's minutes away from you. In fact, I can see you. I'm at the top of the road. You'll see him in seconds. Why aren't you in the pub?"

"Long story. Change of plans. We need to chat to him on the street. If he resists, we'll put him in the back of the car and take him to the club. Thank the Gods it's shut." She stepped into the shadows of a high wall, pulling Vlad with her, and scanning the street, saw a figure heading toward them a short distance away. "I see him. Follow him, and tell the others."

Vlad's hands were stuffed in his pockets, and she slipped her arm though his as if they were lovers, laughing up at him. "We'll intercept him. Ready?"

"Always." He beamed down at her.

She laughed again in response, tugging him along the road.

He grinned. "I am hilarious, right?"

"Not in the way you think," she said through a tight-lipped smile.

They advanced on Jake, who was illuminated by the street lights a short distance away. Just beyond, Jax drove toward them. She hoped Cecile and Monroe were on the way.

"See him?" she asked Vlad, voice low.

"Yep. Not blind, remember?"

Up ahead, Jake paused and stared at them, and then before Domino could blink, he turned and ran.

Domino and Vlad dropped all pretence and sprinted after him, but despite Jake's less than athletic shape, he was making good time. Domino shouted, "Jake! We just want to talk."

He didn't slow. Jax jammed his brakes on and Mads flew out of the car and tackled Jake to the ground, while Jax pulled haphazardly over to the side of the road.

Even from a distance, Domino could see Jake shifting, his clothes splitting as he turned into a dog. Although Mads had got a strong grip on him, Jake wriggled and snapped, his sharp teeth flashing. Mads punched him, just as Domino and Vlad skidded over, landing on top of him.

But Jake shifted again, this time into a snake, disappearing beneath all of them.

"Fucking therians," Vlad muttered, twisting in an effort to see Jake.

"There!" Domino grabbed his muscular tail just as he slithered free of the tangle of bodies.

Trapped under Vlad, she couldn't move, but Mads dived over the top of both of them, wrapping himself around the entire snake, one hand gripped beneath the snake's head.

"Knock him out," Vlad yelled, "before he shifts again."

"How am I supposed to knock out a snake? It has a tiny head. I could smash it!"

But they didn't need to worry about that anymore. Jake was already shifting again, into something huge and furry. Powerful limbs with enormous claws were suddenly thrusting them all off. Domino found herself airborne, just before she crashed into a garden wall. Mads and Vlad were propelled into the road.

Jake had turned into a huge bear. He rose on enormous haunches, no longer intent on fleeing, but on killing them all. He didn't seem to care that they were on a suburban street. His need for self-preservation had taken over. They would have to shift just to be able to match him. With lightning speed, Jake swiped at her, claws ready to rip her throat out. Domino dived to the side, seeing Vlad and Mads tearing their clothes off, ready to shift.

And then, to her horror, pounding footsteps from behind heralded the arrival of three of the four therians from the pub, all spoiling for a fight.

They were going to get one.

With the bear rounding on Vlad and Mads, she faced the rest, Jax racing to her side. She wondered briefly where the fourth therian was, but in seconds, they were on them, and she couldn't think about it anymore. Domino and her team all practised a mix of martial arts and boxing, spending time in the gym owned by Fran's human partner. Fighting as a wolf was easy, but she had to fight well as a human, too. Three against two wasn't an issue. The therians fought well, but they were undisciplined, and with Jax at their side, they were getting the upper hand. But the furious growls and yelps from behind were a distraction, and as she rolled, kicking out the legs from under one of her attackers, she glimpsed the bloody fury of the shifter battle behind her.

This had to end now, before the whole street came outside and the police were called.

Where were Monroe and Cecile?

Suddenly, she heard a series of whumping sounds, so soft she thought she'd imagined them, followed by the screech of tyres. Monroe and Cecile had arrived.

Distracted, she caught a punch to the gut, and it sent her sprawling into the street where she had seconds to take her bearings. She rolled to all fours. Two vans were bearing down on her, one from each direction. Cecile, and she presumed, the missing therian.

Vlad and Mads were wolves, injured, but still fighting, with blood dripping from their teeth. Jake was injured too, his legs torn up, fur ripped away, but he still swung his huge arms, the deadly claws out-stretched, standing upright on his back legs. He towered over her, only steps away, and Domino scrambled to get clear.

But Jake was teetering, his body distinctly swaying, and she saw a series of feathered darts on his body. Not enough to stop him, though. He bore down on her, Vlad and Mads blocked behind him, Jax still fighting the therians.

She backed up and hit the bumper of the strange van.

Bollocks.

Grey was relieved that the club level of Storm Moon was closed that Monday night. It was one less thing to worry about.

He'd had a couple of shifters on patrol around the club all evening, as well as the usual shifter at the door, making sure no one was watching them, or planning a surprise attack. He thought it unlikely, but then again, a few days ago they hadn't expected Kane or Brody to be killed, either.

Fortunately, because it was Monday, the bar was a little quieter than usual. The after-work crowd always swelled the numbers, but it was close to nine now, and the place was half full, a pleasant murmur of conversation blending with the low music.

Despite all that, Grey was restless, mainly because he was worried about Domino. There was still no word from her, although he had no reason to worry. She had a good team with her, and she was a strong fighter and strategist. However, as much as he was good friends with many of the shifters and humans at the club—particularly Arlo, who he liked for his good sense of humour—Domino was probably his best friend. She understood him, and had promoted him to be her deputy over all the other shifters on the team. He appreciated that more than she would ever know.

Getting ahead as a human in a shifter world was hard. They were a pack, and that mentality underlined every decision they made. It made them a strong family unit, whether they were related or not, and he liked that. It echoed Grey's own experiences when he was in the army. It meant, of course, that they clashed too, but that was okay—most of the time. However, their preternatural strengths always outweighed his own abilities. Nevertheless, Domino appreciated the experience he brought to the team, and fortunately Maverick supported her decision. It hadn't been easy in the early days, but now he was as respected in his position as any shifter would be. He'd worked hard for it. So, yes, he was worried about Domino.

He headed into the foyer, and then out onto the street. The huge, wooden doors of the club were shut to keep the cold out, and John stood on the step, surveying the road.

"All quiet?" Grey asked him.

John nodded. He'd been on the security staff for as long as Grey, and was a similar age. Unlike Grey, though, he was married with two kids, both too young to tell if they were going to be shifters or not. "Just the usual passers-by and traffic. Fran has just walked past. No trouble out there, either."

Fran was another female shifter on the security team. "Good. If there's anything that worries you, just call me."

He was just about to join Arlo and Maverick inside, who were waiting on news from Domino, when a familiar man walked along the street and up the steps to the club's entrance. For a moment, Grey couldn't place him, but it seemed that the man recognised him, too.

He held his hand out. "Grey, I believe? Harlan Beckett. I met you a few months ago. I came in here with friends, looking for Blaze."

"Of course." He shook his hand, knowing this was no casual visit. He had a purposeful air about him. "How can we help you, Harlan?"

Harlan looked amused. "Well, I was kinda hoping for a drink and a chat with Maverick, if that's okay."

Grey realised they were blocking the door, and leaving John at the entrance, ushered Harlan into the small foyer. "Sorry. Weird night. You can definitely have a drink, but as for talking to Maverick, I'm not so sure. He's preoccupied tonight."

"I'm actually here to help." He patted his bag. "Well, I'll try to, anyway. Maggie has spoken to me, so I know what's going on."

He cocked an eyebrow. "Has she now?"

Harlan grinned. "We go way back. I'm very trustworthy, and reasonably useful. She's quite the character, isn't she?"

"That's one way of describing her. Are you working for her?"

"Christ, no!" He drew back in mock horror. "I can't think of anything worse. No, she asked me for a favour. Much to my surprise, I'm more invested than I thought I'd be."

Grey knew Maverick was not in the mood for casual conversation, but if Harlan was working with Maggie, and knew all about their issues, then he couldn't really turn him away.

"Follow me." He pushed through the main doors, and led Harlan to the corner booth on the right of the bar. Maverick was sprawled on the long seat, taking up most of one side, and Arlo sat opposite him. Both brooded. "Guys, this is Harlan Beckett, and he wants a word. He's assisting Maggie. Reckons he can help."

"I can." Harlan stepped forward confidently, hand outstretched. "Good to see you again."

Maverick shook his hand and introduced him to Arlo, but glared at Grey resentfully before addressing Harlan again. "This isn't a good time. And Maggie's name, by the way, is not a way to win my company."

"I just want five minutes, and a bourbon. After that, I'll find a table to myself and leave you in peace."

Maverick sighed, and resigned, waved him next to Arlo. "Grey, get us all a top up, and then join us?"

"Sure." Grey turned away, hoping Harlan had something good to share, because Maverick was not in the mood for fairy tales.

Nineteen

Domino's back was pressed against the van's bumper, and she had nowhere to go.

The bear was steaming toward her, blocking Vlad and Mads behind it. On one side, Jax was being attacked by the three therians so fiercely that it was impossible for him to break free, and the fourth therian had emerged from the van and was blocking her other side.

Unfortunately, he was a tall brute, and his lips twisted with malicious pleasure to see her trapped. *Screw him.* She kicked him in the gut, sending him sprawling, and then leaped over him. He rolled and caught Domino's ankle, dragging her to the ground. Twisting as she fell, her hip slammed against the pavement, but she forced herself to her feet and backed up, Jake still advancing.

Why wasn't Jake falling? Weren't there enough tranquilliser darts?

Monroe jogged into view, gripping the tranquilliser gun, and squared up right behind Jake. Domino backed up even further, willing Monroe to shoot again. The therian at her feet rolled away, wary of getting between her and the bear. Cecile had jumped from her van, but had to hang back because she was keeping out of the way of the tranq gun.

But then, with unexpected suddenness, the bear crashed forward face-down onto the ground, finally unconscious, and for a brief second, everyone paused.

Domino yelled. "Get him in the van!"

But that was about as much as she could say. The last dart fired by Monroe, intended for the bear, hit her in the chest. An icy coldness swept through her, and her legs collapsed. The huge therian smirked as he turned toward her, and the world went black.

Vlad's frustration exploded into anger when Domino slumped to the ground, the feathered dart in her chest.

What the hell was Monroe thinking?

The therian lifted Domino into his arms and threw her into the van in one swift motion, before jumping behind the wheel. Monroe charged, grabbing the door. The therian kicked it, sending Monroe sprawling. The therians who were fighting Jax broke off at that, running to their van, too. Mads lay insensible on his side, injured by Jake who had proven to be a formidable opponent.

Fucking therians. He hated them. *Slippery little shits...*

Vlad pounced on one of the fleeing therians, gripping his ankle with his sharp teeth just before he reached the van. Hot blood spurted into this mouth. But the therian was already shifting, and in moments, he had slipped from his grip, and leaped into the waiting van. The door slammed and it reversed down the street with a squeal of tyres.

As much as Vlad tried, he could not keep pace with the speeding vehicle, and within minutes it had vanished down the road, taking Domino with it. He limped back to the street, relieved to find that hordes of angry locals weren't surrounding his team with pitchforks.

Instead, the heavy, unconscious body of Jake had been wrestled inside their own van. Cecile was at the wheel, and only Monroe was in sight.

A wary eye on twitching curtains, he shifted back to human and dressed quickly. "Monroe, you're a lousy shot!"

Monroe visibly bristled with resentment. "I'm a great shot! Jake is out cold because of me!"

"And so is Domino." He looked down the street. "Where are Mads and Jax?"

"Trying to find them in the car. Jax said to call with directions."

"I have vague directions, and that's all." He pulled his phone out of his pocket, relieved to find it hadn't been damaged in the fight. "How's Mads?"

"Fine. Dazed." Monroe slapped the van. "We'd better head to the club. I don't know how long he'll be out for, and I'm out of darts."

Vlad groaned. "You're kidding me!"

"He was a bloody bear, and not a normal one, either! It took a lot to knock him out—and I don't work in a bloody zoo!"

Vlad wrestled his emotions under control. "You're right. You head back, and I'll take my car and try to find them, too." But even as he was saying it, Vlad knew he wouldn't find Domino easily. They had too much of a head start, and he had no idea where to search.

"You have got to be kidding me! You're bringing me fairy tales?" Maverick stared at Harlan, and then the slim leatherbound book on the table. "You know shifters are dead, right? I haven't got time for this."

"Humour me. All you're doing is sitting here, right? We're having a nice drink." Harlan reached for his bourbon. "And they're *shifter* tales, not fairy tales, although admittedly, there is some crossover."

Maverick pressed his fingers to his temples. "Are you for real?"

"Yep." Harlen seemed blithely optimistic, and not even the slightest bit fazed by Maverick's impatience, which annoyed him even more. "Maggie wanted to know if there might be something to the stolen box and crown. She asked me to help."

"They were stolen, and shifters have died," Arlo pointed out. "There's definitely something about them."

"Okay, let me qualify that. What about the box, specifically? Is it true? Does it contain your origins? Where did the box come from? How was it found? What about the crown? Is it decorative, or does it mean something?" He shrugged. "I'm looking into all of that, as is Maggie, but then I got to thinking about myths of *our* origins, and we know there are things in our myths that hold a kernel of truth, so why not yours? Right?" He looked to Grey for confirmation, and then stared at Arlo and Maverick. "You can't tell me that you haven't thought about this, knowing what was stolen?"

Maverick crossed his arms over his chest. "I have, and then I dismissed it."

Harlan leaned in. "You can't afford to. There's a big, dark secret that someone is trying to hide—and you know it. I'm not here to try to get your own secrets out of you, but Maggie needed help. Hell, I haven't even spoken to Maggie yet. I was so intrigued that I came straight to you. And that's all because of this." He flicked the book open. "*The Wolf King and The Witch Queen.*"

Arlo laughed. "Bedtime stories. I remember that one. It was one of my mother's favourites. Interesting, though. I have never seen it in a book before. She used to tell it to me from memory."

Harlan nodded. "An oral tale. They all were once, until someone thought to preserve them. Did you know that bards, storytellers of old, would memorise hundreds of stories? It was their art. They brought worlds to life, sitting around a fire, entertaining people with tales. They were the celebrities of their day. But then, when the tales were written down, they changed, and with each iteration, each new scribe, errors crept in. Or maybe some were changed deliberately, to suit a new audience. But in these stories sometimes lies a kernel of truth." He paused to sip his bourbon, a flush of excitement on his face. Despite his other concerns, Maverick focussed. Harlan was doing a pretty good job of storytelling, too. It echoed his own thoughts that he'd tried to dismiss.

Harlan continued. "Over the last two days I've read what feels like a hundred shifter myths and stories, across maybe a dozen books. Only one book that I found today had this tale in, and it was nowhere near as elaborate as *this* version that's all on its little lonesome."

Arlo laughed. "A dozen? Are you some kind of collector?"

"That's exactly what I am, although this isn't what I usually collect, and I tend to do it for others, not myself. But I do have connections. I went to the auction house to see the rest of Ivan's objects."

Maverick leaned forward, his attention gripped. "They let you in?"

"Sure. I know people."

"And what did you think?"

"The objects are interesting. Unusual sculptures, some nice books—one very beautifully illustrated. And this short story, bound in soft leather, and also opulently illustrated." He cocked an eyebrow and tapped the page. "I'm not sure if this story was in the other book, though. My contact wouldn't let me check that one thoroughly, and to be honest, I wasn't looking for stories on Saturday night. I borrowed this one because something about it caught my attention. It's modern, and my contact said it wasn't that valuable, so I could. The rest of the collection looked interesting, too—the bit of it that I saw."

Maverick frowned. "It feels weird having an auction on shifters, like we don't exist."

Grey shrugged, amused. "There are all sorts of auctions and collections throughout museums on human history. Get over it."

"You know what I mean! We're talked about like we're a myth."

"So, announce yourself to the world, then." Grey's smile spread. "I'd like to see how that would go. What do you think, Harlan?"

Harlan looked at ease, hand clasped loosely around his glass of bourbon, comfortable with his place in the world. A man who was a success. "I know exactly how it would go. Some people would love it, most would be terrified. The world isn't ready. Not by a longshot."

Arlo clinked Harlan's glass with his own. "I agree with you, and I say no thanks. I like anonymity. But, to get back to that story," he nodded at the book. "That's actually from the guy's collection? The one the objects were stolen from? What's got you so excited?"

"It's an origin story. A big one. It's set in the Otherworld—magic, fey, wild beasts, dragons, the fantastical—and it centres on the King of Wolves. But not just wolves. He ruled all shifters—after long and bloody battles, of course. For a while, everything was well, until he fell in love with a witch."

Maverick knew the tale, too, but he'd not thought of it for a long time. "No one liked the witch. Everyone felt he should have another shifter as a mate."

Arlo nodded. "They thought she'd bewitched him to gain power for herself. My mother hated that. She always takes the side of witches."

That explains a lot, Maverick thought. As if he'd read his mind Arlo scowled at him, scratching his eyebrow with a middle-fingered salute.

"Exactly!" Harlan wagged a finger, unaware of the subtext. "Trouble in paradise. But he loved her so madly that he didn't care. He was the King of the Shifters. The Wolf King! He could do what he wanted to."

"I sense an unhappy ending," Grey said.

"Oh yeah," Harlan's eyes widened. "He annoyed a lot of shifters, and eventually after a period of time, some of them laid a trap for him. And here's where it gets tangled in Welsh myth."

Maverick froze. "It does? How? And why are *you* focussing on Wales?"

"Ah! I forgot to mention that. Maggie checked the records of the dead men. They were all in Wales, at one point. A certain spot in Wales."

Arlo had been flicking through the book, but he paused to stare at Maverick. "That's true. We know it is."

Harlan cocked his head, intrigued. "How do you know?"

"Hunter and Domino found some old photos with a Welsh location name, plus some names on them in Riggs's belongings."

"Even better," Harlan said, nodding with excitement. "Another link."

Grey held up a hand. "Harlan! Where's this going with Welsh myth?"

"Okay. The Wolf King is lured into a battle with another trickster shapeshifter, who I interpret as being a therian?"

Arlo nodded, a crease settling between his eyebrows. "I think so. The main enemy, if I remember correctly, of the king."

Harlan's eyes kindled with excitement. "Here's where it gets interesting. The shapeshifter animates a whole forest to help him fight the Wolf King. They march against him and his team. They are overrun. Trapped."

Grey hustled him along. "The Welsh connection?"

"Gwydion is the trickster of Welsh mythology who lives in the Welsh Otherworld—Anwyn. He was bewitched by his uncle and shapeshifts for years. He appears in *The Mabinogion*, *The Book of Taliesin*, and participates in *The Battle of the Trees*. *Cad Goddeu*, in Welsh. I won't even start going into the many interpretations of that, but Gwydion's name translates as 'Born of Trees.' In *The Wolf King and The Witch Queen*, the Wolf King is persuaded to compete in a hunt with a shifter called Mathan. Essentially, the forest comes alive to assist him, and the Wolf King is trapped. Do you see what I mean? The stories blend."

Maverick looked at the glass in his hand. *How many had he had?* His head felt woolly. Arlo, however, was almost bouncing in his seat. "By the great God, Herne. You're right! They're the same. *Ish*."

Maverick stared at Arlo. "You believe him?"

Arlo stretched his arms wide. "Yes! It makes sense. The Welsh tale of Gwydion and *The Battle of the Trees*, does, on first hearing, sound very like the Wolf King's battle with the forest in the fairy tale."

Maverick stared at Arlo. "You've heard two sentences about Gwydion and the trees! How can you possibly make that assumption?"

"I said on *first hearing*! They're similar, and you know it. It's worth investigating."

Grey snorted. "I think you're all barking mad. They're both still fairy tales."

"Deeply rooted fairy tales," Harlan corrected him. "Connected to real Welsh places. King Arthur is in those tales. In fact, the ending reminds me of the Arthur tales. Arlo, tell him what happens to the Wolf King."

"He is grievously wounded, trapped in the forest that has come alive. His men are mostly dead. The Witch Queen, who has not forsaken him, but was waylaid by the treacherous Mathan's men, is able to reach him, but she's too late. He dies in her arms. Furious with grief, she freezes the entire forest in an enchantment, him included, intending to find a way to bring him back to life. And to this day, he lies there still."

"*Voilà*!" Harlan said with a flourish. "King Arthur is taken to the Isle of Avalon, grievously wounded, there to lie until rescued to save the day. See, a mix of tales, all rooted in reality. All origin myths."

Maverick wished he could believe him, but... "You say it like it's known to be true. Despite lots of researchers trying very hard, no one has proven that the King Arthur stories are real. From what I've read—because I have heard of *The Mabinogion* and *The Book of Taliesin*—no one can prove those are true, either."

"But they have persisted through time," Harlan pointed out. "People believe."

"It still doesn't make it true."

"*Someone* believes it now. They stole a box of relics and a crown—which, by the way, was huge!"

"Which is in no way connected to the story *The Wolf King and The Witch Queen*." Maverick sighed with frustration. "You have made a massive assumption."

"Have I? The crown could be a connection." Harlan smiled, ripe with knowledge.

A horrible trickle of possibility coursed down Maverick's spine. *Could any of that be true? And if it was, why were shifters dead?*

His phone buzzed on the table, and Maverick grabbed it quickly, snapping back to reality. "Monroe? What's going on?" His answer lodged fear in his stomach like a rock. "Coming down now."

Twenty

The bitter cold felt as if it was ripping Hunter in two, and despite his thick coat, scarf, and boots, he shivered.

"Bloody hell, I thought Cumbria was cold," he complained to Ollie and Tommy.

"Worried your nuts will freeze and drop off, pretty boy?" Tommy teased him.

"You should worry that I'll rip your nuts off and force feed them to you," Hunter shot back.

"You two are enough to give anyone a headache," Ollie said. "Especially after nearly six hours. That was a hell of a journey."

It had taken longer than they expected. The roads were icy in patches, and snow lay thick on the surrounding mountains, especially the Cairngorms, a range of mountains that rose majestically to the northwest. The scent of snow was strong, but the promise of the wild was stronger. It pulled at Hunter's blood, a primal urge to shift.

The Cairngorms was a national park, the largest in the UK, and covered roughly 4,500 square kilometres. The town of Ballater sat within its bounds, as did several other towns. It encompassed a few ranges, including Angus Glens and the Monadhliath, as well as three major rivers. It was a huge area, and a massive tourist attraction, too.

He surveyed the dark, brooding landscape. "If Emyr is in there, hiding, we're screwed. That's a lot of land to cover. Let's hope Hector is more helpful in person than he was on the phone."

Hector was the pack's alpha, and had tried to dissuade them several times from making the trip. Ollie refused to back down.

"Well, hopefully now that we're here, he'll be more amenable." Ollie pointed up the street to the pub. "That's where we're meeting him. The Balmoral Arms. With luck, that's where we're sleeping, too."

The Balmoral Arms was rustic, but comfortable. A mix of polished wood, tartan fabric, roaring fires, and comfortable chairs. It was a hotel with a bar and restaurant, and Ollie led them to the bar where they had arranged to meet Hector.

It was clearly a popular spot, busy with people casually dressed for dinner. The smell from the restaurant was enticing, and Hunter hoped they could eat soon. Despite the long journey, it was still barely eight in the evening.

A lone figure sat by the fireside in a prime spot, nursing a whiskey in one hand while he stared at the flames, and he gave off a huge amount of shifter energy. As they approached, he stood, turning toward them. "My persistent Cumbrian friends, I presume? I'm Hector Campbell."

Hector was in his mid-fifties, Hunter estimated, but a big man still, solid with muscle. He had a thick head of greying hair, and a huge, bushy beard that hid most of his face. He may have called them friends, but he didn't look that welcoming.

Ollie extended his hand and introduced them, and in minutes they were settled next to him, each with a drink in hand.

"I'm not happy that you're here, I'll be honest," Hector said, a growl to his voice. "You disobeyed my request."

"I'm not under your control," Ollie reminded him, his voice even. "I explained that we needed answers."

"I don't want Emyr disturbed or upset."

"We're not trying to do either," Ollie replied. "If anything, we've come to warn him. I told you what had happened on the phone."

"Aye. I've heard. This is Scotland, not outer space. But that has nothing to do with us."

"It has everything to do with Emyr—if we're right." Ollie had no intention of revealing details, but he would point out the connection between Emyr and the dead shifters.

Hunter settled in the wing-backed chair, half listening to Ollie explain their concerns, and half watching the crowd in the bar. A few of Hector's pack were spread across the room, no doubt keeping an eye on their meeting. A couple caught his eye, and he nodded to show that he'd seen them.

It was unsettling. There was no indication that they would attack, certainly not in the bar, but Hunter wondered what would happen outside. With Hector's blessing or not, they were planning to look for Emyr—somehow. Tommy had spotted their audience, too. He was quiet. Never a good sign.

"Hector," Ollie remonstrated, "I know you're being protective of Emyr, but in these circumstances, you might actually be doing him a disservice."

"I'm the alpha, laddie, I don't think I need you to tell me what to do."

"Eight deaths, all linked, with four in one family. One missing brother—and maybe other missing shifters, too. One old pack that Emyr belonged to. You tell me what this is, then."

"Some idiot with a vendetta."

"A dangerous killer—not an idiot. I'm not sure what playing this down is achieving." Ollie was remaining calm, but only with great effort. His shoulders were set, his jaw clenched, and they all knew what the major issue was. Ollie was a young alpha, and old, grizzled warriors like Hector didn't like that. It upset the natural order of things. Well. *Their* perceived natural order.

Hector clenched his glass, leaning into Ollie's face. "Emyr is old. He doesn't need trouble."

"If we're right, he'll get trouble whether he wants it or not."

Hunter suddenly realised why they were meeting here in a public bar. It wasn't only neutral territory; it also meant that they couldn't create a scene, either. Although, looking at Tommy's brooding features, he wasn't sure that would hold true. Perhaps trying to book rooms in this hotel was a bad idea, after all.

Ollie cast Hunter a look of resignation before turning back to Hector. "Pûcas. Have you heard of them?"

Hector stiffened. "Aye, I have. What about them?"

"They attacked us after we tracked them in Cumbria. They killed some of the shifters—not an *idiot*—maybe all of them. They were vicious. Emyr won't stand a chance. And we think therians are involved."

"He's in a safe place, so leave him be."

Ollie smiled, victorious. "So, he is hiding. I need to know why. It's important. What he knows could save others."

Hector stood, his drink finished. "You won't find him. Go home." And without a backward glance, he walked away.

Arlo stared at the bear that was wrapped in chains in front of the stage, wondering how they were going to deal with this.

"Well, he can't bloody talk as a bear," he remonstrated to Monroe. "And if he comes around, how the hell are we supposed to turn him into a human again?"

"You sent us to capture him! We have! Nearly bloody killed us doing it, too."

Cecile nodded in agreement, seated on the stage. "It was tough. We're lucky Monroe took the tranq gun, or we'd never have captured him."

Monroe paced back and forth in front of the unconscious creature, the tranquiliser gun, now restocked, in his hands. "We could shock him—with electricity. That might make him shift."

"Torture?" Arlo's skin crawled. "Not a chance."

Monroe shrugged. "I don't like the idea myself, but it was just a suggestion."

"Well, forget it. I hate the idea."

Maverick was also pacing, but was on the phone to Jax. He had alternated between calling him and Vlad for the last fifteen minutes, frustrated at their inability to find Domino, and unable to question Jake. Grey was upstairs, and having doubled the patrol on the club, was keeping an eye on Harlan, who was still in the bar.

Arlo addressed Monroe again. "When's he likely to wake up?"

"Maybe an hour? Maybe less? I don't know. It took more shots to down him than I expected it to. Weird shifter metabolism."

"Like he's going to answer our questions, anyway. What the hell were we thinking?"

"Kane is dead." Maverick interrupted them as he ended his call. "That's what we were thinking. Have we got something to wake him up with? Another shot, perhaps?"

"And risk killing him?" Cecile said, appalled. "I don't think so."

"Yeah. I'm not a bloody zookeeper," Monroe remonstrated.

Maverick huffed, running his hands through his hair. "You're right. We have him, that's the most important thing. How do we make him talk?"

"How do we make him *shift*?" Arlo countered. And then he recalled his own injury from the night before. "Morgana can do it."

"No! I will not have that witch here again. And what do you mean, she can do it?" Maverick asked, alarmed.

"When I was injured, I shifted to my wolf to heal, but she needed to dress my wound. According to Grey, she said a spell and it shifted me back to human." He shuddered at the memory. "I was aware of it, sort of. It was uncanny."

"Woah! Seriously?" Monroe stopped pacing, swinging around to look at Arlo. "I didn't know that could happen!"

"Well, apparently it can." Arlo turned back to Maverick. "We can't afford to be picky about this if we want answers. He might know where Domino is, too, if the boys can't find her."

"Fuck it!" Maverick eyes turned molten yellow. "I don't want the witches involved in our business again."

"Why not? Despite my history with Odette, she was only ever helpful to us—so were Morgana and Birdie. And Morgana was really helpful last night. She healed me."

Maverick huffed impatiently. "I'm sure, given time, you would have healed yourself."

"I had a splinter of glass in my wound, Mav! I don't think so." He patted over his injury. "She slapped some of her healing paste in there, too. I think you should cut her some slack. And besides—"

"Don't even suggest it!" Maverick glared at him, and then fell silent, and Arlo let him mull it over. He never liked to be bullied into anything, and that was fair enough. Neither did he. But the other issue that he'd been about to raise was the fact that Kane had been their medic if they needed more serious injuries to be dealt with. Now, they had no one with his level of skill. Employing Morgana on a more professional basis was probably a good idea. He'd just have to deal with seeing Odette more regularly, too.

"All right," Maverick finally said, voice heavy with annoyance. "Call her."

Domino woke in a cold, dark, room, lying on a thin mattress that stank of sweat. Her hands were tied behind her back, and her ankles were secured, too.

She waited for her eyes to adjust to the light, trying to ignore the nausea that rolled through her as she fought to recollect the events that had brought her here. *Why was her memory so foggy? Why was she feeling sick?*

She'd been in a street, fighting a bear, with Vlad. *A bear?* The sting in her chest confused her further.

She focussed on her surroundings, letting her thoughts settle, and knowing it was pointless to try to force things. The room was damp, and it felt small. A window high up on one wall allowed a trickle of light in. She must be in a basement. Distant voices intruded on the silence of her cell. Male voices. It sounded like they were arguing. *Good*. That meant they were distracted, and that boded well for her if they were her captors.

Frustrated, she writhed, trying to break her restraints. If she shifted, would that be enough to free her, or would she likely dislocate something?

With her mind busy, her memory flooded back, and she remembered Monroe and the damn tranquiller gun. She'd been brought down by her own team, making them look like bloody amateurs. But at least she knew who her captors were. *Therians*. She just hoped her own team had captured Jake. He may be a bargaining tool. Although, she'd rather be free herself. Being captured was doing nothing for her ego.

The march of footsteps outside had her squirming to sit up, but they continued past her room. Instead, she heard the clang of a distant door, and voices further along. Angry, raised voices, plus some thumps and curses.

Someone was being assaulted. Her mouth went dry. *This could be her fate.*

Harlan sat across the table from Grey, sipping his second bourbon of the evening. Even though there was a captured therian sitting downstairs, Grey seemed remarkably calm.

Harlan wondered if he should leave, but the bar scene carried on as normal, and he figured he was safe enough there. *As long as a raging bear didn't smash through the door and kill them all.* "So, this kind of thing happens all the time, then?" Harlan asked.

"Hardly. These are unusual circumstances."

"Aren't you worried the therians will attack to get Jake back?"

"No. Not yet, anyway. That's why they have Domino. Insurance. Besides, the bar is busy, and I have strengthened our patrols. They'd be mad to attack here."

"Unless they recruit Pûcas."

"I doubt that. They seem too feral to be roped into any agreements." Grey set his own drink aside, a plain Coke, and pulled the slim volume toward him. "Are you serious about this?"

"The story? Absolutely. I know it seems like a leap, but I've learned not to discount old tales. There are a lot of truths in them." He declined to mention the Nephilim, the *Comte de Saint Germain*, and an immortal John Dee. "You work with shifters. You must know that."

"Yeah, but, the cold reality of that is here. All that other stuff, the origin story and fey, well, it seems a bit airy fairy—forgive the expression."

"I get it. However, I spend my life dealing with this shit, and I would put money on this. I might not be right on the mark, but I'm close." He leaned forward to emphasise his point. "The deaths are doing a very good job of taking the focus off the stolen objects. Where have they gone? Why steal them? That suggests to me that they still have power. Of course, the deaths are important. I get that Maverick wants revenge...but the box of relics matters."

"What would you do?" Grey asked.

"Take a team to Wales. Start investigating the area around Betws-y-Coed."

"Have you ever been there?"

Harlan shook his head. "No, why?"

"I have. It's beautiful, wild, and big. It would be like searching for a needle in a haystack."

"Are there no packs out there that Maverick could approach?"

"A few, but further south, I gather. Unless..." Grey hesitated. "Unless some of the old pack are still there, hiding."

"Or still *guarding* something." Harlan tingled with the familiar thrill of discovery.

"Why do you think they're guarding anything? They could just be a weird cult." Grey smirked. "Holy crap. You actually think they're guarding the Wolf King?"

"It's possible."

"I think you've been doing your job for too long. You're seeing stories where there aren't any."

"I think that if you had experienced the shit that I have, you wouldn't dismiss this so easily."

After a long silence, Grey finally said, "Okay. Say you're right. Why guard him, and what are the consequences of finding him?"

"Before I answer that, I have another question. Who rules the shifters now?"

"No one, not overall. Alphas lead wolf-shifter packs, and I believe the other shifters have similar arrangements, but I'm not sure."

"So, they all have separate allegiances?"

"Yeah, to their own pack, and a healthy respect, more or less, for another's territory. No one likes border wars. Therians don't have territories. They are freelancers, for the most part. Wanderers."

Harlan grinned. "Well, the answer to your earlier question is easy, surely. It will change the balance of power, and someone does not want that to happen. Or, they want the balance swung their way."

Twenty-One

"What now?" Hunter asked Ollie. "There are still half a dozen of Hector's men in this room, watching our every move. There'll be more outside."

Tommy was spoiling for a fight, glaring at the shifters one by one. "I'll take care of them."

"No, you won't, you pillock! There are too many of them," Ollie pointed out. "Besides, we want their help, not their blood."

"Can we get some food first, at least?" Hunter asked. The smell of steak emanating from the restaurant was making him salivate. "And book rooms. We need a bed, and I'm not sleeping in the car."

"Yeah, you book the rooms, me and Tommy will find a table. Maybe we can get out in the early hours of the morning. Work out a way to get through their surveillance. See you in the restaurant."

Hunter headed through the crowded bar to the hotel reception area, aware of eyes on his every move. *Let them stare.* He just hoped the place wasn't run by a shifter who would refuse them a room. Otherwise, they'd have to search around.

In contrast to the busy bar, the reception area was quiet, and only one young man sat behind the counter, working on a computer. A shifter with shaved hair and hard eyes sat on a long sofa in the lobby, making no pretence to read the paper in front of him. He stared at Hunter, but Hunter ignored him, and headed to the check-in counter.

The receptionist looked up as Hunter approached, eyes darting to the shifter and then back again. "Evening, sir," he said in a thick Scottish accent. "How can I help?"

"Evening. I need three rooms, if possible, but we'll take less if you're busy."

"Certainly, sir. I can provide two rooms, but one does have twin beds." *Bollocks.* That meant he would be sharing with Tommy and his outrageous snoring. Although annoyed, he smiled. "That's great. Better than the car."

"Let me prepare your keys." His eyes darted to the shifter again, but when Hunter turned to look at him, he was reading the paper instead. The hotel concierge looked nervous, his hands shaking, and Hunter wondered what was going on.

Hunter waited, back to the counter to survey the room, just in case someone was about to attack, but no one was close.

The man coughed to attract his attention. "Sir. Your key cards are ready. Just sign the paperwork, please."

Hunter hurriedly signed the sheet that had been pushed over the counter, and then exchanged it for the key cards, placed in stiff card envelopes. Hunter went to pocket them, but the man stopped him.

"Please check that they're correct." He stared, wide-eyed. A plea.

"Sure. No problem."

A note was tucked into one of the cards. *We'll come to you at midnight. Be ready.*

Hunter looked up at the man, a silent question in his eyes, and the man's gaze slid to the shifter on the sofa. *Okay. An intermediary.* "Thanks, they look perfect. Have a good night."

Hunter pocketed the keys, looking at the shifter casually as he turned to go back to the bar. For a brief second their eyes met before the shifter stared at the paper again.

Interesting. Either it was an elaborate trap, or some of Hector's pack didn't agree with his decision. Hunter hoped for the latter.

Maverick took one look at Vlad, Mads, and Jax and knew they'd failed. "You didn't find her."

"Not a sign, boss. Sorry," Vlad said, eyes downcast, ready to bear the brunt of Maverick's ire. "We searched all around Clapham. I reckon they have a lockup somewhere, got their van undercover quick."

Mads spoke up next. "We searched on foot, too. Couldn't even pick up a scent of them—except for around the pub where Jake was heading."

Maverick knew it was pointless to shout, as much as he wanted to; they were all furious about Domino's abduction. The only people responsible for it were the therians. He'd save his anger for them.

"Arlo, bring us a map, and let's scour the area. Maybe they're masking their scent with a food market or something. And call Castor," he added as an afterthought. He'd hoped to hear from him about his missing shifter, but so far had heard nothing. "He might know something."

"No problem." Arlo headed to the office, and Maverick turned back to the team. They were covered in blood from their latest wounds—punches, kicks, and the ragged tears of skin from Jake's claws. "I hope you inflicted as much damage on them. Go clean up, and be back in ten. The witches are on the way."

He watched them head to the bathroom, leaving only Cecile and Monroe with him, and all three maintained a healthy distance from the bear. He looked to be still sleeping, but Maverick did not want to risk having his throat ripped out, or a limb torn off.

Maverick grabbed the long pole they used to drop the shutter doors out the back before they were automated, and prodded Jake with it. The bear didn't move. "Bloody lump. Look at him."

"He wasn't a lump when he was conscious," Monroe pointed out. "He was quick and deadly. Is he breathing?"

Cecile nodded. "Yes. I see his gut heaving up and down." She still sat on the stage, thoughtful. "I didn't think therians had packs. They're lone operators. We didn't expect him to have help."

"I know," Maverick said, Cecile voicing his own concerns. "Something has motivated them, and I can only presume it's these recent events."

Monroe shrugged. "Therians have friends, like anyone. They stick together. Just because they don't call themselves a pack, doesn't mean they don't band together."

Maverick nodded. "True. We need a name for one of them. Someone I can call. If they want to trade Jake for Domino, I want that to happen soon."

"Which means we can't hurt him," Cecile said, sounding regretful, and no doubt wanting retribution.

"I don't want to. I want answers." The click of the door and the scent of perfume made him look to the side of the stage. The witches had arrived.

"And you'll get them," a woman said as she stepped into view. "Twice in one week. Aren't I lucky to be back in Storm Moon."

"That's one word for it," Maverick said, a growl in the back of his throat. "Our misfortune, actually. Domino is missing."

Morgana stepped into the light, and dipped her head in apology. "I was making a poor joke. Sorry." She looked at the bear, keeping a wary distance. "He's a big boy."

"No Odette tonight?"

"No. Not now she knows that Arlo is okay." Her face twisted into a smile. "I persuaded her to stay home. It's obvious that he's not comfortable seeing her. And you...well, you hate seeing us. It's a measure of your dire straits that I'm here."

It had been almost two years since Maverick had seen Morgana. She hadn't changed. Her long, brown hair was punctuated by a grey lock that curled around her face like a wing. The grey was a result of a spell, apparently—not a sign of age. He'd never been told the details. He knew Morgana to be a little older than him. Her hazel eyes were sharp, observant, wise with a curious mix of knowledge and humour. They almost seemed to see through him. She was uncanny. The potion maker and Green Witch of their trio. An older cousin to Odette, granddaughter of Birdie.

"I can't lie. I don't like witches, but I'm grateful you came. Thanks for healing Arlo."

"My pleasure—I think. You boys do know how to make a mess of yourselves."

He cut to the heart of the problem. "Can you really make Jake shift back to human if he refuses? Which we absolutely expect him to do."

"I can. The spell works on any shifter, although therians are tricky."

Monroe snorted. "Like we don't know."

Morgana grinned. "It's good to see you, Monroe. Your handiwork?"

"Of course." He wiggled the tranquilliser gun. "He was like a steam train."

"I can imagine." She looked at Maverick again. "I have a few stipulations first. I will not harm him. It's not what I do, understood?"

"Of course."

"Neither will I stand by if you harm him." Her eyes kindled with fire. "It's one thing to defend yourself, quite another to willingly inflict damage. Especially on a captured man. It's torture."

"I want to question him, not kill him!" He hated to be thought of as a monster. Shifters could be violent, but it didn't rule his reason.

She grunted, her expression doubtful, her eyes locked with his. "Easy to say now. But when he resists?"

He'd want to beat the truth out of him. *That was the trouble with witches. All that 'harm none' crap really got in the way sometimes.* "I'll try, but I need answers. Domino is missing, and I doubt they'll be holding back with her."

"Maverick?" She refused to break eye contact with him, and he hated that, too. He was the alpha, and had a reputation to maintain.

"I'll do what I have to do, Morgana, just like you do when you're backed into a corner." He stepped closer, aware of her power. "I hear of the spells of Moonfell, and they are not always good. Do we really want to start splitting hairs here?"

She wanted to retreat, he knew it, but she didn't. He imagined it was taking a great amount of willpower not to, or not to cast a spell on him. They were locked in a battle of wills, neither prepared to back down.

She finally spoke. "You're exaggerating as to our spells, and fishing, too. You have no idea what spells we provide to those who are in need."

He smirked. "Really? You keep telling yourself that. It will be..." He paused, thoughtful, watching her pupils dilate, her breath quicken. "A little mystery between us as to what I know. What secrets I'm prepared to keep." *That would keep her guessing.* "So, what's it to be? Will you help me, or do you want to go home, knowing I'll beat him to a pulp if he won't shift."

After another long moment, in which she stared into his eyes as if she could read his thoughts, she lowered her voice, barely above a whisper. "Fine, but you watch what you do, Maverick. You're not infallible, either." She raised her voice again, all business. "Do you want him to come around first, or shall I start now? It might be easier with him unconscious."

He stepped back from her personal space, wondering just what sort of compromise they had reached. "Do it now, but let the others come back first. They're cleaning up their injuries, but won't be long. Just in case." He didn't need to say just in case of what. That was obvious.

"Wise. I also suggest you have a few traps handy. If he keeps shifting, which is possible, he'll try a few creatures and escape routes."

He groaned, wishing he'd thought of that himself. "Yes, I guess you're right. Cecile, head upstairs and get Grey. This could get tricky."

Domino stiffened as the door to her cell flew open. For a brief moment, a man stood limned against the bright light of the corridor beyond, and then he stepped inside, swinging the door shut behind him.

Her heart pounded, not sure whether it was worse that he had shut the door rather than left it open for his colleagues to join him, but she stayed silent.

"I wonder if you'll be more amenable to questions than our friend down the corridor," the man said softly, a dangerous edge to his voice. It was the man who had challenged them in the pub.

"I doubt it, but it depends on what you're going to ask me. I presume from the thumps I heard that your prisoner is keeping his silence."

The man stepped closer, crouching down in front of her, and the meagre light revealed a blade in his hand. "It seems the death of his friends, and the promise of more to follow, is not motivating him. Perhaps when I kill you in front of him, he'll be more motivated."

Domino refused to show fear. "I'm a stranger. It sounds unlikely."

The therian laughed. "Death at a distance is easier to swallow than one up close. Especially a painful, slow one. But first, I have questions. Why have you taken Jake?"

"We just wanted to talk to him. We'd have done that in the pub, that was the plan, but you didn't want us there."

"No. We don't like wolf-shifters in our pub."

"We didn't know it was *your* pub! It's your fault the circumstances played out as they did. In fact, if Jake would have just talked in the street, that would have been it."

"I doubt he'd have talked to you." His gaze raked over her. "Like I said, we don't like wolf-shifters."

"For the record, I don't have a problem with therians—usually." *She shouldn't say any more, but fuck it.* "You, I dislike intensely."

He backhanded her across the face, snapping her head around and bringing tears to her eyes. "The feeling is mutual."

"Do you want to try that again without me being tied up? Or are you too much of a coward?"

He gave a dry laugh. "I caught you, remember?"

"Only because I was drugged. Would you like round two?"

"Maybe later." He eased back. "I know you're not with the North London Pack, which means you're with Maverick's pack. Having asked around, I now know that you are Domino, the head of his security team. Not a good look for you to be caught, Domino."

"Not a good look for you to be caught with *me*. Maverick will tear you limb from limb."

"He'll have to find me first." He gave her a feral grin. "So, on with the questions." He pulled a wooden chair that was in the corner of the room directly in front of her and sat down, the knife still in his hands. "Again, why Jake?"

She debated how much to say, but knew she had to give him something. "We know he met with Brody, one of our pack members, and we suspect that Brody had something to do with Kane's death—another pack member and a very good friend of mine. We wanted to know what they talked about."

He leaned forward, putting the blade under her chin to tilt her head up. "You've been spying."

"Wouldn't you, if your friend had been brutally killed, and then you found out his family had been, too?" She moved forward, heedless of the knife that pricked her skin. "You would have done exactly the same thing. All we wanted to know was what Jake knew. What did he speak to Brody about? Easy."

He shook his head, tutting, and withdrawing the blade. "Not so easy, you know that."

"I don't, actually. Why don't you tell me why you're beating a man half to death? I can smell his blood from here." She took a chance, knowing it could backfire. "This is about the box, isn't it?"

He froze, but recovered quickly. "Box? What box?"

She laughed. "You're a terrible liar. The box from Burton and Knight. The box of relics. *Wow*. It must be significant to get you all so worked up."

He rocketed off his chair, grabbed a handful of her hair and hauled her half off the mattress. She rose as far as she could, trying to ease the pain from his brutal hold, and vowing she would kill him the first chance she got. "What do you know about that damn box and the crown?"

"Nothing! I never even knew they existed until a couple of nights ago."

Her confusion was obvious, and he abruptly let her go, brandishing his knife. Ice ran through her veins, and she struggled to break free of her restraints. But he wasn't about to stab her, instead he cut the plastic ties that bound her feet. He grabbed her elbow, hauled her to her feet, and dragged her to the door.

"Time to see if Riggs will talk."

At least that explained where Riggs had gone.

Twenty-Two

Grey watched Jake writhe in his restraints, his skin rippling in a myriad of different ways as Morgana cast the spell.

Even for a non-shifter, it was uncomfortable to watch. Glancing at his companions, he saw a mixture of fear and admiration on their faces. Arlo visibly shuddered, even though Grey remembered him saying it wasn't a painful sensation. *Even so...* It must feel like you were being turned inside out.

He and the shifters were gathered around Jake. Jax, Mads, and Cecile were in their wolf; Arlo, Maverick, Vlad, and Monroe were humans. Monroe had his tranquilliser gun fully loaded—just in case. Harlan had desperately wanted to join them, but this was pack business. Instead, Grey had suggested that Harlan find out more details about the crazy fairy story—just in case it turned out to have a kernel of truth in it. He'd also asked Jet to keep an eye on him. Grey didn't have a weapon, instead he held handcuffs and another chain, ready to restrain him again—this time as a human.

Unfortunately, they were doing this later than originally planned, as they had needed to find a new way to secure Jake once he was back in human form. The chains that were wrapped around the bear would be too heavy for him as a human. By the time they were ready, he was already rousing from the drugs, and as Morgana had predicated, the therian was not responding quickly to the spell. Her voice rose, as did her power. A cone of magic whipped around her, lifting her hair in a nimbus, and her eyes darkened with focus. She cracked out a command, and with an almighty shudder and an unearthly roar, Jake started to shift.

At first it was slow, as if he was railing against the spell. He shrank from a bear to a dog, the chains dropping off him, and he darted as if to run. But he continued to shift, falling limp on the ground. He changed to a cat, then a fox, wolf, a stag... It went on and on, quicker and quicker. It was impossible to tell if he was shifting willingly, trying to escape the spell, or if the spell was forcing it. From the howls and grunts coming from Jake, Grey presumed the latter.

But he wasn't shifting to human. Not yet.

Morgana was frozen in position, hands outstretched, face creased with concentration, wrestling with Jake's very being. Just when it seemed that either Jake would collapse or Morgana would, he shifted into human form, limp and barely breathing.

Morgana lowered her arms, plainly exhausted, but no one was celebrating yet. Grey asked, "Is it done? Can he change?"

"Not for a while. But he's strong. I suggest you move quickly."

Grey didn't hesitate. The chains that had restrained Jake had fallen off him and Grey raced in, clamping the cuffs around his wrists, and clipping them to the chain. He threw the end to Vlad who secured it to the wall, and then stepped well out of Jake's reach. Their arrangements were rudimentary, but should hold.

Maverick had a bucket of water in hand, and he threw it over Jake.

Gasping, he took a sharp intake of breath. "What the hell?" He blinked and sat up, scooting back to put more distance between them, his pale skin white under the stage light. He glared at them one by one, rattling his cuffs to test them. His eyes finally settled on Morgana. "Witch! What have you done?"

"Nothing permanent. But I suggest you answer their questions." She retreated, eyes sliding a warning to Maverick.

Grey could feel the tension between them. Maverick was holding on to his anger by a knife's edge.

Maverick stood over Jake, well within his reach, a sign of his need to intimidate and his faith in Morgana's spell. "I have a lot of questions for you, Jake. The sooner you answer them, the sooner you'll be out of here, understood?"

"Like I believe *you*. You'll kill me."

"No, I won't. Not if you cooperate. If we can come to an agreement here, then it could be the start of a lucrative arrangement for you."

Jake's eyes kindled with greed. "Lucrative?"

"Take that any way you like. Money—for information, my help with something, my protection at some future date... But it depends on what you tell me right now."

"Do I get some clothes first? I'm butt naked and freezing."

Maverick cocked an eyebrow toward Arlo and nodded. Arlo grabbed the blanket they had brought from the office and threw it over him.

He didn't thank them, but he did seem less resentful. "And if I don't help?"

"I will find out every sneaky deal you're in on, every contact you've made, and ruin them all. I will make it impossible for you to survive here. In fact, I will make it my personal mission that you become an outcast from your own society."

Jake gave a dry laugh. "That will happen if I betray everyone, anyway."

"But you'll have a new team. Mine."

That was interesting, Grey thought. *Proposing an alliance with Jake? That was one way to get answers.* It seemed Jake was interested, too.

"You would recruit me into your network? Your pack?"

"Maybe *pack* would be pushing it, but yes, I would." Maverick crouched in front of him. "Decide, quickly. Because my most pressing question is, where would your slippery little therian friends have taken Domino?"

Jake's back was pressed to the stage, eyes intent on Maverick. "Domino? Who's she?"

"Don't toy with me. The female shifter who tried to talk to you."

"Oh, her." He looked confused. "They took her?"

"Yes. I want to know where. And then I want to know what you had to do with Kane's death."

"Nothing!"

"Then talk."

Jake swallowed, looking at the cluster of people around him. "Warner's uncle leases a shop in Brixton. It has a basement. Most likely, she'll be there. But I warn you. Warner is on a mission, and he's not easy to stop when he starts."

"Neither am I. I want an address."

"It's by the market. Coldharbour Lane."

"That's a long and busy road. I want specifics."

"I don't know, exactly! I think it's by an Indian restaurant. But it *is* close to the market. A stone's throw, init?" In his panic, his London accent became stronger.

Maverick glanced at the others. "Sound familiar?"

Vlad nodded. "Probably a mile or two from where we were. We'll find it."

"Good. Take the original team with you, including Monroe and his gun. And make sure you come back with her."

Grey was itching to go with them, but knew his place was here. They were as likely to be attacked by the therians, too.

In seconds Vlad left with Mads, Cecile, Monroe, and Jax, and the rest closed their circle around Jake, who twisted, testing his cuffs, and no doubt trying to shift.

Maverick's voice was dangerously soft. "If you're lying, they'll tell me, and the deal will be off, understand?"

"I'm not lying."

"Good. Then tell me about Brody."

Jake sighed heavily, resigned to his fate. "He was a go-between, like me. I think he liked you, so it wasn't personal."

"It wasn't personal when he crashed through the window above us and died right next to where you're sitting now, so all's fair, right?"

Jake swallowed. "'E's dead?"

"Yes. The police are looking into his background now. All of his connections. Where he lived, who he saw... That might include you."

"No, it won't. I barely knew 'im."

Grey was beginning to detest Jake. He had no backbone, and no loyalty. It did them a favour now, but it didn't endear him for the future. Once a snitch, always a snitch.

Maverick continued, his voice smooth but hard. "So, why was he meeting you? Why was he a go-between?"

"He knew Warner from years back. They were mates, of a sort. Warner heard about a crown. Became obsessed with it. Said it was the key to true power. And then...well, he found out something else." Jake's eyes clouded with worry. "I didn't like it. I thought he was mad, actually."

"Go on," Maverick prompted him after he fell silent.

"He found out that a group of wolf-shifters had once guarded this crown, so he decided to find them. But then it all got really messy. He ran into some Pûcas looking for the same thing. *Shit.* That got ugly, until they struck a deal."

"Warner made a deal with Pûcas? That sounds absurd. From what I've heard, they are fey creatures, and don't play well with others. And neither does Warner, by the sound of it."

Jake shrugged. "I know, but they did. Desperate times. High stakes."

Grey exchanged a worried glance with Arlo. It sounded like the crown was more important than the box. Morgana was standing back now, in the shadows, listening and watching. He wondered what she would make of all this.

"And Brody?" Maverick asked.

"He was promised a cut of whatever the spoils would be. All he had to do was tell Warner what Kane was up to. He found out he was meeting his brother."

"His brother?" Maverick's voice rose with shock. "Riggs?"

"Yeah, that's him. He just told me the place." Jake could barely look at Maverick now, or at any of them. "That was 'ere. I just took that message back to Warner, and left it at that."

"That message, you little shit, got Kane killed."

"I was just the messenger! I don't know details. Warner doesn't trust me that much."

Grey's head was reeling. *Nothing made sense...except that Warner didn't trust Jake. That made perfect sense.*

Maverick abruptly stood, and backed away. Arlo, Grey, and Morgana joined him, with Grey still watching their captive's every move.

Maverick's tone was icy. "Does this mean that Warner has Riggs, as well as Domino? Was Riggs a bargaining tool for Kane? Or is he dead, too?"

Arlo shrugged, face creased with worry. "Hard to say. Why didn't Kane ask for help?"

"Maybe," Morgana suggested, "he didn't know how bad the situation was. Or didn't want to involve you. I obviously have no idea what you're all involved in, but it sounds dangerous."

"I have more questions now than before," Maverick complained bitterly.

Grey's worry was a big knot in his stomach. "I'll call Vlad, warn him they might find Riggs, too." And then another horrible thought struck him. "And Pûcas. They might find Pûcas…"

Twenty-Three

After Harlan was left alone in the bar, going mad with curiosity as to what was happening downstairs and wishing he could watch, he decided to catch up on a few tasks.

He phoned Maggie to update her on his theory, and predictably she had scoffed loudly. She also informed him that she had found nothing of use in Brody's flat, and that so far, Irving had found nothing significant about Ivan's collection. It was frustrating, but hardly surprising. Feeling guilty, Harlan had evaded some of Maggie's more pointed questions. Maverick would not like his current exploits shared, and he was not about to be a snitch.

Harlan wished he had his colleague, Olivia, nearby to run his theory past, but she was out of London on other business. He knew what she would say, though. *Follow your gut.* He sipped a beer, already deciding to get a taxi home, and hoping Grey would return soon with an update. However, with every passing minute, he realised that was getting more unlikely.

And then a young, petite woman with dark, almost black hair, tattoos, and smoky eye makeup slid into the booth opposite him. She placed a glass of bourbon in front of him with a smile.

"Hi, I'm Jet. I met you last year, if you remember? I noticed you were almost out, and wanted to make sure you were okay."

"I remember you. The helpful spy." He nodded to the drink. "Thank you, and I'm fine, you don't need to worry about me. I've got plenty to keep me occupied. You're here just to keep an eye on me, right?" He laughed and tapped his head. "Maybe glean my secrets."

Jet laughed. "*Spy* is a little strong. My job is just to help things run smoothly."

"Sure it is," he replied, his voice laced with scepticism as he pointed at her Coke. "But you're not drinking. That alone says volumes."

"I'm at work. I may work in a bar, but it doesn't mean I can drink every night. My liver and my skin would hate me. So would the boss." She nodded at the book. "I'm here more to help you explore your thoughts on that story."

"Ah. A little helper."

"Not so much *little*, thank you."

"Fair enough, that did sound patronising. Sorry." Jet seemed nice enough, and if she was a spy, she'd be a useful ally. She also seemed very clued in on current events. "Have you heard what's happening downstairs?"

"Jake is being helpful, according to Arlo. A team has headed out to rescue Domino." She frowned. "I hope they find her. Domino is amazing. The boys wouldn't thank me for saying so, but she is a huge motivator around here. Everyone looks up to her."

"She seems strong, though." Harlan considered her self-confidence and lithe physique. "Able to look after herself."

"And then some."

"But Maverick is the alpha. His attitude must carry a lot of weight, too." Harlan was very curious about Maverick. He didn't know any shifters, but had assumed they'd be burly and overbearing. While Maverick walked around with a huge amount of self-assurance, he wasn't an insufferable prick.

Jet leaned back, hand resting on her glass. "Ah, Maverick. He's not your average alpha. I mean, don't get me wrong, he swaggers with the best of them, but he's also a modernist, which means he rubs other alphas up the wrong way."

"How so?"

Jet's eyes sparkled with mischief. "He's not a sexist wanker, or I guarantee I wouldn't be here. A few of the older, more traditional alphas resent his modern ways."

"But you're also not downstairs, helping with Jake."

"It's not safe. Look at me." She extended her hands down her small frame. "I'm not a fighter. I'm a party girl, and waitress. I have no urge to brawl. Although, of course, if they needed my help downstairs, I would be down there in a shot. You, however..." her eyes raked over Harlan. "You are not what I expect a collector to look like. I thought you'd be dressed in tweed and wear a monocle." She grinned. "You even work out."

"Ha-ha! I'm American. I don't wear tweed! Being fit is a prerequisite in my job, and to be honest, I enjoy the physical side of it." He rolled his eyes. "Most of the time, when not being terrified I might die..."

"So, you don't always just read through books and negotiate sales?"

"Hell no. I get dirty searching through tombs, dusty libraries, old houses—and let's face it, the paranormal world can be murky... Wherever the job takes me."

"And this job," Jet nodded at the book, "is taking you in a weird direction."

"Very." Harlan's eyes fell on the beautifully illustrated book again, still open on the table. And then his focus sharpened on the page. "Holy crap. There's a crown in this image." He leaned in, taking in the details of the many tined, antlered crown. "It's uncannily like the crown that was stolen."

"You're kidding!" Jet twisted the book so she could see it better, and then stared at him. "That has to be a coincidence, right?"

"Yes? No? It's a very unusual crown." Harlan gave a nervous laugh and scrutinised the image more closely, certainty settling in his stomach like a stone. The illustration seemed to tell a story that wasn't in the text. After the king was killed, his crown was placed on an elaborate throne as a kind of memorial, and an unusual box was placed with it. *A very familiar box...* He looked up, finding Jet's lively gaze still on him. "It's too much of a coincidence. It has to be the crown, and there's a small box next to it, too."

"The box of relics?"

"Maybe." Harlan couldn't believe he hadn't noticed it before, but he'd been caught up in comparing the story, not the illustrations. "But whoever stole the objects didn't put any value on this book." He checked the front of the book, looking for the illustrator's name. And then he noticed something he really should have caught before. "There's no publisher listed, no illustrator, nothing. Like it's a one-off, or a small print run. Or maybe a sample..."

Jet looked puzzled. "But wouldn't that make it more valuable, not less?"

Harlan shook his head, puzzled. "I'm missing something. Something important..."

Vlad had forgotten how much he loved Brixton. It was a vibrant, multicultural place, with market stands, vintage stalls, pubs, restaurants, and music venues. He was in the passenger seat of Cecile's van, with Mads, Jax, and Monroe in the back, having decided one vehicle in this crowded area of London would make life easier.

"Indian bloody restaurant!" Vlad complained. "There are loads around here. I suggest you drop us off, Cecile, and circle around, while we explore on foot."

"Sounds like a good idea." She glanced in the rear-view mirror. "There's a car up my arse, and parking is shit around here."

"It's not shit. It's bloody impossible."

The main roads didn't allow for parking, but there were a few public carparks close by.

Vlad craned to look over the seat into the back of the van. "I think we should get out, guys, and let Cecile cruise around. She can be our getaway driver. What do you think?"

"Good idea," Monroe grunted. "But I need to put the damn gun under my jacket. Getting arrested is not in my plans."

"Where are we?" Mads asked, unable to see the street since the rear had no windows.

"Just turned onto the road. Jake said not far from the market, so it must be one of these restaurants." They had just passed Brixton Market, and the area, despite the late hour, was still reasonably busy. "I'm sure we'll scent something."

Mads's eyes glinted in the low light. "Great. I'm ready."

Cecile gave a dissatisfied grunt. "Fine. I'll keep driving, but let me know when you've found it, and I'll try to park close by." She pulled to the side, double-parking, and in seconds they had piled out onto the street, and Cecile drove off.

"Let's split up," Vlad suggested. "Me and Mads will go this way." He pointed away from the market. "You two head back that way. If you pick up the scent, *call and wait*." He said it specifically to Jax, who had the glint of bloodlust in his eye.

"Of course," Monroe said. "Let's get this done."

The scents and noise of Coldharbour Lane were overwhelming. Not only could Vlad smell curry, but other food scents—Thai, Chinese, and classic fish and chips. In addition, there was the smell of rubbish, perfume, sweat—the ever-present flavour of life. The scent of petrol and diesel didn't help the search, either.

Mads looked none the worse for his earlier injuries, and he paced alongside Vlad. They looked alike, but Mads wasn't as blond as he was, and he was a fraction shorter. They had both left Denmark looking to break away from their old pack connections, and a father who was rigidly sticking to old-fashioned pack values. They had started a new life in London several years earlier, and the city, and the Storm Moon Pack, was now home.

"You know," Vlad said thoughtfully as he peered down a narrow side-passage, "there'll be an alley of some sort running behind these places, or small yards. Somewhere for the rubbish and deliveries. That would be a good way to enter it."

"Let's find the place first." Mads's eyes were hard as he said, "I'll cross over, check the other side."

They progressed slowly for a few minutes, threading through pedestrians, with heads lifted and eyes narrowed as they searched. But then Vlad scented the odd smell they had found with Kane's body. *Pûcas.*

He froze, trying to narrow down the direction, and noted his brother doing the same across the street. Mads pointed. Only a few doors down was a busy Indian restaurant, and beyond that a large hardware shop, closed for the night. But it looked to have a narrow alley next to it, wide enough for a vehicle. *That would make it easy to unload a hostage.*

Vlad pulled his phone out, gesturing for Mads to wait, and he quickly texted Monroe, Cecile, and Jax before crossing the road to join his brother. They waited silently, aware their own shifter scent and voices could give them away, too. Within minutes, Jax and Monroe had joined them, and Cecile passed them in the van, a nod of acknowledgement as she slowed and continued around again. It was too risky for her to pull into the side alley, but hopefully she would find somewhere close by.

They didn't need to discuss their strategy. It was a simple one. Break in, effect a rescue, and get out. In the alley, there were no vehicles in sight, but there was a side entrance, and another alley at the far end that seemed to run parallel to the road.

They progressed quickly and silently. Monroe, Mads, and Jax waited by the battered side door covered in peeling paint. Vlad continued down the alley to check out the rear. He paused, dismayed. It wasn't what he expected. There was a warren of back alleys here, leading off a large square concrete area that multiple buildings backed onto. Alleys that no doubt led to the surrounding main roads. Unfortunately, light spilled from various open doorways—the entrances to the restaurants' kitchens, including the neighbouring Indian one. *Bollocks*.

He returned to the others, speaking in a whisper. "There's a fair amount of activity around the back, but if anything goes badly, that should help cover our escape. Ready?" They nodded, remaining silent, and he tried the door. As expected, it was locked, but now that they were up close, the scent of therians, Pûcas, and Domino was strong. As was the scent of blood.

A quick inspection showed that all windows were locked tight, so while Monroe prepared to break the door down, Vlad and Mads quickly stripped and changed into their wolf. Once through, they had to act quickly. Vlad's senses expanded as soon as he was a wolf. The sharp scent of blood and fear overwhelmed the other scents, but he was pretty sure that wasn't Domino's blood he could smell.

Monroe settled his shoulder to the door, and smashed it hard. It cracked but didn't yield; the second hit smashed the door back, splintering the frame. Monroe raised his tranquiliser gun and raced inside, the rest of the group right behind him.

To their left was the shop, and Jax peeled away to inspect its dark interior, while the others raced to the right, down a short corridor. A quick sweep showed that the small kitchen and toilet at the back was empty, but a door led to a set of stairs leading up to the first floor, and down to a basement. The scent led downward, and this time Vlad and Mads took the lead.

Their immediate surroundings were ominously quiet, but the corridor stretched ahead, far longer than Vlad expected. It obviously extended behind the main shop to the courtyard beyond. With every step, Domino's scent grew stronger. Vlad and Mads progressed on silent paws, hackles raised. But up ahead, noise filtered to them—raised voices and shouts. Wary of attack but worried for Domino's safety, they quickened their pace.

And then a yell echoed from ahead, followed by pounding feet. Someone had heard them arrive.

Twenty-Four

Hunter paced the hotel room, checking the time again. "They're late."

"Chill out," Ollie instructed, sitting on the end of Hunter's bed. "They might be waiting for the guard to change, or something else. We have no idea."

Tommy was at the window, lifting the curtain to look out on the carpark at the rear of the building. "I don't like it. Feels like a setup to me."

"Well, we haven't got any other options," Hunter pointed out, annoyed. "Unless you have a grand plan!"

Tommy snorted with derision. "I don't do plans. I act."

"I know, you idiot hothead."

Ollie snapped. "Shut up. This isn't helping."

They were in the twin room that Hunter was sharing with Tommy, a few hours after having eaten dinner that was as good as the rich aromas suggested it would be. Although, it was an uncomfortable experience. Hector had left a contingent of shifters to watch them, and while to any casual passer-by nothing untoward was happening, it was all too obvious to Hunter and his companions. They were watched with a bristling intensity that Hunter refused to let interrupt his enjoyment of the food.

Besides, Ollie was an alpha, and that meant he carried more power. Their guards shuffled, uncomfortable with every long stare Ollie gave them, and although they refused to back off, Hunter imagined it would take all of their energy to stay put. *Good.*

Tommy finally dropped the curtain and turned to face them. "I told you we should have brought more wolves."

"Shut up," Ollie said brusquely, and then he cocked an ear and stood up. "Someone is coming."

Two people approached the door, and Hunter recognised the scent of the one who had been in the reception area, before a soft tap announced their arrival.

At a nod from Ollie, Hunter opened the door, and the two men slipped inside. The first was the shaven-headed, hard-eyed shifter from the lobby, the other was lean, dark-haired, and bearded with high, sharp cheekbones.

"Sorry we're late," the first man said, eyeing them warily. "It was hard to get upstairs unseen. A couple of the pack provided a slight distraction for us. Nothing untoward." He grinned. "An argument about a woman."

Ollie wasn't amused, and he stepped toward them. "What's going on? Notes passed in a key card? Is this an uprising?"

"Nothing so exciting," the bearded man said. "Just a disagreement as to how to deal with Emyr." He held his hand out. "I'm Regan, and this here is Alastair."

They shook hands as Ollie made the introductions, and Hunter asked, "You know where Emyr is?"

"Aye, and it's not easy to reach him, especially with the weather closing in." He jerked his head upward. "He's in a stone hut in the Cairngorms, a bit wild-eyed after the shifter deaths. I gather you want to speak to him, correct?"

Ollie nodded. "Just some questions. Three people in our pack were killed, and we suspect it's because of something that happened in the past. The people who died all appear to be connected to a place, a good many years ago now. We think someone is hunting them down."

Regan frowned. "Any idea why?"

"We think it's connected to a theft from an auction room in London. It seems bizarre, but we hope Emyr can answer important questions."

"His old pack, you say?" Alastair said, suspicious.

"Yes, and Pûcas are connected, too. They killed our friends, and attacked us in Cumbria."

"We've come across them. They like the wild up here, although we have little to do with them. Strange things, they are."

"What about therians?" Hunter asked. "Any problems with them?"

Regan grimaced. "Not yet. Should we expect to?"

"Perhaps." Ollie ran a hand through his hair, exasperated. "Things are confusing right now. That's why we want Emyr—for answers."

"Good," Alastair said, "so do we. It'll be a tough slog into the mountains tonight, though you all look fit enough."

"We're used to Cumbrian moors, we'll be just fine," Hunter answered, not liking having his abilities questioned.

"And what's in this for you?" Tommy asked, a growl in his voice. "You'll get in a lot of trouble with your alpha, surely."

Alastair answered for both of them. "We don't like shifters dying, and something about Emyr has always felt off to me. And Hector, well, he's a selfish wolf. Doesn't like to get involved in other people's problems, even though they could be desperate. I don't like that. Many of us don't. We shouldn't turn our back on fellow packs."

"How many are with you?" Ollie asked. "Because there was a fair bit of hostility down there earlier."

"Another half a dozen. It's a big pack though, and the rest are with Hector. But I'm pretty sure we've covered our tracks tonight. We just need to get out there."

"And how do we do that?"

Regan grinned. "The positives of a small town are that we all have connections. My cousin works in the kitchen. She's not a shifter, and loathes Hector. She's more than happy to help. She's due off shift, and has pulled her car to the back door. We're all getting in, and she'll drop us off down the road. Easy. After that, we're on foot."

Ollie glanced at Hunter and Tommy, and both nodded in agreement. It was the best chance they were likely to get. "Fine. Let's go."

Domino couldn't get over how much Riggs looked like Kane—or would have, if he wasn't bloodied and bruised.

He was tied to a chair with nylon rope, arms lashed behind the chair back, his legs strapped to the metal chair legs. His chest was bare and streaked with blood that had oozed from his many cuts there. He had been beaten badly, and yet he still grinned like a madman, his teeth bloodstained.

"You can keep hitting me, you therian scum, but I won't tell you a thing. You'll end up killing me, and I don't fucking care."

That earned him another powerful punch from a therian also stripped to his waist. Domino recognised him as one of the four from the pub. He was enjoying this. He had a feral glint in his eye that showed how much he enjoyed inflicting pain on others.

Riggs had visible scars that had healed recently. They had obviously been beating him for a while, and as a shifter he would heal, and then they would start all over again. For now, Riggs hadn't seen her. They were in the doorway of his blood-spattered room, another concrete shell like the one she had been kept in.

"Rox, wait!" Her captor stepped forward, pushing Domino ahead of him.

Both stared at her. Riggs's eyes hardened, and he spit blood onto the floor.

The therian, however, smiled even broader, his eyes sweeping over her. "Nice one, Warner. This will be fun."

Warner ignored him and addressed Riggs. "We'll kill her if you don't tell us where to take the crown. And I'll make it slow, understand?"

"I don't even know who that is!" Riggs said, scowling. "Why should I care about her?"

"Because I'll kill her in front of you. Can you handle that?" He smirked. "I don't think so."

"Ignore them, Riggs," Domino said quickly. "Whatever secret you're hiding, they shouldn't know. They don't deserve to."

Riggs's eyes flickered to her and back to Warner. "She has nothing to do with this."

"She does now. She's been nosing around in our business. Her and the rest of her pack. This will be a message for them all to back off."

"You half-witted moron," Domino said. "You're inviting a storm of trouble you will not survive."

Warner punched her, and she staggered back, her head whipping to the side, stars exploding in front of her eyes. She slammed into the wall, breathing heavily. *Wow. He would regret that.* Her wolf was rising, her senses already magnifying.

The therians were ignoring her, focussing only on Riggs, as if she was a useless piece of meat. It gave her time for her vision to recover, and she studied the room quickly. There was another chair, a grubby, thin mattress on the floor, and a bloodstained blanket. *Not much in the way of weapons.*

But there was also a rusty pipe sticking from the wall with a jagged edge, a couple of feet away. *The remnant of a ripped-out sink, perhaps.* While the men engaged in a pissing contest, she feigned a stagger, and edged in front of it. She slumped down the wall, pretending to be more injured than she was, and started to rub the rope around her wrists across the jagged edge.

"So," Warner continued, "What's it to be?"

"You killed my brother and my family. There's nothing else you can do to make me talk."

"Fine. Let's see how you feel once we start on Domino. Felix, grab the chair, and we'll tie her up, too."

But as Felix swung the chair around to place it next to Riggs, an almighty series of howls echoed down the passageway.

Her pack had arrived.

Vlad charged forward, Mads next to him, meeting the advancing shifter full-on. *A tiger.*

Behind them, Monroe fired his tranquilliser gun, and Vlad kept low. Two darts thudded into the tiger's chest. His pace slowed, and then he dropped to the ground.

Vlad leaped over it, but there was no respite. Another creature was racing up the hall. But this wasn't a therian, it was a Pûca. Its strange scent preceded it. It wasn't shifting, either. Vlad barely had time to take it in. Its gangling figure, all legs and arms, was covered in thick fur, and it moved like a whirlwind. Sharp teeth lined its large jaw, and huge ears stood upright on its head.

Vlad had heard all about Domino's encounter with them, and knew he had to strike fast if he was to have any chance of success. Vlad crunched into it. They both hit the side wall, rolled down the corridor, and in a tangle of limbs and teeth, crashed through a doorway, smashing into old chairs.

He felt teeth tear into his shoulder, but he gripped the Pûca's arm. Bone snapped between his jaws, and the creature hissed. It was strong, its muscles like steel, but Vlad swung his weight over it, pinning it beneath his huge paws, trying to bite its neck.

It struck back, huge claws at the end of its limbs. Suddenly Vlad was airborne, smashing into the wall, and the Pûca launched itself on him again. Frantic, Vlad twisted, springing upward and under the Pûca. He pounded its body to the ground, where it sprawled, neck exposed. Vlad ripped it out, flinging aside the flesh as the creature shuddered and died, and he raced back into the corridor.

Mads was ahead of him, fighting a therian, their bodies twisting and writhing as each tried to kill the other. Behind him, he could hear Monroe's tranquilliser gun popping, and the frenzy of snarling and snapping. *More shifters.* Vlad was about to race in to assist his brother, when an almighty howl signified his victory.

He focussed instead on finding Domino. He slowed, edging forward, the scents of therians and Pûcas almost overwhelming. The passageway snaked left and right, and although Vlad had a good sense of direction, down in these windowless confines, he couldn't work out where he was in relation to the street above. Empty rooms opened on either side, and then he caught a strong scent of Domino ahead.

Before he could advance, a therian appeared at the end of the corridor, raised a shotgun, and fired. With a split second to react, he dived through the doorway to his right.

Jax raced into view and launched himself at the therian. Vlad scrambled after him.

The therian should have shifted, rather than use a gun. Jax was too quick for him. His huge paw ripped out his throat, killing him instantly. From the sounds behind Vlad, the rest of the team were catching up now.

He and Jax burst into a large, central room and immediately separated to either side of the doorway. The female therian from the group who had attacked them in the street was in the corridor ahead, shooting at them as she made a stand. She wasn't carrying a shotgun, but some kind of handgun.

In the seconds before he scrambled for cover, Vlad caught a glimpse of a fight behind her. It was Domino, and another wolf-shifter. He could smell her, and her blood. *A fresh wound.*

Keeping to the perimeter, Vlad raced to the door and the therian guarding it. Under pressure from the two wolves attacking from different directions, she shot wildly to either side. It kept her distracted enough not to notice Monroe arriving behind them.

He fired the shotgun he'd taken from the dead therian. The shot caught her mid-chest and sent her sprawling on her back. Jax reached her first. The scent of blood was strong now, and the pack responded accordingly. It made them more vicious, more focussed.

More deadly.

The woman was already near death, but Jax ended her quickly, tearing her throat out before leaping toward the others. Vlad was right behind him.

As soon as the howls reached Domino, Warner grabbed her elbow, and thrust her toward the door before she could free her arms.

"Rox, time to go. Let's get to the van. Bring *him*!"

Rox swiftly cut the ties to Riggs's legs and chest, leaving his arms bound behind him, then hauled Riggs to the door. But Riggs had been immobile for too long, and he staggered, collapsing against Rox so they both stumbled. Domino seized her moment.

She stamped down hard on Warner's foot, twisted, and brought her knee up into his groin. He turned, and she kneed his thigh instead. He punched her, and she crashed into the wall while he ran out of the door.

Rox, half-staggering under the weight of Riggs, thrust him off and followed Warner into the corridor. Although winded, Domino hauled herself to her feet and followed them.

Vlad streaked past her, racing toward Warner and Rox who had made it through a huge steel door at the end of the corridor. Monroe shouldered past her, gun raised. But both were too slow.

The door slammed shut.

While Vlad and Monroe charged at the door and tried to get through it, Domino turned her attention to Riggs, who was only half conscious on the floor.

"My brother's pack, I presume?" he said, words slurring. "Can we get out of here? There are more of them, and they'll be here soon. We won't beat all of them. Not yet, anyway."

Twenty-Five

The bitter wind carried the scent of snow, as did the thick clouds swirling above Hunter and his companions as they raced along a steep valley that led away from the River Dee.

Regan's cousin, Kirsty, a chirpy woman with a big laugh, hadn't shown any sign of worry at sneaking three strange men out of The Balmoral Arms. She had a large hatchback that stank of dogs. She threw a thick blanket over them, covered with dog hair, which helped to mask their scent. However, with so many shifters around, and the fact that Regan was also in the car, supposedly getting a lift home, they pulled out of the carpark with ease.

They didn't get out from under the blanket until they reached a small place called Crathie on the north side of the River Dee, where Alastair waited for them with another shifter, a woman called Greer. Leaving their clothes in Alastair's car, they shifted and started their trek. They were going to a small stone building that apparently had only three rooms. A living area and kitchen, a bedroom, and a bathroom. It belonged to Hector, but was used by the pack when necessary, especially when they needed a place to rest and hide. A rough track led to it from a minor road, and it was mostly gravel that only a four-wheel drive could access. Most shifters approached as a wolf. The only reason a car was used was for supplies.

The crisp air was invigorating, and after the cramped conditions of the drive and the tension at the hotel, Hunter relished the chance to explore. There were many other scents. Deer, squirrels, hares, birds, many small mammals, shifters, and the occasional therian—hopefully not a therian who was involved with this whole situation.

Alastair led the way, and Hunter hoped they could trust them. They could certainly find their way back to Ballater from here, but if he was leading them to a trap, they might never get the chance. Hunter was suddenly very glad to have his huge friend, Tommy, and Ollie the alpha with him.

Their plan was simple. They just wanted to talk to Emyr. Alastair said that he should be alone. No one thought they needed to guard him, because it was so remote. In fact, according to Regan, Emyr had insisted that he didn't want company, and Hector had honoured his wishes.

But as they progressed up the ever narrowing and steep valley, finally cresting the top to enjoy the vast sight of the snow-topped Cairngorms ahead, Hunter saw a bird wheeling in the sky. They all halted to admire the stunning view, but Hunter couldn't shake off his unease. *Was it a regular bird above them, a therian, or a Pûca?*

Alastair yipped, drawing their attention ahead. A thick wood crawled up the flanks of the hillside, a light fall of snow dusting their branches.

Their destination was close. Alastair raced away, setting the pace again.

Maverick studied Riggs's bloodied face and body, his black eyes, cuts, and bruises, and behind it all, he recognised Kane's features, and ached for his loss.

"I'm sorry we didn't find you sooner," he told him. "We were too slow."

Riggs shrugged. "You had no idea, and that was the point. No one was supposed to know about the missing crown and that damn box."

"I was one of Kane's best friends. He could have trusted me."

"He couldn't. He wasn't allowed to. I'm sorry." Riggs dropped his gaze to his whiskey, his second. The first had been drunk all too quickly.

There were only a few people in Maverick's flat with him and Riggs: Domino, Arlo, and Monroe. They sat on the sofa in the dark living room, lit only by one lamp and the fire in the wood burner, their mood subdued. However, Maverick had to confess to a certain level of peace now that Domino was back. Although also bloodied and bruised, she appeared none the worse for her short imprisonment. Everyone else was downstairs in the club, cleaning up their injuries and watching their prisoner. *Bloody Jake. What the hell were they supposed to do with him?*

Maverick focussed on Riggs again. He had so many questions, but he'd start with the easiest. "What happened on Friday night?"

"Kane had been in touch with me only the day before, telling me that he'd heard about the auction, and we needed to retrieve an item. A very important item. He didn't mention what it was over the phone, but he didn't need to. The crown had been missing for years. Stolen." He sighed heavily, leaning back into the cushioned chair. "The pack searched for that for a long time, but found nothing. It was as if it had vanished into thin air."

"And the box?"

"Important, but nowhere near as important as the crown." He stared into the fire, his gaze vacant. "And all because of some crazy spell."

Maverick couldn't believe that Harlan had actually been right. "Is this really to do with the fairy tale? *The Wolf King and The Witch Queen*?"

Riggs laughed, and then winced, holding his ribs. "Ouch. Yes, it is. Crazy, isn't it? But for me and Kane, we always knew the truth of it. Accepted it completely. It was our legacy to guard it." His smile vanished, and his eyes were haunted again. "But in one night, that honour vanished, and our pack was a disgrace. We had lost what had been preserved for centuries."

Maverick exchanged a glance of disbelief with Domino and Arlo. "I have to ask, what's the big deal with this? An ancient crown from an old wolf king."

"Not any wolf king! *The* Wolf King!" Riggs's hand tightened on his glass. "You don't get it, do you? It's all real. The crown was made of the blood and bodies of our enemies. Because while our kind may rub along all right now, at one point in the distant past, we were at war. The crown is made from a stag's antlers, the fur of a hare, feathers of a bird, and a bear claw, all of it bound with fey magic, tipped with gold and silver, and studded with gems. Whoever wears it gains the power of the alpha—the Ultimate Alpha. Strong, super senses, fast healing—virtually immortal."

"But wolves don't wear crowns!" Maverick scoffed. "We usually fight in our wolf, and if I was going into battle, I wouldn't wear a bloody crown, either."

"I'm not explaining this well," Riggs said, shaking his head. "The Wolf King defeated his enemies, and then had the crown made for him. It was a symbol of his power and strength, and indicated that all should bow before him. He had it *made*. It didn't confer power to him, it bound *his* power into the crown. Of course he didn't wear it while fighting—it was a symbol of victory afterward."

"You've seen it," Arlo said, eyes glinting. "Did it really have that power?"

"Oh, yes. It resonated with it. But only to shifters. I doubt humans would feel the power. Not properly, anyway."

"What about other shifters?" Monroe asked. He had been standing at the window watching the road below, but now he focussed fully on Riggs. "Do they sense its power?"

"Definitely. That's why it was stolen."

Domino frowned. "I've got to be honest. I'm a bit baffled. If we, wolf-shifters, don't know about this crown except as a fairy tale—well, all except for your pack, of course—then how do therians and other shifters know about it? How do they value it when we don't?"

"Because of Pûcas. They are pure fey creatures with long memories and longer lives. I'm honestly not sure how they came to know about the crown's whereabouts at Burton and Knight, or how they came to be involved with the therians, but they are. They didn't talk much while beating me." Riggs's hand shook, more with anger than weakness, Maverick thought, and he placed his empty glass on a side table. "I need to heal. A good night's sleep should do it. These wounds aren't deep. They made sure of that—the longer to keep beating me. Then I'll hunt them down, find the crown, and make them pay for what they did to my pack. My family..."

Domino squeezed his hand and looked to Maverick for support as she said, "You won't be alone. We'll help."

Maverick didn't hesitate. "Of course we will. But, if they have the crown, why were they beating you?"

"Because they need to know where the Wolf King's body is. The legend says that in order to wear the crown and assume the power it holds, it must be done where the Wolf King rests. The fairy tale was true. He fought another therian-shifter, one who commanded forests. It was not a fair battle. Like all therians, he was a trickster, and the Wolf King was killed—most of the pack, too."

"And the Witch Queen tried to save him?" Arlo asked, looking more excited than Maverick had ever seen him. "To bring him back to life?"

"That was the plan. The witch entombed their bodies within the forest, and cast the whole place under a spell. I have never seen it, but it's supposed to be petrified. The wolves, the forest, everything... A perpetual memorial to a fallen king."

"And the witch?"

"Long gone too, I believe. It's quite the tale of woe and lost love, isn't it?"

"And your connection?" Maverick asked, sure he knew the answer.

"We're the descendants of that pack. Some convoluted connections over time, admittedly. Our pack is so paranoid that our births are registered all over the country."

"Wow!" Monroe said, his normally strident voice hushed. "Guarding the old king. Bloody hell. That's insane."

Riggs gave a sad, resigned laugh. "You know, I was a kid when we left. I didn't really get it, but my father drummed it into us over the years, all while insisting we keep it a secret. I've always thought it was a bit nuts, to be honest, and then this happened."

"And the heirs of the Wolf King. What about them?" Arlo asked.

"There are none. They are all dead."

Maverick shook his head, trying to clear his woolly thoughts, and focussing only on the present. "So, they wanted you to tell them where the petrified forest is? Somewhere in *this* world?"

Riggs smiled enigmatically. "Sort of. The therians and Pûcas don't know where it is, but I do. Well, I have a vague idea of where it is," he qualified. "Only one person knew exactly, and I have no idea where he is or even whether he's still alive." He shrugged. "The alpha of our pack back then. Emyr. He made sure to disappear. I think more than anyone he was ashamed of what had happened."

"Holy shit," Maverick said, realising how much danger Ollie and his team could be in. "Friends of your father are in Scotland right now. They've found him. Or are close, at least."

Riggs's voice rose in panic. "The Pûcas have been searching for him. That's another thing they wanted out of me—his location. If they find him..."

Maverick was already reaching for his phone, but knew there was probably no way to reach them now.

Hunter halted next to Ollie and the other wolves at the edge of a clearing in a dense forest of pines, a small stone lodge ahead, smoke idling from its only chimney.

The scent of pine resin, earth, woodsmoke, and snow hung on the air.

And the smell of wolf-shifter. *Emyr.*

Regan nudged Greer, gesturing that they should circle the cabin, and Ollie told Tommy to join them. Communicating as wolves was in part a mental connection, and part gesture. It was the smallest things—a look in the eye, a nudge, a cuff, a growl. It was as easy as talking as a human, once you got used to it. As a juvenile wolf, it was hard, but the more you shifted and hunted together, the easier it became. That's why hunting as a pack was so important. It bonded you as wolf and human.

Hunter was glad Ollie wanted him to go into the cabin. That way, even if there was some kind of trap, at least there were two of them in there. Tommy was big enough and mean enough to hold his own outside. But so far, there was no sign they should be worried. Emyr's was the only scent present.

Alastair led them to the door, but they were barely halfway across the clearing when it opened and a tall, grizzled man with a huge beard appeared in the doorway, a shotgun in his hands. "No further, Alastair. I have nothing to say, not to you or your friends."

Alastair immediately shifted back to human, but Ollie and Hunter remained as wolves, standing to either side of him. "There's no need for the gun, Emyr. We only want to talk."

"Are you deaf? I said I have nothing to say."

"We've travelled a long way to see you. Wolves have died. These shifters say you have answers they need."

Emyr raised the shotgun and pointed it at Alastair. "Don't try me. I will shoot."

Hunter lowered himself to a crouch, wondering how much distance he could cover before Emyr could reload. He was not leaving without talking, and from the smell of fear rolling off Emyr, he had a story to tell.

Alastair raised his hands in a sign of surrender. "If you shoot me, you'll have to shoot all of us. Six of us. You'll never kill us all before one of us gets to you, but if you do survive, you'll be cast out of the pack and will probably start a pack war. You can tell there are three strange wolves here. Do you seriously want that?"

"Hector will never cast me out."

"Because you keep his secrets?" Alastair laughed. "Someone will challenge him, and he'll lose—eventually. Let's not go there, Emyr. Let us in."

Emyr didn't budge, except to raise the gun to his eye. "Leave, now."

Suddenly, a flurry of movement to the right caught Emyr's attention, and he swung around and fired. While he was distracted, Hunter sprang at him, Ollie right alongside, but they weren't as quick as Tommy. Human, and completely naked, he sprinted across the roof and dropped on Emyr from above. They clattered to the ground, the shotgun spinning out of Emyr's grasp, as Tommy's fist knocked him almost senseless.

"That'll teach you to point a gun at another shifter, you little shit!" Tommy yelled, red-faced and yellow-eyed as he raised his fist to hit him again.

Ollie shifted back to human and pulled him back. "No more punches, Tommy. We want him alive."

"Just one fucking more!"

"*No!*"

Tommy, unable to meet Ollie's commanding stare, kept his eyes down and rose to his feet, but he dragged Emyr with him. The old man's eye was already swelling, and his nose was twisted, blood pouring out of it. He tried to break free, but it was obvious he was still dazed.

Alastair shouted, "Regan? Greer?" They both loped out of the forest, uninjured but snarling at Emyr. "Nice moves, guys. You too, Tommy." He smirked. "I certainly wouldn't want you landing on me. Especially naked."

"That's not what the ladies say," Tommy shot back.

Ollie cocked an eyebrow at Alastair as he wrestled Emyr from Tommy's grip. "He wishes." Alastair laughed as he supported Emyr's other side. He could hardly stand upright, but despite his age, he was still a big man. "Tommy, you're back on patrol. Hunter, inside. Grab the shotgun—just in case."

Hunter shifted, picked up the gun, and followed the three men into the stone-built building, shutting the door behind him. The heat inside felt stifling after the biting cold outside, but Hunter was glad of it. It had been a long trek into the foothills of the mountains, and they had crossed racing streams, rocky hillsides dusted with snow, and dense forest. He had checked overhead a few times, but hadn't seen the bird of prey from earlier. It had allayed his worries...slightly.

The door opened into one large room, with a fireplace on the right, and the kitchen at the back. It was comfortably furnished with an old sofa and sagging armchairs. A couple of doors led off to the bedroom and bathroom. There was no running water here, and no electricity, except what was provided by the generator. The heat was provided by the blazing fire in the huge fireplace. Hunter knew that the toilet was a compost one. This was very much living with the basics.

Ollie shoved Emyr onto a chair by the fire, and Alastair disappeared into the bedroom, returning with a handful of clothes. "Here you go, guys."

Hunter and Ollie grabbed t-shirts and tracksuit bottoms. While shifters were comfortable enough around each other naked, once inside they automatically preferred to dress. Hunter then headed to the window and picked up the shotgun. Spotting shells on the table, he reloaded it, just in case.

"Right," Alastair said, sitting opposite Emyr, who was now stemming his nosebleed with a towel, "what's going on?"

Ollie watched, arms folded, eyes fixed on the old alpha.

"Screw you, Alastair."

Alastair leaned in. "I can smell your fear, Emyr. I can see it in your eyes. As soon as those men were killed, you vanished. You know what's happening. You may as well tell us."

"I know nothing. You have a vivid imagination."

Alastair gestured to Ollie. "I'll let Ollie spell it out for you."

Ollie pulled another chair up and sat across from Emyr. "I know about the disbanded pack from Wales. I know you were in it, and were the alpha at one point. I also know that the men who were killed were in that pack. A family—Harry, his wife, and his non-shifter, harmless daughter—were killed, too. They were members of *my pack*. His son, Kane, is dead, his other son missing. You remember them, I'm sure. I've seen a picture of you with them."

Emyr's eyes flickered, trying to look away, but Ollie was exerting his alpha dominance now, power rolling out of him. "Save your energy, you coward. Why were they killed?"

"I don't know!"

"You're a very bad liar. Whoever killed them is looking for you. You know it, or else why are you here, all holed up alone in the middle of nowhere?" He moved closer, his face inches from Emyr. "I know about the crown and the box of relics. The *origins of shifters*." He let the words hang between them as Emyr edged back in the chair.

Hunter already loathed Emyr, and he could understand why Alastair didn't trust him. In his youth, he was probably a bully, a blusterer, using his large frame to intimidate. That's how some alphas obtained their position. Many didn't deserve it. They craved power and dominance, and it was ugly. Always ugly. But Harry never spoke of him. Never badmouthed him. Perhaps that's why Hector liked Emyr. Men like that always stuck together. Alastair had said Emyr kept Hector's secrets. He could imagine that only too well. They probably kept each other's secrets. Hunter shook his head as the thought entered his mind. *Of course. Hector must know what was going on, or why else try so hard to keep them away?*

While Ollie outlined what he knew, continuing to goad Emyr, Hunter studied the clearing. Tommy was circling at the edge of the trees, while Regan paced closer. Greer was behind the house; Hunter could smell her. So far, nothing else stirred out there. He stared at the group by the fire again, noting Ollie's tense shoulders and the gleam in Alastair's eyes. He had his own agenda here. *A wish to overthrow Hector as alpha, perhaps.* Maybe undermining and exposing Emyr was part of that. *Always politics.*

He focused on the conversation again as Ollie asked, "What's the significance of those relics? Why do therians and Pûcas want them?"

"You have a vivid imagination, boy," Emyr said, eyes shuttered. "It's nothing."

"People don't die over *nothing*. They were your friends once. Your pack. Don't you have any compassion? Any guilt for what has happened? Any wish for revenge?"

Emyr sagged in the chair, defiance ebbing, his gaze still fixed on Ollie. "Of course I do. They were family. It was a good life."

The silence in the cabin was profound as a note of regret entered Emyr's voice for the first time.

"What went wrong?" Ollie asked, voice soft. But he didn't break eye contact, keeping Emyr focussed only on him.

Hunter felt it too, the pull to an alpha, as did Alastair. He didn't move either, both transfixed on the conversation and Ollie's commanding voice.

Emyr resisted. "Don't try that on me. I was an alpha once."

"*Was*. You're not anymore. And you're weakened by failure. By hiding. You carry a burden. It's time you shared it."

Emyr finally answered, as if the truth was being dragged from the deepest reserves of his being. "I went wrong. I spoiled it all."

"How?"

"I split the pack up after the relics had been stolen. There was nothing to guard anymore—not really. Except no one actually stole the relics. Well, no one except me. I sold them."

Hunter held his breath. It felt as if the forest held its breath, too.

"*You* sold them?" Ollie repeated. "Why?"

"I gamble. That's my problem. I had no money, and I owed so much... So very much. I saw a way out and I took it." He snivelled, a mixture of snot and blood, his inner defences gone. His face fell into his hands. "I sold our heritage. I betrayed our entire history. But I didn't think it mattered. I sold it to a human who had no idea of its significance. He said he would keep it a secret. Hidden forever. I didn't expect that this would happen!"

Disgust swelled through Hunter. Emyr was pathetic, even more despicable in tears than he was as a defiant blusterer.

Ollie kept his head, though. "What history? Why do other shifters want these relics? Why kill for them?"

"They need the location, but only I know that now. The second in command died years ago. I have never shared it." He lifted his gazed defiantly. "That's one thing I didn't sell. The crown is useless without a location."

"Holy shit," Ollie muttered to Alastair. "This is unreal." He turned back to Emyr, his voice tight with anger. "You knew what was going on and you hid! Do you know how much I hate you right now? You're pathetic. A disgrace. And so is Hector for hiding you. He will be judged for this." Ollie grabbed Emyr's jaw in a steely grip. "What's the significance of the location?"

"They can use the crown to gain dominance over all shifters. We would become subjects."

"I don't bloody think so," Alastair said, snorting dubiously.

"You would have no choice," Emyr answered. "But it's okay! They don't know where to go. One without the other is worthless." He looked pleased with himself. "See? That's why I'm here. Leave me here, alone, and it will be fine. I'll take the place to my grave."

"No. We need to find this place, and the crown, and end any threat for good," Ollie said. "The fact that it's out there now means that the thieves will keep searching. There is no other option. Where is the place?"

"I won't tell." This was a hell of a time for Emyr to find his backbone.

And then an ear-splitting howl interrupted their conversation. Hunter snapped back to the window, and saw shapes flitting through the clearing.

They were under attack.

Twenty-Six

G rey finished his patrol of Storm Moon, and checked in with John on the main door.

"Everything seems quiet," he said, noting his watchful stance. "I doubt anyone will attack while we're open."

"I agree." John stepped aside and opened the door, smiling broadly as a young couple entered the bar. "Evening."

They smiled and nodded, saying "Hey, John," as they passed inside.

"Regulars?" Grey asked, thinking he recognised them.

"Like clockwork. Love the cocktails." His smile vanished. "Yeah, there's too much going on for anyone to risk an attack. Plus, we have a very heavy shifter presence."

"I called in anyone who was free," Grey said, recalling the many phone calls he'd made earlier. "They were happy to help."

"It would be good to get rid of Jake, though."

Grey sighed. "You're right. That's next on my agenda."

He made to leave, but John said, "You're sure Domino is okay?"

"Absolutely. I saw her briefly before she went up to Maverick's flat. She'll be fine."

"Good. The place isn't the same without Domino."

"No, it's not. Call me if you're worried about anything."

"Will do, boss."

As Grey made his way to the club in the basement, he pondered on the staff's fondness for Domino. He realised that although she might not be the pack second, and everyone liked Arlo, if anything happened to Maverick, she would be most shifters' pick for alpha. *Interesting.* Not that he'd discussed that with anyone else, but he knew it.

In the club, someone was playing music using the DJ's station, a subdued dub track that only added to the tension in the room. Half a dozen security staff were gathered by the bar at the far end, and Morgana was with them. Cecile was by the stage, leaning against the wall, arms folded across her chest as she watched Jake, who was still bound in chains.

Because Cecile had been the driver, she wasn't injured like the others, but she stared daggers at Jake. Grey headed to her side. "Is he behaving?"

"I guess so." Her French accent was strong as her words dripped with disdain. "He is an odious man."

Jake, aware of their scrutiny, shouted, "What? I helped, didn't I? You found her. She's fine."

Cecile stepped forward, fists clenched. "If you had talked to her in the first place, we wouldn't have had to find her!" She glared at Grey. "Let me beat him up. Just a little."

"It's tempting, but best not. He did come through, though, and Maverick offered him a deal."

"Yeah, he did!" Jake said, belligerently. "What's going on, Grey? Gonna keep me chained up all night? I think I should have a drink, too, right?"

Grey eyeballed him. "Don't push your luck. I need to check with Maverick, but hopefully, I'll kick you out of here in the next ten minutes."

Jake paled. "You can't turf me out! I'll be in danger. Warner knows you've got me! I need protection. Maverick's protection. 'E said so. I'm part of your pack now." His swagger had come back, and it was intensely irritating.

Cecile exploded. "You are so not in our pack! I would rather kill you first!"

Grey laid a restraining hand on her arm. "Jake, you're the least of Warner's concerns right now. He'll be on the run for a while." *With the crown, while he searched for whatever it was that he needed.*

Jake squinted up at him. "What? Is he? And the others?"

"Yep, with his pal, Rox. His two little friends are dead, and a few Pûcas, too. But I gather there are more, so maybe you should keep a low profile over the next few days. As long as *we* can find you, obviously…"

"Obviously," Jake blustered.

Morgana appeared at Grey's side, having arrived so silently he almost jumped. She drew him away so they could talk privately. "Can I leave, too? I don't think there's anything else I can help with."

"Your spell. Can he shift again?"

"Maybe in another hour. It still holds for now." She cast him an appraising glance. "It would be unfair to throw him out before he can shift. He might need to protect himself."

Grey groaned and rolled his shoulders. "Yeah, we would be leaving him defenceless. Give me five minutes, and I'll chat to Maverick."

In a few minutes, Grey was inside Maverick's apartment, which strangely enough, had a similar vibe to the club. It was like being caught in the calm eye at the centre of a tornado. He winked at Domino, who gave him a beaming smile, before addressing Maverick.

"Sorry to disturb you. I need to know what you want to do with Jake."

Maverick sighed and leaned back, his face mostly in shadow. "Great question. I feel like I've made a deal with the devil. How is he?"

"Cocky and annoying now that he knows Warner is on the run. Before that, he was pleading for the protection of the pack."

Maverick's eyebrows shot up. "I presume you told him where to go."

"Cecile did, quite vociferously."

Arlo sniggered. "He's lucky he still has his balls."

Grey updated them on Morgana's suggestion. "Unfortunately, I think she's right. It means hanging on to him for another hour."

"A deal's a deal. Untie him, get him a drink, and then send him on his way. Just make sure we have his number and know where to find him."

"Will do. I've advised him to keep a low profile—just in case."

"Wise." Maverick gestured to Riggs. "Riggs says there are more involved."

Riggs nodded. "I didn't see them, but I heard voices. More therians, and definitely more Pûcas."

"So, what's the next step?" Grey asked, aware of the basics of what was happening, but needing to plan for whatever happened next. He wasn't sure what Domino was going to do.

Maverick stood decisively, all eyes following him as he walked to the kitchen. He topped up his drink, and leaned on the counter. "We're going to Wales. I'll decide as to who's going with me soon. I want you to stay here though, Grey. Make sure nothing goes wrong with the pack, or the club."

Grey was pretty sure that either Arlo or Domino would stay, too. Although all the shifters liked Grey, a senior shifter needed to stay with him. He'd like to hear that argument, but knew it would take place behind closed doors.

Riggs spoke up. "You don't need to do this. This is my fight. I'll go alone."

"This concerns all of us," Maverick said, his tone brooking no argument. "I admit, I was sceptical, but I can't be anymore. We may not have the crown, but we can stop them from finding the place. You just need to get us close enough." His fingers drummed on the counter. "The question is, do we leave now, or wait until dawn?"

"I don't think we can afford to wait," Riggs said. He was bloodied and bruised, but fire burned within his eyes. A need for vengeance, as well as a desire to put right what his pack had lost all those years earlier. "I don't think they'll waste time here, especially now that I've escaped."

Monroe nodded. "Especially if you think they're going after Emyr."

There was a long silence as Maverick considered his options. Eventually, he said, "Tonight it is, then. Grey, prep the team downstairs."

"And Morgana? She wants to leave, if she's not needed."

From the look of resignation on Maverick's face, Grey knew what was coming next. He stared at Riggs. "You say there's a spell on that place?"

"Supposedly."

"Bollocks." Maverick turned his gaze to Grey. "Ask her, pretty please with sugar on top, if she'll come with us."

"Sure. And if she wants to bring Odette?"

"Why not? Let's have a bloody party." Grey turned to go, but then Maverick said, "What about Harlan, is he still here?"

"I think so. He was talking to Jet, last I saw."

"Send him up, please, with the book. Maybe there are more clues in it that will help us, because if someone gets to Emyr before we do, we'll be in big trouble."

Hunter threw the door to the lodge open, and opened fire with the shotgun. At least half a dozen Pûcas and therians were in the clearing, and they were attacking as a mixture of bears, boars, and wolves.

Hunter shouted over his shoulder. "Half a dozen so far, maybe more to come." He aimed at a bear that was barrelling toward him, waiting until it was close enough to cause maximum damage, and then fired. He hit the beast's shoulder, and roaring, it fell backward. Tommy charged at it from the side, taking it down in a tumble of fur and claws.

Ollie yelled, "Alastair, stay with Emyr!" Then he shifted and raced into the fight.

Because Ollie was the alpha, his wolf was far bigger than anyone else's. He stood as high as Hunter's waist, and in seconds had taken down a therian boar. Hunter fired off a few more shots, but knew he'd do more damage as a wolf.

Greer and Regan were diving in and around their attackers, biting and tearing flesh where they could, but their enemies were inflicting just as many wounds. Despite their good intentions, they had betrayed Emyr's hiding place, and put them all in danger.

But were their attackers planning to kill him, or capture him?

"Alastair. Your turn," Hunter said, turning to him. Flushed with anger, Alastair had left Emyr by the fire and joined Hunter in the doorway. Hunter thrust the shotgun into his hands, and then stripped. "I need to help the others."

"So should I!"

"But Emyr is not fighting. Look at him!"

Emyr sat in the chair, head in his hands, not even making a sign that he would fight. It was as if he was preparing for capture or death. It was the opposite way that a wolf should act.

Alastair grabbed the gun and took aim, but his eyes flickered with doubt. "Are you sure I shouldn't put a bullet in Emyr?"

"No. We need him."

"Fine." He shot at a Pûca instead, fighting in its natural, long-limbed and furry shape. "Good luck."

Hunter shifted and immediately leapt onto the back of a huge boar that was threatening to impale Greer.

The next minutes were a confusion of howls, tearing flesh, and bloodlust. But although they could handle the therians easily enough, the Pûcas were stronger and faster. They kept advancing on the lodge. Fortunately, it had only one entrance and small windows, and they managed to keep driving them back. That is until an almighty screech had them all scattering out of the clearing as a huge bird circled overhead and dived at the house.

Alastair stepped outside and fired straight overhead, but the bird was too big and too fast. It was like a fighter jet swooping down low. Huge, clawed feet raked across the top of trees and ripped into the roof, shredding tiles and sending them flying.

Alastair tried to get back into the building, but the doorway had collapsed, trapping Emyr inside on his own. Hunter attempted to get to his side, but was thrown into a tree trunk by a wild-eyed bear. His breath left him in a rush of bone-crunching pain, but despite his injuries, he managed to get to his feet. Blood poured from his rear leg, and it felt weak. His vision wavered, just as the bear charged him.

Then Ollie came flying from behind him, landing on the bear with such force that they both went rolling back into the clearing. Tommy was a short distance away, fighting for his life against a boar with enormous tusks. Greer and Regan were close by, but Hunter couldn't see them, only hear them. The smell of blood and animal musk was strong, almost overwhelming his heightened senses.

But the bird was doing the most damage. It was abnormally large, like something out of a fantasy film, and Hunter realised the Pûcas were capable of much more than just normal shape changing. Alastair had dropped the gun and shifted, and once Hunter realised Ollie was okay, he raced to Alastair's side.

The building had now lost almost half of its roof, and a beam enabled Hunter and Alastair to run up and worry at the bird, teeth snapping at its wings and legs, but it was too powerful to be stopped. Hunter was caught by its wing and sailed off the roof, crunching to the ground. He was lucky compared to Alastair, who ended up in a tree.

Unfortunately, the bird had spotted what it came for. It lunged down, reaching into the lodge, and when it emerged, Emyr was gripped in its claws, looking pathetically small. The bird flapped its enormous wings and screeched, summoning the others.

Within seconds their attackers had fled, and Hunter, utterly spent, collapsed on the ground.

Arlo had every intention of going to Wales, his earlier plans to hunt on the common cast aside.

His injuries were virtually healed, and he loved the fairy tale. It had stuck in his mind with its vivid imagery, and to hear it again reminded him of his happy childhood. To find out it was true was incredible.

He eyed Domino, who was sitting on Maverick's sofa talking to Riggs, and she met his gaze, a smile playing on her lips. She knew exactly what was going through his mind. Now, however, was not the time to argue. Riggs had lost his entire family over this, and he sat mired in guilt and anger, still looking half dead from his beating. He was healing quickly, though. Cuts that were open an hour ago had already closed.

Arlo was in the kitchen with the others, studying the illustrated short story that Harlan had laid out under the bright lights on the kitchen counter, dispelling the moody air of the flat. He concentrated on the heated conversation, watching as Harlan once again showed Maverick the images in the book, his finger jabbing the page.

"See!" Harlan pointed out. "Not only the box, but the crown is in this, too."

Maverick looked exasperated. "So? He should be wearing a crown. What's the big deal?"

"The detail of it! It actually looks like the *stolen* crown! I've seen the photos that Arbuthnot took. Whoever illustrated this has seen the crown, too."

Monroe grunted with doubt. "But there could be a description in the story."

Harlan sighed dramatically. "I've read it. There isn't, not a detailed one. This suggests to me that the illustrator knows something. I don't know who it is, but it made me think that perhaps there's a clue in here as to where the place is. If," he paused, looking at Riggs, "he doesn't know it."

Maverick shrugged. "He says he doesn't, but if Hunter has Emyr, then it's all good. Without him, we're in trouble." Maverick was trying to appear casual, but his jaw was tight.

Jet had arrived with Harlan, and she leaned against the counter, her booted foot tapping the tiles on the kitchen floor. "Was the illustrator a member of the pack?"

"Must have been," Arlo said. "It explains why they didn't put their name to it. You wouldn't want to advertise the fact that you'd put real details into a story book."

"Again," Monroe pointed out, "who would know?"

Harlan grunted, turning his attention back to the story as he settled himself more comfortably on the barstool. He sipped his bourbon, turning the pages carefully, and equally fascinated, Arlo sat next to him.

The colours of the illustrations glowed in the golden light, almost lifting off the page, despite their age. He took a sharp intake of breath as he noted the gilding on some of the pages. "It's not mass-produced at all, is it? This is probably a one-off, or a small production."

"Exactly what we thought," Harlan said, turning toward him, a glint of victory in his eyes. "In fact, I think it's a backup."

Arlo smiled as he understood Harlan's meaning. "For just this eventuality. A way to find the place when all else fails. There has to be directions in this."

Maverick interrupted them. "A map?"

"Too obvious," Harlan said, shaking his head. "It will be in the images. Maybe an obvious landmark. A rock, perhaps, a tree, a hill..." He trailed off as he turned the pages.

Arlo understood why Harlan was so good at his job. He spotted connections, and was skilled at looking beneath the surface of things. He turned to Riggs, summoning his attention. "Hey, Riggs. Come and look at these pictures. Recognise anything?"

Riggs was blinking in an effort to stay awake, but he joined them anyway, Domino too. One thing was certain—Riggs had to sleep on the way to Wales, or he wouldn't be useful for anything. "What am I looking at?"

"Can you spot any recognisable landmarks in the illustrations?" Harlan asked, angling the pages toward him. "I think this book is a way of ensuring that the place is never truly lost."

A spark of hope flared in Riggs's eyes. "Really? But who would have done this?"

"Must have been someone in your pack—years before your time, though."

As he studied it, Maverick received a phone call, and exchanging a worried glance with Arlo, he walked away to answer it.

Domino took the opportunity to pull Arlo aside. "I know you want to go. That's fine. I'll stay here."

"Are you sure?" He studied her expression, hoping there was no angle here. He liked Domino. He didn't want this to be an issue.

She smiled. "Of course. This story means a lot to you, and although it's intriguing, my place is here. If they have any sense at all, the therians will know that we're not backing out of this yet. They might see it as an opportunity to attack this place. I doubt it, but..."

"Which suggests that as the pack's second, I should stay," Arlo pointed out, feeling the pull of his responsibility, despite his desperate urge to go to Wales.

"I'm head of security. Your job is to support Maverick, and protect our heritage—whatever the hell that is." Her eyes flashed with fire. "Besides, I have an overwhelming urge to take revenge and remind the therians not to interfere with us again, and that includes any Pûcas I can find, too. They crossed a line today."

"You'll do that tonight?"

"Once the club closes, I'll start looking for them, but I suspect I'll need tomorrow, too. As long as Maverick doesn't take my whole team." Her gaze flickered toward him. "He's on a mission. This will be bloody."

Maverick was already ending his call, and in seconds was at their side, his expression bleak. "Emyr was captured by Pûcas." He quickly related the events in Scotland. "Fortunately, although they have injuries, Ollie and the team with him survived. We need to move. Now. I presume you two have argued it out between you?"

Arlo nodded. "I'm coming, Domino has her own agenda here. How many are we taking?"

"Monroe, Vlad, Jax, Mads, us two, and Riggs, of course. That leaves plenty of staff with you, Domino. Plus, we'll take Odette and Morgana." He sighed heavily, eyeballing Arlo. "I don't want to take them, but I think we'll need witches—just in case. Are you okay with it?"

"I went to see Birdie, didn't I? It's fine. Plus, I know we can trust them, despite our...differences." Like a huge row and an almighty falling out that meant they hadn't talked in years. He'd have to deal with that. It wasn't anyone else's problem.

"What about Hunter's team?" Domino asked.

"They'll meet us in Betws-y-Coed. But it's a longer trip for them, and they just had a big fight. They should sleep first, but I think they want to get on the road." Worry clouded his eyes. "They have to get out of Ballater, too. They went behind the alpha's back."

"Let's hope their accomplices can help them. We should get a few hours' sleep, too," Arlo said. "I know you want to get there soon, but the Pûcas will be travelling with Emyr. The giant bird can't fly him all the way to Wales." He still hadn't quite wrapped his head around that image. "Plus, Riggs needs to sleep." He looked over to where he stood at the counter, visibly exhausted. "We must be fit for this. Being knackered won't help us fight well. I'll be back to full strength tomorrow."

Domino looked unconvinced, but didn't contradict him. "Vlad, Mads, and Jax will be fine. As far as fights go, we've had worse. They'll be fired up to finish this. I'm with Maverick. We can't afford to delay."

"Good." Renewed determination settled in Maverick's eyes. "For all we know, they're on the way already. Ollie said it took them a couple of hours to get back to the car to be able to phone, so they have a head start. Arlo, you and Riggs will have to sleep in the car. I'll drive." He checked his watch. "Bloody hell. It's two o'clock already. That's good, I guess. It will be light when we get there."

"I think we should take Harlan, too," Arlo said, resigned to his decision.

"Really?" Maverick watched him, head bent over the book with Riggs on one side and Jet on the other. "Why?"

"He spotted things we didn't. He might do it again."

Domino added her support. "He's right, Maverick."

"He's a collector. He could betray us to the highest bidder," Maverick said, eyes narrowing.

"You're the alpha, and he's a human," Arlo pointed out. "I don't think he'll put up much of a fight. Besides, I like him. I have a good feeling about his trustworthiness."

"Fine, but you keep an eye on him. Let's hope Morgana is ready to leave soon, too." A familiar yellow glow that signalled aggression began to fill Maverick's eyes. "I'd really love to hunt, but that will have to wait." He gave a wolfish grin. "I'll save it for tomorrow."

Twenty-Seven

The journey to Wales proved long and tedious, and Maverick was getting more and more cranky with every passing mile. Only now that they were close to their destination did his impatience ease.

The traffic around London had been busy, despite the late hour when they left, and the motorways weren't much better. Their progress was slow, but once they were out of the city, the traffic thinned and they picked up the pace. He wished he could have waited a few hours as Arlo requested, because Riggs did look exhausted. However, when they outlined the plan to him, he didn't complain once. Despite his injuries, he was as keen to get on the road as the rest of them.

Meeting Riggs was unnerving. He was like Kane in so many ways. He glanced at him in the rear-view mirror. Riggs leaned into the corner of the rear seat, finally awake and looking out of the window, after sleeping most of the way. His bruises were a mixture of yellow and purple, and his cuts had mostly healed. His eyes, however, showed that his thoughts roved a long way from the car, lost in memories. Maverick hoped his need for vengeance would return once they reached their destination.

Arlo and Harlan were also travelling with him, Harlan in the back, next to Riggs. The other four shifters were in Vlad's car, and Morgana and Odette travelled separately. *That was for the best, certainly.* Arlo might proclaim that he was over Odette, but it sure didn't look like it to Maverick. He had a wistful expression in his eyes that suggested his thoughts lingered on their past. Arlo was a romantic, and he'd fallen hard for Odette. Maverick was glad he didn't get romantically involved. Women were fun, and he loved them, but he preferred his life without complications, and women always made life complicated.

He focussed on the road. They were on the A5 now, and only a few miles from Llanrhychwyn, the small village just outside of Be-tws-y-Coed, their destination that was within the borders of Gwydir Forest. It was just after eight in the morning, the traffic busy again as people headed to work. The sun had risen, but it was hidden behind a bank of clouds that promised rain, and the light was grey and murky. They passed through small villages constructed of grey stone, the backdrop green, featuring hills, forests, tumbling streams, and in the distance, Snowdonia.

"Not far now," he informed the group.

Harlan had been scrolling through his phone for the last half an hour, but he looked up, catching Maverick's eye in the mirror. "I've been reading about our destination." He grimaced. "I won't even try to pronounce it. Did you know that it's linked to Taliesin? Another shifter connection."

Riggs finally dragged his gaze from the wild countryside. "There are many such rumours around here, but that's false. A misinterpretation of an old document."

"So I read, but still, makes you wonder," Harlan said.

"Wales is littered with myths. They're so firmly enmeshed with everyday life that sometimes past and present seem to meld together."

"You miss the place," Arlo said, twisting to look at him.

"It's in my blood. My family's blood. Now that I'm back, I can't believe we ever left."

"Did you ever visit?"

"Once or twice, but I never went even close to our old home. My father discouraged it. He thought that we might be watched. I thought he was being paranoid, but now I'm not so sure."

"How old where you when you left?" Maverick asked Riggs.

"About ten. A lifetime ago."

"Are you sure you don't recognise any images in that picture book?"

"Not really, but I'm hoping when we get there, something rings a bell."

Maverick was frustrated, but it wasn't Riggs's fault. He'd been a child when he left. Maverick couldn't remember details from when he was that age. He slowed as the signs for Betws-y-Coed appeared, and within a few minutes, the pretty village was on either side of them.

Even in late autumn and at an early hour, the place was busy. Cars lined the streets and filled the public carpark, and the cafés looked busy. Tourists were dressed in walking gear with thick socks and boots, huge anoraks, and walking sticks, ruddy-faced and unkempt. It was like being on another planet, compared to Wimbledon.

"Just carry on through here," Arlo instructed, after consulting the map on his phone. "The turn for the village is after Betsy. On the right." He pronounced the name like many people did, rather than tackle the Welsh pronunciation. He wound the window down and inhaled deeply. "Good, clean, cold air. No therians yet."

Once through the town, Maverick turned down a narrow lane, and thick vegetation pressed in on either side. He was desperate for a coffee, and the cafés had looked welcoming, but the need to find the place where the crown had once been drove him on.

"Slow down," Riggs instructed, leaning forward. "I recognise this. Our settlement was off this road, somewhere to the left."

Maverick checked the rear-view mirror, making sure the other cars were behind them. He caught Riggs's expression. He looked frustrated. "I'm sure it was here somewhere."

"Was it a proper lane?" Harlan asked, studying their surroundings greedily.

"I thought so, but maybe I was wrong. I think there was a gate..."

"You lived in cabins though, right?" Arlo asked, nose also pressed to the glass. "Made of wood."

"Some were wood, some were stone. But, no, it wasn't like a proper village." He laughed. "It was like a commune. Although, we were sent to the local school."

Maverick kept going, and with every mile they passed, his heart sank. Especially when signs for the village appeared. "Have we missed the turn off?" he asked, slowing down.

"I could have sworn the turn off was earlier." A frown creased Riggs's brow. "Stop the car, and let me out."

Maverick continued along the road for a short distance until he spotted a narrow layby set next to a gate in the hedge, a tight track disappearing into the trees, and he pulled in. The other cars followed, and in seconds they had gathered on the verge.

The rich scent of earth and damp air was a shock after the warmth of the car, but it was also welcome. Maverick's wolf blood responded to it, and he wanted to be out there, all four paws padding the rich loam, exploring the undergrowth. It seemed Riggs did, too. He stripped and threw his clothes in the back of the car, shifted, and loped down the lane.

"What do we do if he can't find it?" Vlad asked, lips pressed into a thin line.

"Not much we can do," Monroe pointed out, "except to watch for therians and Pûcas."

Maverick shook his head. "Not an option. They could be there already, and we're too late. I just wish I understood this better! Riggs made it sound simple. Like you just wore the crown in the right place and assumed the king's power. It still sounds like bullshit to me." He turned to Harlan, who seemed to understand much better than he did. "What else could be involved?"

The American shrugged. "Hard to say. Shifters are magical beings, right? Perhaps there's a ritual that involves some kind of binding magic that would make you obey other shifters. How does it work as a pack?" He looked genuinely curious. "What makes you the alpha, and why do the others follow you?"

Maverick wasn't sure this was the best time to be having this discussion, but with Riggs retreating down the road, he may as well try. "The pack needs a leader, like any group of people do. A government, a family head, someone to make the final decisions or you'll end up arguing forever. Wolves respect power, and that means the alpha has to be stronger than anyone else, and be able to fight. However, there are lots of strong wolves in every pack. Not all want to be alpha."

"True," Arlo said, nodding, and the other shifters agreed. "It comes with a responsibility for the welfare of the pack, and the mentoring of young wolves. If you go off the rails young, don't learn the rules, it's hard. I like a happy, well-functioning pack. I don't want to be an alpha, though. Not at this stage in my life, certainly."

"But not all alphas are so altruistic," Mads said, eyes sliding to Vlad. "We've experienced that. Some will abuse their power. That's ugly. He makes you weaker."

Maverick knew all about that. It was his job to know about his pack's background. And also his job to keep their secrets.

Harlan leaned on the car's bonnet, head cocked. "How does he make you weaker?"

"There's a bond in a pack," Mads explained. "You lend each other strength. Our strength feeds the alpha, and his feeds ours. A happy pack is a strong pack. Everyone flourishes."

Monroe took over. "But in an unhappy pack, only the alpha flourishes."

"So, the alpha can draw on your power?" Harlan asked. "Like your shifter magic? Because you guys heal quick, right? You hunt together, too. Does that mean you sense each other? Because, surely, if someone proclaimed themselves Shifter King, then he would act like a giant alpha?" His face wrinkled with confusion as he worked through his theory.

"Fuck it," Maverick said, realising the full implications of what this could mean. "He—or even she—would draw on *all* of our power. We'd be subjugated in more ways than one."

Odette and Morgana had been listening at the periphery of the group, but now Odette spoke up. "It's a kind of binding spell. An innate one. You're all part of the same family. Pûcas are pure fey. This ritual must be a type of stronger binding to their will."

"But we have free will," Monroe said, perplexed. "Maverick doesn't control my mind."

Maverick shot him a quick glance. "But I could bend you to my will if I wanted to. Make your life unbearable. You'd heal more slowly, would mentally suffer. You might even fear for your family. And because I'm the alpha, drawing on power from the rest of the pack, you'd find it hard to challenge me, too." He didn't need to spell it out to Vlad and Mads. They'd experienced that only too well.

Harlan pressed onward, the bit between his teeth now. "So, anyone who challenges the alpha to be the new one must be a really strong wolf. "

"Or the old one bows out, knowing he's weaker. Then the pack members who are interested fight it out between them," Maverick explained. "I had to fight another couple of shifters for the job. Fortunately, I had the support of the pack." The shifters who lost had left, eliminating future conflict.

They had all been worried and puzzled about the implications of the Wolf King's crown, and it had seemed surreal. A dream. But with every passing moment, the implications became clearer, and as his team stared at him, it was obvious they understood it, too. Their very future was at stake.

Maverick turned to Arlo. "Do me a favour. Call Ollie. See if they're on the way. I think we'll need backup." As Arlo nodded and walked away to make the call, Maverick addressed the others. "Know anyone in the Welsh packs that could help? I certainly don't. They keep to themselves from everything I've gathered, although I think there's a small pack the other side of Snowdonia."

They all shook their heads, but didn't have time to talk anymore, because Riggs raced back to them, swiftly shifting to human. "I've found the road."

"Hold on!" Harlan said, stalling everyone before they rushed back to the cars. "Riggs, if your pack had the crown and knew where the place was, why doesn't one of them rule the others? Why is there no king now?"

That was an excellent question, and Maverick felt a fool for not thinking of it. But Riggs just looked baffled. "I have no idea."

Domino sat on the back step of Storm Moon, behind the stage area, wearing a thick jacket and clutching a coffee.

Weak sunshine struggled through the cloud cover, but it didn't add any warmth to the day. She should be inside, but the club felt claustrophobic after last night's imprisonment, regardless that it had been brief. The strong smell of Jake still filled the room, and coupled with the unusual scent of the Pûca, the place seemed alien to her, and vaguely threatening. Opening the rear doors meant that she could air it out.

Domino had spent many hours during the night searching the surrounding area for signs of possible attack with the remaining team before heading to Brixton, but fortunately had found nothing. The therians had some sense, after all. *Or maybe the strong response to her kidnapping had done that.* That she'd been caught still rankled, and the fact she'd been drugged was not an excuse. Not to her, anyway.

Although it was still early on Tuesday morning, they weren't taking any chances. A few of her team were inside already, the smashed window was being repaired by a glazier, and Cecile and Xavier, her cousin, were circling Wimbledon. Footsteps behind her signalled Grey's approach, and she edged over to make room for him.

"Cheers, Dom." He settled next to her with his own coffee, and leaned against the door frame. "How are you?"

She didn't bother to hide anything from Grey. "Pissed off that I was caught. I feel like an idiot."

"You were drugged accidentally by that huge unit, Monroe. Not your fault."

"Even so..."

"The therians are at fault here. Not you. Not even Monroe."

She sighed, her breath pluming on the air and mixing with steam from her coffee. "I know."

"Did they hurt you?"

"Other than Warner punching me? No." She extended her wrists. "I have marks from my restraints, of course. I think my shoulders have finally unkinked. I was worried that I'd dislocate them if I tried to shift."

Grey sipped his coffee, eyes hard as he studied her injuries, and then he stared at the line of trees on the boundary. "They must be sure of their success to have risked such a thing."

"I think they were jacked up on adrenalin—plus we'd knocked Jake out. It was tit for tat. And they didn't like me and Vlad being in the pub. Worrying though, for therians and Pûcas to be working together. Let's hope it's not a sign of things to come."

"And wolf-shifters. Don't forget Brody, and Castor's rogue members. I presume you're heading to Brixton soon."

"After I finish my coffee. I'll take Cecile and Xavier with me. I want to see if we can find any more clues, or therians, around those shops. That basement stretched quite a way. We can explore the other exit, the one Rox and Warner used. Last night's escape was a bit frenzied." She laughed at the memory. "I think the boys would have liked to mop up—hell, I would have—but we had to get Riggs away."

"Probably for the best." Grey turned his blue eyes on her again. "Retribution feels good at the time, but we don't want a bloodbath. No one does. You did what you needed to do to get out. That's smart."

"But we can't afford to appear weak."

"You made it very clear that we're not weak." He smiled. "Cut yourself some slack."

Domino cocked her head, hearing footsteps. "Oh, oh. I hear Maggie Milne. She sounds determined."

"Because she's like a bloody rottweiler."

"Good. Let's hope she has more leads." They both looked up as Maggie rounded the corner of the building, and in seconds she was at the top of the steps, on the carpark. Domino waved. "Morning, Maggie."

"Morning. Nice! Time for coffee then for you two, despite the death and destruction you cause." Maggie sounded grumpy, but she also looked amused as she joined them. She had obviously slept well, her hair was freshly washed, and she was made up and dressed smartly. "I had a few odd reports last night. Someone said they saw a bear in a street, in Clapham. Were you involved in that?"

Domino shrugged. "We might have been in the vicinity. It's all sorted now, though."

"Really? I'm hoping I don't find a dead bear somewhere."

"No, he's alive and well, and will be helping us in the future, should we have need of a therian," Grey told her.

She frowned, unconvinced. "You better bring me up to speed."

Grey outlined the previous evening's events, including Domino's capture, and Maggie's frown turned into a scowl.

She looked at Domino. "You were kidnapped?"

"Yes, but I'm fine, except for a dented ego."

"And a bruised face."

She smiled at Maggie's concern. "Honestly, don't worry. I've had worse."

"Okay," Maggie sighed, pulling her notebook out of her pocket. "Names. All of them."

"We barely know any, I'm afraid," Domino admitted, which was more or less the truth.

"The bear, then? You must know his. Just so I know," she added quickly. "I'm not tracking him down. I just like to build a database of paranormal creatures. It helps maintain the peace."

"Jake," Grey said. "No surname. Sorry."

"And the stolen objects? Have they turned up yet?"

"No." Domino glanced at Grey, wondering how much to share. "Did you find anything in Brody's place? Or anything about Ivan?"

Maggie snorted. "Nothing remotely useful." She peered over their shoulders into the club. "So, Harlan turned up, did he? Should have known he'd have come right to the source. Where's Maverick?"

"Wales. Harlan went with them. They're hoping to find the crown today. Or whoever has it, at least."

Maggie looked warily between them. "Should I warn my colleagues there? With several deaths already, we don't need more."

"I have a feeling that whatever happens will take place in the wilderness somewhere. If," Grey qualified, "they can even find the place."

"And what happens if you guys lose?"

Domino considered the strange, wild Pûcas who seemed to have their own agenda. "I don't think things will work out well for any of us."

Maggie frowned, pen tapping her knee. "I don't like the sound of that. Pûcas doing their own thing in their own place is fine, but having full fey creatures being more...obvious is a very bad idea. It would cause mayhem. At least you guys know the fucking rules. Flexible though they may be."

"Holy shit, Maggie," Domino said, almost snorting her coffee. "Is that a compliment?"

"Yes, so enjoy it. It's probably the only one you'll get."

Domino grinned. She was warming to Maggie.

"So," Maggie continued, "these Pûcas are in London?"

"There were a couple that I saw last night. Riggs said there were more, he was sure of it, but we didn't see them."

Maggie's eyes narrowed. "At least he's been found. Good work on that. But Pûcas in London...I don't like it. If their natural habitat is the wild, it means they're becoming bold." She studied Grey and Domino again. "This could cause significant issues in the paranormal world, and consequently, have repercussions in the normal one. What are you doing to mitigate this shitshow, and how can I support it?"

"You'll help?" Grey asked, looking surprised.

"Of course! This is my problem as much as yours. More so, even. You just care about shifters. I care about everyone else."

Time to lay their cards on the table. Domino leaned forward, elbows on knees. "We're heading back to Brixton today. I'm sure the rest of the therians who are part of this will still be hiding there—maybe Pûcas, too. But it's a busy area. It's by the market."

"You're fucking kidding me!" She looked between them both. "Bollocks! That place is never quiet."

"I went back last night, with a team, but didn't go in the building. We have to do that today."

Grey's eyes lit up. "What if I get a couple of my boys to help?"

Domino cocked an eyebrow. "Would they?"

"I reckon they'd love a challenge."

"Hold on!" Maggie interjected. "Who the hell are *your boys*?"

"Ex-Services." Grey winked. "Ask no questions, Maggie. It's for the best."

She huffed belligerently. "Don't tell me which bloody questions to ask. I want names!" She held a hand up as Grey started to protest. "Hear me out! I am the face of paranormal policing in this city, and I have a team—not nearly a big enough one, but I manage. We manage. The only way I keep on top of stuff is by working with others and cultivating relationships in the paranormal world. I have witch contacts, occult contacts, bloody Nephilim contacts—and Christ almighty, do they rack up body counts! And you, my lovelies," she jabbed a finger at them, "are my shifter contacts, because that slippery fuck Castor I would rather kill than work with. Get it?" She waited expectantly, and Domino and Grey could do nothing but nod. Maggie might look unassuming, but she had her own power. Domino was impressed. "Good. All of which means that because you are as interested in keeping the peace as I am, and admittedly, have control of your own business, I need to know *who* you work with. That enables me to protect them and you. I haven't got an armed response unit—only if I beg for one, and they don't do this shit, so that always brings more trouble than it's worth. So, that leaves me and my murky contacts." She took a breath.

"But there are things I can do. I am the respectable face of proper law and order, and investigation. I have access to things you cannot get. And now I'll get to my point. I can smooth things over. Use my powers to make things work. If you are going to Brixton today, I can clear some of the area. There'll be a sudden gas leak or some such crap. You will go in there and find them, and I will create the space for that to happen—without you all getting arrested. Do you fucking *comprende*?"

Domino grinned and looked at Grey. "Do we?"

"I think we do." Grey studied Maggie. "You are most unexpected."

"I pride myself on it." Maggie was trying to suppress a smile and failing. "Do we have a deal?"

Domino was still getting her head around Maggie's diatribe. "Just to clarify, you will clear out the area we need so we can search it? And whatever happens, no repercussions?"

"Exactly. You're happy, I'm happy. But, I may require help with future issues that require the skills of shifters—and your mysterious men." She directed that at Grey. "Although—" she jabbed another finger. "It doesn't mean I turn a blind eye to everything that you do. There are still rules…"

Domino would have liked to discuss this with Maverick first, because it sounded like Maggie would hold it over them for future help, but needs must. They needed this. He would surely say yes. She shook Maggie's hand. "Deal."

Twenty-Eight

A s they drew into the ramshackle camp, Harlan shuddered. The thought of living there, in the middle of nowhere, filled him with horror.

Riggs, however, was looking all misty-eyed. "I can't believe I'm here again."

"Please tell me that it has changed, and it used to be so much better than this," Harlan said, grimacing. "I feel unclean just looking at it."

But the car had stopped, and Riggs was already out the door. The rest of them hurriedly exited, too.

Once they found the road through a rusted, old gate that had long been obscured by greenery, it had been a hard slog along a narrow track. Every now and again, Arlo had jumped out of the car and hacked at branches with a machete they'd brought with them, and they crawled another short distance before he had to do it again.

The path snaked back and forth, and up and down rises, and on a couple of occasions, they'd stopped when they met a fork in the path. Riggs had shifted to his wolf to explore, Arlo going with him for safety. The trees on either side were huge, their canopies towering high above them, encroaching on the path every step of the way. The road was in deep shadow, compounded by the heavy cloud cover. Harlan had felt like he was underwater. However, the last few hundred yards had been easier to drive, the path wider and more accessible, until the camp opened up before them—sort of.

Arlo whistled as he surveyed their surroundings. "Wow. This really is in the middle of nowhere. Not your thing, Harlan?"

"Hell no. Is it yours?"

"Maybe for a week when I need to get away, but to live? I doubt it. But," he smiled at Harlan before studying the place again, "you're not a wolf. This place sings to my blood. Listen." By now the other cars had drawn up behind them, and their engines turned off. The sudden silence was filled with birdsong, the creak of the trees, and the babbling of a stream close by. "Stunning. You would totally find your own inner beast out here."

Harlan tried to imagine a fierce wolf at the centre of his being, surrounded by a wild forest and primal nature. They would be as one. Just for the briefest of moments, he was jealous of that connection, but it quickly passed. That was not for him. Maverick immediately took charge, directing the other shifters to search the perimeter. Arlo followed Riggs and Maverick as they explored the closest buildings, but Harlan stayed put, soaking it all in.

Decaying wooden houses were spread throughout the dense forest. The trees, a mixture of pine, Douglas Firs, and Norway spruce trees, were enormous. They towered over everything, sheltering the buildings that had been wedged into the spaces between them—or around them. Some were constructed around huge tree trunks.

At one point, it must have been carefully managed. Cleared enough to allow houses to be built, but still dense enough to provide cover, and shelter from prying eyes above. Now, trees, saplings, and bushes sprouted everywhere. The stone-built buildings had fared better, but all windows were grubby, shattered in places. It both looked and felt abandoned. *But there was something about the place that spoke of secrets...*

"You feel it, too?" Harlan looked around, startled at the woman's voice since she had approached so quietly. She was young and beautiful with creamy white skin, her gaze focussed on the camp. "So many secrets."

"How did you know I was thinking that?"

She levelled her gaze at him, an unnerving, unblinking gaze that also spoke of secrets. "It's in your expression. You live on secrets, so it makes sense that you would know them."

"I guess I do. You must be Odette." He shook her hand. "Harlan Beckett. You're Morgana's sister?" He'd met Morgana briefly last night; she was altogether different to Odette. Earthier, with a no-nonsense attitude, but she also carried a sense of secrets and power. "You're a witch."

"I am, but Morgana is my cousin, not sister." Odette was staring into the trees again, her fingers weaving a pattern before her, words mouthed silently. A window of clarity seemed to open, and the air became fresher.

"A spell?"

"Of protection. Blood has been spilled here. Much blood." She shuddered. "Deception and betrayal have soaked into the earth. There'll be more."

"Hush Odette, you're unnerving Mr Beckett." Morgana had a large leather bag over her shoulder, and it looked full. Like Odette, she had approached silently. Perhaps this place was getting to him already.

"Call me Harlan, please. Can I carry your bag?"

Morgana smiled and shook her head. "No, thanks. I'll keep it close. Besides, you have that intriguing book to bring with you." She gestured ahead to the nearest stone house. "Let's see if we can get a fire going. I'm not standing around freezing out here all morning while they find the place."

"If it's here," Harlan pointed out. "It could be further out—whatever *it* is."

Morgana shook her head. "Oh, no. Odette is right. It's close. I think we're right on top of it."

Maggie had overextended herself this time, no doubt about it. Her boss had looked at her like she'd gone mad, but she had stuck to her guns, impressing on the stubborn, no-chinned wonder that unless she acted quickly, all sorts of weird shit could happen in Brixton.

He—DCI Campion—had pointed out all sorts of weird shit happened in Brixton anyway, but when she warned it would get worse, he had agreed to clear the immediate area around the building where Domino had been held captive. They had gone with her initial suggestion of a fake gas leak, and had even commandeered a British Gas van to drive into the courtyard behind the buildings. However, it was filled with shifters, two very hardened ex-Services men, and Grey.

It had taken a couple of hours to complete the evacuation, and the locals had complained. *A lot.* She'd had to draft in extra PCs to help man the perimeter, and most of them were unaware of the real reason for the subterfuge. It was easier this way, and she wasn't even sorry for lying. Sometimes in her profession, lying was a whole lot easier than telling the truth.

Maggie had also insisted on being there, with Stan, despite Domino suggesting otherwise. Now they just had to hope that it was worth it. Irving was investigating the owner of the hardware store.

Maggie and Stan exited the narrow alley into the courtyard, and found the van already unloaded. Domino had earlier introduced her to Cecile, Xavier, and Fran, and Grey had introduced all of them to Clint and Ray. The three humans carried large knives, and two had shotguns. She felt like she'd made a deal with the devil. *He'd probably be easier to deal with.*

Cecile and Xavier, the two long-limbed French cousins, were already stripping off, and in seconds had changed into two huge, beautifully thick-furred wolves.

Stan muttered next to her, "Bloody hell. That's impressive."

Maggie had more pressing things on her mind, and she voiced her concerns to the group. "The likelihood is that the therians will have evacuated, too. I might have overcooked it with the gas leak."

"But it means we can get in and search it properly," Domino said, shrugging. "If we find stragglers, so be it. It's like Grey said this morning, we don't want a bloodbath. We just want to clarify our boundaries. And stop their plan, of course."

"Okay. Which way?"

"The hardware shop," Domino said pointing down the alley. She turned to Clint, a huge, square-jawed man with lively eyes, and a crew cut, and pointed across the square to another narrow alley that led to a different street. "Last night we found an exit over there, if I remember correctly. I think I was being held right under our feet. I'll check it out with you, because if these guys flush any out, I want to catch them. Fair enough?"

"Suits me."

"Good." She turned to the rest, her eyes glinting with excitement. "I'll also take Frances."

"And Stan, too," Maggie said, nodding at her sergeant. "Good luck."

As Domino led her team away, and Xavier headed in the other direction, Maggie had a final word with Stan. "Keep your head, but don't risk your life. If need be, shoot first. Understand? And keep an eye on Clint."

"Will do, Guv."

Maggie hurried after Grey, hoping she'd made the right decision. Hoping, in fact, she'd be around to regret, or not, making any decision at all once this was over.

Arlo had explored most of the abandoned settlement when he sat on his haunches to breathe in the crisp, cold winter scent of pine trees and leaf mould. The scent of shifters was thick on the air too, mainly from his companions, but there were also the ghost scents of other shifters.

Every time they explored a building, another wave of smells emerged. It was surprising how much remained, considering it had been abandoned so long ago.

But they had also found a fresher scent. Someone had recently returned to this place. Maybe to tend to it, maybe to see if the secret place was still hidden. Or maybe to find it. So far, however, they had found no sign of any secret *anything*, and the fresher scent was everywhere, so that didn't narrow anything down, either.

The smell of woodsmoke caught his attention, and he followed it to one of the houses close to where their cars were parked. He shifted and dressed, then entered the small house. The smell of fire and dampness warred for supremacy. Dampness was winning. As in many of the houses, soft furnishings had been abandoned here, and most were ruined by mould and decay. Leaves littered the floor, and the ceiling sagged from rot. The floor was of slabbed stone, so that had fared a little better than the furnishings.

But a crackling fire was burning in a small fireplace, and someone had placed a table and chairs in front of it. Harlan was once again studying the book with Odette, and for a moment they were both so absorbed in their task, they didn't notice him. Arlo felt a stab of jealousy at seeing Odette so close to someone else. Her slim frame was wrapped in a thick jumper and coat, and her hair fell forward across her face. Seeing her again reminded him that he still had feelings for her, feelings he'd rather not harbour.

His annoyance made him grumpy, and as he crossed the room to join them, he asked, "Found anything useful?" He sounded brusque, even to his own ears.

Harlan, however, was so distracted that he didn't seem to notice. "Now that we're here, I'm even more convinced that whoever illustrated this has been here. It's too accurate." He huffed, shaking his head. "The types of trees, the mixture of buildings..."

Arlo was very confused. "They've put this place in the story? That doesn't make sense. It's not part of the tale." He peered over his shoulder.

Harlan twisted his head and grinned at him. "It's clever. The story talks about the Wolf King and his pack. After his victorious battles, when the other shifters were subjugated to his rule, they lived in the forest in the Otherworld, at one with nature. Their houses were part of the forest. Sort of like treehouses."

Arlo groaned, remembering the story. "Of course. It was at the beginning. It sets the scene. The Wolf King had brought stability to the shifters. His home was a kind of idyll. A city in the forest."

"Exactly. It was a place fed by streams, situated amongst trees that were hundreds, if not thousands of years old. Fey forests, filled with dryads, water nymphs, and all sorts of fey creatures—including the fey themselves. This place," he gestured around him, "is just like that, but less fanciful. The story describes *very* fantastical buildings, while the illustrator has, unusually, made it less fantastical. Far more *human*."

Odette's eyes sparkled as she looked at Arlo, and he found it hard to look away. "He's right. Fantasy illustrators always play up the fantasy, and the rest of the illustrations do. But not that."

Arlo felt a glimmer of intrigue and hope stir within him. "Okay. Fair point. But how does that help us?"

Harlan smoothed out a double-page illustration that covered most of the visible space, with only a few lines of text underneath. "For a small part in the story, this is a big illustration. The Wolf King lives in a kind of treehouse, in the centre of the forest city. It's surrounded by gardens, and is by far the biggest place. It's described as the seat of his power. Not a palace, exactly, but he received visitors there."

"Like a royal reception room," Odette added. "And he wears the crown in a picture depicting that."

"Of course, that's where the trickster shifter challenges him," Arlo said, able to relate parts of the story from memory.

"Exactly!" Harlan flipped the pages to show him. "This part of the story reminds me a little bit of Sir Gawain and the Green Knight. You remember I kept saying about how it reminded me of the King Arthur myth? This is another link. Do you know that story?"

Arlo shrugged. "There's a big Green Knight who challenges Sir Gawain."

"He challenges *everyone*. Marches into King Arthur's court and throws down a challenge that was impossible to refuse. Sir Gawain is the only knight brave enough to accept. In this story, Mathan, the shapeshifter trickster who also reminds me of Gwydion, challenges the Wolf King to the ultimate hunt. A battle in Mathan's own forest. He phrases this challenge in such a way, in the centre of a great feast, that the Wolf King is obliged to accept it."

"Of course." Arlo grimaced. "He doesn't want to, and he has nothing to prove since he is already the king. But to refuse would make him lose face. That part of the story always worried me as a child, but equally, the Wolf King is the hero. He can't die."

"Until he does," Harlan pointed out. "Anyway, blah, blah, blah, cut to the chase. The trees help the Gwydion character. *The Battle of the Trees*-thing. The Wolf King is defeated. Mathan unfairly wins the crown—until the witch steps in. So far, so good. We've talked about that. But how did they get to the forest? And how is that *here*? In the story, the Wolf King leaves his own forest, and travels to Mathan's. But we know that once, the borders between this world and the Otherworld were thin. Fey and humans crossed all the time. The story says he crosses out of the Summerlands to a place of cold and ice. A forest rimmed with hoarfrost, and full of ravines. Very Green Knight, again. And very much like this place is right now. Anyway, the trees come alive, and the king is killed. The Witch Queen had followed him, unbeknownst to both the trickster and the Wolf King, and arrives too late to save him. She was so grief-stricken by his death, so furiously angry with the trickster, that she placed the whole place under a spell, and sank it deep within the earth, right?"

Arlo nodded. "Yes, she said it should never see the light of day again. She clothed it in darkness that was as black as Mathan's soul. A place of great power, bound by magic, the Wolf King's old power caught within it. And Mathan's magic was trapped there, too."

Harlan looked at him, eyes wide. "I think it's beneath our feet."

Arlo snorted with disbelief. "A whole forest?"

"Yes. We are in a narrow valley here. Hard to see with the trees towering around us, but we're in a bowl. Almost as if the earth had collapsed."

As much as Arlo wanted this to be real, and as much as he loved the story, this sounded nuts. He looked at Odette. "Do you agree?"

"I do. As soon as I arrived here, I sensed loss, love, and blood. This place feels haunted. The land is scarred."

"But this is Wales! You, Harlan, said that it has a huge, rich history. That feeling could come from anything, not just this...fairy tale."

"But here we are, chasing a crown, and a lost king's resting place."

Arlo decided to roll with it. "And the entrance?"

"Beneath the biggest house here," Harlan said. "Which was the alpha's house, and equates to..."

Arlo nodded in understanding. "The Wolf King's palace. I've explored around the biggest place here. It *is* in the centre of the village. A huge spruce towers over it."

Harlan stood up, putting the book into his messenger bag, and shouldering it. "That's where we need to look. I'm convinced the entrance is beneath it—somehow. We need to gather the others. If we can find it first, we can defend it." He rubbed his stubble. "Maybe I have lost the plot."

"If that's true, then we all have," Arlo said, heading to the door. "I'll summon the others."

But before he had laid his hand on the door handle, a huge howl ripped through the forest, quickly picked up by another and another, until they were surrounded by deafening noise.

The battle was back at their doorstep.

Twenty-Nine

As Grey advanced down the corridor beneath the hardware shop, he took the time to check his surroundings thoroughly. So far he'd passed a couple of general storerooms packed with old boxes, spare supplies for the shop, and a small office that was sparsely furnished, but clean. Cecile and Xavier, both wolves, scouted ahead. Maggie was behind him, having spent time investigating the shop, and Ray was on the other side of the corridor.

He turned into a small room that contained an old bed covered in dirty sheets, and not much else. It smelt of Pûcas. Even as a human he could pick up their different scent, unlike the smell of wolves and therians, which he could not detect at all.

He heard footsteps, and Maggie appeared in the doorway. He nodded at the bed. "Looks like someone has been sleeping here. Must be a place to hide when things get tricky." He dropped to his knees and looked under the bed, but a cursory sweep showed a box of clothes and nothing else. After making sure there were no hidden papers in there, he pushed it under the bed again and stood.

"I wonder if Pûcas need beds?" she asked, half watching him, half looking down the corridor.

"It depends how human they are or not, I guess. I have yet to see them, so I have no idea." He took in her size. She didn't look much like a fighter. "Are you sure that you're okay to be here? If they are around, it could get ugly."

She looked amused. "You don't think I can handle myself, you cheeky bastard? Or would I just get in the way of some unsavoury behaviour?"

He laughed. "If your self-defence skills are as strong as your language, I'm sure you'll be fine. And I do not have unsavoury behaviour."

"I'm glad to hear it." She didn't look convinced, though. She looked up, face wrinkling with concern as she studied the ceiling. "That looks solid. Nowhere to hide up there."

She headed across the corridor to another room, this one stacked with old office furniture, and started to hunt through it, as Grey went to the next room. Another one with a bed in it. He called out, "You know, I think this is some kind of base. A retreat, when things get tricky."

"For what, though? Illegal activity? I can't check any of this for stolen goods. I'm here without a license."

That gave him pause, and he walked to the doorway of the room she was in. "You're sticking your neck out for this. For us."

"For me." She finished her search and joined him in the corridor. "I don't like the way these guys—creatures—work. Besides, my senior officer signed off on this. It's not like I'll be taking them to court, is it?" She grinned, and slid past him to the next room. "What we need are other addresses, or phone numbers...other places they may hide."

"Somehow, I doubt we'll be that lucky. They're sneaky, not stupid." Another thought struck him as they continued to the next room together. "What about the owner of this place?"

"It's a big corporation. The building is rented to a guy on a long-term lease. First inspection says he's fine. My team is following it up. He may have more shops—"

"Which could mean more bases."

A strangled cry broke into their conversation, and they both pounded up the hall, Grey quickly shouldering past Maggie. His old friend, Ray, rocketed out of a room up ahead, a small, furry creature attached to his chest and throat.

It took Grey a second to work out what it was, and he blinked with surprise.

A monkey?

A very strong monkey, whose fingers were wrapped around Ray's throat. Not hard enough to stop him from cursing, though.

"Get this little shit off me!" Ray rolled over, trying to squash the creature, but even as he was doing it, the creature shifted, becoming something much bigger, uglier, and far weirder. It had to be a Pûca.

Before Grey could even take it in, instinct took over, and he lifted his gun. But Ray was in the way, and the creature wasn't letting go.

Maggie rushed past him, arms raised, yelling, "Duck!"

Ray had barely time to keep his head down before Maggie swung a broken chair leg, smashing the Pûca in the face and sending it sprawling. The impact of her follow through swing had her falling over Ray, and it gave Grey the shot he needed.

He fired the shotgun just as the Pûca sat up, spitting and snarling, and it fell back, blood splattering everywhere. But there wasn't time to celebrate.

A hiss and strong waft of Pûca scent indicated that another one was behind him, and Grey spun around, catching a glimpse of it as it launched at him. He fired, catching it in the chest, and it slumped to the floor. But howls were sounding in the centre of this underground lair, and he spun again. Ray and Maggie had already found their feet, and together they jumped over the Pûca's body, Grey reloading as he ran.

Another Pûca dived out of yet another room, but Ray was ready for it this time. He fired, both barrels, and the Pûca was blasted backwards. They jumped over its twitching body, and for one moment, Grey allowed himself hope that there were only a few and that they'd killed them all.

That is until they hit a large, central space and found at least three fighting Cecile and Xavier, with more advancing behind them and down the corridor on the far side.

It wasn't just a base. It was a nest, and now they were trapped in the middle of it.

Vlad scented them first. *Therians and Pûcas.* They were a distance away, but were advancing quickly through the forest.

He debated the best course of action. If he howled to alert his pack, the enemy would know they were there. But then again, if their sense of smell was as acute as his was, they would know anyway. He opted for the former approach, and his howl was picked up by the others.

The trees seemed to tremble as if they recognised the sound, and he was sure he felt a ripple of unease beneath his feet, but he hadn't time to consider it. Arlo's howl rose above everyone else's, summoning them back to the base.

Vlad raced back to the collection of buildings, aware he needed to protect the humans amongst them. As he rounded the cars, he saw Harlan and Odette running away from the end house toward the centre of the buildings, Arlo with them, and he flanked them.

A slink of dark movement in the trees caught his attention, and he moved to intercept it, but Arlo howled again, and the command made him ignore it.

By now the pack had emerged from the surrounding trees, drawn by Arlo's summons. Monroe was behind him, shifting into human form and grabbing a bag of weapons. Vlad had thought they had a little more time. He was wrong. However, his early warning had bought them some breathing space. Morgana ran from the trees, her huge bag on her shoulders, the scent of cut herbs and roots strong.

In seconds, their destination became clear, as Arlo led them toward the largest building in the community. Stone built, it was the sturdiest, the roof still holding and most of the windows intact. He waited at the bottom of the set of steps while Harlan, Odette, and Morgana ran inside, Harlan shouldering the door wide open.

Maverick must have been exploring further afield, but he arrived, too. His calm, powerful, and commanding presence immediately settled Vlad. They all raced into a large living area, and the door thudded shut behind them. Immediately the pack shifted to human, and Vlad positioned himself by the window, looking out while they talked.

Maverick spoke first. "Arlo, explain."

"Harlan thinks the Wolf King's resting place is beneath our feet, and the entrance is somewhere in here."

All eyes turned to Harlan. "It's sounds crazy, but honestly, there's logic behind my decision. Odette agrees."

Vlad had always been unnerved by Odette's cool beauty, but there was no doubt she was a clever witch. She immediately backed Harlan up. "I do, and I'm happy to help him search, if you can keep the others away."

Maverick turned to Riggs. "Does this ring any bells for you?"

Riggs shook his head. "None at all, so if Harlan thinks he knows…"

Maverick focussed on Harlan with that intent gaze of command that Vlad was very familiar with. "If you're wrong, they'll be ahead of us, and it will be too late."

Harlan didn't flinch. He straightened, jaw lifting. "I'm not wrong."

"Then do it. Summon us when you've found it. The rest of us will keep them off the scent—out there. But if we spot Emyr, or the crown, we'll try to get them."

Vlad spotted movement in the trees, much closer this time. "They're almost on us."

"Then let's not waste time." Maverick threw the door wide open, shifted, and leapt outside.

Domino heard gunshots at the same time as she scented the Pûca behind her.

She sprang around, snarling, ready to attack. She thought she was prepared after her last encounter, but the Pûca's strange fey appearance, all furry limbs and huge claws, still caught her off-guard. It jumped on her, pinning her to the ground, its wide jaw with razor sharp teeth snapping at her neck.

However, she was a powerfully built wolf, and she rolled and clawed at the Pûca, bringing her back legs up and raking her claws along the creature's flank. She wouldn't hesitate again. As it drew back in pain, she doubled down, seeking the creature's soft neck. A slash of daggerlike claws tore into her arm, but she lunged regardless, and with a satisfying bite, severed the creature's major blood vessel, killing it swiftly. It seemed the key to fighting Pûcas was speed and accuracy. And perhaps the confined space was an advantage for her, too. This wasn't the forest. It was her world.

But there was no time to celebrate her victory. Clint was under attack from a therian who was mid-change, shifting from dog to bear. He fired his shotgun, and then used that as a weapon, swinging it sharply to crack the creature on the head. It fell limply to the ground, and he jumped on it, securing its head under his arm, and breaking the creature's neck.

Fran was engaged in her own battle, and Stan was under attack, too. But Domino was surprised. Stan, for all his skinny, meek appearance, had demon fire in his eyes as he assaulted his attacker.

They were all trapped in the narrow confines of the rear corridors that led to other exits. It was a warren, and Domino realised that the therians and Pûcas must have hidden as small animals, secreting themselves in hiding places, ready to emerge only when they needed to. Their scent was already so strong down here, it had masked their presence.

They obviously hadn't bought the whole gas leak ruse, and must have expected that Domino and a crew would return. Despite their preparations, they had walked into a trap. Domino hadn't wanted bloodshed, but it seemed if they were to leave alive, they had no choice. But while the narrow corridors made fighting difficult, it worked both ways. The Pûcas and therians couldn't shift into huge animals, and that put them at a disadvantage.

Potentially, they could take one captive and try to bargain for its life.

She shifted back to human form, yelling at Stan and Clint, "Try to capture one! We need a bargaining tool!"

"Are you insane?" Clint yelled back, repelling yet another therian with his huge fist, and promptly slamming it into the wall. "It's trying to kill me!"

"But it's another shifter, and despite what they're doing, I actually hate the fact that we're killing them!" As she said it, Stan was under attack again from another Pûca. Sharp claws had raked gashes down his arms, and blood poured onto the floor. He had escaped death by pure luck. She sprinted down the corridor and threw herself onto the creature's back. Securing her arm around its neck, she dragged it away. "Stan, help me bind it somehow!"

She grimaced as its thick fur rubbed against her bare skin. It felt oily, greasy, and its musky scent was unpleasant. She tried to reason with it, not sure if a fey creature could understand a word she said. "Stop fighting! I don't want to kill you!"

It spat and snarled, hissing a strange, sibilant language, and both of them crashed to the floor. The cold, hard ground was pressed against Domino's back, but the creature was still wrapped in her arms, and she wrapped her legs around the rest of its flailing body. For some reason, it wasn't shifting, and she wondered if it had understood her.

"Stop struggling! Call off the attack!" She eyeballed Clint and Fran further down the corridor. Fran was badly wounded; she could see that even from this distance. Blood was pooling around her paws, and her fur was matted with more along her flanks. *Shit. This was risky.*

"Clint! Do not kill that creature! Fran, go tell the rest!"

Clint held back his second punch, and Fran limped down the corridor to the commotion further in the complex.

Very slowly, the creature fell still in her arms. *Was it a ruse? Would it strike her if she lessened her grip?* Stan must have discerned her doubts. Rather than aim the shotgun and risk shooting both of them, he grabbed a broken chair leg and raised that, poised to strike. He nodded.

"Okay," Domino said, "I'm releasing you now. Do not attack! Do you understand?"

It nodded, and mumbled a strange, elongated, "*Yesssss*."

As Domino unclenched her legs and arms, the creature rolled free. For the first time, Domino was aware she was stark naked in front of a very startled Stan, who quickly kept his gaze fixed firmly on the creature.

He took over the interrogation. "We do not want any trouble. Understand? We want to stop fighting."

Domino crouched at Stan's side, ready to shift at any moment, and observed the strange creature properly. It was about four feet tall, with gangling limbs and a furry body. Its face was long, also covered in dark fur, with a jaw like a dog's. It had two huge green eyes, and long, twitching ears. It glared, teeth bared, but didn't attack.

Stan continued to speak, his voice low and soothing. "That's good. We just want to talk. I'm going to put my weapon down, understand?" The Pûca gave a wary nod. "Good." He bent down and gently placed the chair leg on the floor. "What is going on here?"

The Pûca's mouth moved in an odd way, as if it was trying to form words, and eventually, in a deep, creaky voice that sounded like a rusted hinge, it said, "The Wolf King's crown offers strength. We want it."

"So I gather," Stan said. "But the strength it will give you seems to come at the expense of others." He pointed at Domino. "The wolves would be weak. They don't want that."

It turned its huge green eyes that shone like crystals in the dark corridor on Domino. When their eyes locked Domino felt a connection, like a charge of electricity that zapped between them. She felt its power, but also its fear. There was something behind its search for the crown. "What are you so frightened of?"

"Death. The death of our race."

"Death?" Domino thought she'd misheard, and wanted to look to Stan for confirmation, but she didn't want to break her connection. "Why would you die?"

"Because there are few of us. We are weak because we are fey. Weak in the world of men."

"That's not true. You're one of the strongest creatures I have ever fought."

"But we don't exist in this world. We are unseen. Invisible."

Compassion flooded through Domino as she understood the creature's fears. "I get that. Humans wouldn't understand you. The world has changed since you came here."

"Too much. And we are dying, slowly." The Pûca was becoming easier to understand the more it spoke, as if its vocal cords were getting used to human language.

"You don't breed?"

"Not enough."

Stan spoke up. "What will having the crown achieve?"

"It gives strength. The more strength we have, the more likely we can breed and survive."

"So," Stan spoke slowly, "just to clarify, you don't want dominion over others?"

"We don't. The therians do."

"But you're working together, right?" Domino asked, confused.

A spark of mischief entered the Pûca's eyes as it focussed on Domino again. "For now."

Domino groaned in understanding. "I get it. Therians can do what you can't. Move around in this world easily. You're using them until you don't need to anymore." Domino finally turned away from the Pûca and looked at Stan. "A double-cross. Shit." She stared at the Pûca again. "You're planning on betraying them?"

"For the crown. Yes."

Stan heaved a sigh of relief. "That could change everything."

"Then I need to call Maverick." Domino addressed the Pûca again. "We will help you, if you help us. Sound fair? We do *not* want the therians to succeed."

"Fair, yes."

"Do you have Pûcas in Wales? Looking for the crown?"

It nodded. Domino had no idea if it was male or female. "They are close now."

"Can you contact them?" *That sounded dumb. Did they use phones?*

The creature, however, just tapped its own head. "We contact this way. Through our thoughts."

"Good. I will speak to my boss, and you speak to yours. Let's see if we can turn the tables on the therians. Together."

Thirty

H unter felt like an impatient child as he stared at the vast expanse of trees and hills surrounding the winding lane they were travelling along. "Are we there yet?"

"For fuck's sake, Hunter," Ollie exploded. "Will you stop asking that?"

Tommy sniggered. "You're a dick."

"Piss off! I feel like I've been in this bloody car for most of my life!"

"As opposed to just the last day or so?" Tommy grinned at Ollie. "And you think I'm annoying."

"You're both infuriating." Ollie shot them a quelling glance and focussed on driving.

Ollie was annoyed for good reason. He was knackered. They all were. They had lost a fight, Emyr had been kidnapped by a giant bird, and then they had to sneak back into the hotel, grab their bags, and make a very public exit to make it clear to Hector's pack that they were leaving. A car had trailed them for miles. A very tense few miles, in which they hoped no one would discover they had found Emyr and were responsible for his disappearance.

Fortunately, once they were well away from Ballater, the car following them had disappeared, and they breathed easier. The only thing they were worried about now was Alastair and his friends. Hunter sensed a coup was imminent. He'd experienced one of those. It was bloody and unpleasant, and success wasn't guaranteed.

Ollie pulled to a stop in a layby. "Okay, I think we're close. Who wants to go scout for the gate? I'll cruise along behind you. You should be able to smell them."

Hunter was already halfway out the door. "On it." He quickly stripped and shifted, and then loped along the lane.

It was close to midday, but the day was still dark and overcast. Scents and sounds competed for his attention. He was starving after only grabbing a burger from a motorway service station, and the scent of rabbits made him salivate, but he remained fixed on the job. He was searching for Riggs's scent. He'd smelled him at his house, and he'd know it again. Maverick's pack was at least a couple of hours ahead of them, but it wasn't long until he caught shifter scent on the wind—including therians. He ran along the lane, and in minutes found the break in the trees, a rutted path beyond a rusted gate that looked freshly disturbed.

Hunter lifted his head and inhaled. *They were ahead, moving swiftly.* He howled, a brief, clipped yip, and Ollie, a short distance down the road, accelerated and turned toward the gate. Hunter shifted and opened it for him, glad that the lane was so quiet, with little chance of being seen. As soon as Ollie was through, he shut the gate and followed the car along the overgrown path until Ollie pulled to a halt.

Hunter leaned through the open window. "I'll carry on as a wolf. There are scents everywhere around here. I think we're too late."

"In that case," Ollie said, "we'll both go with you. I'll jam the car between some bushes. We'll all be quicker on foot along this track. The less time we waste, the better."

Harlan scoured the living room floor, looking for signs of a trap door or loose boards, while Odette and Morgana searched the other rooms.

The howls and growls from wolves and other creatures circling the camp were unnerving, and Harlan tried to ignore them. Unfortunately, a distant engine was getting closer. *What if he was wrong? What if they knew the real location, now that they had Emyr? Was he even still alive?*

As he pulled back rugs and shoved aside sofas and chairs, a phone started ringing from another room, and he heard Odette's voice. Harlan ignored it. *Think. If it were him, and there was a hidden entrance to some lost world beneath his feet, how would he hide it? A trap door would be easy, but obvious. But how was the place accessed? A stone stairway? A sheer cliff that required scaling? A narrow cleft in the rock?*

He tried to be logical. If the Witch Queen had indeed destroyed the whole valley, sinking it into the earth, it would have been sealed. Which meant that someone surely had to make an entrance to get in it. Or perhaps she had made one to get out. From the story, it seemed the Witch Queen hadn't buried the forest beneath a mound of earth and rock, she had sealed the area in some kind of pocket. A cave, witch-made.

Harlan paced the room, continuing to search as he considered his options. He tapped walls, opened cupboards, and then wondered if there were cellars somewhere. Odette broke into his thoughts, Morgana on her heels.

Odette wagged her phone. "That was Domino. The Pûcas are on our side."

Harlan straightened, brushing dust off his jacket. "Since when? Murderous bastards."

"Since Domino found out they are planning to double-cross the therians. They need the crown to strengthen their race. They do not seek to enslave the wolves—only the therians want that."

Harlan stared out of the window, seeing a wolf streak by in front of the house, teeth bared. "Well, you'd better tell them, because it's about to get ugly out there."

"The thing is," Morgana said, hands on hips and lips pursed, "we need to keep up the pretence until the last moment. Lull the therians into a false sense of security."

"Well, sure, but that's hard to do if the wolves start killing Pûcas. Our truce will be over in seconds."

Odette was already moving to the door, and she threw it open and yelled, "Arlo! Maverick!" The door slammed behind her as she waited on the porch.

Morgana sighed. "What a mess. Bloody shifters. Drives me mad. As much as I like Arlo, and Maverick, to be honest, although he's not so keen on me, I was relieved when Odette split up with him." She gave Harlan a knowing smile. "I think, however, it's far from over for them. Anyway, it's not my business." She jerked her head over her shoulder. "We've searched everything back there. There's nothing in the kitchen, the storeroom, or even the wood pile at the back. Although, interestingly, we did find a pile of dynamite."

"Really? Okay..."

"We left it there, obviously. If I'm honest, that's raised even more questions. I guess if we get in trouble, it's another weapon."

"Let's leave that until we're really desperate." Harlan didn't relish getting blown up. "I'm running out of options here, though, and wondering if I've got this wrong. But..." The word 'wood' gave Harlan pause, and he stared at the fireplace, studying it properly for the first time. "That's a *very* big fireplace for an ordinary cottage, wouldn't you say?"

The stone fireplace was as tall as a man and very broad. It had a stone-flagged base with a large iron grate for holding wood, and ashes littered the floor. Soot smeared the back and sides; it had been well used. He stepped inside it and tapped the walls.

Morgana immediately joined him, investigating the other side. "You're right. This is a huge fireplace, but logically..."

"I know. It'll be under our feet. Just wanted to make sure." He dragged the iron grate aside, wincing as it scraped along the floor, creating streaks in the ash.

"Let me help."

Together they placed it on the living room floor. Harlan grabbed a small brush next to the fire and swept a thick layer of ashes aside. Right in the centre, under where the grate had been, was an iron ring. Expanding his search, he kept brushing ash away until he had exposed the four seams where a large, central slab met the others.

"*Voilà*!" He looked up at her, eyes wide. "Fingers crossed."

He planted his feet, grabbed the ring, and heaved, grimacing at its weight. Morgana sprang to his aid, wedging an iron poker underneath to help lever it up.

"Herne's horns. I'll give myself a hernia," he grunted.

Morgana's lips moved in a soundless spell, and suddenly the slab felt much lighter. With renewed excitement, he hauled it to the side, exposing a large, black space beneath it. Cold, damp air swirled up, carrying the scent of decay. Morgana threw a ball of golden light inside, revealing a craggy shaft that ran down, and down, and down, crude steps cut into it.

Their eyes met, and relief swept through him. "Let's hope this is it. Either that, or Emyr had a dungeon fetish. Better call the others..."

Maverick detected another wolf-shifter, someone unknown. He moved slowly, stiffly, as if injured. And he was surrounded by therians and Pûcas.

It could only be Emyr.

A growl started low in the back of his throat as he monitored their advance, his belly low to the ground. His pack was spread around him, protecting the hut, and waiting on his signal. He had been torn between wanting to lead them away, which would leave the humans unguarded —although, the two powerful witches were hardly vulnerable—or staying and drawing attention to the building. In the end he opted to stay. To hold the entrance put them in a position of power.

He estimated there were about a dozen therians, and perhaps a similar amount of Pûcas. For all that he had an excellent sense of smell, the Pûcas blended well with the forest, their earthy scent mixing with loam and leaf mould. His intention was to let them draw close, and then he would try to bargain. But that depended on them being right.

With every passing minute, he doubted Harlan's reasoning. This whole thing was insane. He should be in London, preparing for the week, overseeing the repairs of the damage to his club, not slinking about a forest indulging in some whimsical bloody fairy tale. Although, he had to admit, this wild forest offered much better hunting ground than Wimbledon, and for the first time in a long time, he wondered if settling in London was the wisest choice for him. And then he thought about the women. There were a lot of women in his club. More than he'd meet in the wilds of Wales.

Decisions, decisions.

The shifters drew closer, fanning out, and the sound of the engine that whined up the hill stopped suddenly, and doors slammed. They had brought something with them. Something that resonated with power and age.

The crown.

Everything came into sharp focus. *This was real. This was shifter history.*

Odette's shout broke his concentration, and he reluctantly left his spot in the undergrowth and headed to her side, Arlo following him.

He shifted to human, frowning with impatience as he looked down at her. "This better be good."

"I thought I'd offer you a cup of tea! Of course it's bloody good!" Her voice dripped with sarcasm, and Arlo hurriedly subdued a smirk. "Domino has phoned." Anxious, she looked around, caught Arlo and Maverick's arms, and pulled them inside the building. "The Pûcas are planning on double-crossing the therians. They're on our side."

"What? How? Why?" And then other pressing concerns pushed those questions out of Maverick's mind as he saw the hole in the fireplace floor. "Holy fuck! You've found it!"

Harlan, streaked in soot and ashes, grinned. "Just this second. Well, we think this is it."

Morgana, similarly filthy, said, "It seems to go down a long way."

Arlo didn't hesitate. "Let me go first. I can check it out, before we try to come to any sort of agreement. Or fight."

Maverick nodded, running through his options. "Odette, tell me everything. You three," he eyed Morgana, Harlan, and Arlo, "check it out together—and be careful!"

Hunter and his companions were making good time; after hours trapped in the car, they were desperate for a big run. This rugged landscape was perfect.

Not needing to stick to the narrow, rutted track, they headed through dense forest and undergrowth, heading higher and higher. On the way, Hunter caught a rabbit, which helped allay his hunger, but he didn't linger. Ollie was up front, and he set a fast pace. The scent of therians drew them onward.

They were close now, and Ollie signalled them to stay back. They were on high ground, at the head of a shallow valley. Hills rose on either side, the entire area clothed in gigantic spruces and pines.

They headed left, keeping downwind, so they flanked one side of the therians. Wolf-shifters were ahead, but not many. Not nearly as many as there were therians and Pûcas. Hunter's skin crawled. He was keen to exact his revenge for their last encounter. He could scent Emyr now, too. The wind was stronger up here, the branches rattling and mixing with the chattering of streams. So far, however, there was no sign of a fight.

And then a piercing whistle cut through all other noise, and a loud voice shouted, "Wolf! We need to talk. I have someone here I think you will want to save."

Maverick shouted back, his calm, authoritative tone sounding unimpressed. "Why would I want to save a traitor?"

"Because if you don't, I'll kill him, and I'm sure you don't want that on your conscience."

"And what would you want in return?"

The man barked a laugh. It was ugly, jubilant, as if he held all the cards. "You know what. You're sitting on the entrance to the Wolf King's resting place. I have the crown. I don't need your agreement.

You're outnumbered here. But I promise not to kill all of you, *if* you let us through."

"I'm the alpha, you worm. Not just anyone. You think you can get through me?"

"I'd put money on it. Your pack didn't fare so well last time."

"Neither did yours. You're Warner, I presume."

The man's voice was sharp. "Yes, I am. All the more reason for me to seek my vengeance today."

"And what happens when you take the crown to our king's resting place?"

"You will bow to the therians. We are marginalised in the shifter world order. That needs to change."

"You marginalise yourselves. But you're getting ahead of yourself. You've hardly brought an army with you."

"I don't need an army. I have the crown. After that, everything will change. In exchange for not fighting, you'll survive, and will have a high place in our new society."

There was a short silence, and then Maverick said, "I need a moment to think."

"Don't take too long. I'm impatient."

Hunter looked at his two companions. The look they exchanged said it all. The man was a joker. *A new society?* He was barking mad. *But then again, he had the crown. A story of myth and legend.* Hunter tried to fathom how it could possibly work. *A ritual? A spell? A sacrifice, perhaps.* Nothing really made sense.

The longer Maverick's silence stretched, the more worried Hunter became. *What was going on?*

Thirty-One

Arlo went first, leading Morgana and Harlan down the narrow, twisting stone staircase between the seam of rock. He was back in his wolf, sure-footed, swift, strong.

The stench of decay and dampness grew stronger as he descended. Moisture dripped off rocks and pooled on the steps. Small niches had been cut into the rock at intervals, holding candles, and Morgana lit them as they progressed, but her witch-light still bobbed overhead, and Harlan's torch pierced the darkness.

However, the stairs twisted and turned, and Arlo's eyes adjusted to the darkness that the lights couldn't penetrate. He picked up the pace, both eager and also dreading to see what was ahead.

"Hey, Arlo, slow down!" Harlan shouted behind him, but he ignored it.

Finally, the path levelled out into a tunnel, still rough-walled, as if chiselled out by hand. And then the tunnel emptied into a huge space and Arlo stopped abruptly, unable to understand what he was looking at for a moment.

Large columns filled the space in front of him, as if he was in a gigantic cathedral. They spread to either side, and he couldn't see the far end of the cavern. He estimated it was as big as the valley above, which made a certain sense, if they thought the entire place had been destroyed by the Witch Queen. Then he realised he was actually seeing tree trunks, enormous petrified tree trunks, the branches knotted overhead to form the canopy of a forest.

Harlan and Morgana finally caught up to him, and they gasped. The beam of Harlan's torchlight combined with Morgana's witch-lights to light the ancient woodland in patches.

"A petrified forest," Harlan said, his voice full of wonder. "She sank the whole forest—encased it in a cave. This is insane!"

"But where is the Wolf King in all of this?" Morgana asked. "This place is vast."

Arlo could smell wolves, death, and other shifters. But he'd also seen something with his heightened vision. He shifted back to human. "There's a path ahead. Snaking through the forest."

Harlan nodded. "That makes sense. This pack was guarding it. They would have come down here, perhaps paid their respects. Maybe just the elders, which is why Riggs wouldn't know about it." He angled his torch so that it picked up the start of the path. "Looks like there are torches along it. I guess we need to follow it."

"For some reason," Arlo said, shivering in his nakedness, "I'm a bit worried about stepping in there, but I don't know why. There's no reason to think there's a trap. The pack came down here, that's obvious."

"And presumably," Morgana said, "the place to use the crown is at the end of that path. However, we need to tell Maverick that we've found it." She turned to Harlan, looking impressed. "Well done. Everyone thought you were mad, but here it is!"

"Yeah, but it's not over yet. You two should go on, and I'll head back up. Perhaps you should consider hiding—just in case. Unless, of course, you want to leave?" Harlan asked Morgana.

"I'm happy to stay. I want to see if I can find out more about this Witch Queen."

Arlo nodded, considering their options. They needed to know the layout of the place if the others were to come down here. Even if it seemed the Pûcas were now on their side—sort of. "Fine. We'll continue, and I'm sure we'll hear you return. Just be careful up there. I don't trust them."

"No, me neither," Harlan called over his shoulder, and he was soon swallowed by the darkness.

Maverick was stalling for time. *Where the hell was Arlo?*

His pack was becoming restless, and so were their enemies. They inched forward as his silence stretched. Maverick had drawn his team closer to the building, and he could clearly see them now. Vlad and Mads were to the left, Riggs, Monroe, and Jax on the right, while Odette was behind him, on the porch of the building. He hoped that Ollie and his team were close.

What he hadn't had proper evidence of, though, was Emyr. He called softly to Riggs, and he loped to his side, and shifted back to human. "Would you recognise Emyr again?"

Riggs nodded. "It's been a long time, but yes, I likely would. His scent is familiar, so I think it's him."

"Good." Maverick shouted, "I need to see Emyr, to make sure he's alive!"

A rustle of leaves ahead indicated movement, and in a short while, two men stepped out of the clearing, a younger man pushing an older man who was covered in blood ahead of him like a human shield. *Talk about paranoid.*

"Emyr?"

The old man nodded, only defeat in his eyes.

Riggs sighed, and kept his voice low. "That's him. He's changed. He used to seem so huge to me. Imposing. He's a shadow of himself."

"That's what betraying your pack and hiding for years will do," Maverick said bitterly.

Riggs shook his head. "It's not just him. It's this place. It seems smaller, too."

Maverick felt sorry for him. This was Riggs's childhood home, and no doubt in the summer it would be spectacular, but all adults tended to view their past through a rosy glow.

"Happy?" His captor shouted. "What are we waiting for? I suggest you move aside and let us through." He tightened his grip on Emyr's neck. "Or I'll kill him right now."

Maverick couldn't stall anymore, and to attack anyone would be suicide. But then Odette shouted, "Maverick!"

He turned, catching Harlan's scent. Taking Riggs with him, he headed to the porch. "Tell me good news."

Harlan was breathless, but he looked excited. "There's a big, fat petrified forest down there! Arlo and Morgana are exploring it. I don't know where the crown goes, but..."

"Good enough." He turned back to Emyr and the therian. "Okay. We've found it. We'll let you through—no tricks. But we're coming, too."

"Oh, don't worry. You'll be there to witness our ascendancy. I insist on it." The therian released his grip on Emyr, and with a quick whistle, summoned the others.

Maverick called his wolves to him as the therians and Pûcas emerged from the trees. *Time to update the team with the new plan.*

Maggie dunked her arm under the tap, sluicing off the blood and dirt from a jagged cut she had sustained during the fight. It stung like hell, but she looked in much better shape compared to some.

Frances, the wolf-shifter who was part of Domino's team, had a huge wound to her thigh, caused by razor-sharp claws that had almost ripped through muscle to the bone. She was dealing with it stoically, though. She had shifted to her human form and Xavier, her cousin, cleaned the wound while she cursed loudly. Maggie was impressed. She almost swore as much as she did.

Xavier must have been used to her colourful language, because he poured neat alcohol into the wound and said, "You'll thank me later."

"You are a bastard, motherf..." The rest of the swear was lost in a yell. Within seconds, she shifted back to her wolf, and Xavier sighed with relief. "Good. She'll sleep for hours once we get home." He jerked his head around the room, his lips pursed with distaste. "We're leaving soon, right?"

He was addressing Grey more than Maggie, but she answered anyway. "Just want to make sure we haven't missed anything. And catch my breath before I have to complete endless paperwork on this."

Grey laughed. He was patching up his own injuries, as were Clint and Ray. They all had varying numbers of cuts and bruises, and Grey had the shotgun on the table, ready just in case something else appeared.

Maggie scowled at him, trying not to let her gaze linger on his impressively defined arm muscles. *And everything else muscled.* "You can laugh, but I'll be filling in bloody forms for hours."

They were still in the underground network of corridors beneath the Brixton shops, most of them gathered in the central communal area. Stan and Domino were finishing a last sweep of the rooms, and Maggie had called in her specialised SOCO team to assist. The therian bodies would head to the morgue, but the Pûcas wanted to dispose of their own dead, and she thought that was fair enough. They had vanished, using what Maggie presumed was some kind of fey magic.

"Talking of forms," Clint said, finishing off his own dressing that he made from a first aid pack under the sink, "Ray and me would like to leave now, if that's okay. Before it starts getting official."

"Oh! Something to hide?" she asked, eyebrow cocked.

"No. Just have better things to do with my day. Right, Ray?"

"Too right, mate."

Grey looked at her, clearly amused, as she said, "Fine. But *you'll* find them for me if I need them, okay?"

"Yes, ma'am." Grey saluted.

"And don't call me fucking ma'am."

Clint and Ray didn't wait, and with a quick nod and goodbye to the group, they trudged up the corridor and out of sight.

Grey sat on a wooden chair, one of the only pieces not broken in the fight. "How will you explain all this?"

She patted her wound dry, and then leaned against the counter. "Fortunately, I don't need to explain too much to anyone. No one likes the grubby details of paranormal stuff. But I will have to file reports to my boss. He'll just be glad to know it's been dealt with. And that he can justify shutting part of Brixton off." She would also need to update the Paranormal Division, but Grey didn't need to know that. Potentially, Layla Gould, the PD's doctor and pathologist, would take one of the therian bodies to her own morgue, but she could negotiate that on her own.

"And that will be it? No repercussions for us? The pack, that is," Grey asked.

"No. You helped me deal with this. No repercussions. And as long as that wanker, Castor Pollux and his merry band of cutthroats keeps his head down, none for him, either—for now." She smirked, but it quickly became a grimace. "He can never keep his hands clean for long, though. But, there have been so many deaths. I can't bring Pûcas to justice, but if they withdraw, and we can stop the therian ringleaders, then everything will settle down again."

"Well, we killed a few today, and more the other night, so I guess it depends on Maverick now." Grey gave her a weak smile. "He's never let me down thus far."

"Yeah, but I bet he hasn't had a situation like this, either."

Thirty-Two

"I don't like this place," Arlo said to Morgana as they hurried along the marked path through the petrified forest. "It feels cursed."

"It is cursed, sort of. What you're feeling is the Witch Queen's grief." Morgana paused, face etched with pain as she struggled to overcome her emotions. "I can feel it now, even all these years later. It was so great, her body couldn't contain it. She unleashed all her fury here."

She paused, bent double, hands on knees as if the weight of it was too much to bear, and Arlo took a moment to study his surroundings more closely. Ever since Harlan had left, they knew they needed to make good time and hadn't stopped, but the further they walked, the more the trees pressed closely. Morgana had cast several witch-lights, and they bobbed overhead, but instead of seeming magical, they had somehow made the forest darker, more sinister.

The tree trunks were as black as the cave walls, and felt like stone, too. They had the texture and appearance of bark, but were cold and damp to the touch. What would have been grass and shrubs beneath their feet looked like blackened, frost-damaged plants, and the canopy overhead was a giant cobweb of branches. However, the path they walked on was clear of undergrowth, as if it was well maintained at one point. Arlo shivered, wanting to change back into his wolf for warmth, but preferring to talk to Morgana. The conversation dispelled some of the menacing silence. He adjusted Morgana's thick scarf that was wrapped around his waist. She insisted he wear it for modesty. He wished he had something warmer, but had refused her jacket, not wanting her to be cold. She had been kind when he split up with Odette. He would always like her for that alone.

"Morgana?" He touched her elbow to draw her attention. "We need to go. Are you okay?"

She took a deep breath and straightened up. "I'll survive."

"You know, it just struck me," he said, quickening his pace as he saw the path widen ahead, "according to the fairy tale, these trees came alive. Is that something that could happen again?"

"Bloody hell, Arlo, this place is creepy enough. Haven't you noticed that they're petrified?"

"Well, yes, but I doubted that the whole place could exist, so... Wow!" He stopped abruptly, thinking his eyes weren't seeing properly, and then hurried forward again. "Is that for real?"

They paused on the edge of a clearing, in the centre of which was an enormous throne on a dais, easily twice a man's height, carved of wood and gilded with metals, featuring huge antlers crowning the back of the throne. Hardly daring to breathe, they both stepped forward, spellbound.

The throne was intricately carved with all sorts of flora and fauna, some of the faces grotesque—wide eyes and mouths open as if they were screaming.

Arlo swallowed. "Do you think the Witch Queen made this?"

"I doubt it. I think it seems more likely that it was made afterward, probably by the wolves. The pack that guarded it."

"I don't know. This doesn't make sense to me..." Arlo trailed off as he looked at the surrounding forest, and then his blood ran cold. From this angle, he saw things he hadn't seen before. Things he couldn't unsee now. There were bodies trapped within the trees. Bound within warped branches that clutched them like arms. And strange lumps protruded from the earth. With dawning horror, he realised that they were bodies wrapped in an endless embrace of gnarled tree roots.

"Holy shit, Morgana. We're in a freaking graveyard!"

The witch raised her hands, power balling in her palms, and she backed toward the throne. "The Witch Queen sealed *everything*. The battle was far from over when she arrived. No wonder I can feel it all so strongly. We're surrounded by death."

Arlo was used to death, and a certain degree of violence. Wolves hunted and killed with their teeth and claws. They were dominant and aggressive, even those that weren't alphas, but even so, to see this... He could almost experience their final moments. But now they had to focus.

"Just—let's forget those for now. Where is the Wolf King? He must be beneath our feet. This is why the throne is here. I presume it's a grave marker. How does this crown-thing even work? I presume someone sits upon the throne, right? You said you can feel a spell. This is her doing?"

Morgana's eyes were haunted when she finally turned back to him, dragging herself back to the present. "It must be, yes. A king is crowned on his throne, but as to how it works, and how we can stop it—"

"But Domino says we *shouldn't* stop it. The Pûcas need it. We just need to stop the therians from using it."

"I'm not sure any of this is a good idea. Harlan posed a very good question earlier. The pack that guarded this place had ample opportunity at any time to wear the crown, and have someone proclaim themselves the Wolf King. Why didn't they?"

Arlo didn't think he could feel any more dread, and yet... "It is an excellent question." He considered the story. "Perhaps they did, and it only responds to certain people. No one has deserved it yet."

"Or maybe there's another part of the story that no one knows. A part that no one wants to happen..."

The clatter of feet and the sound of voices announced that the others had arrived. Arlo grabbed her arm and pulled her aside. "Come on, time to hide and think this through."

Maverick bristled as the escort of therians surrounded them, a ragtag bunch of men and women whose stances swaggered with the promise of victory. But he was biding his time for the right moment to strike. If Warner, that cocky little shit, thought he was just going to sit back and bow down, then he was a bigger idiot than he looked.

Warner had, however, surrounded Maverick with a guard of the strange, hairy Pûcas. They had powerful limbs and sharp teeth, and even if they didn't shift into larger animals, they would be a tough opponent. If Domino was right, however, that wouldn't be an issue.

Looking at their implacable faces right now, it was impossible to tell. Their huge, green eyes gave nothing away, and they barely looked at him. Perhaps they hadn't received the message, as Domino's contact said they would.

Warner had crowed when he saw Riggs again, and pure fury radiated from Riggs in return. Maverick had insisted he stay by him, his alpha presence command enough for Riggs not to fight right now. It took all of Maverick's dominance to control him. His pack were itching to fight, too, but they were well trained and disciplined, and obeyed Maverick's instructions. He hoped the ones on the surface were, too. He'd left Vlad and Mads outside with a couple of therians that Warner had stationed at the exit. Insurance that they could get out again. All the shifters knew the consequences of not obeying him at times like this. They would be immediately thrown out of the pack—end of discussion.

As soon as they were in the petrified forest, Maverick detected Arlo and Morgana's presence; they were keeping well away. He glanced behind him at Harlan and Odette. Both were quiet, watchful. Harlan caught his eye and gave a barely-there nod. He hoped he wouldn't disappoint him, either.

But with every step they took along the path, Warner's cockiness diminished. Especially when they reached the throne, and the bodies became apparent. The entire party had fallen silent at that point. The throne was spooky in the torch light, the shadows of the antlers like fingers reaching across the ground, and the contorted bodies of the dead seemed to writhe.

Emyr had slunk along silently the entire way, walking behind Warner. His eyes darted everywhere, and with every step, his gait stiffened. He had not spoken again since his outburst on the surface, but as soon as they reached the throne, he again appealed to Warner. "Please! Listen to me! This is not meant to be. This is not what the crown is! You're making a mistake."

Warner tutted patronisingly. "Just because the wolves were scared to reclaim the Wolf King's power, doesn't mean I am. You have clearly weakened over time. All of you huddled in your own little packs. Pathetic!" He turned to his sidekick. "Rox. Unlock the crown."

"No. I beg you!" Emyr said, voice rising in panic. "I did a stupid thing, so many years ago. I should never have done it. I was weak.

Desperate. I never thought it would be seen again!" He turned, staring at Riggs. "You must understand the dangers of this?"

Riggs growled. "I understand nothing. I was a child. I was told nothing, except to secure the crown if it ever came to light. Your rules, Emyr. And even now, you're too weak to have stopped them from coming here. You're pathetic. I don't even understand how you became alpha."

Emyr showed the first sign of anger. "I was different back then. A better man. I was a good alpha."

"You're a *liar*. It was all an act! My father thought as much, but didn't voice it for years. To disband the pack, abandon this place..." Riggs's words dripped with scorn. "And now, almost everyone is dead—including my family."

"Shut up! Both of you," Maverick commanded. "Now is not the time."

Rox and another therian whose name Maverick hadn't caught had carried a wooden box between them, but now they placed it on the ground by the throne, unlocked the lid, and lifted the crown out.

A ripple of unease ran around the watching group as the magnificent crown was held up for them all to see. It was beyond ancient, and far bigger than Maverick had imagined.

The crown was constructed mostly of antlers and bones. They radiated outward, the tines tipped with silver and gold and other precious metals. The antlers were bound together at the base within a double golden circle, also studded with gems and engraved with curious figures. But inside the base, cradled by the antlers, was a wolf skull, its empty eye sockets staring out. Small bird and mammal skulls and the jawbones of other creatures nestled around it. Maverick realised that the relics stored in the box must have been part of the crown, and Warner had combined them.

It was macabre. A symbol of power and control, and the need to subjugate. Maverick knew one thing for sure. He would never want to wear that crown.

It suddenly became clear to him. Like every fairy tale, this one had utter darkness at its core. *The Wolf King was cruel. So was the Witch Queen. Perhaps the trickster therian had done everyone a favour.*

But if Warner had any doubts, he wasn't revealing them. "Rox, my cloak! The rest of you, light the torches."

From the bottom of the box, Rox pulled out a cloak of fine fur, and Warner draped it around his shoulders dramatically. "I thought I should look the part."

While his team planted torches into the hard earth, the flickering flames adding to the eeriness of the place, Warner turned aside to prepare himself.

Emyr pleaded, "Let me join the wolves. You don't need me now."

Warner nodded, waving his hand imperiously. "Fine, go join them."

Emyr threaded through the therians and Pûcas to reach Maverick's group. But Maverick was focussing on the Pûcas who weren't making a move, other than to shuffle Maverick and his team to the side of the clearing. Maverick exchanged an anxious look with Monroe and Jax. *What were they waiting for?*

Maverick took the opportunity to speak to the Pûca closest to him, keeping his voice low. "Is this the time?"

It looked at him for one long moment and finally spoke in an odd, husky whisper. "*No.*"

"Well, when? Because we're running out of time!"

"The energy must be right. The therians will do that. Then we strike."

"So, you *are* on our side?" He studied the Pûca's odd features. He had never seen anything like it before, and he was used to the paranormal. He *was* paranormal. He had magic in his veins. But the Pûca was *odd*, especially here in this surreal landscape. He wondered if this was the Pûca that had killed Kane. Part of him wanted to kill it on principle, but he knew they needed them. Domino had made a deal.

It studied him with equal interest, and what looked like amusement. "We're on *our* side. But yes, we do not seek to rule all shifters. Just survive."

"Wait!" Emyr was confused. "You made a deal?"

"Unfortunately, yes," Maverick confirmed, still staring at the creature. "I'm assured that our interests are compatible."

It nodded. "They are. But you must be ready to run."

Maverick thought he'd misheard. "Run?"

"We will endeavour to make you time."

"What? You mean because of the therians? We can deal with those."

It will be my pleasure.

Emyr interrupted them, his laugh harsh. "He means the trees."

Monroe snorted. "The fucking what now?"

Emyr shook off his apathy, his tone urgent. "The Witch Queen's magic keeps them in stasis. The crown raises *the* Wolf King. It doesn't establish a new one—therian, wolf, or otherwise."

Harlan stuttered. "But he's dead!" He flapped his bag with the book in it. "It says so in here."

"She arrived as he died. She couldn't save his body, but she could save his spirit. It's trapped here, bound in some complex way with his crown. She planned to bring an army to defeat the trees and resurrect him properly, but died herself before she could complete the task. Our stories say that she made the throne, ready for his ascension. But no one," Emyr looked at all of them one by one, Pûcas included, "wanted to save him. He was a monster. So, he's stuck in here, trapped in a spell, and this place is cursed forever."

Maverick was temporarily struck dumb, but Monroe wasn't. "We're stuck in the middle of a bloody forest that's about to come alive! I am not going to become bloody tree fodder!"

The Pûca snarled. "We need the energy of the old fey forest and the wolf-shifter. Whatever you may think of him, he was powerful!"

Maverick ignored them both, appealing to Emyr. "You told that idiot, Warner, what will happen, right?"

"He thought I was just trying to scare him. Riggs," he turned to him apologetically, "I wasn't being completely honest. I did sell the crown. I was a gambler, and I owed money. But there were other issues. There is always someone in a pack who wants to wear the crown—*always*. And he or she must be managed. Steered away. But it was getting harder and harder, and my weaknesses weren't helping my cause. I sold the crown to make money, but I also sold it to lose it."

"Smashing it with an axe would have done it," Harlan pointed out.

"No. It's indestructible. I couldn't even burn it." Emyr looked at Warner as he settled himself on the throne. "All it requires is a simple incantation, according to our lore, at least. There's just the shifter on a throne wearing the crown, and a word of command."

"And you actually told him?" Maverick asked, unable to believe his ears.

"It's time to end all this. One way or another. This will do it."

Odette gasped. "You have a death wish. You wanted this to happen!"

"I have no death wish. I wanted to end my life in the mountains in Scotland, well away from this hellhole, but I've learned the hard way that someone will always want to resurrect this. The thing is, the cavern was indestructible, too. I planted charges and detonated them. I knew miners from around here, it was easy to source dynamite. I failed. But once the trees are alive, and her spell is broken, I think it can be brought down. We'll bury the place. Or rather, you will." A steely reserve that Emyr had been keeping hidden suddenly flared into life. "I don't know how long we have. Minutes only. As soon as this starts, you must run for the exit. I have dynamite upstairs, in the woodshed. It's fresh. I kept it ready, just in case."

Odette nodded. "Yes! We found it. It's dry and ready to use."

Maverick suddenly understood. "You're the one who visits."

He nodded. "I never forgot my obligations here, despite what it looks like. I'll delay them, and," he stared at the Pûcas, "I'll even buy you some time. But it's scarce minutes. Are you sure you need to do this?"

The Pûca hissed. "We're sure."

"Then start running as soon as Warner begins." He stared at the gathered therians in a circle, ready to anoint their new king. "They won't notice for a while. They'll be too exultant—until it all goes wrong."

Maverick nodded, not fully understanding what the Pûcas needed to do, but at this stage not really caring. He gathered his team close, and they began to edge backward. No one was watching them.

He grabbed Jax's arm. "Arlo and Morgana are here somewhere. Find them now, and then leave."

Jax nodded, shifted, and loped into the trees.

Thirty-Three

H unter was tired of waiting, and so were Ollie and Tommy.
They had overheard the exchange between Maverick and
the therians, and watched the group head into the stone building,
leaving two wolf-shifters and two therians waiting by the entrance, a
wary distance apart.

But that wariness didn't last long. The therians baited the two
blond shifters, shouting and insulting them for being cowards. Neither responded, instead backing off, shifting into their wolves, and
settling on their haunches. Hunter and the others descended the ridge,
deciding to get closer. Hunter had no idea what was going on inside,
but everything felt very wrong.

And then, the therians shifted into two huge bears and attacked the
wolves without any provocation at all. The wolves fought back, but
taking on two bears was not a fair fight.

Ollie howled, and all three raced to help them.

Game on.

Arlo and Morgana retreated into the petrified forest, far enough so that they disappeared into the inky blackness of the cave and contorted trees, but close enough to see the activity around the throne.

Morgana extinguished her witch-lights, and they huddled together. Neither could work out a way to help. They decided their role had to be to support the attack when it came. Fortunately, it didn't seem as if the therians knew they were there. Unfortunately, there was no sign of an attack.

Morgana whispered in his ear, "Why aren't the Pûcas attacking? What are we waiting for?"

"There must be a reason. A change of plans, perhaps…" Arlo didn't take his eyes off the group. He knew he could see much better than Morgana could. "Maverick is retreating, very gradually. He's sent Jax out. Come on, we need to move."

"But we'll be too far away…"

"Trust me."

Wordlessly, Arlo edged through the trees at an angle that would intercept the main path, knowing it was taking them deeper into the forest, but trusting it would get them out quicker in the long run. He quickened his pace, making sure Morgana stuck with him, just as he heard Warner's voice. He was almost shouting, exultant, as he said a command that was muffled by the trees and distance.

The air shifted around them, as if a breeze had found its way into the cavern. The earth rumbled beneath his feet. Morgana clutched his arm. "Did you feel that? Something is very wrong."

"I felt it, but I can't see them at all," Arlo complained. "I don't know what the hell is happening!"

Warner's voice rose again, and this time they both heard him distinctly. "Grant me your powers! I will rule the shifters. Give me your strength!"

An almighty crack split the air, quickly followed by a succession of pops and creaks. Branches moved, and roots trembled.

Jax cannoned into the pair, moving so swiftly that Arlo hadn't seen him approach. He shifted, face white with terror. "New plan. Get out, now! We're going to blow the place up."

Harlan cursed as he ran down the path, ducking and weaving under the creaking of tree branches, and hating the howls of the wolves that arose around them. Not Maverick's pack, either. *Other wolves…*

"Why do I insist on getting involved in these things. I could have stayed outside, but no, I had to come in. Let's see the petrified forest, see the throne of the Wolf King, it'll be fun, we'll have a few laughs. Something to share with Shadow and the Nephilim. Hey, guess what I've been getting up to. Right? So much fun!"

A root lashed up, whipped around his ankle, and dragged him to the ground as the earth opened beneath him. The root's grip was so strong, Harlan knew if he resisted, it would break his leg.

Odette blasted a slash of fire that sizzled the root. She hauled him to his feet, and started to run again. "You talk to yourself, you know that?"

"This situation is making me crazy!"

"You led us here!"

"You followed me!"

"Will you both shut up and move!" Monroe yelled, running back to them. A branch swung into him and he smashed it with his fist. "If you haven't noticed, we're all going to die unless we get out of here."

Another root snaked across the path, and more and more followed, as if they were tracking them. Harlan groaned. They were *so* tracking them. He was prey.

Odette blasted them again, wielding fire like lightning bolts, before sending a wave of it rolling across the ground.

The roots withdrew, but instead branches cracked around them, and they all dived to the ground.

Monroe yelled, "Get up and run, now!"

Harlan scrambled to his feet again, and with an agility he didn't know he had, rolled and ducked, desperate to reach the exit and get to the dynamite. He had no idea where anyone behind their small group was. Jax had left, Arlo and Morgana were gone, and Maverick was behind him with Riggs and Emyr. *What the hell was happening?*

His torch light sliced the blackness, giving him flashes of movement only. Odette's witch-lights offered some illumination, but the thrashing branches obscured them, too.

And then Monroe skidded to a halt, and Harlan and Odette crashed into him. The trees had blocked their path.

There was no way out.

Maverick made sure his team was out of the way, and then waited with Emyr and Riggs, who had refused to run. They watched Warner with rapt fascination as his acolytes placed the crown on his head.

It was huge, and must be heavy, made for a monstrous king. Warner braced himself, his hands gripping the arms of the throne as he steadied himself beneath the weight. The torch light flickered, animating the throne and the crown, and long, twisted shadows writhed across the clearing onto Warner's face.

He uttered the words of command, and the change was instantaneous.

His features rippled, and his team edged back. But Warner either seemed unaware, or didn't care. He shouted his plea again, ending with, "Give me your strength!"

The chair became alive. The carved plants erupted, vines wrapping over Warner and trapping him in place. His eyes widened with horror as his body started to shift.

Emyr growled a warning at Maverick. "Get out of here!"

But Maverick was transfixed. "What's happening to him?"

"The Wolf King is possessing him, and now is the time to stop it. I'm not leaving this place—I know that now. *Go*!" He pushed Maverick with such force that he stumbled, and it brought him to his senses. Emyr stripped, shifted, and launched himself at the therians.

The moment seemed to be what the Pûcas were waiting for too, because they attacked Warner, just as the Wolf King's features took over his own.

For a second, Maverick looked into the black eyes of the king, seeing his fierce intellect and naked ambition, before the Pûcas swept him off the throne and onto the ground, the crown rolling away. There was nothing else he could do here.

He grabbed Riggs. "Come on!"

Riggs shook his head. "No. I'm staying."

"You're not needed. You'll die here." Maverick gripped his arms, staring him down. "Don't do this. Join our pack, or go back to your own. Help us finish this up top."

"I haven't got the heart to, but I trust you will. This isn't your fight. It's mine and Emyr's. Our responsibility. I'll fulfil my family's oath. Go!" And he too pushed Maverick, shifted, and dived into the fight.

Maverick knew he couldn't save him. He shifted and focussed on his own survival. Only then did he see the full impact of releasing the spell.

The trees were alive.

Not only were their branches writhing and snapping, but their roots had dragged from the ground, and the trees were moving. Injured wolves tumbled from their grip, and they were fighting, too. Howls echoed off the cavern walls.

Maverick kept his head down, and ran.

Arlo, Jax, and Morgana were scratched, bruised, breathless, and almost witless with fear when they reached the path that was hardly visible anymore.

They were a fraction ahead of Harlan, Odette, and Monroe, and saw the trees block their friends' exit.

"Damn it! They're trapped!" Arlo said, desperately trying to see if Odette was okay.

"You know," Morgana said, her eyes burning with fury, "I generally love trees, but not these. I *hate* these!" She swelled with power and unleashed a wall of white-hot fire all around her.

It raged and crackled, and a hideous, piercing shriek ripped from the trees. Arlo stepped back from the searing heat. Jax was back in his wolf, and he howled. He was calling Maverick and the others, and from somewhere far back in the forest, Maverick responded.

Arlo was dumbfounded. "He's trapped! Why the hell is he so far away?"

But Morgana hadn't finished. It was clear that the forest hated the fire. Already the trees were retreating, but it had also made them more dangerous. Branches whipped toward them, mouths and eyes appearing in their trunks. Morgana lobbed fireballs high into the air, so that they dropped across the whole forest.

Odette must have joined in, because more fireballs cascaded up above them, before plummeting into the forest's depth. As the trees ignited, it was far easier to see the horror of their surroundings.

Monroe, Harlan, and Odette burst along the path that was accessible again, and they all ran to the stairway of rock that led to the entrance. Pockets of flames reached higher and higher, but there was still no sign of Maverick.

Arlo had no intention of leaving without him, and was eager to shift to search for him. "All of you, up now. I'll find Maverick. Jax, you said there was dynamite? Start preparing it. Although, to be honest," he looked at Morgana and Odette with new appreciation, "you've done a pretty decent job of destroying this place."

"Not enough." Morgana watched the havoc she'd wreaked with troubled eyes. "It's a big place, and there's a lot of magic here."

"Then hurry!"

Monroe hung back as the others vanished up the stairs. "I'll help you."

"No. Go. I'll find him."

Monroe was haunted with indecision. "We'll wait until you're both out."

"Ten minutes, that's all. If we're not out by then, we didn't make it."

Then Arlo shifted and raced into the forest.

Harlan emerged from the narrow stairway to the roar of bears and the howls of wolves.

"Fucking great. This just keeps getting worse."

"Ignore them," Monroe rumbled from behind him. "Get the dynamite. We'll sort the bears out."

The front door was open, and Jax had already joined the fight. Monroe grabbed the shotgun that had been left on the table.

Harlan stepped back as he saw Monroe's eyes. They were molten gold, his fury barely contained, a swift reminder that he was in close confines with a wild beast.

He caught Harlan's surprised expression and growled, "Dynamite!"

Harlan was not ashamed to run. The wood storage was at the back of the house, partially sheltered beneath a large porch. Only a small stack of wood was there, and together, he and the women threw the logs aside to access the trap door that Odette and Morgana had found earlier.

As Emyr had promised, bundles of dynamite were stored in a large metal box.

"Crap! That's a lot of dynamite!" Harlan said. He thought the witches had been exaggerating earlier.

Odette asked, "Do we need it all?"

"You saving some for a rainy day?" Harlan hauled the box inside.

"But we could bring the cave down!" she protested, running after him.

Morgana gave a dry laugh as she headed to the window. "I think that's the plan, Odette. We'll get the cars started. We don't want to hang around, and it looks like the boys have wrapped it up out there."

Harlan gingerly extracted a pack of dynamite. "I have no idea how this works! I could kill myself."

"Lucky you have me, then," a booming voice said from behind him.

Harlan jerked up in shock, almost whacking his head on the stone fireplace. A huge man, bearded, gruff, and very naked, stood in the doorway, grinning at him.

"Who the hell are you?"

"Tommy." His face split into a broad grin and he rubbed his hands together with glee. "Oh, yes! This is how to end a fight. Move aside, small American man. Let the master work."

"I am *not* a small American man!"

Another man appeared, also very naked and clearly very comfortable in his skin. He was dark-haired, lean, and with a killer physique. "Don't worry, Harlan mate. He's with me."

"*Hunter*?"

"Aye! Step aside, sunshine. Let the fun begin."

Maverick howled a warning for Arlo to stay back. He would find a way out without endangering his friend.

With every howl, Arlo responded, and he followed the sound closer and closer to the edge of the forest.

But it wasn't easy. The forest was a live, thrashing thing, consumed by rage, pain, and fire. Pockets burned all around him, the flames bright against the pitch black of the cavern. The floor moved, roots lashing out, but Maverick was moving so quickly that the roots couldn't get a grip.

Plus, they had other things to occupy them. Like the old wolves that had been brought back to life, the Pûcas, and the therians that ran screaming through the undergrowth. By the time he found Arlo on the outskirts of the wood, he felt half dead; he was scorched, his paws were burnt, and his fur was matted with blood.

They were within sight of the tunnel when a scream of appeal had them both spinning around.

Rox was clawing his way out of the forest, or trying to. Roots were dragging him into the earth. "Help me! Don't just leave me here!"

But Maverick knew all about Rox and what he'd done to Riggs, and what he was going to do to Domino. He stared him down pitilessly, then turned and walked away. Rox had brought this on himself.

Vlad watched Arlo burst out of the stone stairwell, Maverick on his heels, both stinking of smoke and singed fur, wild-eyed and savage. He'd expected as much, and had sent the humans back to the cars, ready to flee.

The members of his pack who'd been down in that hell hole had emerged scarred and scared, and that always made a wolf vicious. It tampered with their judgement. He'd seen it when Jax threw himself into the fight, and Monroe too, taking pot shots with his shotgun. They were savage. Arlo and Maverick would be worse.

The less they had to distract them, the better.

Fortunately, Ollie had imposed his will on Jax and Monroe once they had their fill of killing therians. He was out there now with them, supported by Mads. He might not be their alpha, but he *was* an alpha, with all the power they wielded. Everyone was ready to flee.

Only Tommy and Hunter were with Vlad now, and as soon as Maverick and Arlo emerged, they flew downstairs, armed with the dynamite.

Maverick shifted back to human, eyes blazing. "Are we ready?"

"We're ready. It's okay, Maverick." He held his gaze, calmly submissive, not challenging him. "The dynamite is ready, and Tommy knows how to set it. They're doing it now."

"I want it all gone. *All of it*!"

Vlad stared at the ground, unable to meet the weight of Maverick's anger and pain. He was glad he hadn't witnessed what the others had. He eventually risked raising his eyes again. "It will all be destroyed. The others are waiting in the cars. Tommy has rigged dynamite up here, too." He risked a glance at Arlo, who had also shifted back to human. "Unless, of course, you'd rather leave as your wolf. We'll meet you further down the road."

Maverick growled. "You think I'm not in control?"

Vlad stared at the floor again. "I sense your need to hunt. That's all. Monroe and Jax have." He kept it simple, heart pounding.

After a moment's pause, he knew Maverick was calming. He clearly fought to keep his tone even as he said, "It's a good suggestion, Vlad."

Vlad looked up to find Arlo and Maverick both looking less feral—slightly.

Arlo asked, "Odette?"

"In the car, and fine. We need to leave, though. Tommy will be minutes only. I suggest you start hunting now."

Maverick didn't argue, and neither did Arlo; they both shifted and left.

Within another minute Tommy and Hunter emerged, white-faced and grim. "Done."

The cars were a good distance down the track when the first explosion boomed behind Harlan and the witches, and then there was another and another. The ground shook beneath them.

"Floor it!" he yelled.

Morgana was already driving fast, the car bouncing over ruts. "I'll rip the bottom of the car out!"

"Can you make it fly?"

Morgana focussed on the road, but Odette twisted around and scowled at him. "That is slightly beyond my abilities, although..."

"We are not making a flying bloody car!" Morgana said. "Besides, I'm knackered after incinerating a forest."

Harlan braced himself as the car bounced again and the rear fishtailed. "I don't think we would have got out of there if you hadn't done that. Either of you."

"Well, I certainly can't thank you for taking us there. What was your name again? Harlan?"

"Yep. Collector with The Orphic Guild. You know, I could do with a couple of reliable witches among my contacts in London..."

Odette spluttered, looking at him in amazement. "You must be kidding me? We're barely escaping with our lives, and you're suggesting you might call on us again? Nope."

"Oh, come on." Harlan's natural enthusiasm for life was reasserting itself. "We'd have fun! And we'll make money."

Morgana met his eyes in the mirror in a fierce glare. "We already make money, thank you. We're fine."

"Well, keep me in mind, at least. I'll give you my card." He glanced out the rear window, seeing a cloud of dust above them, and the other cars right behind. "I think the valley might have collapsed. "

"We're not going back to look!" Morgana shot back.

"I didn't say we should!"

The closer they got to the main road, the stabler the ground felt, and Morgana slowed.

Harlan thought he'd risk another question. "Any chance I can get a lift back to London with you? The wolves looked a bit...wolfish."

Odette turned to look at him again, her face softening with a smile. "Yes, anger does that to them. It must be something to find out a fairy tale is actually a nightmare. Of course you can."

"Thanks." He sat back, relaxing for the first time in hours, and vowed not to get involved in wolf business again.

Thirty-Four

"So, it's over? Done? This bloody issue won't darken my door again?" Maggie asked Harlan, scowling at him.

"Why are you glaring at me? I didn't start this! That crazy-ass therian, Warner did. Well, him and the Pûcas. I helped end it. You should be eternally grateful to me!"

"Yeah, well, tough."

"Just to remind you," he said, scowling back, "you banged on my door, you're drinking my bourbon, and sitting on my sofa! You could have gone anywhere else!"

"And who else am I supposed to talk about this to? Stan is at home with his missus, Irving is doing whatever Irving does, and I am not heading to that club today. I've had enough of shifters to last a lifetime. Who does that leave me with? *You*!"

"Oh, great. So I'm a last resort. Even better."

"You understand this job better than anyone, and you're a human! I'm sick of the paranormal!"

"Well, you've got the wrong job, then!"

"Shut the fuck up and pour me another bourbon!"

"Pour your own damn drink!" He gestured to the table in the corner of his living room. "If we're having this weird friend vibe, in which you make yourself at home in *my* home, then you can help yourself."

"Fine. I will."

"And top mine off, too." He held his glass out.

"You're a cheeky shit."

"It's after eleven at night. I'm exhausted, and I was going to bed! You nearly knocked my door down. And you did not experience what I did today."

Maggie took pity on him. He really did look terrible. He may have showered, but he still smelled like smoke, and she was pretty sure some of his hair was singed. And she had banged very loudly on his door.

She topped his drink up. "But you know, I also had an experience today."

"So you told me. Was it a forest that came alive? No. I don't think I'll sleep for a week. Maybe a month."

"Then you must be glad I came."

He took the replenished drink off her and said, "I don't know if I'd go that far."

She laughed. "Liar. This isn't going to put you in good stead with Burton and Knight."

"Hey, I'll buy the book, and recompense them for the crown. It'll be fine. I make them a lot of money."

She eased back into Harlan's very comfortable armchair and wriggled her feet by the fire as she sipped her drink. "Would you work with them again? The shifters, I mean?"

"If I had to. They were okay, actually. The job...well, that was different. But this career does that, right? You never know where it will take you."

"You have a lot of money now. Would you ever give it up?"

"I asked myself that question a few months ago." He swirled the amber liquid. "No. I like it too much. Everything else seems tame. Boring."

"You don't regret not having kids, or a family life?"

He snorted. "No! Does it look like it? Do you?"

She considered his question. Like Harlan, she had her own place, her independence, kept erratic hours, ran into danger. Also, no kids and a ruined marriage. *But even so...* "No. I love it. Are we mad?"

"I think we're probably the sanest people I know." He raised his glass. "Bottoms up."

Hunter laughed at Tommy dancing on the table in the bar of The Slaughtered Lamb. "You'll break your bloody neck, you idiot."

Tommy threw back his head and howled, and then jumped down and plonked on the chair next to him. "You're just mad jealous of my dynamite skills."

"I'm not sure *mad jealous* is the phrase, but I am impressed. All thanks to your miner dad, I presume?"

"Aye! Always knew that would come in handy." He grinned at the other shifters gathered in the pub. Hunter, Ollie, Hunter's siblings, and Evan. "You should have seen it blow. It was spectacular!"

"I saw the aftermath, you madman," Piper said, shaking her head, eyes wide. "It were on the news! A bloody helicopter hovering over the devastation in the Welsh hills. You sank half a valley!"

Tommy rubbed his hands together again, his face alive with glee. "It was the most fun I've had in years!"

Once Tommy had laid the charges down the stairway, and threw the remaining dynamite into the writhing forest, the image of which Hunter was sure would give him nightmares for days, they had fled into the hills and onto the ridge to watch the destruction before joining the others.

The land jumped and churned as if it was alive, a few houses exploded, and then a deep, thunderous rumble preceded rocks exploding from the ground like a volcano was erupting. Earth, trees, and the remaining settlement had vanished into an ever-widening pit, and at that point they had fled. They had heard that Emyr once planted old charges, and wondered if they had exploded too, finally, all those years later.

At least it was done now. No more Wolf King and Witch Queen. No more living trees. No crown. No throne.

The only thing Hunter now had to decide was whether or not he should do what his heart was telling him. He needed a change. A big one, if only for a while. His family was in Cumbria, and maybe his future, but he was all upside down after Briar. The family business could manage without him, and he found that he liked Maverick and the Storm Moon Pack.

Ollie was sitting next to him, and while the others ribbed Tommy, he nudged Hunter. Ollie always knew what he was thinking, and he knew he wasn't himself. He tapped his pint glass to Hunter's. "Whatever you need to do next, you'll always have a place back here."

Hunter smiled, the decision made. "Cheers, Ol."

It was close to midnight by the time Domino was able to join Maverick and Arlo in the office overlooking Storm Moon's dance floor.

Once again, the club heaved with customers, the DJ playing an eighties setlist. Eighties Night was always popular. It made her smile, a sense of normalcy returning as she climbed the stairs and entered the office.

Well, it had almost returned.

The office window had been fixed, the place cleared of glass and blood, but the music in the office was far moodier. Instead of Duran Duran, a dub beat was playing, the lights were low, and the conversation was hushed. She met Maverick's eyes across the room. He nodded, an acknowledgement of what had passed. She turned her attention to Arlo, and noted the same. Both were calm, their rage evaporated.

When they had arrived at the club only hours before, they still held their pain and anger. Monroe and Jax carried it, too. Fortunately, Vlad and Mads were not that far gone. Maverick had ordered everyone home, and given the four pack members the rest of the day off. But now they were back. All four were upstairs in the bar, winding down and talking through the experience. She was fine with that; they needed to process. To sit at home, mulling over events like these on their own was unthinkable.

She had done much the same with her team after they left Brixton. They had showered and cleaned up, and then sat in the deserted bar before opening, talking things through. It was a kind of healing. Grey and Jet were with them now. She could always rely on Grey to keep an even keel. He had been fantastic that day. They needed humans in the club, as part of the pack. They helped tame the animal inside the rest of them. And no one could stay mad around Jet for long.

Domino helped herself to a gin and tonic before sitting next to her alpha and his second. "I'm *very* glad you're okay, but I'm so sorry to hear about Riggs."

Maverick's jaw clenched, and he topped up his whiskey and sipped it before answering. "I couldn't stop him. I knew it. He was too far gone. Wrapped up in guilt, and grief, and anger. So much anger. At Emyr, at the situation. At the fucking therians…"

Arlo exchanged a worried glance with Domino. "But like you said, you couldn't stop it. I think he'd probably already made his mind up before we went down there. When his family was killed, all he wanted was revenge."

"But I could have stopped it," Maverick argued. "I could have refused the Pûcas' request. Stopped everything before that stupid crown was put on the idiot's head. I would have happily ripped his throat out. The forest would still be petrified, and the Wolf King would be a distant memory."

Domino stepped in. "If we're blaming anyone here, blame *me*. I was the one who agreed to the request. Hell, I invited it. I was sick of killing. Unfortunately, I had no idea of the consequences of that. I didn't know what that required. And now, well, are they dead? It doesn't sound like they left with you."

"We saw them," Arlo told her, "on the hillside, afterward. Some of them, at least. I guess that being fey-shifters, they found another way out."

"But did they benefit? Did they get the power they wanted?"

Maverick huffed. "I saw them rip into the therians, especially Warner, who was half Wolf King at that point. I think they ate him. I'm pretty sure that was how they absorbed the power."

"Ate him?" Domino blinked. "How does that benefit them?"

"I don't know and I don't care," Arlo said. "I just hope I never have to meet them again."

"They killed Kane," Maverick said, eyes kindling again. "I should have killed them all. Their needs did not justify their means."

"They did what they had to. We all do sometimes. The therians held no such ideals. They just wanted power. You really left Rox behind?"

"Yes. Shithead." Maverick leaned back and put his feet on the coffee table, one hand behind his head, one hand resting his drink on his abs. "And what about Odette, Arlo?"

He shrugged. "What about her? She helped. Her and Morgana. You should cut them some slack."

"I didn't criticise them. I merely asked about you and Odette."

"There is no me and Odette."

Maverick cocked an eyebrow at Domino. "Right. By the way, Hunter says hi."

"Oh, really? Well, hi to him." She remained impassive, knowing Maverick was desperate to ask questions. *But really, what had happened?* They'd flirted, nothing else.

"I offered him a place in the pack."

She almost slopped her drink. "Why?"

"He said he might need a change, and asked if I would accept him. He's a great wolf—clever, takes orders, thinks on his feet. Of course I said yes. Not sure if Ollie will thank me, but I didn't poach him." He grinned at Domino, a tease in his eyes. "I guess we'll see."

Domino decided to change the subject. "What are we going to do about the Assistant Manager job? It's vacant, now that Kane is dead."

"I'd like to ask Vlad," Arlo suggested. "I think he's ready for more responsibility."

"He's on my staff!" Domino protested.

"And we'd still use him, obviously, for security issues." He winked. "Although, it frees a job up for someone else."

Maverick shrugged. "I have no objections. Although, Cecile would be good, too."

Domino did not like the way this was going at all. Hunter might join the pack; she might lose Vlad or Cecile. *Fine. Time to really throw the wolf amongst the rabbits.*

"Well, Kane was also our medic. I think we should ask Morgana to fill that position." She smirked as she saw their expressions.

Oh yes, that would be fun...

Thank you for reading *Storm Moon Rising*. I hope you enjoyed reading it as much as I enjoyed writing it. Please make an author happy and leave a review here.

The second book is released on February 22nd 2024. It's called *Dark Heart*, and you can buy it here: https://happenstancebooksho p.com/products/dark-heart-storm-moon-shifters-book-2-ebook

Newsletter

If you enjoyed this book and would like to read more of my stories, please subscribe to my newsletter at tjgreenauthor.com. You will get two free short stories, *Excalibur Rises* and *Jack's Encounter,* and will also receive free character sheets for all of the main White Haven witches.

By staying on my mailing list you'll receive free excerpts of my new books, as well as short stories, news of giveaways, and a chance to join my launch team. I'll also be sharing information about other books in this genre you might enjoy.

Ream

I have started my own subscription service called Happenstance Book Club. I know what you're thinking! What is Ream? It's a bit like Patreon, which you may be more familiar with, and it allows you to support me and read my books before anyone else.

There is a monthly fee for this, and a few different tiers, so you can choose what tier suits you. All tiers come with plenty of other bonuses, including merch for the top two tiers, but the one thing common to all is that you can read my latest books while I'm writing them – so they're a work-in-progress. I will post a few chapters each week, and you can read them at your leisure, as well as comment in them. You can also choose to be a follower for free. I will also post polls, character art, and some of my earlier books are available to read for free.

You will also be able to join our exclusive Discord community, where you can comment on my books, and chat about spoilers.

Interested? Head to Happenstance Book Club.

https://reamstories.com/happenstancebookclub

Happenstance Book Shop

I also now have a fabulous online shop called Happenstance Books where you can buy eBooks, audiobooks, and paperbacks, many bundled up at great prices, as well as fabulous merchandise. I know that you'll love it! Check it out here: https://happenstancebookshop.com/

YouTube

If you love audiobooks, you can listen for free on YouTube, as I have uploaded all of my audiobooks there. Please subscribe if you do. Thank you. https://www.youtube.com/@tjgreenauthor

Read on for a list of my other books.

Author's Note

T hank you for reading *Storm Moon Rising*, the first book in the Storm Moon Shifters series.

I always wanted to explore the shifters at Storm Moon, and to write more about Hunter. I love his character, and wanted to develop him further. There are more stories to come, and although I'm not exactly sure what the next one will be about yet, you can guarantee that it will be action-packed. The next book should be released in December 2023.

I owe a big thanks to four of my readers who provided names for the occult shops I mention in Chapter Sixteen. Last year I asked TJ's Inner Circle, my Facebook group, for some esoteric names, and some of them were used in the Hunters series. This book was a great opportunity to use some more. Thanks to Jo Bevis for Seekers by Stealth; Veronica Chafer-McNally for Keepers of Magical Artefacts; Dawn Fortune for Silver Hawker; Sharon Clegg for House of Hecate. They're great names! Thank you.

If you'd like to read a bit more background on the stories, please head to my website www.tjgreenauthor.com, where I blog about the books I've read and the research I've done for the series. In fact, there's lots of stuff on there about my other series, Rise of the King, White Haven Witches, and White Haven Hunters, as well.

Thanks again to Fiona Jayde Media for my awesome cover, and thanks to Kyla Stein at Missed Period Editing for applying her fabulous editing skills.

Thanks also to my beta readers—Terri and my mother. I'm glad you enjoyed it; your feedback, as always, is very helpful! Thanks also to Jase, my fabulously helpful other half. You do so much to support me, and I am immensely grateful for that support.

Finally, thank you to my launch team, who give valuable feedback on typos and are happy to review upon release. It's lovely to hear from them—you know who you are! You're amazing! I also love hearing from all of my readers, so I welcome you to get in touch.

If you'd like to read more of my writing, please join my mailing list at www.tjgreenauthor.com. You can get a free short story called *Jack's Encounter*, describing how Jack met Fahey—a longer version of the prologue in *Call of the King*—by subscribing to my newsletter. You'll also get a free copy of *Excalibur Rises*, a short story prequel. Additionally, you will receive free character sheets on all of my main characters in the White Haven Witches series—exclusive to my email list!

By staying on my mailing list, you'll receive free excerpts of my new books and updates on new releases, as well as short stories and news of giveaways. I'll also be sharing information about other books in this genre you might enjoy.

I encourage you to follow my Facebook page, T J Green. I post there reasonably frequently. In addition, I have a Facebook group called TJ's Inner Circle. It's a fab little group where I run giveaways and post teasers, so come and join us.

About the Author

I was born in England, in the Black Country, but moved to New Zealand in 2006. I lived near Wellington with my partner, Jase, and my cats, Sacha and Leia. However, in April 2022 we moved again! Yes, I like making my life complicated... I'm now living in the Algarve in Portugal, and loving the fabulous weather and people. When I'm not busy writing I read lots, indulge in gardening and shopping, and I love yoga.

Confession time! I'm a Star Trek geek—old and new—and love urban fantasy and detective shows. Secret passion—Columbo! Favourite Star Trek film is the *Wrath of Khan*, the original! Other top films—*Predator*, the original, and *Aliens*.

In a previous life I was a singer in a band, and used to do some acting with a theatre company. For more on me, check out a couple of my blog posts. I'm an old grunge queen, so you can read about my love of that on my blog: https://tjgreenauthor.com/about -a-girl-and-what-chris-cornell-means-to-me/. For more random news, read: https://tjgreenauthor.com/read-self-published-blog-tour-thin gs-you-probably-dont-know-about-me/

Why magic and mystery?

I've always loved the weird, the wonderful, and the inexplicable. Favourite stories are those of magic and mystery, set on the edges of the known, particularly tales of folklore, faerie, and legend—all the narratives that try to explain our reality.

The King Arthur stories are fascinating because they sit between reality and myth. They encompass real life concerns, but also cross boundaries with the world of faerie—or the Other, as I call it. There are green knights, witches, wizards, and dragons, and that's what I find particularly fascinating. They're stories that have intrigued people for generations, and like many others, I'm adding my own interpretation.

I love witches and magic, hence my second series set in beautiful Cornwall. There are witches, missing grimoires, supernatural threats, and ghosts, and as the series progresses, weirder stuff happens. The spinoff, White Haven Hunters, allows me to indulge my love of alchemy, as well as other myths and legends. Think Indiana Jones meets Supernatural!

Have a poke around in my blog posts and you'll find all sorts of posts about my series and my characters, and quite a few book reviews.

If you'd like to follow me on social media, you'll find me here:

facebook.com/tjgreenauthor/

pinterest.pt/tjgreenauthor/

tiktok.com/@tjgreenauthor

youtube.com/@tjgreenauthor

goodreads.com/author/show/15099365.T_J_Green

instagram.com/tjgreenauthor/

bookbub.com/authors/tj-green

https://reamstories.com/happenstancebookclub

Other Books by T J Green

Rise of the King Series
A Young Adult series about a teen called Tom who is summoned to wake King Arthur. It's a fun adventure about King Arthur in the Otherworld!
Call of the King #1
The Silver Tower #2
The Cursed Sword #3

White Haven Hunters
The fun-filled spinoff to the White Haven Witches series! Featuring Fey, Nephilim, and the hunt for the occult.
Spirit of the Fallen #1
Shadow's Edge #2
Dark Star #3
Hunter's Dawn #4
Midnight Fire #5
Immortal Dusk #6

White Haven Witches

This is an Urban Fantasy series all about witches! It's set in the fictional town of White Haven on the south Cornish coast in England. It's my most popular series, and features female and male witches. Low on romance, high on action and magic! I also blend lots of English myth and legend into the stories. And they'll make you laugh, too!

Buried Magic #1

Magic Unbound #2

Magic Unleashed #3

All Hallows' Magic #4

Undying Magic #5

Crossroads Magic #6

Crown of Magic #7

Vengeful Magic #8

Chaos Magic #9

Stormcrossed Magic #10

Wyrd Magic #11

Midwinter Magic #12

Moonfell Witches

This series features the mysterious and magical witches who live in Moonfell, the sprawling Gothic mansion in London. They first appeared in Storm Moon Rising, Storm Moon Shifters Book 1, and then in Immortal Dusk, White Haven Hunters Book 6, and features characters from both series. However, this series can be read as a standalone.

If you love witches and magic, you will love the Moonfell Witches.

The First Yule #0.5 Novella

Printed in Great Britain
by Amazon